## ABOUT THE AUTHOR

Australian writer FELICITY DOWKER was born in Tasmania in 1980 and now lives in Victoria with her husband, their two children, and a distinct lack of cats. In addition to her day-job in the finance sector, Felicity has also certified and worked as a Doula (professional non-medical birth attendant).

Writing has always been her madness of choice, and since she began submitting her work in 2008, over 20 of Felicity's short stories have been published in Australian and international journals and anthologies, most recently in *Aurealis*, Morrigan Books' *Scenes From the Second Storey*, and Ticonderoga Publications' *Scary Kisses*, *More Scary Kisses*, and *Damnation and Dames*.

Felicity won the Ditmar Award for Best New Talent in 2009, and her work has been reprinted in *The Year's Best Australian Fantasy & Horror*, Honourably Mentioned in Ellen Datlow's *Best Horror of the Year* (Volumes 2 & 3), collected two Chronos Awards, and been shortlisted for both the Aurealis and Australian Shadows Awards.

World Fantasy Award-nominee Angela Slatter on Felicity's writing: "She is one of those rare and talented writers of horror who can creep you out while still making you admire the graceful construction of her prose."

# BREAD and CIRCUSES

# BREAD and CIRCUSES

stories by
## FELICITY DOWKER

T≋
p≋
Ticonderoga
publications

*This, and everything else, is for my mother, who always called me a bookworm as though she were bestowing the greatest compliment in the world upon me—and she was. She gave me life, words, and love; it is the absolute least I can do to give her a dedication that she will never read but I will always feel: thank you. I love you. I miss you.*

Designed and edited by Russell B. Farr
Typeset in Sabon and Berylium

A Cataloging-in-Publications entry for this title is available from The National Library of Australia.

ISBN 978-1-921857-07-2 (hardcover)
 978-1-921857-08-9 (trade paperback)
 978-1-921857-09-6 (ebook)

Ticonderoga Publications
PO Box 29 Greenwood
Western Australia 6924

**www.ticonderogapublications.com**

10 9 8 7 6 5 4 3 2 1

ACKNOWLEDGEMENTS

*The author would like to thank Russell B Farr,
Elizabeth Grzyb, Trent Jamieson, Stephen Gray,
Aiden Gray, Layla Gray, Alan Baxter, Andrew
McKiernan, Paul Haines, Martin Livings,
Jason Crowe, Mark Farrugia, Amanda Pillar,
Pete Kempshall, Stuart Mayne, Jason Fischer,
Kirstyn McDermott, Ian Mond, Jason Nahrung,
Simon Petrie, KV Taylor, Mark S Deniz, Baden
Kirgan, David Kernot, Stephen Clark, Stephen
Studach, Robert Shearman, Talie Helene, Chuck
McKenzie, Dave Hoskin, Brendan David Carson,
Rocky Wood, Gillian Pollack, Angela Challis,
Shane Jiraiya Cummings, Angela Slatter, Brenton
Tomlinson, Marty Young, Stephen Dedman,
Ellen Datlow, Will Elliott, Leigh Blackmore,
David Conyers, Ion Newcombe, Jeff Ritchie,
Stephanie Gunn, Tim Martain, Kareena Vicari
Hoy Poy, Malcolm Saltmarsh, anyone who
ever encouraged me (because you're lovely),
anyone who ever tried to discourage me (because
you only make me work harder), anyone I've
forgotten (mea culpa), and, of course, you, dear
reader.*

*Thank you.*

# CONTENTS

Time to be Scared, by Trent Jamieson ........................... 13

Bread and Circuses ........................................ 19

Jesse's Gift .................................................... 39

From Little Things . . . ...................................... 55

Us, After the House Came Back ............................. 77

The Bearded Ones .......................................... 89

Berries and Incense ........................................ 103

To Wish on a Clockwork Heart ............................. 121

Phantasy Moste Grotesk ................................... 137

The Blind Man ............................................. 165

Red Delicious .............................................. 179

After the Jump ............................................. 195

Rota Fortunae ............................................. 209

Nepenthe .................................................. 225

The Female of the Species is
    More Deadly than the Male ................................ 233

The Emancipated Dance ................................... 249

# TIME TO BE SCARED

*It's terrible, but it's beautiful, and I want to see. I need to see.*
"The Emancipated Dance"

This is a book filled with monsters, magic, and revenge, and it is awesome. As such and, in the tradition of all writers of introductions to collections as good as this one, the sort of collections where the stories are far far better than anything the introduction can ever do justice to, I implore you to skip over these words and just get to the stories themselves. All I have is my pride being asked to write the introduction to what is one of the best short story collection debuts of recent years. And, honestly, pride's not a good starting point to any writing endeavour.

Hopefully, you've all gone. At least, I can imagine you have, which makes this much, much easier.

*It's the people that matter. Their empty, broken bodies.*
"After the Jump"

Felicity Dowker understands horror, she understands its subtleties—the mechanisms that are part craft and part art. She's wise to its tricks. Because, you see, most of the best horror doesn't celebrate monsters or madness or death, it celebrates life. Life in all its messiness, life in its stupidity, wisdom, meanness and joy. Good horror, good fiction, is generous enough to produce life in all its shades. It makes us think even as it administers the shocks. It's rich, it's terrifying and you can't look away.

*I'd been living in the abyss with monsters for too long, and it showed,* says the protagonist of the story "Us, After the House Came Back". And the irony is, of course, that those monsters are human. I won't tell you what happens afterwards, but it's both bleak and deliciously ironic, and in less talented hands would have been told utterly differently. But we are in the talented hands of a talented writer: a writer that gets monsters and their various uses, and isn't afraid to use them.

There's a dark heart in her stories, but it beats perfectly in time with your own. She knows how to draw you in, gently, gently, layering the detail, bringing a world to life until you care, and better yet, you fear, for her characters and what she will subject them to, because she understands horror's subtleties, and she understands its hard edge. Felicity pulls no punches.

You don't know how rare a thing that is, unless you do, and then, like me, you can't help but sing her praises. There are very few writers whose work I would at once class as whimsical, magical and utterly harrowing. Felicity is one of those writers.

*Marc met the clockwork fairy on his way home from the pub.*
"To Wish on A Clockwork Heart"

Her stories come at odd angles, familiar enough that you'll take the first step thinking you know where a story is going, but then, Felicity won't so much as throw a twist at you, but her story shifts, and you find yourself on another path altogether, or on the same path only now it is dark and things are moving behind the trees and you have to know what happens as much as you don't want to.

Felicity understands relationships, their making and their breaking and she charts this truthfully in her stories. Her dialogue is divine, and funny, and dances like all good dialogue should. It's read out loud good.

*It's a Santa Claus beard,* his mother said, her voice hushed and reverent. *Blow it away and make a wish. It's magic.*
"The Bearded Ones"

And then there is the magic. It's costly, intrusive, it's never tacked onto the story, and it elevates her fiction in a way all great fantasy does. She takes it seriously, prods it when it's ridiculous, lets it rage or silently creep up on you when it's not. It permeates her stories with its promises and deceits. It's the magic of a universe flawed, rough and magnificent. It's the sort of magic you could imagine in a world as flawed, rough and magnificent as our own. Takes real skill to do that, and she does.

*Rage, hatred, revenge, sorrow . . . these are great and ancient things, bigger than just one man.*
"The Blind Man"

Revenge runs through these stories, but like magic it rarely comes without a cost. It's transformative, brutal, never celebrated, and ultimately wounding. It opens doors that shouldn't be opened; it shapes those that are hurt into monsters. It benefits no one, but it makes for a hell of a good story.

And there are damn fine stories in here: powerful, unforgettable stories.

You'll encounter clockwork fairies, houses that go and come back again, zombies on the cusp of change. You'll see love bloom, fade, burn, rage, kill or be killed. You'll find desperate people doing desperate things and you'll wonder how you might react in such a situation? Just how far you might be from the monsters that we all fear, if just given the right push, the right hurt?

*It hurts, and it's horrible, and it's beautiful . . . and we might as well enjoy it.*
"Bread and Circuses"

It's all these things and more. Felicity is a truly talented writer, and seeing these stories together, feeling them resonate against each other, I can't help but be impressed by her talents anew. A good collection is hard to come by, this is a great one—easy to be excited about, easy to force onto the unsuspecting, because I know they will love it.

May this collection be the first of many for her! We deserve her stories, we need stories this dark and vital. For, like Stephen King, or Shirley Jackson, Felicity Dowker has made horror not just an emotional response but high art.

Now, you've tarried here far too long, it's getting dark, and there are darker places ahead. The circus lights are burning, the carousel is spinning to the steaming calliope's crazy tune, and the shadows that its racing gyre hurls out might just eat you whole. Lucky you have Felicity as your guide. It's time for bread and circuses. It's time you started to be scared.

TRENT JAMIESON
BRISBANE, MAY 2012

# BREAD and CIRCUSES

# BREAD AND CIRCUSES

*"Already long ago, from when we sold our vote to no man, the People have abdicated our duties; for the People who once upon a time handed out military command, high civil office, legions— everything, now restrains itself and anxiously hopes for just two things: bread and circuses."*
—*Satire X, Decimus Junius Juvenalis*

We live in the graveyard. It's the only place they won't go.

It's not religious. There are no Gods left to frighten evil away. It's not even physical. We've dragged a few of them in to see what would happen. Nothing much did. They just get pissed. They get so worked up that they can't function, not even in their usual shambolic, brainless fashion. And they cry gooey, pink-tinged, meaty tears. We think they have cellular memory of being truly dead and buried underground, and they don't like it—can't *bear* it.

They would rather stand gazing in and starving. Better that than to enter the place where the dead used to be imprisoned. So they lurch outside the cemetery, and we cower within.

My bed is a tomb that was once occupied by SLOAN, MARJORIE, MAY SHE REST IN PEACE. I guarantee that where ever she is now, SLOAN, MARJORIE doesn't rest in peace. Nor do I. My lullabies are shuffling thick feet, wet smacking lips, wretched groans oozing from putrescent throats.

It's poetic, I suppose. The outcome of the final revolution. We were the ruling party for so long: living, roaming the world in arrogant freedom. They were the oppressed: dead, planted in dark earth for an eternity of decay and neglect. Perhaps it was always a matter of time until they rose up and fought for our place at the top of things. Maybe their vacant, endless striving for our downfall is fair punishment for our presumption.

It doesn't matter anyway.

I don't hate them. They're too empty to feel anything about, other than fear, revulsion, and crawling fascination.

I hate the graveyard, and the Game.

◆　◆　◆

The Game started a year ago, when we realised we graveyard citizens would survive. That left us with one question: now what? We were alive, there was food for us to stay that way. The countless casualties left behind a lot of non-perishable foodstuffs, and the wilderness brimmed with wild animals for us to hunt. The zombies didn't come inside our graveyard

*(prison)*

sanctuary. We would endure.

But what was the *point?*

There were suicides. People strolled out of the graveyard and offered themselves to the zombies. Our leaders—men and women for whom managing our village was reason for living—saw their

*(minions)*

community slipping from their grasp. Morale wasn't low, it was subterranean.

The zombies began the destruction of the human race, but we were willing to finish the job ourselves rather than face empty futures.

No religion survived in the age of the walking dead. A few random crazies clung to their philosophical opiate, but most of us understood that eternity and divinity were cancelled when the first reanimated corpse erupted from its grave. Which left . . . nothing. Just years of well-fed graveyard life, with zombies at the gates.

The lack of joy was killing us more efficiently than any gnashing teeth and tearing fingers could. Our leaders were desperate. In a last-ditch effort to fill our agonising hollowness, they gave bloody birth to the Game, and my fellow cemetery-dwellers were satisfied. That disgusts me more than anything else: they all love the Game. Even though they understand that one unfortunate day, they may be the participants, they're willing to risk it for the rush they get from watching. The proletariat still have to work it for the pleasure of the powerful people, even in the cemeteries of the new world— and *they agree to do it*. I want to scream. I want to die. But I don't want to give them the gift of watching me.

I'm alone since they sacrificed Noelle, and I'm an easy target. The only reason they haven't played me in the Game is because it's amusing to let me live. Every grinding day I spend here is a joke. They're taking bets on when I'll crack and give myself to the zombies. Or, better yet, when I'll try to attack our little community, take revenge for them killing Noelle. They love a good death-battle. It doesn't matter whose blood is shed. Human, zombie, it's all the same.

A full belly and entertainment. That's all the savage human virus has ever been about, but we've hidden it beneath intricate webs of civilisation until now. In a world ruled by the dead, what need is there to conceal our base selves?

I'm as primitive as the rest of them. The same adrenaline spurts in my bloodstream like liquid fire with each new Game, and I despise myself for it. But I feel something they don't seem to.

Love.

I love Noelle. I miss her.

I don't think they remember love. In that regard, they're already zombies themselves. Every last stinking one of them.

◆ ◆ ◆

She was my girlfriend of five years, and I still thought she was Goddess incarnate. She was tall, dark-skinned, and tough. Without her, I never would have survived the zombies and made it to a cemetery community. I don't know now if that's a good or bad thing. All I know is that Noelle was my angel, my protector, my inspiration. There was beauty in our species while I could stare into her black eyes and kiss her soft pillow lips.

She called me Curly Sue. It wasn't original. It was trite and common. But it was all mine, and sounded so sweet tumbling from her tongue. Nobody calls me anything much now. I'm not sure they know my name anymore. Sometimes I think I've forgotten it myself. I'm empty and alone. Who cares what my name is?

Noelle did. She cared that my name was Susan, enough to twist it into something that was her own, and make *me* her own.

So I try to remember that I'm Susan. Curly Sue. Not for me—for Noelle.

It happened like this.

◆ ◆ ◆

There was no Monday, Tuesday, Wednesday, whatever. Just random time, a series of sun-ups and sun-downs set to the music of milling zombies. Nobody had anywhere to be, so time became redundant. We were cut loose, set adrift in space.

It was horrific.

She kept me tethered to Earth. We lay in the pit we'd dug with our bare hands, five feet into the soft soil in a tree-lined corner of the graveyard. It was warm in there, wrapped around each other. We rose only to eat and defecate. Noelle had been out of the graveyard on food detail. They sent her because she was so strong, she had a good chance of returning. She went without protest. She thought it fair to do her bit. I lay trembling in the pit every time she left, convinced that she wouldn't return. She always did, and I buried my face in her thick dark hair, sobbing tears of relief.

"Relax, Curly Sue," she'd say, stroking my back like the mother-sister-lover-friend she was. "I'm a big girl. I'll always come back to you, little girl. It's fate, and love, and the way things are. Understand?"

I believed, but I worried, too. I knew she was amazing, and amazing things were given only to be taken away.

So they took her, and I can't tell you what day it was, because I don't know. I can't pinpoint the moment it happened, because every moment is the same. That's the most profane thing about it—someone like Noelle deserved to have her death noted in the turning cogs of time.

We were making love. Her long brown legs were coiled around my white ones, intertwined like writhing snakes. She gave off baking heat when we coupled. I basked in it. She was slippery with sweat. I gloried in sliding my fingers around the slick skin of her back. Her tongue danced around my lips, teasing me, and the hard blasts of breath from her nose were a delicious assault on my face.

I ground myself against her, thrusting up, our bodies consumed by a hunger that rivalled the zombies who listened to our carnal sounds. Death and sex, the timeless marriage.

"Two lesbos getting it on in a graveyard while the world goes to shit. Don't that speak volumes," a voice drawled. I looked up over Noelle's shoulder. She grabbed my chin, steering me back towards her, lips roaming my face.

"Ignore them," she breathed in my ear, her breath a wisp of temptation.

But I wasn't that strong. Besides, they'd never intruded on us like this. Something felt wrong.

"Go away," I said, glaring up at the figure above us.

Tom Sheehan. He usually restrained his boorishness to leering at us from the shadows. He was a coward and a bigot. Most of the survivors were. It took a special sort of selfish desperation to evade zombies. Unless, like me, you had a Goddess to deliver you.

"That's not nice," Tom hissed. Several figures appeared around the rim of our pit. They reached in and laid their hands on Noelle.

"Leave her alone!" I screamed, digging my fingers into the flesh of her back, trying to hold on. She was oily with our lovemaking, and I couldn't keep her safe from them. She thrashed, muscles bulging and the white of her furious eyes vivid.

She didn't speak. She just fought.

It took ten of them to haul her out of the pit. She was big, strong, and enraged. They were all men, the tallest and broadest. They'd known she'd resist. She was powerful. They knew their best chance was to sneak in a mob.

Gutless bastards. Slimy cretins.

Tom still crouched next to the pit, staring at me. I struggled to my feet, covering my naked breasts and pubic mound with my hands. I felt his piggy gaze skittering across my flesh like loathsome flabby bugs. I forced myself to meet his eyes, and he grinned. I could see saliva glistening on his lips.

"Your hellcat gal pal is for the Game," he said, winking. "She's gonna put on a helluva show. Don't worry, I'll keep you warm at night, after. I've always been a charitable guy."

I grabbed the edge of the pit, ready to pull myself out and go to Noelle's aid. Tom stood and brought his steel-capped boot down on my fingers. The pain was brilliant and nauseating. I heard a crackling sound as the delicate bones in my hands snapped.

I wasn't strong like Noelle. I screamed.

"Stay in there," he said, drawing his boot back and aiming at my face. I cradled my broken hands in front of my heaving belly and tried in vain to see Noelle above ground. All I could see was a mass of jerking backs as the men closed in around her. She still wasn't making a sound.

"Please," I whispered. Tom laughed.

I tried to scrabble out of the pit without using my screaming hands. I must have looked pitiful—naked, crying, climbing using my elbows and feet. Noelle wouldn't have been so pathetic if our roles had been reversed.

"I said, *stay*," Tom snarled, and kicked me in the head.

Instant blackness.

◆　◆　◆

I woke up folded in a corner of the pit. A sharp scent stung my nostrils, and after a moment, I realised what it was. Ammonia. My hair and face felt wet, and I shivered in the cold air. The sun was high, but shed no warmth.

He pissed on me. They took Noelle, broke my hands, knocked me out . . . and pissed on me. This is what was at stake, this was humanity. As far as I was concerned, the zombies were a preferable future.

I inspected my hands. They were swollen lumps, skin stretched taut and shiny and already a vibrant shade of purple. As if on cue, my head began to throb and complain. My right eye viewed the world through a thin curtain of crimson where the blood from my head trickled down.

I stood up. They had Noelle. I couldn't do much about it, but I couldn't stay in the pit and let it go unchecked, either.

I used my hands to climb out. I bit my tongue to swallow the pain, gagging on the pulsing blood that flowed down my throat. Everything was red agony, but they had Noelle, and that eclipsed it all.

"Right on time," Tom called as I staggered across the graveyard. He leant on a tree, smiling and beckoning to me like an old friend. Behind him was our entire village, clustered in a thrumming mass near the gates. As I neared them, Tom grasped my elbow, guiding me through the crowd. They parted for us, staring with exhilarated eyes. I was crying again. The salt of my tears stang my ravaged face. Tom's hand was a claw, digging cruelly into the tender flesh of my arm.

I didn't think about the zombies stumbling nearby. They were a daydream in contrast to the grotesquery of my fellow humans.

Noelle stood in front of the open gates, groaning zombies pawing the air less than a metre from her. She was still naked, her dark skin mottled with blood and bruises. I saw the imprint of a boot

*(I'll kill you Tom, I swear, somehow I will)*

in the small of her back and thought I might die from my grief and fury. A ragged sob choked out of my throat, and Noelle turned around, looking at me. One of her beautiful eyes was swollen shut, her bottom lip torn. They'd beaten her. The Game worked better if the participant was bloody and fighting their injuries. Besides which, they liked beating on people.

She raised one long arm and pointed at me, resting her other hand over her heart.

"I'll always come back to you, Curly Sue," she said. Her voice was calm and clear. She was impossibly strong. "I love you. Remember."

"Aw, it's so fucking sweet I could cry," Tom said, but he was weak against the force between Noelle and I. I felt it, sparking, connecting us. I pointed at her with one ruined hand, and placed the other on the hollow space that was my heart. They let us stand like that for a moment. Then the machine gunners stepped forward.

Their job was to mow a path through the zombies, to create a space for the Gamer to run through. Noelle stood motionless, watching while they fulfilled their role with aplomb. The undead fell in jittering mounds as the bullets tore into their heads and reversed their reanimation once and for all. The gunners whooped and hollered, sweating, excited, and giddy with the thrill of the easy kill. I covered my ears against the *rat-a-tat-a-tat* of the guns. The result was a bizarre silent movie of exploding zombie heads and falling undead bodies.

The zombies were horrible dead things that should be underground instead of staggering around trying to kill everyone . . . but they were people, once. They were abhorrent, but mostly they were people who were different to us, and we were mowing them down. They were without intellect, driven by irresistible hunger. We were intelligent, supposedly. We used our advantage to kill easy targets. We were evil.

Although maybe the zombies weren't entirely unintelligent, because after a few minutes of watching their comrades being slaughtered by the gunners, they hung back. The path cleared by the bullets stayed open.

It was time for Noelle to play the Game.

They gave her a hunting knife and machine gun. I saw her arms shaking under the weight of the gun, and knew how badly they had hurt her. But she walked forward, not looking back, not even at me.

If she'd refused to play, they would have gunned her down where she stood and thrown her corpse out for the zombies to devour. She had a gun, but they had several. The Game was not voluntary. Once chosen, you left the cemetery and greeted the zombies—one way or another.

She left with her battered head held high.

Hidden in the woods outside the graveyard was a metal ball— the Prize. Noelle had to find the Prize and bring it back to win the Game. If she did, she'd never have to play again. She'd never have to go on food detail, muck out a lavatory hole, or venture out for ammunition and blankets and the other primitive and technological miscellanea our village coveted. She'd live in the graveyard with her community taking care of her, revelling in her heroism.

It sounded like a good deal, but nobody had ever won a Game. Nobody except the zombies, the undefeated champions. As I stood watching my love march out the gates and into the sea of churning undead, I dared to hope.

Noelle bolted for the trees. The zombies were cautious,

*(unintelligent my arse!)*

making occasional grabs with fetid hands, but not rushing forward. She slashed at their seeking fingers as she sprinted past. She looked fearsome, a gore-clad Fury with flying hair, sinuous muscles, and wild eyes. I should have walked away then, sunk into our pit and remembered her in her prime. But I couldn't.

They lunged as she neared the edge of the woods. A pack of twenty surged forward and tackled her to the ground. I saw a child zombie lift Noelle's flailing foot to its mouth and bite off her toes. A dozen sprays of blood arced into the air around the snarling, biting, tearing zombies.

"I thought she'd get further," Tom complained. The crowd was disappointed. I thought I would explode from the hate bubbling and festering inside my veins.

She was dying for their amusement. How could they be so cruel? I loved her, and she was dying, and they didn't care!

But incredibly, my warrior queen was rising to her mutilated feet. In a volley of gunfire and a flash of knife play, she emerged from the clump of undead. They fell like marionettes whose strings had been cut. I saw the child-zombie's blonde head burst open in a cascade of white and red pulp as Noelle took aim and fired. I screeched, a primal cry of bloodlust and triumph.

*"Run! Get in the trees and run until you find the Prize and get back here!"* I shrieked to Noelle through the bars of the cemetery fence. A man-zombie swiped at my face on the other side, and I laughed at him. I felt spittle trickling from my lips, and knew I was crazy.

For she was lost, whether she made it back or not. They had bitten her, torn at her, infected her. She wouldn't be Noelle for much longer. It was over.

But the Game wasn't over, and she was still my beloved. So I watched, cried, yelled, and screamed. Through it all, she never made a sound, never looked back. She was something else, some other species elevated above humans and zombies. She was perfect.

And still she ran.

She was enveloped by the trees, and as if heeding some psychic call, every zombie turned and followed. They clambered, straining forward, crushing their kin in their rush to chase Noelle. Their groans were jagged and urgent. They had been hungry for a long time, and they, too, loved the Game, for it meant food and purpose for a brief while. They were past their momentary fear of destruction, and their focus was fixed on Noelle.

There was a loud beeping sound, and the crowd gasped.

"I'll be damned. The bitch-giant has done it. Too bad for her that it doesn't matter now." Tom spoke in my ear. I didn't care. I was euphoric, delirious.

It was the Prize monitor going off. She'd picked it up and flicked the sensor switch. She'd got it. Nobody had ever done that before. She was special. She was coming back, and everything would be alright.

*Noelle . . .*

◆  ◆  ◆

I stood at the fence for a day and night. Everyone gave up and wandered back to their idle business after a few hours, but I refused to accept it. She had the Prize. She'd won the Game.

She'd said she'd always come back. She made a promise, and she was a Goddess. Somehow it would be ok.

A few women with something vaguely resembling decency left in their shrivelled hearts picked me up and carried me to my

*(our)*

pit. I think they wanted me out of sight. It was offensive to see me keeping a pathetic vigil at the fence. They didn't want the reminder of their guilt.

The zombies didn't emerge from the woods for several days. Noelle must have been a delight of epic proportions for them. They were even more slow-moving and vacant-eyed than usual after their orgy of ghoulishness. Peeping over the edge of my pit, I could see her blood smeared on them. One held a severed hand, dark-skinned and long-fingered, nibbling on the weeping wrist stump like a juicy canapé.

I couldn't stay in the pit. She should have been there with me, it was our place. Instead, she was spattered across the replete undead. Nothing was right out there, and nothing was right in here. I climbed out and found the most exposed, uncomfortable tomb to lie in (thank you, SLOAN, MARJORIE). It was penance, the least I deserved for doing nothing while they took Noelle. There was nothing I *could* have done, but *she* would have fought for *me*.

I was barren, null and void. Another zombie had been made, without so much as a bite.

My world was dead.

◆  ◆  ◆

I don't know how long it's been. I tried keeping track, but the days and nights are greasy things that slip through my clutching mind, and I find myself lost in them. Maybe it's been a year.

When I woke up curled in the foetal position in my dead-bed, I knew today was Game day, and they were going to play me at last. I'd dreamt it, and in the new dead world, dreams didn't lie.

Tom sat on the edge of SLOAN, MARJORIE's slab, staring at me. Was it pain I saw in his moist eyes? He was disgusting, but perhaps even he felt emotion in this weird place. He'd made several advances since Noelle had gone. I'd rejected them. Now they'd sent him to collect me, and he was less than ecstatic about it.

I hated him all the same. If I'd thought I stood a chance of success, I would have tried to pluck the eyes from his murdering skull with my deformed hands that had never healed right. Hands that *he* had ruined.

"Wake up, sleepyhead," he said, voice hard. His eyes continued to give him away. "Today's a special day."

"Is it?" I yawned, knuckling the crust of sleep from my eyes. "Am I meant to be shocked? Scared? Sad? Sorry, I'm just bored. You have that effect on me."

His mouth twisted, and one of his hands jerked as if he'd like to slap me.

"You're a stupid bitch. You know that? I could have looked after you. They would have left you alone if you were with me. I tried, but you won't be saved. Will you? Still hung up on that Amazon woman of yours. Well, fine. Take what's coming to you, then. Get up."

"Oh, they'd leave me alone if I was with *you*?" My laughter was a bitter bark in the chill morning air. "*You're* safe from the Games? I think you'll find out one day just what utter bullshit that is, Tom. We're all meat for the beast. Nobody here cares about anyone. Nobody is safe. Nobody is *special*. Nothing matters, not even you—*especially* not you."

He did slap me then, a solid blow that sent my head reeling and thickened my brain. It hurt, but I laughed again. I knew that would bother him.

"Come die then. We'll send you to join your bitch girlfriend. Isn't that what you want, *Curly Sue?*"

He knew how to stop my laughter.

He reached to pull me up, but I waved his hands away. I was determined to go with pride and strength, like Noelle had. I was so terrified that I thought I might lose control of my bladder, but

I wouldn't let *them* see. I wouldn't do anything to intensify their enjoyment.

They stood at the gates, waiting. I was clothed, and Noelle had been naked, but I couldn't muster the quiet dignity she'd emanated. My lower lip was trembling, and my breath was shallow and rapid. I could feel sweat rolling in beads down my brow, despite the morning cold. The gunners stood tensed and ready. Nobody moved toward me. Nobody beat me. It wasn't necessary. I'd been bleeding and broken ever since Noelle died.

I felt hard metal in my hand, and realised Tom was pressing a knife into it. I took it, and he placed a machine gun in my other. It was ridiculous. I had no idea how a gun worked, and couldn't operate it whilst wielding a knife with my other hand—not with my mangled paws. I was no warrior, not like Noelle. The weapons felt heavy and cumbersome, and as useful as if I had been brandishing a frozen fish and a banana. But all that mattered was that I didn't break. No tears. No pleading.

"You're all going to die," I said. They stared back at me, saucer eyes in moon faces.

"We know," a little boy said. I looked at him, and he met my gaze. His face was blank. He couldn't have been more than six years old.

"If I can, I'll come back and kill you all," I said, knowing it was ludicrous.

"Maybe we could give her a break." Tom's voice was behind me, always behind me. They looked at him, pleased. *Here* was some palpable pain. *Here* was the entertainment I was withholding. "She . . . her girlfriend died this way. Maybe she should be exempt."

Marion, our leader, stepped forward. She was smiling. She looked like a kind old woman, with plump arms you could step into. She had thought up the Game, and she selected who played. She was Grandmother Death.

"Are you volunteering to take her place, Tom? Is that what you're saying?"

There was a pause, stretching out into eternity while I stood holding my useless weapons. Tom coughed. The little boy who had spoken giggled.

Then: "No. I was only saying . . . I'm sorry. Go ahead. I didn't mean to interfere."

"No, I didn't think you did," Marion said, still smiling.

"Cowards," I hissed through chattering teeth. "You're all cowards."

"Show us bravery, then, Susan," Marion said. She waved one of her small hands at the gates and the zombies loitering beyond. "Serve your community. Show us heroism, and exhilaration. Entertain us. Feed them. There are no better causes. There is nothing else."

I spat at her, and one of the gunners raised his weapon above his head for a blow. Marion stopped him with a look, and he fell back, glowering. She wiped my spittle from her chest and fixed her pale blue eyes on me.

I looked away first. What good was a battle of wills to me with this death-queen now?

Marion nodded at the gunners, and they set about their noisy, bloody work. Standing here, so close to them, the sound was deafening. I could hear the cries of the undead with unbearable clarity from my vantage point near the gates. I'd never noticed how animalistic they sounded when wounded. Their cacophony was violent and terrible. I forced myself not to block my ears. This was *my* death, too, and I wanted to be present for it. Every gun blast, every *thock* as bullets tore into zombie flesh, every scream and whimper from the dying undead—I took it in and made it my own.

The legion of walking corpses outside the cemetery fell back. A clear path opened amongst them, snaking towards the woods. The grass was green and fragrant out there, and I remembered that the *world* wasn't dead, only the part of it that was human. Everything else was fecund and free. I had no more time to reflect, because I was nudged forward.

I dropped my gun. It was no good to me, and would weigh me down. The knife I kept, though I had little chance of using it productively.

"What the fuck are you doing?" Tom's voice was a buzzing insect in my ear. "You don't stand a chance without the gun! Are you crazy?"

I ignored him. He was as dead as I was.

I crouched, allowing energy to coil in my haunches . . . build . . . climax . . . and *release* as I sprang into a full-blown sprint. I was out of the graveyard for the first time in years. My feelings were not fear, but giddiness. I'd escaped! Here was *life*!

Then I felt the first cold, moist hand pawing at my torso, and my skin leapt in disgust. I waved the knife wildly around me as I ran, feeling it connect more than a few times, shuddering at the wetness that soon coated my slashing hand. I kept my eyes fixed on the narrowing strip of grass in front of me, and the woods beyond. I didn't want to see the zombies. Confronting them so closely would bring an abrupt end to my running. My legs would seize with horror. So long as I refused to acknowledge their proximity with my eyes, I could keep going.

I heard the villagers cheering me on. They sounded crazed, overjoyed, stunned.

I didn't run for them. I was looking for my Prize, and it was in the woods. It wasn't that stupid metal ball.

I was small and fast, even after years pent up in the graveyard. I could see trees that marked the edge of the woods metres away. I stretched out my hand, straining for them.

A zombie's hand clamped on my wrist like a stone manacle, and I was wrenched by the force of the grab and my forward momentum. I slammed into the creature, my face smacking into its own. I gasped a lungful of air, felt bile rise in my throat as the thing's dead-stench flooded into me. Its mouth snapped at mine, trying to take in flesh. One of its eyes dangled on the stem, bouncing and brushing my skin as the other stared in frenzied malice. It had no nose, just a ragged flap of skin where it had been. Worms writhed in its patchy black hair, and lice burrowed in its ears. Its flesh was green-grey and damp, coated with mould.

I didn't know if it was male or female. It was just a zombie.

"Rargh," it moaned, a flaccid sound flopping from its rotten throat. "Urgh!"

"Get your hands off me," I said, bringing the knife up with my free hand and pressing it against the thing's soft neck. "I'm sorry, but I have to get in the woods. Let me go."

It mewled, still trying to bite my face, the hand that wasn't gripping my wrist gouging at my chest hard enough to lift the skin in bloody, burning furrows. I could sense its comrades closing in. I had seconds before they were on top of me.

"I'm sorry," I said again, plunging the knife into its throat. It gave easily, the flesh collapsing like moist soufflé. In two stabs, the head dangled by a thin string of mildewed skin. One more rip, and the head toppled off. The zombie's hand came undone around my wrist, and its body slumped to the ground.

A score of hands caressed me, trying to grab, tear, devour. I shrugged them off and threw myself forwards, into the cool darkness of the woods.

My legs spasmed and gave way, and I tumbled to my knees, falling into the aromatic grass and dead leaf mulch on the forest floor. My head span and my body trembled. I couldn't think straight. I retched until a flood of hot filth poured out of my mouth and painted the undergrowth around me.

My traumatised body had betrayed me. I couldn't even crawl. I flopped onto my back and stared up at the leafy canopy above me, whimpering. I waited to feel the first defiling hands on my body, sobbed as I anticipated the first snaggle of teeth penetrating my skin. My knife lay next to me, useless, accusatory.

I waited a long time, and eventually realised the zombies hadn't followed me.

But *something* was coming for me, shuffling across the ground in lopsided steps. It approached behind my head. I rolled my eyes back as far as they would go, ignoring the watery sting, but saw only a blur.

"Come get me, then," I croaked, throat tight and dry. "I'm an easy meal. Dinner's served. I can't move, and I don't care. Not anymore." "Curgh-ee Shoooooooo," the thing crooned, and something in the deepest parts of my brain exploded.

*(my Prize)*

My visitor reached my side, edged forward, stood over me. I could see it

*(her!)*

in glorious perspective, a living dead Goddess, looming above me in terrible beauty.

"Noelle?" The word left my mouth before my brain registered it. I couldn't breathe, couldn't think. I was pure emotion, trapped in my fleshy shell.

She was still divine. Her dark eyes were intact, boggling at me from the mess that was her face. Half the skin on her head had torn, and dangled in a large sheet from her chin. But it was *her* skin, that glossy mahogany casing that enclosed everything that was Noelle. It was mottled, and savaged, and paler, but still hers. Her large teeth grinned at me like rickety fence palings. One of her voluminous lips dangled with the skin beneath her chin. Her matted hair was flecked with gore. One of her arms was gone from the elbow down, leaving a stringy stump of gristle and bone. All her toes and parts of her feet were gone. The downy pad between her legs was a mish-mash of blood and maggots. All over her I saw teeth marks, gaping wounds, dangling flesh. A loop of sausage-like intestines protruded from her open belly, wound around her waist like a belt.

She was carnage, pestilence, and decay. But she was still *something else*, something above humans, zombies, and the whole damn mess. She was dead, she was hungry, and she was different, but she was Noelle. My love for her was alive.

No matter what.

Her throat bulged, and she hacked a few times, like a macabre cat trying to dislodge a fur ball.

"It's ok," I said, reaching up to her with shaking hands. "Don't hurt yourself. You don't need to—"

"Uhm bach fuh yoooooooo . . . " she clawed at her neck, frowning. Frustrated. "Ah-wash uhm bach fuh yoo. Curgh-ee Shoo."

A thought occurred to me, and it gave me the strength to sit up.

"Noelle, are you scared of the graveyard?"

She stared at me with lurid eyes. The skin dangling from her face swayed like a grisly beard as she shook her head. *No.*

"I didn't think you would be. You're different, aren't you? Different to us all. That's why you can talk to me. That's why you remembered me. You've kept a lot of *you* in there. And maybe, with you by my side, I could do the same."

I saw that her hands were trembling, and every now and then, they would twitch toward me. She kept grabbing at herself—stopping.

"You're hungry, aren't you?"

The enormous flap of skin jiggled again as she nodded, eyes sorrowful and vicious.

"No . . . .urt Curgh-ee Shoo . . . "

"It's ok, my darling. I *want* you to. It will only hurt for a while, and then I'll be with you forever. And we'll have food and vengeance. We'll go to the graveyard. We'll sneak up on them. We'll give them the best damn Game they've ever had. And for you and me . . . the food, the Game, and the love will last for eternity. Remember? It's fate, and love, and the way things are."

She had fallen to her knees, and her fingers were fumbling at the blood on my hands and arms. She brought her hand to her mouth and sucked, eyes rolling in her head. I knew she couldn't control herself much longer.

"You're the first Noelle," I said as she bent her face down to mine. "You're the start of something new. I'm lucky enough to come along with you for the ride, but it's always been you that counted. And you're better than all of them. No matter what happens, you're better. *We'll* be better."

We kissed, my lips sliding deep inside the gaping, corrosive wound that was her mouth. Her tongue was furry and soft, and her breath was cold. I felt her hand at my neck, tentative at first, then squeezing, gouging. Her fingers burrowed, laying my throat open under their insistence. She was moaning and panting, like so many times before at the height of passion.

It was going to hurt a lot, but I thought she'd make it quick.

"Uh luch oo," she gurgled against my cheek as her teeth met my skin for the first time. The pain was sharp and brilliant, searing my senses. My face was raw and my nerve endings were aflame. It was so much worse than I had expected, and it was only a little bite. Just the beginning.

"I . . . love you, too," I gasped, digging my nails into my palms, fighting my urge to scream, to run, to fall apart. Noelle was chewing on a piece of my face, making small sounds of ecstasy in the back of her dead throat.

Her hand around my neck was so tight. I couldn't breathe. I couldn't think. The world was receding to bright pinpricks of light in dancing blackness, and in the centre of it was Noelle.

I still had love, and hate, and I took them both down into oblivion.

*Remember the graveyard,* I screamed inside my fading brain, desperate to cling to purpose. *Remember Noelle, and be with her.*

*And kill them all. Humans. Zombies. Just kill them.*

I found meaning, purpose and vitality at last as Noelle tore my chest open and grappled with my ribcage to get to my heart—which was always hers.

Now comes the joy, at last. And food, always food. Steaming, dripping, throbbing flesh and red-hot blood. I want it already. I want to see them run, toy with them, hear them beg.

Bread and circuses. Even unto infinity, it's all there is. Even for me. Even for you.

It hurts, and it's horrible, and it's beautiful . . . and we might as well enjoy it.

# AFTERWORD

*This is probably the most well-known, well-liked, award-nominated piece I've written to date, and as you've doubtless spotted, it lent the collection you're reading its title. It is, ultimately, just another zombie story (which isn't a bad thing!) and I wrote it very early in my still-fledgling career. It shouldn't have worked. I don't know why it did. Perhaps the bleakness spoke to people. Perhaps the focus on the human tale rather than the zombie tale helped—that's certainly what I'm more interested in as a reader. Perhaps the fact it's a story of love-amongst-the-zombies (a surprisingly untapped well) added a little spice. All I know is that Noelle and Susan came to me fully formed, as did the concept of the Game, and the graveyard communities. As an individual, I, like Juvenalis, hold a somewhat pessimistic view of humanity as a whole. It was actually very cathartic to be able to funnel "the blackness of man's heart" into this story. I hope a little of that same catharsis can be found in reading it.*

# JESSE'S GIFT

Being a child is perilous; predators lurk around every corner, and we have so few tools with which to defend ourselves. So many of my friends didn't make it—and those who did didn't always make it intact. Their scars aren't always visible, but they're there.

*I* made it, barely (though I can't claim to be unscathed), and now, at 36, I've forgotten most of my close shaves. Forgotten them, was ignorant of them in the first place, or have just blocked them out.

Except for one.

The Ice Cream Man took my best friend when I was eight, and he almost took me too. Jesse gave his life to protect mine that night, and I won't forget that. I promised Jesse I would remember him. Him and the Ice Cream Man.

And I have kept my promise. Decades later, I still keep it. Even on the nights where sleep won't come, and I convulse with grief and fear in my cold bed, and a strange song seems to dance in the air around me, and I think I truly might be insane . . . even then, I cling to my memories, and I keep my promise.

I love you, Jesse. I love you still, and I will always remember.

◆ ◆ ◆

The apple was enormous, a hard red boulder. It hurt like hell when it thumped into the back of my head, and my eyes began to tear immediately. I spun around, holding my throbbing scalp, feeling the sharp sting of rage in my chest.

A tall boy grinned at me, white teeth dazzling in his grimy face. He had olive skin, hazel eyes, a snub nose dotted with freckles. His brown hair was clotted with mud, his scabby knees winked at me from below his shorts. He already had that coltish look boys get just before they hit puberty; all long limbs and awkwardness. But he wasn't at all awkward; he could move those gangly limbs as quick as lightning. I knew it just by looking at his whippet-thin form.

He was graceful and beautiful and bold, and I adored him at once.

"My name is Ann, and I'm not scared of you," I said, standing with my legs parted, hands on hips. I glared into his eyes, daring him. If I had unclamped my hands from my hips, he would have seen they were trembling. But I wasn't that stupid.

He stared at me a moment longer, taking my measure, and then laughed. A generous sound. I wanted to be the cause of him making that sound again. Often.

"Kid, you're ok," he said, closing the gap between us with a few lanky strides. He stuck his dirty hand out, and I took it. We shook in the solemn manner of children who understand that everything in life is serious, especially the things that don't seem so. "My name's Jesse, and if you ever need a hand with anything or anyone, just say the word."

I smiled up at him (he was a full head taller), and hoped he couldn't tell that I was blushing.

"Thanks," I said, "I will."

"You're new," he stated. This was a kid who had no questions about the goings-on in his neighbourhood; he knew it all. "I live at number 36 too, with my mum, in the flat at the top of the drive; you're at the bottom. We're neighbours."

We were standing on the street, just past the steep driveway leading down to the four little freestanding flats where we both lived. Fitzgerald Court was a cul-de-sac atop a formidable hill; mum said our little two bedroom flat was cheap because nobody wanted to scale that mountain every time they needed something. Few people in the area had cars, and many of the flats were housing commission. The street was full of single parents (like my mum) with their kids (like me).

I had been walking back from the shop at the bottom of the hill, where my mother had sent me for cigarettes (they didn't care so much about selling them to minors back then—in fact, in that area, I'm sure they still don't care). I didn't know where *he* was returning from, but I wished I had been there. With him.

"Yeah, we moved in yesterday," I told him. "I start school on Monday."

"Rose Gardens Primary?" He knelt down for a moment, and resurfaced holding the apple he had lobbed at me. He bit into it, crunching with relish. He held it out to me, offering a bite. I leant forward and took one while he kept hold of the apple. The fruit was sweet and crisp, but not as delicious as the intimacy of the shared moment. "It's a posh name, but not a posh school. But I reckon you guessed that."

"Yeah. I'm in grade three. You go there too?"

"Yep. Grade five. I'll walk with you on Monday." Another not-question. I nodded. He returned my nod, and we walked side by side back to our driveway. A grin, a wave, and he was gone, consumed by his flat's bright yellow door.

I'd been in the neighbourhood for five minutes, and already a kid that oozed coolness and capability was going to hang out with me. Well, for the walk to school (and maybe on the way home, too, if I was lucky), anyway.

"What are you smiling about?" Mum took the cigarette packet from my hands and began to unwrap it as I walked into our lounge room. She was still in her dressing gown, curled into a ball on the couch watching Oprah.

"Nothing," I said. "Just happy."

"I think we'll both be happy here, Ann." She was already sucking on one of the cigarettes, her eyes flitting to me in quick hope. "I really think maybe we will."

"I think so too."

As long as Jesse was nearby, I had a feeling everything would be alright. Better than alright, even.

I still feel that way now, if I sense Jesse near me. I don't feel him often, but sometimes, I think he's there.

I choose to believe that, anyway. I've *got* to.

◆　◆　◆

Jesse walked me to school on Monday, and home again. He did the same on Tuesday, and by Friday, I was pretty sure I could safely call it a regular thing.

We didn't see each other much during the school day; he was a big ten year old, and I was a much smaller (and less well known and important) eight year old. We passed on the oval or in the corridor from time to time, and he always gave me that radiant grin, and sometimes reached out a hand to ruffle my hair as he walked by.

God, I loved it when he did that. Especially when everyone *saw* him do it.

True to his word, he was suddenly *there* if I needed him. When the biggest girl in my grade took a dislike to me, shoving me around behind the bike shed, Jesse materialised and whispered something in her ear. I don't know what he said (he refused to tell me), but it made her swarthy face blanch, and her lower lip shudder. I even thought I spotted moisture in her piggy eyes.

"Sorry Ann," she blurted, running away before I could reply.

He was my self-nominated protector, and soon enough, everyone knew it. I was off limits for bullying and all the other mundane violence and torture that make up a large portion of school life. I was safe, and the name of my safety was Jesse Willis.

◆ ◆ ◆

Don't get me wrong, he gave me a rough time himself on occasion. He liked to challenge and provoke me, and he enjoyed a good battle—physical or mental, it was all the same to Jesse, though I think he preferred non-physical sparring with me. I was so much smaller than him that there was no fun in beating me as we wrestled on the concrete of our shared driveway; it was a foregone conclusion that he would be the victor. Jesse liked to be genuinely tested, and he played some of the most vicious mind games I have ever encountered. No one could push my buttons like Jesse could.

But I knew he would never *really* hurt me. Jesse just had an angry core, burning away deep down inside where few people could see it. It flamed in measured bursts, but he was always in control. Because he was *good*, in every way that mattered.

Our backgrounds were so similar we barely bothered talking about them. We had a brief exchange of words and were done with it.

"My dad put my mum in hospital a couple times, so we left him, and then we moved here," Jesse said, dropping a stone into the puddle below us. We were sitting on scaffolding up on the building site at the end of our street. Jesse told me it had been "under construction" for about five years. The house was an empty shell with no roof; the owner builder had gone bankrupt and had simply stopped work. We called it The Mansion, and it was one of my, and Jesse's, favourite places.

*Dad tried to kill mum on my seventh birthday,* I thought, willing him to hear me. *From my bedroom, I could hear every punch, and her screams. Then there was a crash and the screaming stopped. I thought she was dead, and I knew he'd come for me next. I jumped out the window and ran to a neighbour's house, and they called the police. Mum was in a coma for a week, and I was in foster care for a while. Then we were in a women's shelter, and now we're here. Sometimes mum locks herself in the bathroom with a bottle of wine and her cigarettes, and I can hear her crying and moaning in there, and I'm scared she's going to kill herself.*

But all I said was: "Same here."

He knew. I knew that he knew, and he understood.

We had sleepovers every now and then; I loved curling up with him in his little red metal bed, him under his boyish racing car doona, me on top of it—and I could just walk the few steps back to my own house the next day. We spooned with the innocence of kids who don't yet know what spooning is, and we told ghost stories until the wee hours. We talked about school; I loved to hear his tales of life as a grade fiver (he had less interest in my retellings of grade three life).

It was a small and modest Utopia we created, Jesse and I. We were poor kids in many ways, but we weren't bothered by that.

Jesse's mother yelled at him a lot, and I'd seen her slap him in the face once; he'd stormed past me into his bedroom, and when I followed, his tight lips and blazing eyes told me not to discuss it. But she loved him, and he loved her—fiercely, like everything he did and felt. I loved my mother too, with all her neuroses and flaws.

Our mothers couldn't afford to buy us stuff the other kids had, but we had The Mansion as our personal plaything, more than any other kids could claim. And we had each other.

For the briefest moment in time, we were happy.

Then the Ice Cream Man came, and saw our frailty. Maybe he sensed it, *smelt* it on us.

And all was lost.

◆ ◆ ◆

Of the simple pleasures afforded to your average kid in those days, the pinnacle was an ice cream from the van that made its musical way around the neighbourhood streets.

On hearing that tinkling in the distance, every child shared a Pavlovian response. We sat bolt upright, stopped whatever we were doing as the saliva flooded our mouths. We descended upon our parents in a flurry of demand, clamouring for the right amount of change. We hopped from foot to foot, hearts beating furiously, as our parents took their sweet time gathering the money. Then we tore out the door and onto the street, coins in hand, standing in hopeful bunches, peering down the road, each vying to be first to spot the van as it came around the corner toward us.

That was exactly where Jesse and I found ourselves the day the Ice Cream Man came.

"I'm getting a soft serve with a Flake," I said, craning my neck, determined to see the van before Jesse did. The hot pavement was scorching the soles of our bare feet, a pleasant association with the treat to follow.

"I'm getting choc dip on mine," he said, blocking my line of sight with his frame, as I scuffled for position with him.

*Greensleeves* played on a loop; the tinny melody echoed, ricocheting off neighbourhood nooks and crannies.

"There it is!" I yelled, and danced in the gutter as Jesse hissed in disappointment.

*Greensleeves* was suddenly a cacophony, blasting down our street. I always think of that van's tune, reverberating through my every fibre. Jangly. Evil is a jangly thing, and its wares are sweet and cold.

The ice cream van was a battered beast, once white, but now a chipped grey. Its side was covered from top to bottom in photos and descriptions of wondrous confections. SHAKES TOO! brightly painted letters informed us. The window in the middle of the van's side was open, like an eager mouth.

The van shuddered to a halt in front of us, and was immediately swarmed with children. I rushed forward, but Jesse pulled me back.

"Better to hang back until those vultures are done."

We watched the wriggling backs of the other neighbourhood children. They looked like mewling newborn kittens, clamouring at their mother's teats.

When the last kid had scampered off, licking the melting sweetness from their hand, Jesse and I approached the window.

The Ice Cream Man had his back to us, re-stacking the cones. He was huge; *broad*, a hulk of a man. The top of his bald head brushed the van's ceiling, the back of his white shirt stretched almost to breaking over the expanse of his shoulders. A sheen of sweat coated the back of his head, and I felt oddly repulsed; for a moment I thought I might vomit.

We should have run away then. I wish we had.

He was humming *Greensleeves* as he turned around. His eyes, a shocking venom green, widened when he saw us. His cheeks were round and red, like a painted doll. His tongue darted out from behind his small pointy teeth, moistening his plump lips as he smiled. His translucent skin stretched tautly over him like a full body mask. Which is what it really was, after all.

"Why, *there* you are! I thought all my customers had gone for the day." His delighted voice was shrill and nasal. "You two certainly hid yourselves well!"

His choice of words and the recognition in his voice started the slow flip-flop of unease in my belly.

"Yeah, it's better to just wait until everyone else is done," Jesse said, and I had the sudden urge to wrench him away from the gaping maw of the van's window; run back into my flat with him and hide until the van was gone.

"A very wise approach," the Ice Cream Man said, his eyes fixed on Jesse's. "Very wise indeed, young man."

We stood there for a moment, and when it became apparent that the man wasn't going to speak again, I cleared my throat.

"Um, can I please have a single cone, soft serve, with a Flake in it?"

He kept staring at Jesse, and then his eyes *shifted* somehow, and he was looking at me—*and* Jesse.

"Of course you can, little lady. And you, young man? What can I do *you* for?"

"The same, but with choc dip."

"Oh, mmmn, yummy!" the man giggled, and it sounded like a pig screaming. I looked sidelong at Jesse, and found him already looking at me. He shook his head slightly. *Don't freak out,* he seemed to be saying.

By now I knew I wouldn't eat my ice cream. And I didn't want a single melted drop of it to touch my skin. I sensed danger, and I wanted to run, and run, and run.

But Jesse was never a runner; he would stand there until the danger backed down or consumed him. And I wouldn't leave his side.

My knees began to shake as the man turned his back on us once again.

"What names do you two kids go by?"

"Jesse and Ann," Jesse said automatically, and I yelped.

*He shouldn't have done that. He shouldn't have given it our names.*

"Well, Jesse and Ann, I go by the name of Vincent when I'm here. These two treats are on the house, ok? When I see smart kids, I want to reward them. And you two are smart kids; any fool can tell that, even an old fool like me." He squealed his hideous laugh again, and stretched his arms towards us, offering the two dripping confections.

*I can't take it from his hand. I* won't.

Jesse gave me a quick glance, and then reached for both of the ice creams. Always my saviour. Always my protector.

The man who was Vincent *when he was here* lifted his long fingers and caressed Jesse's hands as he passed the ice creams over. Jesse shuddered, and his head snapped back on his neck, lolling. For a moment he looked like he was about to fall over, and I reached my arm around his back, ready to try and hold him up; but he seemed to regain his equilibrium quickly, and flashed me a smile.

"I'm ok. Just felt a little bit . . . faint."

"You should go sit down and eat those," the man said, beaming at us, showing off his sharp teeth. "They'll cure what ails ya!"

He flipped a switch to his left, and *Greensleeves* resumed its canned noise. I hadn't even noticed it had been silenced until then.

"Be seeing you, Jesse and Ann," the man called over his shoulder, heading for the driver's seat. "Be seeing you real soon, I hope!"

Another murderous shrieking giggle, and he was driving off; turning a circle in the cul-de-sac and disappearing around the corner.

Jesse and I both looked down at the ice creams he held. As they gleamed in the sunlight, melting white liquid trails snaked towards Jesse's skin.

"Don't let it touch you," I said, but Jesse had already flung the ice creams on the asphalt, stepping back from them with a grimace.

"Were they poisoned?" I huddled close to Jesse's side, and we stared at the gooey carnage on the road.

"I think maybe they were, but not in the way you might think," he said.

I nodded. I knew just what he meant.

"There was something wrong with him, Ann. When he touched my hands, something happened. He's bad. I don't think he's even human."

I heard a moist sniff, and realised to my horror that Jesse was crying.

"He's gone now," I said. But it was a question, not a statement.

"I hope so. I really hope so," Jesse said, squeezing me.

We gave the fallen ice creams a wide berth as we made our way down the driveway.

"Stay at my place," I said to Jesse, and he nodded.

He shivered all night. I knew, because I stayed awake, holding him, keeping watch. A few times, he whispered: "No . . . leave her alone . . . you stay away from her!"

My protector, even in the murky depths of his own worst nightmares. Always my hero.

◆  ◆  ◆

*I scream, you scream, we all scream for* ICE CREAM!

I want to forget, and if I choose to, I can. The blissful fog of adulthood can descend over those sharp-toothed childhood memories and erase them as if they never were.

But it would mean forgetting Jesse, and I won't do it.

◆  ◆  ◆

Mum was going through another black mood. She hadn't dressed in days; her dressing gown was badly food-stained. Her hair hung lank on her pasty face and she stared into the middle distance, eyes glassy and vacant. She still made our meals, and she kept our little flat in decent shape, but she simply wasn't there while she did it. I didn't know where she *was*, but I knew it was somewhere I couldn't go to bring her back.

"I'm going to have a bath," she said tonelessly, moving around the lounge and kitchen area, collecting her cigarettes and a half-full bottle of cheap wine.

*Oh no.*

She shut herself in the bathroom, and, as usual, turned her cassette player up loud. She seemed to think the noise blocked out the sound of her weeping, but it never did. I think that sound can be heard through anything; detected by some deep, primal sadness sensor in our brains.

The music I heard blaring from the bathroom, while my mother cried, was *Greensleeves*.

And in the moment between my eyelids falling and rising in a blink, Vincent the Ice Cream Man appeared next to me on the lounge-room couch.

"She's going to kill herself in there this time, Ann," he said in his high-pitched twang, and he chortled his slaughtered-pig laugh.

I leapt off the couch, terrified keening rising from my throat, and backed up against the lounge room wall, keeping my eyes on him. The seat of the couch bowed under his bulk, almost touching the floor. His arms were spread across the backrest like pterodactyl wings, and his ankles were crossed. He looked casual; comfortable; vicious. Even through his smile.

"You're not real," I hissed at him through clenched teeth. "You're not here, you can't be here, you're *not real*!"

His tongue flickered out from his bulging lips, and I saw that it was forked. Not just forked, but forked over and over again, with at least ten tips. And *long*.

"Why, of course I'm real, Ann. I'm sitting right here talkin' to you, aren't I? I'm one of the realest things in this world right now; the oldest, too." He winked at me, and I realised with horror that his eyelids closed in from the sides, not top-to-bottom.

"What are you?"

"I've come to drink your mother's blood, not to chat with you, on this particular occasion." He pronounced it *per-tickle-uh*, like a demonic Colonel Sanders. "She's slicing herself up good in the bathroom, and I'm going to help you clean up afterwards." He waggled thin brows at me, grinning.

"She's not. You just want to scare me." But I threw a glance toward the bathroom anyway. *Greensleeves* was still blasting through the door . . . but beneath it, I could hear her sobbing. She was so very sad, but she was well and truly alive.

"Oh, but I *do* scare you, don't I, Ann?"

And suddenly he was in front of me, towering over me, leering down. And he was *cold*. I felt a bone-numbing chill gnawing at my bones.

I knew he wanted me to scream, but I wouldn't give him that. Whatever else he wanted from me, he could just *take*, and I probably couldn't stop him; but I wouldn't give him my screams.

Not today.

"Your mother is dead, Ann. There's nothing left here for you. Why not come with me now? It's better where I come from; you'll like it there. All the ice cream you can eat, and there's music, and it's never too hot. In fact, it's deliciously *cold*. Your mother's there now. Don't you want to come, Ann?"

"My mother is not dead," I said, hating the tremor in my voice, "and even if she *was* I wouldn't go with you. I have Jesse."

*Why, oh why, did I say* THAT*?!*

"Yes, your little friend. He's there too, Ann, boogeying on down to *Greensleeves*. Or he soon will be, so who's counting, eh?"

I shook my head at him, over and over. He reached around behind his back, and produced three ice cream cones jammed into his huge fist.

"One for each of you. Your favourite ice creams, and why don't you have a SHAKE, TOO!"

And he threw them into my face, and they *burnt*, with an icy cold fire that ate into my skin, blazed into my eyes, probed my brain, consumed me . . .

I screamed then, as he squealed with delight. I slipped down the wall and hit the floor, cold fire scorching me as the world tilted, spun . . . and fell away completely.

◆ ◆ ◆

When I woke from my faint on the floor, there was nobody in sight, and my face had not been melted off by the caustic coldness of Vincent's ice creams. For the briefest moment, I wondered if I had imagined the whole thing.

But I knew better than that.

I never told Jesse about the Ice Cream Man paying me a special visit. Maybe I should have. I can't see how, but maybe things would have been different. I never told my mother, either. Vincent had lied about her hurting herself in the bathroom. And it hadn't even been Greensleeves she was listening to—she'd had her Joe Cocker cassette playing.

◆　◆　◆

We sat on The Mansion's scaffolding, dropping leaves into the dirty puddles below and watching them settle lightly on the surface.

"You're my best friend, Ann," Jesse said suddenly, and I looked at him, startled.

"You're my best friend too, Jesse."

He put his arm around my shoulders and squeezed me, and I let my head drop onto his bony shoulder. We stayed like that for a long time.

"I'll be going away soon," Jesse said after a while. I jolted upright, instantly terrified.

*Vincent paid him a visit too,* I thought, but I didn't ask, didn't want to make it real.

"Are you moving?"

"No, nothing like that. Forget I said it. I just want you to know that you're the best person I've ever met. I just . . . wanted to tell you."

*I love you, I love you, I love you, please don't let him take you away.*

"You, too," I said.

We watched while the sinking sun dappled The Mansion and us in amber, then crimson, then dusky purple. That is how I like to remember us; in that perfect last moment together, for all time, just Jesse and me, in our safe place.

When the air's chill began to bite and we heard Jesse's mother calling out his name, we clambered down from our lofty perch and ambled, arm in arm, to our steep shared driveway.

"I love you," Jesse said, and then he was gone, running into his house without a backward glance. I had seen the embarrassed flush rising in his cheeks, even in the dim glow from his flat's outside light.

I stayed standing there, looking at Jesse's bedroom window, until my own mother called me home.

Something called to Jesse that night (probably with ice cream that burnt, and SHAKES, TOO!), and it must have called *loudly*, because Jesse was gone in the morning.

And I know why. Jesse had slipped a note under my front door.

But I think I would have known, even without that note. Even if my dreams that night hadn't been set to the tinkling of *Greensleeves*.

◆　◆　◆

It's the only tangible thing I have left of him; left of *us*, and I've treasured it all these years. Treasured it, kept it safe, but never read it again. I only ever read it that one time, the morning after Jesse was gone.

If my mum had found that note, she would have told Jesse's mother, and that would only have hurt everyone more. Better for them to think he was kidnapped by his father.

Better anything than the truth.

◆　◆　◆

ANN,

I HAV 2 GO WITH HIM.

HE SAYS THAT IF I GO WITH HIM, HE'LL LEVE U ALONE. I DON'T THINK THAT HE WANTS 2 KILL ME, I THINK I WILL STILL BE ALIVE OVER *THERE*. I THINK THEY NEED KIDS THERE, AND IT'S HIS JOB 2 GET THEM.

LOOK AFTER YOUR MUM, AND MINE. SHE WILL MISS ME. I WILL MISS HER. BUT I WILL MISS U THE MOST.

U R WORTH IT.

JESSE XOX

◆　◆　◆

I wonder if he still lives in that Other place, where Vincent took him in the dead of night. I wonder if he regrets

(*U R WORTH IT*)

not putting up a fight. But I'm not sure fighting would have helped him anyway. I suspect it had mostly been Jesse the Ice Cream Man wanted, not me. If Vincent had tried to take us both, we could not have prevented it. I can't imagine the negotiations Jesse must have had with the Ice Cream Man. But I *believe* that note. Somehow, Jesse managed to take the horror from something horrific, even to give it some beauty. For me, for us. How Vincent must have hated that.

I was safe, and the name of my safety was Jesse Willis.

This was Jesse's gift to me, and it will stay with me.

I wonder if he is still ten years old. I think, maybe, he is.

Most of all, I wonder how anyone can hear the eerie jangle of ice cream van music without going insane. Even before Jesse was taken, even before we saw Vincent grinning out at us from his van, I knew that music for a Wrong Thing.

There aren't so many ice cream vans cruising our streets now, when we're too paranoid to send our children onto the streets to receive sticky gifts from strangers.

No, not so many travelling ice cream vendors . . . but I think that somewhere out there, there is still a battered grey-white van rattling down the streets, the window in its side panel gaping open, *Greensleeves* blaring on a loop from the loudspeaker mounted on the roof. Inside is a man who is not a man at all, and *his* ice cream is something really special.

# AFTERWORD

*This piece was inspired by three things: the Girl Overboard song* Jackie *(if you've never heard it, hunt it down—it's simple, beautiful, and sad); my husband's remark that I should "write a horror story about an ice cream van, 'cos those things are* creepy"; *and my own brief childhood friendship with a boy called Jesse. I remember the real life version of* The Mansion *in this tale, endless treasure buried in its mud and mess. I remember the joy of sitting on a skateboard and rolling at high speed down a steep driveway, using my feet as brakes until the soles of my shoes no longer existed. I remember being a kid who wasn't quite like other kids, I remember my mother's sadness, I remember the excitement of an ice cream van approaching to the tune of* Greensleeves . . . *and I remember anything being possible, and how that wasn't necessarily a comforting thought.*

# FROM LITTLE THINGS . . .

There's a dragon in my pantry.

Well, it's not really *my* pantry; it's my sister's husband's. I'm staying with them, courtesy of being done over by a lying, cheating, overspending ex fiancé. She got the house, car, and cat. I got a bad credit rating, a broken heart, and my trust in the human race cancelled without a refund.

It's not a regular dragon (the one in the pantry, not my ex, although if the shoe fits . . . ). It's tiny, around 15cm long, with iridescent purple scales mottled with glitter, flashing emerald eyes, and a silver belly. The triangular tip of its tail is amethyst. It's a beautiful thing. I've always thought so. That's why I bought the candle holder that, until yesterday, the iron dragon was entwined around.

I found the dragon when I opened the pantry to get some cereal at 10am this morning. I enjoy late breakfasts because, as my brother-in-law Dwight will readily inform you, I don't have a job. I was fired, but it wasn't my fault. Dwight would probably omit that part.

The dragon sat on a jar of chutney, tail poised above the cling wrap lid, sharp amethyst tip aimed downward. We stared at each other. Not being accustomed to ancient mythical creatures (particularly not miniature ones that should be inanimate on candle holders like good little iron figurines), I had no idea what to do. I gaped while the dragon watched me with cool green eyes.

"Hello," it said after a while. It sounded like a pack-a-day smoker. A flame shot from its mouth when it spoke. The cling wrap on the chutney bubbled and went black.

I raised a hand in dumb greeting and then, feeling impolite, opened my mouth. Nothing came out but a strained wheeze.

"I'm very hungry. It's theft, but I only intended to take a little. Since you're here, may I seek your permission?" Seeing my glazed eyes and slack jaw, the dragon wiggled its tail, indicating the chutney.

"Oh," I croaked, finding my voice. "Uh, shall I open it for you?"

"Thank you."

The dragon flapped its tiny purple wings, lifting off the chutney and alighting on a can of chickpeas instead. I reached in. Intensely aware of the proximity of the dragon to my naked and vulnerable hand, I fumbled, peeling the cling wrap back to expose the orange jelly. The dragon licked its lips. It sounded like the world's smallest piece of sandpaper rasping on the world's smallest piece of wood.

I withdrew my hand with relief, and the dragon gave me a courteous nod before securing itself to the rim of the jar with its talons. It dipped its head, then paused, staring at me.

"Oh," I said, and, grabbing the cereal, shut the pantry door. I pressed my ear to the wood. Faint lapping sounds came from within, followed by a small belch.

Not being equipped with a manual entitled 'Things to do When You Find a Miniature Dragon in Your Pantry', I sat down at the dining table, poured myself a bowl of cereal, and began to eat.

♦ ♦ ♦

*Joe,*

*Work do 2nite, home v. late—free alcohol, woot! Dwight @ faculty dinner, home late 2.*

*Quiche in fridge, heat @ 180/half hour.*

*Pretty please do dishes & washing & keep house tidy? U know Dwight. Really want u 2 get along. Please?*

*Stacey is oxygen thief. Love.*

*Feebs*

My sister, Feebs. Phoebe Marson, who got married and became Mrs Dwight Frontbottom. Yes, that's really his surname. No, I'm not shitting you. Yes, it suits him.

Feebs works in a huge shiny office for a global insurance broking firm. Dwight is the Lapis University groundsman. Referring to himself as part of the faculty is one of his favourite pretences. Feebs earns way more than Dwight. He wears plaid patches on his sleeves in an attempt to resemble a professor. She's smarter. He works less hours. And yet, her night out is merely a work do compared to his *faculty dinner.* Yeesh.

Stacey's my ex, in case you're wondering.

For the record, I do clean up after myself. The way Dwight carries on, you'd think I enjoy smearing snot on the walls and peeing on the carpet.

I opened the fridge to peek at the quiche. The dragon flew out in a burst of shimmering violet. I squawked and leapt back. The dragon settled atop the range hood across the kitchen, smiling. It had a lot of very sharp teeth. It had grown to at least three times its previous size, now looking less like a figurine and more like a plump purple puppy. With wings. And scales.

I hadn't opened the pantry for a week. Takeaway had been my friend, and denial had soothed my brain. I'd gone with the explanation of vivid hallucination, and the dragon had helpfully abstained from reappearing—until now. I had no idea how it had gotten into the fridge, or what it had been up to for the past week. Eating would be my guess; eating and expanding.

"Thank you." The dragon had slivers of carrot and lettuce in its bristling fangs. "I've been in there for hours. Any longer and the temperature might have caused problems. Cold blood."

I nodded. My fingers tingled and my head swam. I thought I might faint.

"Look," the dragon said, gesturing at me with razorblade claws, "I understand how difficult this must be. It's a shock. Shall we make proper introductions?"

"Um. That would be nice."

The dragon flew past my head. It smelt like a freshly extinguished candle wrapped in copper. I turned and followed, and found it perched on the back of a dining chair, tail coiled around its haunches like a contented cat. I sat facing it across the table. I had to fight the sudden urge to offer it tea and scones.

"My name is Jasper. That's not my real name, but it's the closest I can get to it in words you'll understand and be able to pronounce. I am, as you can see, a dragon, and a humble and appreciative guest in your home. And you are . . . ?"

"Er. Joseph. Call me Joe. This isn't my home, I'm just staying here. It's my sister's—well, her husband's. Are you a figment of my imagination?" I was babbling and my voice held the tinny shrill of panic, but I thought I was doing well, given the circumstances.

Jasper the not-quite-so-miniature-anymore dragon chortled. Plumes of smoke erupted from his flared nostrils with a little *whoomph* sound.

"Pleased to meet you, Joe. I'm not in your head. I'm as real as can be. I am somewhat . . . diminished, at present. It's going to take me a while to return to my proper size. There was a spell—but I'm getting ahead of myself. *Not* your house—your sister's husband, you say?"

"Yeah. Dwight Frontbottom."

"Ah. I see. Your brother-in-law—your relative, then. Not by blood, but related, all the same. Very good. Perhaps this time I've chosen wisely, after all."

I had no idea what he (based on the dragon's name and the deep gravel of his voice, I assumed he was male) was on about, but something warned me not to ask him to explain. Something inside my brain that cared about my sanity and knew just how much I could take before I came unhinged and ran screaming and drooling down the street.

"And . . . you *were* the iron dragon on my candle holder?"

"Yes and no. That isn't my true form. I was imprisoned a long time ago—that spell I mentioned."

"And you're getting bigger."

"Yes. And shall continue until I reach my true size. I suspect we will have parted company by then."

"And you're here talking to me because . . . "

Jasper exhaled a vermillion blast of fire. Dwight would have had kittens at the sight of the flames licking the glossy finish on his dining setting—paid for by Phoebe, but *his*. Of course.

"If you'll forgive me, Joe, I'd like to ask a few of my own questions now. This Bigbottom fellow—"

"—Frontbottom—"

"—I'd like to hear about him, if you'd be so kind."

"He's not the most interesting guy. What would you like to know?"

Jasper bared his growing teeth in a wide and jagged smile.

"I'd like to know how *you* feel about him, Joe. It's quite important."

◆  ◆  ◆

Remember that instruction manual I said I didn't have—'Things to do When You Find a Miniature Dragon in Your Pantry'? I was being glib, but I really *do* have that manual now. Except it's called *The Bynding of the Lavender Wyrm*, and Dwight gave it to me.

"Here," he grunted as he slouched into the house, slinging something at me.

I sat up (I'd been lying on the couch, reading—something Dwight had done several times in his life, and then only to decide what he wanted from the McDonalds menu) and grabbed the heavy tome just before it crashed into my face. It was dusty, and I sneezed. The cover was coarse, shrivelled brown leather, and it stunk like bin juice. The many pages were thin and gilt edged. The title was black, seared into the front cover as though by a sizzling brand.

Below the title was a picture of Jasper.

He was bigger in the picture

*(it's going to take me a while to return to my proper size)*

but it was unmistakably him, perched on a rocky outcrop, looming over a town below. Hundreds of humans ran in panic, tiny faces contorted in horror as they looked up at him. Jasper leered, black tongue dangling obscenely from his mouth, gobbets of drool making stringy patterns on the dusty rocks beneath him. His talons were harbingers of doom stretched out over the vista of terror.

A little jolt shot through me. Dwight had a book about the dragon living in his kitchen. Did he know? It was hardly the sort of thing Dwight could keep quiet about.

"What is it?" I said, pleased to discover my voice was casual despite my crawling unease.

"A book." Dwight burst into snuffling laughter at his own wit. I gave him a sick smile as he settled into the armchair opposite me, muddy work boots smearing the lemon fabric.

"I see that. But why'd you give it to me?"

Dwight Frontbottom was a big man who favoured flannel shirts and jeans as his uniform of choice. I had to fight the urge to sing *I'm a lumberjack and I'm OK!* whenever I saw him. He kept his orange hair cropped close to his skull, blazing above his pale freckled skin. His eyes were a muddy brown, barely noticeable above the bulbous slab of his nose. Amid all that largesse, his mouth was almost invisible, a small thin slash of lip and teeth. It stretched now in smugness.

"Don't try it on with me, kiddo. You're a tool, but not as sharp as me. I found it in my car. You're the only one round here who reads queer crap like that. I've told Phoebe I don't want you in my car, but she's soft. I'm not, though, catpiss?"

Dwight had just referred to himself as a tool—albeit a *sharp* one. He'd also substituted feline urine for the Italian word *capisce*. This would normally have resulted in uncontrollable laughter on my part, but not this time.

"You found it in your car," I repeated his words slowly, seeing how they felt on my tongue. They felt just fine. He was telling the truth.

"What're you, an idiot? That's what I said. Now keep outta my car. Otherwise you and I'll have words, kiddo."

I was five years older than Dwight. I hated him calling me kiddo, but even that didn't penetrate my fugue.

"*My* book. Sure, of course it's my book."

Dwight shot me an acid look, then hefted his broad-shouldered bulk out of the armchair, shaking his head in disgust.

"Loser," he muttered. I heard him clumping up the stairs, no doubt leaving a trail of swampy dirt for Feebs to clean.

I stared at the book. It looked ancient. The leather cover was busy, roiling under my fingers. A memory flashed into my mind— lampshades made from human skin during the Holocaust—and I shuddered. I pulled my sleeves down over my hands before touching the book again.

I'd start reading it tonight. If I put my mind to it—and I had a feeling I *would* put my mind to it—I could probably finish it in a week.

For no apparent reason, a thrill ran through me like low voltage electricity.

◆ ◆ ◆

That job I mentioned earlier? Dwight got me fired. Stacey helped. Phoebe knows. She and Dwight had their worst row ever when I told her, and that's why Dwight *permitted* me to stay here in *his* house. Because if he didn't, foolish as Feebs is when it comes to Dwight, I think she might have left him. Dwight knows it, too. He knows that without Feebs to foot the bills, he wouldn't make the house payments, or sustain his myriad of other bills. Nobody wants to lose their meal ticket.

It happened like this.

I was a salesman at a large store. I liked it. I'd been there five years, and given another year, I would have made department manager. I got along well with my boss, Lara, and my workmates.

It was a slow Friday afternoon. I leant on the counter, watching Dr Phil on one of the monstrous plasma screens mounted on the far wall of the showroom. I was pleased when the phone rang.

"Electrical, Joe sp—"

"You dirty *bastard*!"

Stacey. We'd broken up a fortnight ago. I'd arrived home early and found her in bed with another man. Now she rang me—at home, at work, on the bus, on the john—to inform me I was pond scum on a regular basis.

"Always a pleasure to hear from you, Stace."

"Don't get smart, Joseph Marson. It doesn't suit you. You're going to *unlock it*, that's what you're going to do. D'you hear me?"

I heard her. There was enough wretched love and lingering pain in me to ensure I would hear her in my dreams for a long time to come.

"I have no idea what you're talking about."

She snarled, a curl-lipped hiss that rasped in my ear.

"You coy jerk, yes you *do*. The credit card, Joe. It's mine. You had no right to tell the bank to lock it. You're going to fix this. Right. Now."

"Actually, darling, that card—like all the others you've maxed out—is in *my* name, and therefore mine to lock, cancel or set aflame as I see fit. I'm in debt up to my eyeballs from the car payments—you know, the car *you're* driving? And the electricity bill, the telephone bill, the—"

"How am I supposed to *live*?" Her voice was timorous now, pleading, soft. Hey presto, watch Stacey the magician change before your eyes! "I've got no money for *food*, Joe. No money for petrol—how am I to get to work? Would you have me starve, Joe? Would you see me destitute? Is that what you want? Will that make you happy?" She gave a moist sniff, a sterling imitation of a wronged woman bravely holding back her tears.

"Your six figure salary is sufficient to keep you fed, Stacey. And I'm sure your loving man will take care of you. Not me, of course— your *other* loving man. You know, the one you were banging in our bed while I was at work."

She waved her magic wand and changed again.

"You'll unlock it," she said, enunciating each word with whipcrack sharpness, "or I'll come down there. I'll tell Lara you *hit* me. I'll bloody my face up real good, I'll lose you your job. You want to dance? Fine. I'm a much better dancer than you, Joe. You really don't want to take me on."

Idiot that I am, I told her to go right ahead—come down in nothing but her birthday suit with JOE BLOWS GOATS written on her belly in blood—but the card was staying locked.

She showed up within 15 minutes.

Her blonde hair stuck out at wild angles, a clump of it missing from the front of her scalp. Chunky globules of blood nestled on inflamed skin there, and a purple bruise had begun to swell. One of her green cat's eyes was puffed shut, the other eye weeping and torn. Her button nose was broken, pointing East at a jaunty angle. Her bottom lip was mashed and bleeding. Through the blood, bruising and swelling on her cheeks, a handprint blazed.

As I gawped, she leant into my face and whispered. Her breath smelt like iron filings.

"One more chance, Joe," she said with obvious difficulty, her burst lip twitching. "Unlock the card."

I shook my head, a silent exclamation at the insanity of her appearance.

"Fine," she said, straightening and taking a step away from the counter. "Just remember you *asked* for this."

She threw herself on the floor and began to scream. Stacey the magician, working her deceptive spells again. I stood staring down at her. Shock makes fools of us all.

"What's going *on*?"

Lara hit the floor at full sprint, leaping down from the stairs and racing across the showroom. She was a tall woman, and she closed the gap between us in a few loping strides.

"Joe! Are you alright? I heard scream—"

Lara saw Stacey, and her eyes widened. She fell to her knees beside my ex, who had curled herself into the foetal position and sobbed brokenly into cupped hands. Lara put a tentative hand on Stacey's forearm, jerking away as Stacey screamed again.

"My God," Lara looked up at me, "what *happened*?"

"He attacked me," Stacey moaned. "I told him there was no future for us, and he tried to *kill* me!"

I shook my head as Lara stared at me and Stacey continued her ragged sobbing on the floor.

"Is this your fiancé?" Lara said.

"*Ex* fiancé," I corrected her, and wished I hadn't. It must have sounded cold and incriminating. "Yes, it's Stacey, and Lara, I *did not do this to her*. I don't know who did, but it wasn't me."

Stacey gave an ear-splitting howl, and Lara got to her feet, stepping toward me.

"Call an ambulance," she said to my startled colleagues, then she turned back to me. "Joe. This is bad. I need you to look me in the eye and tell me you had nothing to do with it. I know you, and I don't think you're capable of this. But all the same, you need to *tell* me."

I looked into her eyes and told her. She held my gaze as Stacey whimpered behind her, and then she nodded.

"Alright. I believe you. The important thing right now is that we get this woman to the hospital. She's hurt badly and maybe she's not thinking str—"

"He did it," a male voice boomed, and my job was gone.

Can you guess who it was? Of course you can. It was good ol' Dwight of the Frontbottom descending upon us, storming down the aisle in between the white goods and TVs, ginger hair bristling and cloudy eyes narrowed in mock fury.

He wasn't a good actor, but he was *there*—the only "witness"— and he said I did it. Everything Stacey said as they wheeled in a stretcher and lifted her onto it, he corroborated. Together they told Lara that I leapt the counter and reduced my ex's pretty face to a heap of shattered bones and bloody flesh. Never mind that my fists were clean and my clothes unmarred, they said I did it, and that was that.

Lara's eyes fixed on me in horrible disappointment as store security escorted me out ("your fiancé doesn't want to press charges, but if we see you here again, we'll press you in our own way," the big guys grimly informed me), so I know she didn't see the strands of bloody blonde hair wrapped around Dwight's sausage fingers. Strands that, minutes earlier, had been planted in Stacey's scalp. I wondered if Dwight had gotten over enthusiastic and broken a few more bones than Stacey requested. I thought perhaps he had.

So now you know how I lost my job, but there's one thing left undisclosed.

The man I caught in bed with Stacey. If you haven't already got it figured, I'll spell it out for you: Dwight. My sister's husband, sleeping with my (EX!) fiancé. They'd been doing it a long time— months, maybe years. They were *in love*, and as far as I know, they remain so to this day. Feebs works long hours. There's plenty of time for Dwight to pay visits to Stacey the magician for her special kind of sorcery. Now that her bones have mended and her face is pretty again, that is.

I loved Stacey. She was a cruel and selfish bitch, but I loved her, all the same.

I told Feebs how Stacey and Dwight lost me my job, but I didn't tell her why. Dwight still insists that I beat Stacey up. That's why he and Feebs fought so badly—she just won't believe I did it, bless her.

And the reason I won't tell her about Dwight's affair?

Because if I open my mouth and break her heart then her beautiful face, so full of trust and love and everything good (so like our mother's), will crumple and fall in on itself, and never be the same again. I can't do that to my sister. I won't.

Cowardly? Maybe. Am I doing the wrong thing? I don't know. I know that I love her and want her to be happy. And as long as she doesn't know, she is happy, in her own way.

I'll tell you one thing. I plan to make Dwight pay. I don't know how, but I'll wipe that smug smile off his ugly face.

I've been dreaming about it for the *longest* time.

◆　◆　◆

Curled up in bed in the spare room that had become *my* room, I stared at the bedside table. A lamp and digital alarm clock stood atop it. Not interesting. But in front of them were two things that were very interesting indeed. An iron candle holder, *sans* the dragon that had been wrapped around it when I purchased it from a garage sale a year ago, and a thick book bound in withered, pungent leather.

I reached out and picked up the book. I needed both hands to do it—the thing was *heavy*.

*The Bynding of the Lavender Wyrm.* What was this, Shakespeare humping Poe's leg?

I opened the book. There was no publishing information, just a table of contents. Even that hardly seemed necessary, since all it said was:

*The Bynding of the Lavender Wyrm*
*Book One: The Wyrm*
*Book Two: The Bynding*

Strangest of all, the book seemed to be handwritten. Extravagant black ink swirls snaked across the parchment pages.

I rested the weighty book on my chest and grasped the inner pages so that I wouldn't have to touch the crawling cover. I began to read.

I finished *Book One: The Wyrm* and, blinking in the light, glanced at the clock. I'd been reading for fifteen minutes. Impossible. The pages weren't numbered, but there were easily a few thousand in the book, and I'd just read half of them.

I knew a lot more about my reptilian friend in the kitchen now. Jasper was the most notorious dragon ever to have lived. He'd brought fortresses crashing to the ground with a flick of his barbed tail. He'd devoured countless towns, earning the name World Eater. At full size, each of his teeth was the same size as the average family car (how a book that was so old could possibly know about cars seemed the least strange thing I'd come across so far). His silver belly reflected light with such intensity that anybody looking upon him when he reared up would find their eyes an exploded mass of pulp in their skull. His scale glitter was corrosive, eating into the flesh of any being it touched, reducing them to smoking bones. There was no point of weakness on Jasper's body—nothing could pierce it. His flashing green eyes could paralyse people, rivers, even the clouds in the sky. His talons were so sharp that they need only part the air in anger within a few metres of their prey for it to fall, cut to ribbons. A single flap of his wings could cause a storm halfway around the globe.

In addition to this frenzied medieval hype came the usual dragon stuff—breathing fire, cave den filled with bones and treasure, various failed attempts by brave souls to vanquish the Wyrm and end his reign of terror.

Apparently Jasper was so intelligent that he was revered as a God in many countries. He'd been known to speak to humans, animals, and the very earth itself, and could command all. He slumbered for years after he ate, sometimes centuries. Some cultures regarded him as nature incarnate, dishing out a grisly, indiscriminate form of population control and restoring balance to the world.

*Book One* of *The Bynding of the Lavender Wyrm* was a complex, meandering catalogue of Jasper's life and times. It was fascinating and frightening, but seemed unrelated to the small dragon that had once been a figurine on my cheaply bought candle holder and was now a garrulous chutney-and-salad munching resident in the kitchen below me.

I thought that *Book Two: The Bynding* might shed more elaborate light on how Jasper came to be here, and why he was relevant to me. I was right. In addition to retelling Jasper's Bynding (wily and courageous sorcerer of unparalleled power manages to ensnare dangerous dragon with a clever spell, etc), *Book Two* contained details of the ritual for *un*Bynding.

I began to smile.

◆　◆　◆

There was an absence of dragon in the kitchen.

A few telltale crumbs lurked at the bottom of the pantry, and every egg in the fridge had been cracked and drained, but no dragon.

I was halfway around the kitchen, opening cupboard doors, when I realised my search was futile. Jasper would be too big now. He'd need to find somewhere with room to move and grow. Somewhere safe and inconspicuous.

I thought I had a pretty good idea where Jasper had relocated to. The garage was a dark place, filled with cobwebs and dank oppressive air. The steel door hadn't opened in years. Dwight's house had an undercover carport at the rear which was easier to manoeuvre in and out of, so the garage had become a dumping ground for unused exercise equipment, clothes that would be donated to charity "one day", and broken junk.

I knew Jasper was there before I flicked the dangling overhead bulb on, shedding weak light on the dirty room. It was the acrid sulphur-and-metal scent. Still, when I saw him, I couldn't help but gasp.

He was *huge*.

He'd shoved the debris over to the roller door and stacked it high; it towered to the roof. Cleared of the detritus that choked it, the garage was large enough for two cars with room to swing a cat on either side. But there was no space now. Jasper obliterated it with his immense presence.

His eyes were green satellites, perfect circles in the hardness of his face. His scales were big as roof shingles, cluttering his body in thick purple slabs. His body snaked along the garage, sinuous muscle tapering from the flat plate of his brow to the amethyst barb at the end of his meaty tail. His wings were veined purple tarpaulins, folded on the hump of his back. He smiled at me in friendly recognition, and I almost turned and ran at the sight of his teeth. Not the size of a family car yet, but on their way.

He scratched at one eye with a gleaming talon and nodded.

"I hoped you'd pay me another visit, Joe. As you see, I can no longer fit into the kitchen to obtain my own food. I wondered if you might assist me."

"I—I don't think we have enough food to feed you, Jasper."

I was frightened. Jasper exuded abrupt and blatant menace that I hadn't noticed when he'd been tiny. But I felt we had an unspoken agreement: I'd be cordial to him, and he'd be cordial to me. I hoped that part of that gentleman's agreement was the condition that he wouldn't eat me. Or touch me. I'd rather he didn't even look at me.

He was still smiling. I had the sudden feeling that he knew what I was thinking. Maybe even what I *would* think, in future. The book had said he was a God.

"You're right. I require substantial nutrition. But I haven't eaten in weeks, Joe—you've been keeping yourself quite busy—so at this point, I'll eat anything."

His words were a thinly veiled threat.

"What's in the house won't sate me, but it will take the knife edge off my hunger. I'm *ravenous*, Joe. Bring me everything—and I mean *everything*—from your kitchen, and I'll eat. Then, when I can think straight, without the drumbeat of starvation pounding in my brain, we can talk. You want to talk, don't you, Joe?"

"I've been reading," I blurted, and stopped. His jovial smile didn't falter.

"Of course. You'll want to talk about that. But first things first."

I felt Jasper's palpable need throbbing in the stagnant air, and I pitied him. Was he using me as a puppet, a minion, as the book had told me he could? I didn't think so. He needed me to act of my own free will. The book had told me that, too.

"I'll bring everything I can carry," I said. Jasper gave me his slow nod and dropped his head to the concrete floor, conserving energy.

He ate it as quickly as I brought it out. If the food was packaged, he ate the packaging, too—cardboard, plastic, glass, it didn't matter. He loved meat. His rows of ivory teeth crunched through frozen beef, chicken and lamb and he swallowed with guttural groans of pleasure. Now and then a flame escaped as he huffed and sighed.

After the fridge and every cupboard in the kitchen were bare, I made myself a cup of tea—I'd saved one teabag and a dash of milk. I knew I'd be in the garage with Jasper for a while. Feebs and Dwight weren't due home for hours. I extracted a fold up chair from the mountain of miscellanea piled behind Jasper, giving him a wide berth. I slid the door into the house closed behind me and settled in the chair a metre or so from Jasper's food-spattered muzzle.

I sipped my tea and forced myself to look into Jasper's glowing eyes.

"Did that help?"

Jasper chuffed smoke out the horny spheres of his nostrils. The image of a distinguished gent puffing on a pipe after a good meal flitted through my mind.

"Yes, it did, more than I expected. I feel much stronger. Thank you, Joe. As always, you've been gracious."

We stared at each other, my puny blue eyes pitted against the endless depths of his huge green orbs.

"There're only a few things I want to know." My voice sounded bold and loud. I jumped.

"Then ask, Joe, and I'll try to answer. Go ahead. I won't bite." Jasper's laugh was sudden and genuine. I couldn't prevent the smile that bubbled to my lips. I *liked* this formidable creature. Feared him. Loathed him. Wanted him gone. But liked him, too.

"The book Dwight found in his car. You put it there?" I figured I'd start with basic puzzles.

"No. Yes. I didn't, but it was there because of me. It put *itself* there. It's part of me. It goes where I go. It tells everything about me to those who need to know—in this case, you. The man who imprisoned me—the sorcerer—didn't trust me to tell my story to his satisfaction. Do you understand?"

I didn't entirely, but I nodded. It wasn't the most important thing. I was working up to that.

"It was in Dwight's car, rather than just coming straight to me, because . . . "

"I don't know. I don't control it; couldn't if I wanted to. I think it simply misses its mark sometimes. It travels through many years with the power of a long-dead sorcerer propelling it. Perhaps the force that motivates it has grown weak." He growled deep in his throat. "I'd like to think so."

"Is everything the book says true? All those things it says about you . . . things you did . . . what you *are* . . . what is required—"

"Yes"

"So the sorcerer's spell—the Bynding that imprisoned you in iron. The loophole in the spell that could free you, and what it involves . . . "

The great purple head rose and fell in yet another nod. "It's true, but you misunderstand the intention of the man who Bounde me. He didn't create a loophole in the spell. His intention was not to offer me a chance at freedom, but to deepen my torture and drive home the lesson he meant me to learn. Three times I could quicken, break free of my iron prison and become the pitiful creature you discovered in your food closet those weeks ago. Three times I could seek the assistance of the human who possessed the trinket I was forced to meld with. I've used two of those chances, and failed. This is my third and final opportunity. And the sorcerer intended for me to fail every time. But he was human, and humans are not farseeing."

"But why did he offer chances to you if they were futile?"

"To have me smell life and freedom, and be deprived of it. To vanquish me thrice more over. To teach me that humans rule this world, and they revile me—they prefer their imaginary human Gods to a real dragon God. To make me suffer, Joe."

There was a curious tone of respect in Jasper's voice. He admired the guy who did this to him. He didn't enjoy being the victim, but he appreciated the ingenious cruelty.

"And Dwight . . . "

"Yes, I thought you'd appreciate that aspect most, Joe. The other two humans I tried to enlist to help me were foolishly chosen—most people aren't keen on sacrificing a relative, for obvious reasons—but with you, I was prudent. You're willing? You understand your part?"

I nodded. My cup sat cold in my hand as Jasper got to his feet, long body writhing and shifting into place. He was careful to keep his silver underbelly hidden from my view. Kind of him. I did prefer my eyes non-pulped.

"It has to be soon, Joe. I can't stay in here much longer—it will become physically impossible. I'd suggest you select a time for the ritual with all possible haste. Ensure the absence of your sister. If she is here, she will be destroyed, one way or another. It doesn't matter to me—I *am* hungry, after all—but I tell you this because I know it matters to *you*. I am many things, Joe, but ungrateful is not one of those things. I can't reward you—yet—but neither do I seek to cause you pain. But I can't have anyone seeing me and running tales—not yet, while I'm still small and weak."

"I'll make sure she's not here," I said.

"That would be very wise, Joe."

◆ ◆ ◆

*Joe,*

*Won't be home tonight, @ Martha's place. Casserole in fridge, heat @ 180/40 mins.*

*Dwight home @ normal time.* BE NICE.

*Stacey yellow matter custard dripping from a dead dog's eye. Love. Feebs*

Tonight, then. Jasper was getting impatient. He wanted to be done with the unBynding. I was eager, too. He'd promised me I was safe, but my senses screamed whenever I was near him. He reminded me of the story about the Navajo woman who is shocked when the snake she'd rescued bites her, so the snake reminds her: "Look, bitch, you knew I was a snake".

I wondered how his previous two would-be-allies had refused him, and what had happened to them. I couldn't imagine telling the gargantuan thing in the garage that I wouldn't help. I wondered if he was sentient while he was a bauble on a candle holder. I think the man who put him there would have wanted him to feel his captivity for all time.

It was irrelevant, because I was willing to play my part in the unBynding. I needed no reward. The ritual was prize enough.

Humans are not farseeing.

I slid into the garage to tell the dragon the good news.

◆　◆　◆

Overpowering Dwight had been a concern, but it was easy. I'd gone through plot after plot in my mind. In the end, I figured something would present itself when the time was right. And it did.

He'd walked in the door earlier than usual. I'd been poring over *The Bynding of the Lavender Wyrm* one last time. Revising, you might say. He'd taken me by surprise, creeping up behind my chair.

"*Boo!*" he'd shrieked, and I'd leapt up in fright, rounding on him with the heavy book raised high. He'd bent over double, laughing, big hands gripping his knees.

"Fag," he'd hissed through giggles. I hadn't thought about it, I'd just brought the book down on the back of his skull. The impact reverberated up my arms, jarring my skeleton and snapping my teeth closed on my tongue. I'd stood for a while, tasting blood in my mouth, contemplating how strange it was that hitting someone else seemed to have caused *me* pain. Then I'd realised that Dwight wasn't laughing anymore. Wasn't even on his feet. Was, in fact, face down on the rug, breathing in little gasps with his eyes closed.

I hadn't wasted a moment after that. I had no idea when he would wake up, but I knew he'd be angry. He was bigger, stronger and dumber than me, and I didn't want to give him a shot at retaliation. I also didn't want to give myself a moment to think. I'd done all the thinking I was prepared to do. This was about *feeling*.

I'd dragged Dwight to the garage by his ankles, ignoring the screaming muscles in my chest and back as I lugged his dead weight through the house. Once there, I'd used the last of my strength to heft him onto a table. He'd gotten smashed around, but since he was in the last moments of his life anyway, it didn't matter.

I'd lashed his wrists and ankles to the table legs with black electrical tape. I didn't think even *he* could break through a dozen layers of tight bonds, but just in case, I hoped the awkward angle would remove the power from his struggles.

There was just enough room for the table, Dwight, and me, squeezed up against the wall. I held *The Bynding of the Lavender Wyrm*. The rest of the garage was now bursting with Jasper. Everywhere I looked were shimmering purple scales, long claws, membranous wings, and flashes of white teeth. The triangle that tipped Jasper's tail rested on the floor in front of the makeshift dais Dwight lay on, pointing at him, twinkling in the light cast by Jasper's luminous eyes.

I opened the book and looked at Jasper. He was still and composed, his lizard face inscrutable.

"Begin." His voice was the sound of a match igniting at one million decibels. I felt the air in front of my face shrink as his breath scorched it. I held the book open above Dwight's unconscious body, and cleared my throat.

"I, Joe Marson—"

"Your whole name, Joseph."

I felt absurd.

"I, Joseph Marson, take part in this unBynding of my own free will and with full understanding of what I now do. The man I come here to sacrifice is the husband of my blood sister, and thus my relative. His name is—"

"Mother*fucker*!"

Dwight resumed consciousness in fighting form. He roared, face red and knotted as he bucked and writhed. I watched in alarm as the table leapt under his exertions, steel legs clattering on the concrete floor in a rocking dance. The tape around his limbs seemed looser, and the table gave an ominous groan as he thrashed.

"Be swift," Jasper murmured, voluminous eyes fixed on Dwight. I recited the words as quickly as I could without them being reduced to gibberish.

"—his name is Dwight Frontbottom; the Bynding is broken and the unBynding is completed with the snuffing out of my relative's life at my own hands. I do this to return the Lavender Wyrm to his full power."

Simple words. They were formality—it was the intent and act that mattered. Dwight seemed to agree. I could see my intentions mattered a great deal to *him* once he saw me pull the long knife out from the waistband of my jeans. His eyes widened and the flush of rage drained from his face, replaced with deep pallor. He stopped fighting and lay motionless. Then, in a slow movement, he rolled his head to the right and looked at Jasper for the first time. The dragon smiled. Dwight lay like that for a moment, then his face rolled back toward me. His lower lip spasmed violently.

"You—" he whispered, but I didn't give him a chance to say anything else. I lifted the knife over my head, *The Bynding of the Lavender Wyrm* thudding to the cold floor.

◆  ◆  ◆

*Joe,*

*Do u know where Dwight is? He hasn't been home in 10 days. He's taken off before without telling me where he was going, but never for this long. Something doesn't feel right. I wanted to ask u face 2 face, but u've been locked in ur room whenever I've been home. U've been crying in ur sleep. I hear u through the wall.*

*Talk when I get home from work 2nite, k?*

*I love u.*

*Feebs*

◆  ◆  ◆

You've got bloodlust, haven't you? You want to know what happened in that garage. You want *details*. I'm sorry, but I can't give you much. Most of those moments are dead air in my memory. I'm glad, because what I can remember ain't pleasant.

Just three things.

The sounds: loud sucking every time I pulled the knife out of Dwight, moist punching every time it went back in.

The screaming. His. And mine.

And Jasper, closing in on my dying brother-in-law, licking his lips. Still smiling.

The rest is silence.

I didn't see Jasper leave, but he's gone, along with every trace of Dwight. The garage is back to its former messy glory. There's no sign of the ritual that took place there.

I'm beginning to wonder what will happen when Jasper reaches full size and strength. I should have thought about that before, but at the time, the question of what a world decimated by a dragon God would be like seemed far less important to me than my revenge on Dwight.

I never claimed to be clever, or to have admirable motives. I was just hurt and angry, and the Wyrm knew it. I was the perfect assistant: I had reason to want Dwight gone, and nothing much left in my life.

I don't regret what I did to Dwight, not for *his* sake. I've never once dreamt about him. I've only had one dream, over and over, since the unBynding. In it, a Jasper so enormous my mind's eye cannot fully see him smiles at me with teeth the size of the Empire State Building and chants the same phrase on an endless loop:

*you knew I was a snake you knew I was a snake you knew I was a snake . . .*

◆　◆　◆

I heard the clink of glass in the kitchen as I pressed my ear to my locked door, and knew Phoebe was sitting at the dining table, alone, getting drunk on cheap wine.

I felt guilty. Of course I did.

Until I heard her laugh.

"I don't miss you at all, you bastard," she said to nobody, and then, raising her voice: "I knew, Joe. I knew about Dwight and Stacey. I know you're in your room listening to me. So hear this: *I knew about them, and I don't care what happened to him.* I'm not going to make a fuss about it. I was freaked out at first but now . . . I don't want to know. Ok?"

Well, well, well. Perhaps my sister wasn't as fragile as I'd thought. Not even close.

◆　◆　◆

*Joe,*

*Did u break my bookend? Don't mean 2 b anal, but it was from mum. Means a lot 2 me.*

*Come out of ur room tonight, please.*

*Love. Feebs*

Humans may not be farseeing, but I knew what was going on before I finished reading her note.

I remembered mum giving that bookend to Phoebe on her eighth birthday. An ornate pewter slab, engraved with magical creatures twisting through clouds and stars. And standing atop them all, wand outstretched, a figurine of a man in a billowing robe with a long beard and hard eyes. Jasper's sorcerer. The one who had Bounde him, whose spell I had reversed with the blood of my brother-in-law.

My heart began a slow dive within the flimsy walls of my chest.

The bookend sat on top of Phoebe's note on the kitchen bench. There was a chipped indent where the sorcerer figurine had been.

I felt something small and sharp jab my ankle, and yelped, looking down.

"We have a lot to talk about," the scowling little magician said, withdrawing the tip of his wand from my leg. "You have no *idea* what you've done. I'm going to help you understand—whether you want to or not. And then you're going to help me clean up the mess you've made. Your sister is going to have to get involved, I'm afraid. Regrettable, to be sure—but you should have thought about that before you set your poisonous little plans in motion."

*You've got a shock coming your way, you miniature cretin,* I thought, grinning down at him. *I don't care about you or your Wyrm, but I care about my sister, and involving Phoebe may be the worst mistake you'll ever make, because she cares about me too—and we've both underestimated her. But that's ok. We shall see, eh? We shall see.*

"I suppose you want some food," I said.

# AFTERWORD

*Ah, I do so love a good revenge tale. It's a personal obsession and thus a bit of an accidental theme throughout my work. This piece was tremendous fun to create. It started out as innocuous urban fantasy (something I don't normally write, and wanted to try my hand at) and then transformed into something much nastier. Oh well. From little things, dark things grow.*

# US, AFTER THE HOUSE CAME BACK

I pushed my bedroom window open and leant over the sill, surveying the territory below. A sorry excuse for a garden bed, a few tufts of thirsty grass, and, most importantly: a *lot* of concrete. My window was at least three metres off the ground. It didn't look very high when you stood down there and looked up, but when you were up here looking down, it was frightening. I wasn't sure I'd make the jump in one piece. My hands and feet tingled. It was too much. I couldn't do it.

Down the hall, in the kitchen, the noise kicked it up a notch—banging, scuffling, and fleshy thuds. When women are attacked in movies, they always scream. My mother didn't. She grunted and gasped, loudly. Somehow that was worse than screaming.

Worse still was the fact that this had been going on for hours now, and I hadn't done anything about it yet. Guilt clotted my veins. Part of it was that I was struggling to accept that it was really happening. Kevin had pushed mum around before, yelled a lot, hit her a few times, but nothing like this extended brutal assault.

Something different was happening tonight, something cold and alien. I was more scared than I'd ever been in my life. There wasn't room in me for all the fear. It overflowed, filled my room, immobilised me. I could smell it in the air, acrid, like burning blood.

Earlier in the evening, as my mother sobbed, I'd heard Kevin take a break from beating her to pick up the phone and calmly order Chinese. When it was delivered, he'd had a polite chat at the door with the driver, then taken the food into the kitchen and taunted my mother while he poured the food all over her and rubbed it into her hair and eyes. I knew, because he'd narrated every second of the torture for my benefit as I cowered in my bed, not wanting to listen, but unable to ignore it. He'd also described his actions in amplified loving detail as he'd broken two brooms over my mother's back, and as he'd dragged her outside by her hair, slammed the door on her feet until her toes broke, and then yanked her back inside to punch her teeth out.

I'd told mum last time he hit her that if it happened again, I'd jump out my bedroom window and get the police. I thought she'd beg me not to, but I don't think she believed me. I didn't believe me either. I was too scared to do it, and too scared not to do it. I was stuck. And somewhere, deep down, I was furious. This was all wrong. I shouldn't have to protect my mother. It was meant to be the other way around.

Sweat trickled down my spine, tickling like spider legs.

"I'm going to kill you," Kevin told my mother. He didn't shout, didn't even raise his voice. He might have been announcing he was popping out to the shop for some milk, for all the stress in his words. But those words carried through the closed kitchen door, down the hall, through my closed bedroom door, and squeezed the air from my lungs. Because he meant it—he was going to kill her. I had no doubt. Had known it all night, really, but had tried not to believe it.

It was my twelfth birthday, after all. My stepfather couldn't murder my mother tonight. But he would. And, fair or not, there was no one else here to do anything about it. I had to move. *Now.*

I grabbed my white cotton nightdress from the floor and pulled it over my head and arms. I'd torn it off when I'd gone to bed. It stuck to my skin now, quickly soaking through with sweat. I looked down and saw it was inside-out. I knew my hair must be heat-frizzed and tangled into knots. What a mess I was. Some hero.

I grabbed the window-frame and eased myself onto the sill until I sat, dangling, over the drop below. My legs swung, skinny and pale in the moonlight, and the ground looked impossibly far away. In movies, people rolled when they hit the ground after a big jump. I pictured myself slipping off the sill, plunging through the air, and melting into a graceful somersault upon impact that carried me smoothly to my feet once more, unharmed.

Yeah, right. Once again, I reminded myself that this was not a movie.

I couldn't do it. I slumped, tears mingling with the perspiration on my cheeks. It hurt so much—this powerlessness—that it stupefied me, provided its own pain relief. My chin dropped to my chest and I stared, sightless, into space, as my body filled up with a glorious floaty feeling. Blessed numbness.

Then there was an astonishingly loud bang, and my mother did scream, at last. The scream cut off before it reached its peak, and a chilling silence descended. The kitchen door was wrenched open and heavy footsteps rushed down the hall toward my bedroom.

Conscious brain shrivelled into a ball and released control. Lizard brain took over without words. I launched myself off the windowsill and hurtled toward the ground. I hit hard, but managed a clumsy roll that left a good portion of skin from my bare arms and legs behind me on the concrete. Nothing felt broken, and I stood up, shaking not with fear now but with pure adrenaline. Without looking back, I sprinted up the driveway and onto the street. It had to be after midnight, and most of our neighbours' houses were dark, except one, across the road. I ran for it and hammered on the door with both fists, panting.

The door swung inward, a thirty-something man and woman staring out at me in surprise and concern.

"My stepfather is trying to kill my mother," I said. "Please help me."

◆　◆　◆

I sat in a soft armchair, tucked under a doona despite the stifling heat, a cup of steaming Milo in my hands. An old movie played on the TV, a man and woman, arguing. The couple who'd let me into their home—Rob and Sarah, they'd told me as they'd ushered me inside—exchanged glances, and Sarah flicked through TV channels until an innocuous cartoon filled the screen.

Such kindness in people. Such evil, too. Such a lottery as to which shone through.

Rob stood suddenly, striding to the door. Sarah leapt after him.

"Where are you going?" she said.

"I'm going over there," Rob said, shrugging into a jacket.

Sarah clutched his arm, shaking her head. "No! It's too dangerous."

"I can't just sit here and do nothing!"

"The police are on their way," Sarah said, then, "It isn't worth Max and Jack waking up to find their daddy has been hurt, or worse, Rob."

So they had kids. I bet their little boys never had to shove their fists in their ears at night to block out the sounds of their father throwing their mother around. For a moment, I hated those faceless children. For all that they had, and all I never would.

Reluctantly, Rob took his jacket off and allowed Sarah to lead him back to the couch.

Minutes ticked by. Rob called the police again, once, twice, was told they were on their way. He slammed the phone down and cracked his knuckles, frowning.

"They always take a long time to attend domestic disputes," I told him. He stared at me, his eyes wide, and I knew he saw me as a foreign object, a strange not-child who shouldn't know the things I knew. It was flattering, in a way, the status afforded me by my trauma, the elevation from preteen to old soul. I'd been living in the abyss with monsters for too long, and it showed.

I was worried, of course. I loved my mother. She was all I'd had for as long as I could recall, and she was the sun around which my world revolved, my tragic queen, victimised by a tyrant king. I ached with the separation from her, the distance between us, even in this house just across the street. It was horrific, not knowing what was happening to her right now. Was she . . . ok? Assuming she was—because she *had* to be—would she ever forgive me for what I'd done tonight? The shame I'd let in, the spotlight I'd put on us, the rage this would engender in my stepfather, the demons my actions would force her to face. The strength I'd shown that she had not. The mothering I was giving her that she'd failed to give me.

I had no idea what I'd done. I just knew I'd had to do it.

Finally, finally, sirens wailed in the distance. In moments, they were a cacophony, so loud it seemed incredible that the windows didn't rattle. Tyres squealed on the road outside, car doors slammed, voices murmured. The room we sat in lit up like a disco, strobing red around the edges of the closed curtains.

Rob and Sarah helped me stand, wrapped the doona around me, and led me to the door.

◆ ◆ ◆

My house was gone.

The tired old garden and ramshackle fencing remained, but nothing sat amid them now, save for empty concrete foundations, bright and smooth in the moonlight as if they'd just been laid. I gaped. Was I hallucinating? Was I confused, looking at someone else's property and mistaking it for my own? I looked side to side, taking in the street. No. That was definitely where my house had been, and it wasn't there anymore.

I turned to Rob and Sarah. I opened my mouth to say something—I don't know what, what *could* I say?—but stopped when I saw them. They stood close together, Sarah still holding Rob's arm, but their faces were slack, their eyes closed. Their chests rose and fell slowly. As I watched, Rob began to snore.

"Rob! Sarah!" I clapped my hands in front of their faces. Nothing. They just went right on sleeping on their feet. Maybe I, too, was asleep. I pinched my arm, hard. It hurt. Nothing around me changed one bit.

This was all my fault. This was what happened when you *told*. Well, at least the police were here. They'd help me.

I turned away from Rob and Sarah. In my shock at the disappearance of my house, I hadn't really looked at anything else. I'd seen red flashing lights and movement in my peripheral vision, had heard sirens and voices, but I hadn't focused on any of it. Hadn't, for that matter, actually seen any police at all, and weren't their flashing lights usually blue, anyway? And now, the street was empty and still. Humidity hung in the air, dense and oppressive.

Belatedly, it occurred to me to wonder: where, then, was my mother?

My heart sped up, hammering at my ribcage. Once more, adrenaline shot like fire through my veins. I struggled to breathe.

A tear slipped down my cheek as I hesitated on Rob and Sarah's front doorstep. I had no idea what to do next. I wanted my mother so badly, I thought the need might kill me.

"Come back inside," small voices said in unison behind me. I jumped, a shriek escaping me, and spun toward the sound. Two boys stood in front of Rob and Sarah, looking up at me. Identical twins, their dark hair rumpled from recent sleep, their plump faces almost silver in the moonlight, pillow creases still visible on their cheeks. They couldn't have been older than five.

. . . *waking up to find their daddy has been hurt . . . or worse.*

"Are you Max and Jack?" My voice was too loud in the unnatural quiet. I wondered if the whole street were sleeping like Rob and Sarah, unconscious in the middle of whatever they'd been doing, unable to be roused. And if so, why not the whole suburb? The country? The world? Nobody left awake but me, adrift in an ocean of stars and silence.

Me, and the twins.

"Come back inside," one of them repeated. A black M was embroidered on the chest of his pyjama shirt. Max. Jack's pyjamas bore a J.

"What's going on?" Why was I asking *them*? They couldn't possibly know. And yet, they didn't seem bothered by their parents standing unconscious behind them, didn't seem to find my presence there—a crying stranger, in the middle of the night, in an inside-out nightgown and with crazy hair—surprising.

"Come back inside," Jack said again, holding his pudgy hand out to me. "Everything is going to be alright. Next time you come back out here, it will all be as it was. Only better."

"We've done an exchange," Max said. "It's a fair one."

I put my hand in Jack's, suddenly quite sure I *was* dreaming. Max reached up and took one of his parents' hands in each of his. He led them into the house. They didn't open their eyes. Rob continued snoring. Jack pulled gently on my hand, and I followed the strange procession.

The door swung shut behind us.

I was asleep in Rob and Sarah's chair. I *must* be. But it was time to wake up. My mother needed me. Always, she needed me. I felt guilty about betraying her secrets, and this dream was because of that.

Only a dream, and nothing more.

◆ ◆ ◆

I awoke to Tom and Jerry capering homicidally on the TV, dancing about with hammers and knives, carving each other into amusing shapes. Funny how that was ok, but a man and woman shouting was not. Funny, how humans thought. None of it made sense, none of it did any good. It was all nonsense, really, and yet we were so adamant about our reality.

And where had *those* thoughts come from?

"Sweetheart." Sarah, kneeling at my elbow. "Time to go. There's a car waiting for you outside. Your mother's in it."

"A car?" I stood, rubbing my eyes, the doona I'd been bundled in falling to the ground. My Milo sat on a table near my chair, cold now, a dusky skin forming on its surface.

Sarah looked awkward. "The police." I don't know why she was so uncomfortable. I knew what had happened, knew why I'd come to this stranger's house. No need to pretend it was a social call, no need to pretend anything. Maybe she wasn't sparing *my* feelings at all; maybe, now that it was all over, she just didn't want to remind herself of what she'd let in tonight.

"Oh." I reached out a hand. "Thank you so much. For helping."

Sarah took my hand, wrapped it in both of hers, squeezed. She held it for a moment, looking at me as if considering keeping me, then thought better of it and released her grip.

"Good luck, Fiona," she said, walking me to the door. Lights strobed lazily outside, and they were blue, not red, and I had no idea why I thought they'd be otherwise. My mother was in that car, my *mother*, and I was already on the front stoop dashing toward her when I realised Rob was absent. I turned back to Sarah.

"Where's Rob?"

"He fell asleep. He's got a big day at work tomorrow, so I didn't wake him, but I know he'd wish you all the best."

"Oh. Well, tell him thanks, too. I hope all the commotion didn't disturb the twins." I waved as I pulled the car door open and slid inside. I was so absorbed in the awful first sight of my mother that I didn't fully notice Sarah's hesitant return of my wave that wilted before her hand was fully lifted, the way she wrapped her arms around herself as if cold, and scurried back inside, slamming the door.

Later, much later, I realised she'd never told me her boys were twins.

◆ ◆ ◆

A bundle of wet red sticks sat on the backseat of the police car, wrapped in a blanket, reaching for me. My mother. God, she'd gotten skinny. They hadn't cleaned her up any; blood dribbled and spread on her pale skin, soaked her blanket, spattered her fingers and bare, broken toes. Her mouth was a sunken crone's grin, her gums almost black with gore. Her face was swollen, one eye completely shut, Chinese food congealed in her hair. She glinted when she moved; tiny shards of broken glass bedecked her skin like distant stars.

The thought of stars scared me for some reason. Silly to be frightened of such nonsense, given what was in front of me right now.

She was my mother, and I loved her, and I needed her to love me back. Nothing else mattered, none of this horror, none of our pain. I could bear this sight, live through this disaster, if only she would tell me it would be alright.

"Did I do the right thing?" I begged her, seeking absolution, needing the blessing of my Goddess.

"You *thought* you were doing the right thing," she said, with terrible kindness, and it turned out my pain did matter. Guilt, rage, loss and regret flared in me. I'd done bad. Somehow, I was wrong, and Kevin was right. What he'd reduced my mother to was true, and my view was a lie. Here and now, with what she did and did not say, she absolved him and damned me.

I was just a child after all, not the sage creature I'd considered myself hours before, and I knew nothing of these adults. Except that they were unfair, and I hated, hated, *hated*, and loved, and there was very little space between those feelings. Very little difference. Just like those distant, inexplicable stars that were so far away and yet so close.

The two police in the front of the car kept their silence, and I joined them in it. I looked out the window and watched the dark night slide by, as my mother's breath whistled through her missing teeth and she gasped with every bump in the road that jolted her injuries.

◆ ◆ ◆

The police station. A kind woman, taking notes, photographing my mother's ravaged body. A women's shelter, full of smiling, broken women and their glassy-eyed traumatised children. I was one of them, I supposed. A halfway house, a cosy little unit where my almost fully healed mother and I could live alone together in a safe, humble bliss.

They were the moments after, and they were gone so fast. A sniff of freedom, a breath of fresh air and sunlight, and it was over.

When my mother announced she was reconciling with Kevin, that he was a changed man, that she knew I'd see what she meant for myself, I wasn't surprised. It was always coming. In a way, it was comforting, the familiarity of the story, the ending that never changed. I went with her. What else could I do? My own father was a worse option even than Kevin, and then there was my mother. I wouldn't leave her, couldn't. Unthinkable, like severing a limb, like cutting out my heart. Like snuffing out the stars.

Who would look after her, if not me?

So back we went. Kevin greeted us at the door. When I walked in, he pulled me close to him, and whispered in my ear: "Don't be afraid, Fiona. We'll look after you now."

I pushed him away. The most he'd ever said to me before now was *get me a beer*. He didn't frown, didn't smile, only maintained a beatific blankness that almost looked like open-eyed sleep. My mother clasped her hands under her chin, beaming.

"I told you," she said. "Didn't I tell you he was a new man?"

I thought of red flashing lights, the empty space where my house should've been, and eerily calm twins telling me they'd made a fair exchange.

"Yes," I said. "You did tell me that. And you were right."

◆　◆　◆

It's amazing, the wrongness you can live with, the utter disconnect you can ignore. For so long, I'd gotten up, dressed, gone to school, come home, slept, rinsed, and repeated; all against the backdrop of Kevin shouting at my mother and beating her. I'd lived with the anxiety, never sure what might set him off, when the calm would break and the stomping and smashing and abuse would begin, never sure where it would lead that time.

Now, I lived with constant, unchanging serenity, and even if I knew the thing that looked like my stepfather wasn't Kevin—was an *exchange*—well, what of it? How was that disconnect worse than the one I'd endured for so long? My mother was happy and unhurt, for the first time in so long, her bones covered in meat rather than fractures. My nights were silent and I need not leap out my bedroom window and hammer on the neighbours' doors, pleading for succour.

Sometimes Kevin stares into space for a long time, and we can't rouse him. Sometimes he snores and sleeps while he's standing up. Sometimes there's blood on his boots—not mud, but blood, like he's walked through a slaughterhouse—and he says it's red cement mix, from his concreting business, and we say we believe him, because it's not my mother's blood, and that's good. And sometimes, rarely, but sometimes, he unplugs the phone, then talks into it in a language I've never heard the likes of before. And I hear someone talking back, faintly, on the other end of the disconnected line. ET phoning home never looked like this.

My English teacher had once set us an assignment to read Anthony Burgess' "A Clockwork Orange". She'd gotten in trouble; a bunch of parents and other teachers banded together to declare her choice of reading material unsuitable for our fragile minds, and the books were taken off us—but not before I'd had time to devour the story, wash myself in the language, bind it to my heart and *feel* it. The author's point seemed to have been that a man who can't choose ceases to be a man, that it's better to choose to be bad than to be forced to be good.

I must respectfully disagree with Mr Burgess. I don't know much about men, but I'll tell you what a child thinks. A child thinks that it doesn't make a lick of difference *why* her stepfather isn't beating her mother; all that matters is that her mother is not being beaten.

I don't know where Kevin went, I don't know *why* something took his place, I don't know what that something is, and I don't need to know. I was already living with a monster. This—whatever "this" is—is better. It couldn't possibly be worse.

There *are* no monsters worse than men.

In a movie, there'd be some big reveal here, some spaceship descended to Earth with insectile creatures boiling forth from it to announce their purpose, some penalty to pay for the peace my mother and I now enjoy, some cosmic lesson driven home with ray guns and the demise of the human race.

But this isn't a movie.

This is us, after the house came back, and I like it much better this way.

# AFTERWORD

*I've heard it said that horror writing can set the wrong things right. That horror literature is—at its finest, at its core—about justice. I totally agree. I agree so much that it hurts. For me, though, justice is often (sometimes only) found in revenge. I know that's a contentious view that many disagree with, and I'm academically aware of its flaws as a theory, but a lot of my writing doesn't come from logic. It comes from an unquiet place that just rages. And so, often, I write horror for revenge. To set the wrong things right, yes . . . but also to punish the bad guys. That's where this story came from—a little girl who was once utterly helpless in a situation not of her making, who grew up and, through the magic of words, went back in time, no longer powerless, and fixed what was broken. If only real life were so simple.*

# THE BEARDED ONES

The memory haunted Eli's dreams: the dandelion seed head, white and fuzzy against his small palm. *It's a Santa Claus beard,* his mother said, her voice hushed and reverent. *Blow it away and make a wish. It's magic.* Eli's breath hit the downy ball a fraction of a second before it left his hand, and he felt it swell with heat and life as it puffed away from him, carried on the life force thrust from his lungs.

His mother sighed.

Eli felt suddenly afraid. He wanted to chase the fuzzy thing, snatch it out of the air and crush it beneath his feet.

Too late now.

◆ ◆ ◆

Eli's mother told him the truth when he was five years-old. He forced her, really. He'd always been a bright boy. His mother found that irritating, but she tolerated it most of the time.

"Mummy, how can Santa be over there handing out lollies, when we just saw him across the road having his photo taken?" He tugged on her sleeve, and she looked down at him, her bottom lip tucked between her teeth. Finally, she knelt before him, decisiveness shining in her eyes.

"I'm going to tell you something big, Eli. I'll leave it up to you what you do with the information, but it might be kind of you not to tell any of your friends. Sometimes it's better for people to find things out in their own time, or not at all." Her hand was cool and gentle on his shoulder, and he smiled into her open face, honoured by her honesty.

"I won't tell anyone, Mummy. Not a soul. Never ever."

"You will, eventually. And that's ok. Just not too soon, alright?"

"Alright," he'd agreed easily, already picturing the awestruck and—most importantly—*jealous* looks on Sam Jacobs and Richie Santoro's faces when he passed on his treasured adult knowledge to them. He jiggled with excitement. His mother watched him carefully, and something changed in her face, as though she'd taken a different direction at the last minute with the words that next flowed from her lips.

"Eli, there isn't just one Santa in the world. There're lots. You knew it wasn't *really* possible for one Santa to get everywhere he needs to be and do everything he needs to do, didn't you? So, all the Santas split the Christmas duties. That's why you can see a Santa here, and then another across the road."

"Lots of Santas. Like an army," Eli breathed. It felt right. Why hadn't he figured it out himself?

A shadow fell across his mother's face, and she ground her lower lip so hard between her teeth that a smudge of blood marred the pink surface. She licked it away, and grimaced.

"Well . . . not an army. More like a friendly team, or a very special family. They all cooperate and everything works like a well oiled machine. You know what that means, don't you, Eli?"

"It's like when I throw the ball to Sam and he throws it to Richie and none of us drop it," he said.

"Yes, like that. So now you know."

"Lots of Santas," Eli murmured. He thought about it through the hours spent traipsing the shopping centre, and when his mother bundled him into the car and leaned over him to click his seatbelt into place, her lemon-and-honey perfume tickling his nostrils, another thought leapt into his mind.

"Mummy, what happens to the people who aren't nice?"

She stood up too fast, her head smacking the top of the doorframe.

"What do you mean?"

"Y'know, the Santas only bring presents to people who are nice. What do people who are naughty get? Is that why there's an army of Santas?"

"People who are naughty just get nothing, Eli." She wrenched her door open and slid behind the steering wheel, her jaw set in a tight line. "And it's *not* an army."

Good people got presents. Bad people got . . . nothing? But surely, with so many Santas working together, that couldn't be right? When Eli was naughty, he didn't just have *nothing* happen to him; a host of punishments awaited him. Time out. A smack on the back of his hand. No TV. No dinner. That was how things worked, wasn't it?

"Enough questions now, Eli." His mother started the car. "Just . . . stop thinking about it, ok?"

He grinned at her and nodded, eager to please. He was going on the Nice list this year. He wanted that shiny blue bike with the red handlebars under the tree on Christmas morning, thank you very much. But Santa couldn't know what he was *thinking*, could he? Not the stuff that was just in his head and never came out his mouth.

So Eli didn't stop thinking about it.

Ever.

◆ ◆ ◆

Richie threw the fat file on Eli's desk with a flourish. It knocked Eli's cup to the floor, slopping cold tea on the carpet and Eli's ankles. Richie shrugged, smiling lopsidedly.

"Sorry," he said. Eli sighed, and grabbed a handful of tissues to soak up the liquid.

"S'ok. What is that, anyway?"

"The Thompson file. I can't make sense of it. You're good with that technical stuff. You'll sort it out in a quarter of the time it would take me to stuff it up."

"Rich! I'm . . . busy tonight. I can't—"

"Please, Eli. I really need your help." Richie's eyebrows bunched together in earnest pain, and the easy grin slid from his face like a dead bird from a window pane. Guilt twisted in Eli's chest, and for a moment, he wanted to leap the grey partition and choke Richie.

*He's manipulating me. He always does. But I'm too gutless to stand up to him.*

"Rich. I've got plans tonight. You . . . you know that. I've had plans for a week."

"Oh, God! Your date with the chick from Accounts Payable . . . Cindy? I'm so sorry, man. How can I make it up to you? D'you want me to call her for you?"

"Sally," Eli corrected, his guilt replaced by a bright flare of panic. Rich call Sally? He knew how that would go. Richie's honeyed voice would murmur apologies into her ear, and before she even knew what was happening, she'd be on a date with *him* instead, struggling to remember who Eli was and why it mattered. "I've wanted to take her out for months. And no, I don't want you to call her. Just . . . stay away from her."

"Geez, man, I was just trying to help. Calm down. Look, I really appreciate what you're doing for me. You don't need to martyr yourself, though."

"Martyr *myself*? You—"

"Thanks. Really. I owe you." Richie was already walking out, jacket dangling rakishly at his shoulder from one hooked finger.

God. And it was a week until Christmas. Eli would need to reschedule his date—if Sally would still see him—and then what time was left for gift shopping? The Thompson file was a mess. It would take days to set it straight.

Knuckling his stinging eyes, Eli picked up the phone.

"Hi, Sal? Yeah, look, I'm really sorry, something's come up . . . "

◆ ◆ ◆

It was late. The office was dark and eerie. A dandelion head

*(Santa Claus beard . . . magic)*

rolled across his desk like a tumbleweed.

*There's no breeze in here . . . and where did that come from, anyway?*

Eli reached out and closed his hand around the dandelion head. Something squirmed wetly in his palm. Pain lanced up his arm as claws needled his flesh. Swearing, he opened his fist. Empty. Unhurt.

*Okayyy . . .*

A Christmas song careened through the office, warped and canted slightly offbeat, like the battery powering the music was dying. Eli stood up, staggering as the room tilted sideways. Arms out like a blind man, he crossed the office, stepping carefully, head pounding. "Hello?" he called. His voice sounded thick and strange. No answering voice called back.

The music was coming from the staff kitchen. Eli walked in, and found that it wasn't the staff kitchen anymore; it was the lounge room of his childhood home, faux cellophane fire in the hearth, Christmas tree lights twinkling like mischievously winking eyes. A carrot and glass of milk adorned the hearthstone, and a stocking hung flaccid on the mantel. *ELI*, it said in jaunty red cross stitch lettering.

"I'm not seeing this," Eli whispered.

The tune blasting through the lounge was *I Saw Mummy Kissing Santa Claus*, and Eli did not want to look. He'd looked once before, and once had been more than enough. He'd worked hard to forget. He tried to turn away, and found he couldn't. His legs wouldn't move, his head wouldn't turn, and his eyes wouldn't close. Powerless, he watched.

His mother sat in her chair near the hearth, head bowed over her tapestry, humming. His father snored in his chair next to her. On the TV, Molly Meldrum expostulated silently—muted. In the fireplace, a large black boot appeared, stomping on the fake flames. Another boot joined it, and then a large man in dirty red and white wool clambered into the lounge. The glass of milk shattered as he kicked it out of his way. The carrot withered to a husk as he passed.

Eli's mother looked up and screamed.

The man in red tore the tapestry from her hands and, grasping her wrist, pulled her to her feet. His beard was not white but grey, mottled with putrescence and filth. His eyes were bulbous and bloodshot, the pupils large and black. His teeth protruded through his lips like tusks, misshapen, yellow and cruelly sharp. He leered into Eli's mother's face.

"You've been naughty, love! Haven't you?" the man twisted Eli's mother's arm until a sharp *crack* parted the air, and she cried out again, a high wheezy sound this time. "You've been telling secrets to little boys, and you've been plugging up chimneys, and leaving pathetic little circles of protection around your house! Did you think you could hide? Did you think we wouldn't find you?"

Another pair of black boots appeared in the fireplace, and another man—taller than the first, his face longer and even more savage—unfolded from the hearth and stepped into the room. And another, this one round and chuckling. And another. And another. And another. They crowded the room, their stink clotting on the air, their laughter low and mad.

"Please," Eli's mother whispered. "Please, I won't . . . "

"You won't what?" The fat Santa snarled, taloned fingers stroking Eli's mother's back. She shuddered at his touch.

"Got something to say?" The lean Santa snapped at Eli's father, who had woken and was boggling up at them. Eli's father shook his head slowly, not moving from his chair. Eli's mother stared at him for a moment, then burst into hopeless tears. Eli gaped, at once a frightened little five year old boy peeking through the lounge door and a stunned thirty year old man frozen in his staff kitchen.

The first Santa sang along to the tune, his voice bubbling like a dead stream. "I sawwww mummy kissing Santaaa Clausssss . . . do you wanna kiss Santa Claus, love?" The thing pressed its bristling lips to Eli's mother's, its teeth tearing bloody trails in her skin. Her screams were muffled now. Tears slipped from Eli's father's eyes, but he didn't move, didn't speak. "Underneath the mistletoeeeeee last niiiigghhhttt . . . " the other Santas closed in like wild animals around a fallen carcass. Eli's mother was lost in a shuffling sea of red and white.

Five year old Eli crept up to bed and huddled beneath the covers, clutching his teddy bear like a talisman, blocking his ears to the noises drifting up from downstairs. Thirty year old Eli opened his mouth to scream, and coughed instead, choking on something dry and dusty at the back of his throat. Hacking, he spat the obstruction into his palm. A dandelion head, spotted with blood. *No*, he told himself, but he knew it was futile. *Not happening. Not real. No.*

The kitchen was a kitchen once more. The office was still.

Eli woke up.

◆ ◆ ◆

Wiping drool from his mouth, Eli's fingers brushed something damp and furry. He plucked it from his cheek and stared at it. The dandelion head from his dream. Too much work; he'd passed out at his desk. But he *had* been dreaming, hadn't he? Remembering— but asleep? He dropped the sticky thing in the bin, grimacing. A telephone rang across the office, playing *I'm Too Sexy*.

*Richie's mobile. He's left it behind. Maybe he's calling it to see where he left it. If I don't answer . . . he'll know I was here and ignored it.* Sighing, Eli stood and hurried to Richie's office. The purple mobile phone jittered around on the desk, flashing and warbling.

"Hello?" Eli caught it just in time.

"Richie?" Static crackled on the line.

"No, it's—"

"Sorry, darling, I'm running late, I'm getting on the train now. I just got off the phone from . . . Richie? This is a bad line. Are you there?"

"Who is this?" Eli spoke at the same moment his brain recognised the voice. The woman gasped and hung up on him. He listened to the silent phone for a while before slowly setting it down on Richie's desk.

Sally had sounded so sympathetic when he called her earlier. Had she been rushing for the train then, dressed to kill, cheeks flushed with excitement? Had they planned their betrayal ahead of time, or had it been spontaneous—a phone call, a proposition, a hasty agreement?

Eli sat down heavily, rubbing his brow with his fingertips. His head was pounding and his throat was dry. "You've been naughty, Richie," he murmured. "What will Santa bring you?"

◆　◆　◆

"I don't have a fucking chimney, Eli," Richie said, sucking juicy meat from a lobster leg with aplomb. "My house is hardly Christmas party material. Eggnog, roast meal, roaring fire, carols . . . I'm not into that whole thing. I'll probably be here, working."

Eli tore at his lobster with more force than was necessary, his teeth coming together painfully. "I have a chimney," he said, forcing himself to speak calmly. "Not that it matters—it's too hot in Melbourne for a fire at Christmas, but I have a great fake fire. I have a big empty house. It was my mother's, you know. We had a lot of Christmases there. It's perfect for a party. Sally's already agreed to come. Sam, too. And—"

"Well," Richie interrupted, blotting his greasy mouth with a napkin, "If the Samster is going, I have to come, don't I? We haven't caught up in ages. And Sally's going? You two seeing more of each other, then? I haven't seen her around this past week." His casual tone was too smooth.

"I haven't seen her lately, either, but I spoke to her yesterday, and she hasn't got plans. Her family are all interstate. She was going to be alone." He emphasised the last word so that it meant *not with you.*

"Yeah, cool," Richie muttered. He screwed his napkin into a ball and tossed it on his plate. His knuckles were white. "Ok, whatever. I'll see you at your place, tomorrow night, 7pm, then."

"You can bring a date if you like," Eli called to Richie's departing back with petty glee. Then, plucking his phone from his pocket, Eli dialled Sally's number.

"Sal, hi. It's Eli. I know you're probably screening my call, but I just wanted to let you know, I know everything, and I'm fine. We only had one date planned, right? No big deal! No need to make things weird. In fact, I want you and Richie to come over tomorrow night for Christmas dinner. Richie's already agreed, and I've got a date myself, so it really will be fine. 7pm, ok? I'll text you the address. Let's bury the hatchet—Christmas spirit, and all that. See you then!" She would come. She was guilty. She'd called in sick all week to avoid them both.

Eli had stitched Richie and Sally's names with painstaking care into two bright new stockings last night, the needle sliding through the fabric like a hot knife through butter. He'd hummed *I Saw Mummy Kissing Santa Claus*, and thought about dandelion heads stained with blood, as tears glittered on his cheeks.

◆ ◆ ◆

They captured children's breath. Eli figured it out when he was six. His mother had taken a month to recover from the previous Christmas, and she'd been different since then. She was twitchy, jumping at shadows, her eyes hooded and furtive. Eli's father couldn't look at her. Her bruises and broken bones had healed fast, but her eyes never again lost that sly look of fear.

Eli caught a dandelion head, floating on the summer breeze, and pursed his lips to blow it away. His wish was half formed in his mind when his mother came screeching across the lawn, her hands hooked into claws, her face wild. She slapped the dandelion head from his hand and clutched his shoulders, shaking him back and forth like a rag doll. "Don't! Don't ever do that again!" *Shake, shake, shake.* "It might make no difference, it's probably too late, but by God, don't make it easier for them!"

She'd let him go then, sent him reeling across the grass as she ran inside sobbing. He'd landed hard on his butt and bit his tongue. As his tongue pulsed and blood filled his mouth, he stared at the dandelion head, buffeted on invisible currents, winging its mysterious path home . . . and he understood.

What child wasn't taught to blow on dandelion heads and make a wish? What child didn't implant its breath on those Santa Claus beards before sending them flying to their destination? They captured every child's breath that way, and perhaps a little piece of every child's soul. They tracked them, traced and watched them—*caught* them, somehow.

Magic.

◆　◆　◆

"Hi." Sally looked up at him from beneath her lashes, bashful, hesitant. "I came."

"So I see." Eli ushered her in. He took her coat, planted a chaste kiss on her cheek, fought the urge to throttle her. "Welcome. I'm glad to have you. Richie's in the lounge."

"It's so cosy here," she said, hurrying toward the brightly lit room. "So festive. Your old family home, Richie said."

"Yeah. My mother died when I was seven, but I remember Christmas with her here. My dad went kinda nuts and was shipped out to a home when I was ten. After that, it was a combination of uncles, grandparents, and family friends, all taking turns looking after me . . . but I don't know why I'm telling you this." He laughed, wiping away the look of unease that had been blooming on her face. "Just relaxed, I guess."

"You lost your mum when you were seven, huh? That's rough. Mine died when I was eighteen." She touched his shoulder briefly, her warmth like gangrene against his skin. He forced a smile.

"Hey, Sally." Richie's laugh was confused. "I thought you might be someone else. Eli said there was a cast of thousands turning up, but seems it might be just you and me." A look passed between Richie and Sally. Eli slipped into the lounge behind Sally and pulled the door shut, locking it before slipping the key in his pocket.

"Yes, just us three. Funny number, three. We three kings. The three witches. Mummy, Daddy, and Eli. Three's a crowd."

"What're you talking about, mate?" Richie was on his feet now. He'd noticed the door being locked. It didn't matter.

"Eli? Are you alright?" Sally reached for him again. He knocked her hand away roughly. Richie was at her side in an instant, his face dark.

"I'm fine. Really good. You two have been very naughty. It's bullshit, you know. Naughty people don't just get nothing. They get something, alright. As long as the Santas can find them."

Richie pulled Sally behind him and pushed his face into Eli's. "Listen, Eli. I know you're pissed off, but you're being ridiculous. You didn't have any rights over Sally. We like each other. It's just one of those things. You're being rude."

"Rude?" Eli giggled. "You're in my house now, Richie. I do have a chimney. See?" He pointed at the hearth, at the stocking with RICHIE and SALLY sewn on them in blood red lettering. Richie stared at the stockings, then back at Eli, frowning.

"You're not making any sense, Eli," he said quietly. "You're obviously very worked up. If you'll just let Sal and I out, we'll go home. You can get some rest and we can talk about this later."

"See, you always lived in expensive apartments, Richie. You and your rich family. You never had chimneys. You never had a garden, and you weren't the type to chase dandelions and make wishes. Your family were too busy to propagate ancient myths for you. You were always safe, you bastard. Naughty and safe." Spittle flew from Eli's lips and spattered on Richie's face. The red and orange cellophane fire seemed to crackle and blaze higher, and a single black boot stepped into it.

"Eli, what the fuck are you talking about?"

"Richie . . . " Sally's voice shook. She was looking at the fireplace. Eli grinned at her.

"Did you have a chimney growing up, Sal? Did you make wishes on dandelion heads? Did Santa come for you?" She gaped at him, her lower lip trembling. Knowledge flashed in her eyes.

"My mum . . . " she whispered.

"Were you naughty when you were eighteen, Sal? Did they get your mum then? They do that, don't they. They punish you in all sorts of ways, and they start with the things you love." Eli clapped. "Oh, that's perfect. We're more alike than I thought. We could have been great together."

"Don't encourage him, Sal." Richie turned to look at Sally, saw her stricken expression, and followed her gaze to the fireplace just as a short, rotund Santa stepped out and grinned at them all. Where his mouth should have been was a grossly elongated dog's muzzle, matted and dark with filth. Sally shook her head from side to side and backed up against the wall, her hands fluttering in front of her face like frightened birds.

"No," she whispered. "Not again. You're not real. I've never seen you before, I'm not seeing you now, you're not—"

"Little Sally Richards," the man in red said, his canine lips writhing like snakes. His forked tongue flickered as he spoke, bloated and obscene. "My, you've grown. Oh, yes, you've grown quite well. Do you want a kiss, Little Sally? Your mummy liked kisses. She liked them a lot."

"Nice gag." Richie glared at Eli. "Very funny. You're sick, you know that?"

Eli chuckled. Something in his mind tilted, bent, and finally snapped. He rounded on Richie, snarling. "You think I'm doing this to her? Oh, no, my fine friend. Anything that happens to Sally is your fault, because you connected her to you, made her betray me for you. She's collateral damage, but this is all for you. It's always about you, isn't it? Why should this be any different?"

Another pair of feet tramped through the cellophane fire and carried their owner into the room. This Santa had the body of a hulking wrestler and the face of a gargoyle. His red costume looked like ill fitting skin, stretched to the point of desperation, on the brink of splitting open and spewing forth whatever stinking innards lurked within. He shouldered past Eli, and clapped a gnarled hand on Richie's arm. Behind him, a growing number of Santas stepped out of the fireplace in a grisly procession, closing in on Richie and Sally as Eli wordlessly stepped back, smiling.

"Fancy a kiss?" Gargoyle Santa puckered up and smacked his hoary lips in Richie's face. Richie swung a short punch at the Santa, whose mouth yawned wide, teeth crunching neatly into Richie's fist. Blood arced like a geyser across the wall. Richie gave a small, surprised shriek and tried to pull his arm back, but Gargoyle Santa reeled him in like a large, screaming, fleshy fish. In the background, Eli saw Sally curled in a ball on the floor, hands over her ears and eyes tightly closed, before a wave of red monsters closed in on her and she was lost.

Time seemed to twist and slow to a crawl. Eli leant on the wall and watched as a sinuous ballet of gore played out before him. After a few moments, the screaming and laughter sounded identical, and then there were no screams at all. Everything was red and white. Suits and beards. Blood and bone. "Naughty," Eli giggled to himself. "Naughty, naughty, but oh, so nice."

When Dog Santa approached him and wordlessly handed him a folded red-and-white suit, Eli dipped his head in acknowledgement and took it. The fabric writhed and pulsated in his hands, straining toward him. This was a suit that would wear Eli. As he shrugged the living material onto his body, a dandelion seed head floated out of the hearth and bobbed on the air until it reached him. Eli hesitated for only a moment before snatching it and pressing it to his chin. He felt it prick him, worming beneath his skin, finding purchase and anchoring itself. Another dandelion flew to him, and another, until the hearth was vomiting a constant stream of the things. As they decorated Eli's face and became his beard, he saw his own blood speckling the ground at his feet, and smiled. His face was warm, and he could hear—no, *feel*—the voices of countless children singing in his veins. He knew their every move, their every thought, their darkest wishes. He knew where they were, and how to get to them.

Eli had a singular purpose now, and for the first time in his life, he was not afraid.

# AFTERWORD

*The whole Santa thing is creepy. Aside from being a big fat lie that parents tell their trusting children (and I include myself in that statement), think about it: an oddly dressed, obese, hairy old stranger with supernatural powers sneaks into your house while you're asleep. He likes children to sit on his lap. He has an army of small minions who live solely to do his bidding. He's everywhere, simultaneously. He keeps a list of who is naughty, and who is nice. We know that nice people get presents, but what the hell does this pervy entity do to those who are naughty?! Nobody wants to talk about that . . . so I thought I would. Also, revenge. Again.*

# BERRIES AND INCENSE

Rowan ran the cobblestones of the night in a ragged purple dress made of hope. Her red foliage hair, long and dotted with berries that glowed like coals, rustled and shed pieces of itself as the wind plucked at it with sharp fingers. Waxwings and thrushes raced each other in the starlit sky, marking her passage on the earth below, their beaks snapping in anticipation of her soft fruit. She knuckled her white flower eyes with bark fingers, wiping away the pollen tears that dusted her stiff cheeks.

Oh, but she hurt. She hurt *so* much.

She took huge gulps of air as her wooden legs pumped. Her lungs burnt and her muscles ached and her chest pounded like a drum being beaten from the inside, but still she ran, screaming wordlessly into the dark. The birds above her shrieked back, delighted.

Finally she reached the ornate bridge that straddled the banks between Here and There. On the peak of the bridge, suspended in the aether, was where Rowan wanted to be. That place was Nowhere, a platform cushioned by the splayed tail feathers of sleeping peacocks and lit by winged yellow lanterns. There she could let the Mother Bear lick the sap from her wounds with ancient tongue.

She climbed the bridge, digging her twig toes in for purchase, singing, as one always should when going Nowhere. Mother Bear waited for her, massive arms outspread, warm paws waiting to hold her tight. Rowan ran into the Bear's embrace with a dry kindling sob, pollen exploding from her eyes in earnest. Mother Bear held her and let her cry, the Bear's own beady eyes moist, a protective growl rumbling in her throat.

Eventually Rowan was hollowed out and done, and Mother Bear released her.

'Why don't you visit me more often, Rowan child?"

"I would if I could, Mother. I've tried. But I can't find my way here, save for times when the pain becomes almost enough to destroy me. I wish it weren't so."

"Well, what is, is. Tea?" The Bear pulled a red teapot from one of her many furry folds. Rowan nodded, as she always did, and the kettle steamed and whistled on cue. A waxwing alighted on her leafy hair, dipping its head and taking a berry in its beak before she shooed it away.

"What flavour tonight, Mother?"

"Salty mountain ash, the desiccated remains of a tree-girl's broken heart, mixed with sweet glass, the preserved lies dripped from a lover's tongue, served cold and bitter in an empty cup, the discovery of a lover's betrayal most foul."

The bear handed Rowan her tea, and Rowan cradled it, sipped, sighed. Peppery spices filled her nose and tingled on the back of her throat, their taste muted by Rowan's lack of a sense of smell, an absence she'd carried with her as long as she could remember.

"Drink it all. Let it sit heavy like a glacier in your belly."

Rowan did as she was told and handed the cup—which had always appeared empty, but was lighter now—back to Mother Bear. She clambered onto the peacock's feathers, lying on her back and staring at the stars, brilliant green fireballs in the dark sky.

After a while, the feathers whispered against each other as someone lay beside her.

"Delight of the eye," he said, his voice like boiling honey.

Rowan gasped, turning her head to see her visitor.

"Don't look at me," the voice said quickly, "at least, not just yet. I don't want you to see what I am and spurn me before I've had even the slightest chance."

Reluctantly, Rowan obeyed. She hungered to hear that smooth, warm voice again.

"This is my place," she said.

"Yes, yours, Rune Tree, Quickbane, Thor's Apple. You beautiful thing. You don't even know how special you are. How exalted, throughout all places and all times."

"Nobody thinks I'm special. They call me dogberry. They threaten to burn me. They laugh. They desert." Except for Crow, poor pitiful fellow slave, and, like Rowan, she counted for little.

"They're fools." Rowan felt him rise to his feet, the weight of him gone from their shared featherbed, leaving her too light, untethered, addled. "I love you. I loved you before, and I love you now, and I'll love you after. I love you Here and I love you There. I love you Everywhere and Nowhere. *Don't* look at me," he added as Rowan began, again, to turn her head.

"You're leaving," she said.

"Yes. I'll be missed, and so will you, and this is not my place, as you pointed out. It's hard to leave so soon, but harder still to stay—impossible, in fact. I followed you here, this once, after many failed attempts. But this place is wise to me now, and I can never enter again."

Mother Bear snarled, a low, deadly sound, emphasising the visitor's words.

"I will come for you, Rune Tree."

"Wait!" Rowan cried, looking despite his admonitions, but he was gone.

Nowhere remained undisturbed, which was of course the charm it had always held for Rowan. Wind chimes tinkled. The water frothing under the bridge made pretty sounds. Mother Bear relaxed into slumber, and she and the peacocks snored. The winged lantern's flames sputtered and crackled, high in the air where their fire posed no threat to Rowan.

This was her lullaby and her medicine, and despite herself, Rowan was soothed. Soon enough, her own snores joined Nowhere's song.

◆ ◆ ◆

"You've got to stop running away at night." Crow held out a guano bowl to Rowan, waiting as Rowan snared a few warm berries from her hair and dropped them in. "It only makes the Seamstress angrier at you. She threatened to take your hope-dress from you, and make you new clothing, of fire and pesticide! She threatens your death, Rowan." Crow put the bowl of berries on the counter and added a pinch of spices, plunging her talon-fingers into the mix, piercing the berries and swirling the juicy mess around. Her beak opened and shut in small, pathetic movements on her otherwise human face, giving away her constant hunger, as if her emaciated frame weren't hint enough. It was torture, pairing her with Rowan, tempting her with fruit she could never touch. The Seamstress had Crow's droppings checked regularly for evidence of berry consumption, and her punishment was worth starving to avoid.

"I don't care what she does to me. I'm already dead." Rowan fingered the hard lines of dried sap that gnarled the bark of her arms, scars left by the Seamstress' needle fingers.

Crow cawed, the sound loud and harsh in the small, musty kitchen.

"You must care. We belong to her. The sooner you accept that, the better."

"I don't belong to anyone!"

"You can rage against it as much as you like, but the fact is, the Seamstress bought us, and that makes us her property. She can destroy us and it won't bother her or anyone else one bit. She can find more of us. We're just Wyrd Women, Rowan, offensive to the eye and worth nothing. We don't have any valuable skill or purpose to redeem us, like the Seamstress does. Just do what you're told, and don't run off when you're not supposed to, and the best you can hope for is to be fed enough to continue your sad life. Where do you go when you run, anyway?"

"Nowhere."

"Fine. Don't tell me. But I know you met with a man last night. You smell of his smoke. Surely that's too dangerous for you? Taking up with one who burns?"

The yellow centres of Rowan's flower eyes widened. "You can smell him? He smells like . . . like smoke? What does that smell like?"

"Charred sandalwood, drifting patchouli, the glowing embers of a stick of finest vanilla cinnamon. He is strong flavour that is eaten by the nose. He reeks of the incense makers."

Rowan closed her eyes. Nothing could be done, then. She was wood and leaf. He—whoever he was—was a fragrant flame.

"Here." Crow shoved the bowl into Rowan's brittle fingers. "You take it to her. Throw yourself flat before her, grovel and weep, make your most poetic and moving apologies. She may take pity on you."

"There's no pity in the cold stuttering engine that is her heart. It beats only to remind her to beat *us*," Rowan muttered, but she went to the Seamstress' chamber. Tears would come easy to her today, thinking of the molten voice of her forbidden visitor. It was ridiculous—she'd not even seen him, had heard only a smattering of words from him—but all the same, the pollen flew from her eyes.

Maybe Crow was right, and that would be enough for the Seamstress today. Maybe she wouldn't require sap as well. For once.

◆ ◆ ◆

"Stupid, diseased little dogberry. Weed, pest, unpretty unwanted creeper!" The Seamstress shoved Rowan's berries into her mouth, her rows of needle teeth mutilating the fruit as its red juice trickled down her chin. "Your *ex*-lover whispers tales of your inadequacies to me as he kisses my lips, licks my throat, and moves inside me! Such a poor boy is he, but handsome, and he brings me riches of amusement at your expense. We laugh about you together. That's when he can even remember you at all, which happens less and less often. Not surprising—he's certainly traded up. You're nothing, aren't you, Witch Wood? A dirty thing crawling with stinking mildew and sightless grubs! Be thankful that you're designed so you can't smell anything, for I assure you, your own stench would slay you where you stand!"

Rowan pictured herself safe on the tail feathers of the Nowhere peacocks, and swallowed her rage as if it were Mother Bear's tea. "Yes, Seamstress," she said.

""Yes, Seamstress"", the Seamstress mimicked in a high, cruel voice. "You speak like a snot-stuffed mutant child with gangrene of the nose. How ugly you sound. And where were you last night, my useless shrub? Where are you *every* night?"

"Nowhere, Seamstress."

"Don't defy me, girl. I'll score your bark until you scream for mercy." The Seamstress threw the unfinished bowl of berries aside and rose from her seat, looming over Rowan on her eight needle legs. "Get down on your knees and put your face to the floor so that I don't have to look at it."

Rowan did as she was told, grateful for the reprieve from the blank glare of the Seamstress' eight black thimble eyes.

"Now, I'll ask you once more. Where do you go at night?"

The truth wouldn't do. Not the small portion Rowan was willing to surrender, anyway. She thought quickly. "I go to the incense maker's den."

"What—madness! Why?"

"I . . . " Rowan hadn't thought quickly enough.

The Seamstress sneered. "Either you're lying to me, in which case I believe I'll claim one of your gormless eye buds, or you've been meeting with a new lover there, being that it's the place you're least likely to be discovered, in which case—"

"In which case *what*?" Ah, a voice like that could not be mistaken or forgotten. Rowan's breath quickened, her hands trembling where they lay splayed in supplication on the floor. She kept her forehead pressed to the ground, not trusting her limbs to support her weight if she moved.

The Seamstress yelped at the unexpected intrusion. "Who are you to enter my quarters, uninvited and unannounced?" She sniffed. "Aha! Incense! Well, that is altogether *too* coincidental. This virulent weed cowering here on my floor must have spoken the truth for once in her—"

"Enough." The voice moved closer, until it was right next to Rowan. "I didn't come to listen to your histrionics. I'd tell you that you're repulsive in your cruelty and arrogance, but there's little point, as you're incapable of understanding, let alone changing. So I'll tell you the one thing that will get through to you: I'm here to give you a lot of money."

"How *dare* . . . what?"

"There's the bobbin dropping now. Yes, money. A great deal of it."

"Why?"

"Because you're going to sell me your two Wyrd Women, Rowan Redberry and Crow Blackbeak."

Silence stretched like gum until tension forced it to break.

"Leave us, Witch Wood," the Seamstress barked. Rowan rose to her feet.

"Don't look at me," the visitor murmured as Rowan's leafy head lifted, but he needn't have bothered. She didn't want him to rush away this time, didn't want to botch the miraculous deliverance he seemed to be offering. Her eyes remained fixed on the floor as she exited the room. Her dress itched against her prominent shoulder blades and ribs, the hope-threads ablaze for the first time in the years Rowan had worn the thing. It had, after all, been just another perverse amusement the Seamstress had dreamt up to toy with her two playthings—hope, the eternal punishment.

Crow waited in the tiny kitchen, agitated, having heard everything, her beak agape, her clawed fingers in the black feathers of her hair. "Is it true? Is he here to save us?"

"I don't know," Rowan said, but she took Crow's quivering hands in her own, held them to her chest, and squeezed.

"I can smell him. He smells like jasmine, pine, and musk. He smells like love. He's your burning man, isn't he?"

Rowan didn't answer, for she didn't know what to say. It was answer enough. They stood, entwined, listening. But the visitor and the Seamstress talked in low tones now, their words no longer audible.

Eventually, Crow pulled her hands away from Rowan. "Best get on with the day's chores." The thrill had already faded from her voice, the reality of years of hunger and pain drowning it out. "Who knows what comes."

Rowan nodded, took up her bucket and scrubbing brush, and went outside to clean the marble courtyard. It was a lengthy task that needed repeating every day. The Seamstress' silken webs hung from the walls surrounding the courtyard, her sought-after wares dangling on the gossamer strands. Below the webs lay the gelatinous waste the Seamstress secreted from her fat arachnid body as she sewed. It gleamed in the magenta sunlight, thick puddles of it everywhere Rowan looked. Sighing, she once again got down on her hands and knees and did what she had to, grateful that the stench couldn't touch her.

◆　◆　◆

It happened fast, as decided-upon things tend to do.

Crow tumbled out of the kitchen door into the courtyard, landing hard on her hands and knees, beak agape, the nubs on her back where the Seamstress had long ago torn off her wings twitching wildly through her threadbare dress. The Seamstress appeared at the door a second later.

"You're dismissed from my service," she said through gritted needle-teeth, and was gone.

Rowan helped Crow to her feet, tutting at the pinpricks of blood where the Seamstress' fingers had punctured Crow's skin beneath her feathers.

Then *he* entered the courtyard, and this time, Rowan looked at him.

Prismatic smoke rose in a constant hazy stream from black hair, ashen skin, and clothes that burnt like the sun. He was tall and thin, with fine features and long, articulate fingers. His eyes blazed orange, surrounded by sooty lashes. Tiny balls of flame rolled off his tongue as he spoke.

"Rowan Redberry and Crow Blackbeak. Will you come with me?"

"Where?" Rowan was glad she couldn't smell him. The sight and sound of him was overpowering enough. He smiled at her voice, and she smiled back.

"You, Rune Tree most divine, will accompany me, if you are agreeable, all the way to my home—to the incense maker's den. You, Crow Blackbeak, I will take to the smithing district. There are metals that can only be hammered into shape by beaks such as yours, and tools that can only be made from the guano of your kind. I know this, because I've seen another Blackbeak there. Does the name Macaw mean anything to you?"

Crow's eyes moistened and her beak gaped open. She crossed her hands over the ruffled feathers on her chest and cooed.

"My mother," she said. "I haven't seen her since I hatched."

"Well, you shall see her by this day's end," the burning man said. He bowed low before them, sending the smoke that surrounded him into frenzied eddies. "I have been remiss in not introducing myself. My name is Incendere Resin. I am a Libanomancer. This is the highest art of the incense makers, and I am well paid. Money opens doors, and it has allowed me to walk through one such door today, to stand before you and offer betterment to both your lives."

Crow looked from Rowan to Incendere and back again. "However you came to be here today, freeing us, I am—we are—grateful," she said.

"I'm not entirely freeing you. I can't change our society's culture, or its attitude to your . . . uniqueness. But I can offer greater comfort for you, and," he stood from his bow and looked at Rowan, "higher purpose."

Rowan inclined her head in a slight nod, and followed Crow and Incendere to the incense maker's flame-powered coach. They rocketed through the streets of Here, the townspeople leaping aside, shaking their fists and cursing as the incense maker and his Wyrd cargo shot past.

It was nightfall before they reached the smithing district, and Rowan was exhausted. Her petals rolling with fatigue, she embraced her long-time slave-sister and watched Crow rush from the coach into the brightly feathered arms of a large bird-woman who could only be her mother. A heavyset man, with a face both stern and kind, approached the coach and handed Incendere a hessian bag tied with twine, coin clinking audibly within. Incendere nodded at the man, who returned the nod before walking away, ushering the two bird-women inside with him.

Rowan was fast asleep when the coach finally reached the incense maker's den. Incendere reached to wake her. Rowan's bark skin blackened and blistered under his touch, her eyes flying open as she recoiled. The Libanomancer looked horrified. Rowan waved a twig-hand at him. She was well accustomed to pain.

But as she staggered tiredly into the den, the air heavy and mysterious with incense smoke, her skin throbbed and complained at the memory of Incendere's scalding touch, and pollen dusted her cheeks.

◆ ◆ ◆

Incendere worked from sunrise to sunset each day, locked away in a cavern of the den, while Rowan was free to wander, her duties so light as to be ridiculous—dust an earthen ledge, polish a brass doorknob, fluff a velvet cushion. She was not permitted entry to Incendere's Libanomancy cavern, and she still didn't understand exactly what he did. Whenever she asked, he would laugh, flames spurting from his lips, and smile indulgently at her. "The nuts and bolts would bore you," he would say, and he'd point out another wonder of the den to distract her—a whorl of pulsating smoke in the shape of a heart, a net of dreams to capture the odours of life, a Dragon's Blood joss stick as tall as a man smouldering ruby-bright in a corner of the den.

Incendere forgot time and again that Rowan couldn't smell the incense, and after a while, she stopped reminding him.

Their kisses were painful and infrequent, always initiated by Rowan. Incendere would kiss her back for a time, but all too soon the sound of bark popping and sizzling would become too insistent to ignore. He would cry out in dismay and shove her away, but too late—her lips would already be swelling and splitting. She would smile sadly as he commanded another Wyrd Woman—Aloe, a healer—to apply soothing balm to her wounds. He would stride away, head bowed, but Rowan could still see the tears that rolled in tiny fireballs down his cheeks.

Love should not hurt, but in Rowan's experience, it always had. This time it hurt her more than usual, and more visibly, but surely that only meant it was stronger, and more honest?

Rowan slept in a large soil-filled cot, the dirt cool and black and comforting around her. Incendere didn't sleep, but he would enter Rowan's bedchamber and sit—at a distance, of course—and tell her fascinating stories, about oracles, scented altars, scrying shapes in rising smoke, reading signs in the crackle of incense on coals. In this way she pieced together the meaning of his work, the uses for what he created—what it was to be a Libanomancer—but she still knew nothing about the practicalities of the work, the nuts and bolts that he insisted would bore her.

And it became too much, this unsatisfactory endless talk, this gaping space between them. The burn was worse when he *didn't* touch her.

◆　◆　◆

When Incendere entered Rowan's room one gloomy Saturday evening—the rain hammering at the little stained glass window over her bed, the air damp and cold—she was ready for him. She threw herself into his scorching arms, and he held her for a moment as he always did. But this time, she would not allow him to discard her. She fell backwards, and dragged him with her. They tumbled together into the chill dirt of Rowan's bed. Incendere propped himself up above her, his hands planted in the soil, his orange eyes searching her face for acquiescence even as he shook his head.

"Wait! See?" she said, lifting clods of dirt in her twig fingers and smearing them on her lips before she kissed him again and again. "The soil cools your kisses enough for me to take them without too much pain, certainly without burning beyond repair. We can be together, here, in the dirt. *Fully* together, for the first time."

Incendere murmured protests, whispered fears and doubts, but his hands were at her bodice, ripping and burning, and his lips remained pressed to hers. She rubbed gritty soil over both their bodies, and soon enough the Libanomancer's words were dampened to moans. Smoke rose around them in thick clouds as they rolled and twisted together. Soon the only sounds were the rasp of flesh on bark and the hiss of burning wood tempered with soil.

◆ ◆ ◆

"I have a favour to ask of you." Incendere trailed a finger through the air above Rowan's foliage hair, a painless gesture of affection, though some of her berries still withered from it. As the lovers talked, Aloe slathered Rowan's skin with balm, as she did every morning after the burning man and the tree-woman had lain together. Some of the deepest burns on Rowan's bark skin would not heal, and left deep black craters that oozed sap. Aloe packed these with a soothing poultice. It was all that could be done. Rowan didn't even flinch anymore as Aloe's fingers dug into her wounds.

"Then ask," Rowan said.

"I would like you to help me with my work."

Rowan opened her mouth to respond, but Incendere held up his hand.

"Don't say yes yet," he said. "There is much you must know. I don't want to lose you. I am only able to keep you here because you are valuable, my love. It is because of your value that my masters, who own this den, have provided the funds to allow us to be together. I wanted it to be forever, but if it can only be for now, then I want that, too. I have searched for another way. I cannot find any."

"Stop, you make it all sound so dire!"

"But it is." Incendere waved Aloe away. The healer left quickly, as if relieved.

"Then don't tell me."

"I must," Incendere said, hot tears blazing forth from his eyes. And the Libanomancer told the Rune Tree a tale, just as he had on countless nights before.

Once, a burning man saw a beautiful Wyrd Woman buying supplies for her mistress at the market, a tree-girl with hair of red leaves and berries, and eyes of soft floral beauty. He'd never seen such a thing, and he was spellbound. He asked about her, and learnt of her plight. He watched her from afar, saw her run the night streets in pain as birds trailed her through the sky, witnessed her climb a bridge and disappear at the peak, appearing hours later from Nowhere and running back to her cruel mistress. After many nights, he finally managed to climb the bridge himself, to lay with her, briefly. To whisper kindnesses to her and caress her with his voice, though he wanted far more than that.

And finally, the burning man hatched a plan. His work had led him to discover the secrets of a powerful divination incense, one that had never successfully been made before, one that would be worth an inestimable fortune to whoever produced it. His masters were hungry for fame and riches, and they commanded the Libanomancer to produce the divination incense, at any cost. The key ingredients were difficult to obtain, but he gathered them all— except for two. The berries and sap of a tree-girl. This wouldn't have been difficult if any tree-girl would do, but they wouldn't.

It had to be a Rune Tree. It had to be Rowan. This was good, because it led to a way for the burning man to have her. But making the incense would require *all* Rowan's berries—her beautiful crowning glory—and *all* her sap.

"But I'll die," Rowan cried, for surely Incendere didn't know. "My berries you could take, and I would give them to you freely, but my sap is my life. I can't survive without it."

He only looked at her sadly, and she realised—had realised long ago, if she was honest with herself, had known this moment was hurtling toward them—that he understood the price he was asking her to pay very well. She wept yellow pollen tears and shook her head, back and forth, unable to stop her negation.

"I love you, Rowan. This is the only way for us, however short our time may be. What is your alternative? Another Seamstress, a life of pain and starvation? I would be gentle, oh, so gentle. I would take only a little of you at a time, so carefully you wouldn't even notice, and we would make something magical in the process. Isn't that truly love? The fruit of our union would last forever."

Incendere reached for her, but she shrank away, lost to her weeping. He gazed at her for a moment, and then stood and left, wisps of dark smoke trailing in his wake.

◆ ◆ ◆

Rowan was pulled from the agony of her dreams by a gentle hand on her shoulder. She opened her eyes to see Aloe kneeling beside her dirt bed.

"You're not the first," Aloe said. Her voice was cool and soft. Rowan had never heard her speak before, had assumed she couldn't.

She sat up, frowning. "What do you mean?"

"There have been other great and secret incenses that Master Resin has been compelled to make, other essential ingredients, other girls he has immortalised through his work."

"You shouldn't be here. And you're wrong. He loves me, and I love him. This is torture for us both."

"Oh, yes, he loves you. I don't dispute that. Master Resin loves deeply, and often. And all of his love goes up in smoke."

"No. You're infatuated with him. Or you're misguided, thinking to help me, when I don't need your help. There is a way out of this, and Incendere and I will find it together."

Aloe shook her head, and beckoned for Rowan to move away from her bed. Rowan did, stepping out and standing over Aloe, who, still kneeling, leant forward and began to remove handfuls of moist soil.

"What're you doing? You're destroying it, stop!" Rowan reached for Aloe's arm, but the girl shrugged her off, digging at a furious pace. Within moments a hole several feet deep gaped. Rowan leaned down to look. The soil thinned until what Aloe pulled out wasn't soil at all but skulls, ribs, teeth, and fistfuls of ashes, amassing the charnel wares into a pile that grew until Rowan could bear no more. "Stop," she cried, "Please, stop. Leave them alone. Cover them."

Aloe did, replacing the remains and swaddling them in dirt. She wiped her hands on her thin dress and stood. "He has me bury them, and the new one always sleeps atop them. I try to heal them after death, every time. And every time, I fail."

"I love him," Rowan whispered, knowing herself for a fool even as she also knew the truth of her words. He'd coupled with her, there atop the buried tower of his murdered lovers—Wyrd Women, like her, all of them. Like Crow, and Aloe. How deep did the mass grave go? "I love him!"

Aloe stood, her face close to Rowan's. "Love should not hurt! It should never take everything from you, never steal your light and demand your life. And if it does, well, then, where are you, and what have you got? It is far better to be nowhere, with not even the clothes upon your back, than anywhere near *that* kind of love." She shook her dirty finger in Rowan's face. "I will not bury you, Rowan Redberry. I will *not*."

"We're Wyrd, Aloe. Offensive to the eye and worth nothing. We don't have any valuable skill or purpose to redeem us, like Incendere does. We're lucky someone like him wants us."

Aloe gaped. "Do you think me without skill or purpose? How much pain have I eased, how many wounds have I healed? I'm still alive because of my convenient value to his ongoing "work". Rowan, you're the most beautiful creature I've ever seen. Your sap contains the secrets to life itself. You reek of magic, so much so that I need to breathe through my mouth when I'm around you, lest I be overpowered. Why do you suppose you can't smell anything yourself? Why do you think those who claim to own you are so eager to convince you of your worthlessness, but so reluctant to part with you?"

Rowan squeezed her eyes shut, rubbing the bridge of her nose with one trembling finger. "It doesn't matter. Where can the Wyrd go if we run, anyway?"

"Nowhere," Aloe said. "A place that, as you know, isn't as frightening or desperate as it sounds."

Rowan knuckled her eyes. "I'm tired. I need to . . . to sleep, to think. Please . . . I'm grateful for what you've shown me, and I appreciate your words and your care, but I need to be alone."

Aloe touched Rowan's arm as she passed. "Remember: I won't bury *you*," she said. Her careful emphasis was not lost on Rowan, who sank to her knees and stared at her dirt cot as Aloe left, closing the door softly behind her.

◆ ◆ ◆

The night stretched on forever, as nights full of loss and confusion tend to do. By luck or fate or sheer mindless coincidence, Incendere didn't visit Rowan's bedchamber. She lay on the floor, facedown, her head cradled on her arms. If her thoughts were blood, then the hours that she'd passed tonight in this way were drenched in gore, exhausted half-dead things that staggered ever onward, defeated again and again by paradox and snare.

She loved Incendere, but could not stay and let him kill her. Nor could she leave and let him kill others. And, selfishly, she could not live without him if he lived without her. What was more, she cared for Aloe, and could not leave the healer to this endless dark cycle. Nor could she ask the healer to kill for her, or to clean up afterward even if she could bring herself to kill Incendere—which she couldn't.

Round and round the cogs of her mind spun, crushing her rather than carrying her forward, getting her . . . nowhere.

A place that was not as frightening or desperate as it sounded.

◆ ◆ ◆

Rowan ran the cobblestones of the night, naked, all hope left far behind her. Her foliage hair hung brown and wilted without her berries to offer it colour and radiance. No birds shrieked above her, swooping for her fruit. She ran alone and in peace.

She had passed through the smithing district on her long journey, and had seen Crow through a candlelit window, her head resting on her fluffed up feathers, her eyes closed in peaceful slumber, her mother stroking her beak, as the stern but kind man smiled at them. That picture had been true love. Stopping, Rowan had plucked a single petal from her right eye—*she loves me*—and dropped it on Crow's doorstep, knowing her slave-sister would understand.

"Live long and be happy," she'd said, and ran on once more. Her flower eyes were wide and dry, no yellow pollen dusting them now, though sap leaked in a thin amber runnel from the space where the missing petal had been. Her bark skin was ghost gum in the moonlight, Wyrd and strong.

She hurt, oh, she hurt so much, but she did not weep.

She ran faster than she ever had before, but her breath came easy, her heart troubling her not at all despite her exhausting pace, for she had left that behind, too, and found she could live without it. Eventually, she reached the wrought iron bridge, cherubs and serpents smiling at her from the railing, the water beneath burbling its delight at her return. She sang as she climbed the bridge, her voice broken and raw—but *there,* not lost, surrendered, or stolen. The lanterns nudged her head, their wings landing butterfly kisses on her cheeks. The peacocks snored, glossy tail-feathers twitching in dreams. And waiting with arms outstretched was the Mother Bear, tears streaming down her fuzzy cheeks, giving Rowan's pain a face.

Rowan smelt it all. Tallow, feathers, fur, and so much more. The scents flooded her. They'd been here all along, waiting for her to claim them. In time, she would be ready to face her own scent, too.

"Welcome home, our darling," the Mother Bear said. "How long will you stay this time?"

"I'll never leave again," Rowan said, falling into the Bear's arms.

"You never really did, child," Mother Bear said. "But you know, there's a price that must be paid to stay here. It requires a selfless sacrifice and a selfish solution. Nobody has ever stayed, because until now, the toll has been thought impossible. How find *you* this toll, my beautiful daughter?"

Rowan pulled away and looked up at the Bear's face. "Are you hungry, Mother?"

The Bear smiled with shark-teeth. "Always. I am a Mother, but I am also a Bear."

Rowan nodded. "Plant his remains deep in the soil bed in my room, which you will know by its smell. I've left him a gift, the last and greatest one I could offer, a shining red pile of myself. Place it atop his grave, which was always the only place berries and incense could ever be together anyway. And he'll lie there with the others, which, if they feel as I do, may please them, though for different reasons."

With a roar, the Mother Bear charged off the bridge, disappearing into the aether. Rowan lay on the peacocks' tails and hugged herself. She watched the implacable stars wheel overhead and when sleep called to her, she sang herself toward it with gently murmured truths.

"I loved him before, and I love him now. I love him Here and I love him There. I love him Everywhere but, most of all, forevermore . . . I love him Nowhere."

# AFTERWORD

*Once again, I decided to toy with fantasy here, and once again, it got nasty. There is an awful lot woven into this piece, most of which you probably won't care to know about, so I'll just skim the surface. I wanted to write something quite different. It's a curious thing: the more fantastic your fantasy, the more real issues you can deal with. I wanted my protagonist to be an extreme misfit, even within the weird and wonderful world in which she dwelt. I wanted her to be flawed and thus real—she doesn't always make wise choices when it comes to love, doesn't always respect herself, doesn't always see herself and her surroundings for what they really are, isn't always someone we can admire or relate to. She needs others. She fears the void. She is a strong female figure, but not in an idealised fashion. Similarly, her love interest is not a one-dimensional "bad man"; he is not good for her, but nor is he pure evil without sincere emotion. As usual, revenge got thrown into the mix, although not just for our protagonist, but for all her fallen sisters who went before her. Also, I got to play with incense, which is fabulous stuff—hand me a stick of Nag Champa and I'll be a happy camper. I'm burning it while I write this, actually.*

# TO WISH ON A CLOCKWORK HEART

Marc met the clockwork fairy on his way home from the pub. That wasn't surprising, as he was always on his way home from the pub these days. The bitter wind reddened his cheeks and made his nose run. The dark street glistened, a blackened blister lanced by the moon and streetlights. Marc felt neither the wind's bite nor the night's gloom. He'd worked very hard for some time now on feeling as little as possible.

"Forget I ever had a wife and daughter. Maybe she was right. It hurts too much. But Mary . . . oh, Mary, my little girl . . . I'm so sorry. Daddy's sorry."

Tears blurred his already challenged vision. Marc staggered, leant on a telephone pole for support until the beer bees quietened their buzzing in his brain, and *clunk*, the clockwork fairy appeared on the footpath in front of him in a cloudburst of iron filings.

"I need oil," she said, her voice the shriek of rusty nails being dragged down a dented car door. Two huge wings rose like bridges above her shoulders, intricate spirals of metal laced with sluggishly turning brass cogs. Oversized brown aviator goggles dangled around her neck on a cracked leather strap.

"I'm drunk," Marc pointed out, somewhat redundantly, wiping his tears on the back of his sleeve.

The clockwork fairy tried to roll her eyes, but they made a sick whirring noise and refused to move, so she settled for hissing like a broken kettle instead.

"I don't have time for this. I need oil *now*. Do you live nearby?"

"I'm not really seeing you," Marc persisted. "It's the beer talking."

"Oh, for sobbing out loud." She stepped towards him, rattling audibly with each movement, and extended her hand. "I'm Pendula. Shake my hand," she instructed when Mark didn't move and, after a moment, he did as he was told. Her hand was dry and hard in his, and generated a rapidly dissipating superficial heat.

"Nice to meet you. I'm Marc." The inside of Marc's head gave itself an alarming twist, and the street tilted dangerously beneath him, threatening to pitch him to the ground. "Whoa," he muttered.

"Listen to me as carefully as your ale soaked senses will allow, Marc. Look at me!" Pendula screamed the last words, and Marc snapped to attention, one hand fluttering to his mouth in surprise. "See this?" Pendula stabbed a creaky finger at her forehead. A small heart-shaped clock-face hung there, suspended from a thin gold chain that hugged her forehead before disappearing into her frenzied russet curls. "Time is fleeting. If my heart stops ticking, I'm dead. That's true for humans and it's true for me, too. It's already running way too slow. Oil is the answer. I'll get you home, but you have to ask me for a ride. I can't give you one until you ask, or someone asks for you. Stupid rules."

"A—a ride?"

Pendula's glowing eyes—convex copper coins with lightning strikes of silver—narrowed, the movement making the heart-clock on her forehead drop and swing like a wrecking ball. Dreading that blood-curdling scream again, Marc waved his hands in a placatory gesture that almost cost him the last of his balance.

"Alright," he said. "I live three blocks from here. 30 Avondale Terrace. Could you give me a ride? But I gotta tell you, my place is kinda messy. I haven't had guests since . . . haven't had guests for a long time."

"I'll need oil as soon as we get there," Pendula said, pulling the goggles up from around her neck and snapping them in place over her eyes, managing to look both ridiculous and terrifying all at once. "But I'll make it worth your while. I have to. More stupid rules."

"Yeah, yeah, oil. Look, I'm about to pass out, and you're not real, so can we just get whatever it is you want over—"

Marc was swept off his feet, Pendula cradling him in her arms like a baby. He felt something cold and hard biting into his arm where it pressed against Pendula's torso. Turning his head, he saw a corset-like structure that appeared to also be Pendula's rib cage. It was made of bars of iron, and sat on the outside of her clothing. His arm was wedged in between two of her ribs.

Then they were in the air, rushing up toward the stars, Pendula's junkyard wings groaning and thrashing, cogs whirling. Marc's brain twisted again, too far this time, and he slipped gratefully into stupor.

◆ ◆ ◆

He awoke supine on his bed, the wind toying with his naked body with thick icy-pole fingers.

*Why is it windy in my bedroom?*

Turning his head to the left—gently, gently, as greasy worms playing bongo drums filled with alcohol slopped queasily inside his skull—Marc saw the broken window, curtains flapping, moonlight glinting off glass shards scattered on the hardwood floor.

*Ah. I didn't do that. Who did? Don't recall getting undressed, either. Don't recall much of anything. Good. That's good.*

Something soft and wet caressed Marc's penis. He jerked as blood slammed into his groin with sudden force; gasped as the soft-wet-something lapped at him again. It slid up and down his length as he hardened beneath it, then he was enveloped, small sharp nubs adding an intense edge to the sucking, stroking, all-consuming bliss.

*Who is that oooooh don't care!*

Marc orgasmed within moments. He cried out, spasming and twitching as he gushed inside the *something* that had an expert hold on him. It suckled him greedily as he spurted, his hot fluid gone the moment it left him.

Marc sighed, but the sucking didn't stop now his semen was spent; quite the opposite. It intensified, grew painful. The pull was irresistible, and darker fluid began to flow from him, deep crimson blood, salty and thick. Marc squirmed and moaned, the scorching, tugging pain in his groin quickly becoming unbearable, but he couldn't lift his limbs, couldn't fight, and soon, couldn't move at all. Could only lie there as the life—*oil*—was drained from him through his traitorously rigid cock.

After an eternity of silver bright agony, Pendula gave one last satisfied slurp and released Marc, her jaw moving smoothly, all creaks and rattles gone now. Marc was lost again, spinning unconscious through air filled with gold dust and industrial noise, his heart hammering in his throat.

◆ ◆ ◆

*. . . tickticktickticktick . . .*

A clock running fast as a hummingbird's wings thrummed near Marc's ear. He blinked his way back into the world, sleepily, cautiously. Sunlight illuminated the dancing dust motes in his bedroom. Pendula lay next to him, her face inches from his own, the hands of the heart-shaped timepiece on her forehead spinning in a perpetual blur. Her mouth curled at the corners, little fangs tipped with gold peeking through, her high cheekbones jutting as she smiled. The bongo drum worms in Marc's brain had downgraded now to millipedes playing rotten keyboards with their soft-shoed feet. It was bearable and he could move without needing to be sick. He wasn't in pain. He felt . . . well.

His daughter's face sprang immediately into his brain, and he pushed the image her along with the pain it brought down deep into his subconscious, with the practiced skill months of self-obliviating had given him. No use dwelling on things you couldn't change, and Marc couldn't change shit.

He pinched the bridge of his nose between thumb and forefinger, squeezed his eyes shut, frowning, cramming his brain with mundane thoughts *(milk, I need milk, better take some aspirin too, gonna have a headache later, feel great now but might not later, bread, need bread too)* to stop another image flashing behind his eyes.

Fiona. BELOVED WIFE TO MARC, DEVOTED MOTHER TO MARY. That was what her headstone said, and he didn't want to think about that, couldn't . . .

"Thank you," Pendula said. Marc opened his eyes, gazed at Pendula's pink tongue, nestled in her mouth like an ill kept secret. "You saved my life."

"Er . . . you're welcome?"

"I owe you a boon now." Pendula sat up and slid off the bed. Her wings were folded against her back like collapsed outdoor furniture, cogs still twirling in the complex structure. A steel bustle arced over her buttocks, attached to the ribcage corset around her chest and back. Beneath it she wore what looked like a black leotard, with a short striped tutu. Throwing daggers were lashed to her exposed thighs with leather straps. She wore chunky black boots with gold laces reaching to her knees. Her hair was a corona of red-brown double helixes, orbiting the planet of her head.

"What *are* you?" Marc propped himself up on an elbow. His eyes touched on his penis, wilted but otherwise unmarred and intact against his thigh, and then he gazed at Pendula. No matter how hard he looked, he couldn't take all of her in. New little details kept appearing. A dozen chunky wristwatches strapped to each of her forearms. A button pinned to her left breast—SUCK MY COG! A spanner, tucked inexplicably alongside the knives on her right thigh. A gust of steam, propelled from her magenta lips when she exhaled.

"A clockwork fairy. You get one wish." Pendula shook herself, and her wings clicked and popped into position, spread out behind her in a latticework of impossibility. "Do you want it now or later? I've got places to be."

"Later," Marc blurted, only wanting to stare at her some more. "How often do you do . . . this?"

She laughed, the sound like a knife being sharpened on a grindstone. "Typical man. I'd love to tell you that you were my first, Marc, but that would be fibbing. Rest assured that I only *need* oil once every so often, though I *want* it all the time. You're lucky I figured out a way that's at least partially pleasant for both of us, and that I was in a generous mood. Had I met you under different circumstances . . . " Pendula motioned to the knives strapped to her thighs. "Your experience would have been much different."

"What *is* a clockwork fairy, exactly?" Marc was stalling now, trying to keep her here, keep the thoughts and images behind his eyes at bay. She arched an eyebrow and smirked, then turned away from him. A large brass key, the handle shaped like a heart and styled in the same intricate patterns as her wings, jutted from the small of her back just above her iron bustle.

"Clockwork," Pendula said over her shoulder, reaching behind herself and running one long-nailed finger around the rim of the key. "Fairy," she added, flicking her finger upward, pointing at her wings. "And as for any other information about me, that's not for you to know. Unless that's your wish? I could show you . . . " Her voice was eager. Marc sensed danger.

"No," he said, and she hissed. She grasped the key in her back and pulled. It slid out of her with a sound like a tin can being grated into fine shreds, and Marc winced. *Oh yeah,* there's *that hangover I thought I'd skipped this time.* Golden blood dripped from the end of the key, falling to the wooden floor and solidifying into strange nuggets.

"When you're ready for your wish, you can call me with this," Pendula said, turning and flinging the heavy thing at Marc. He rolled, and it thudded onto the mattress beside him, denting it visibly. "But don't wait too long. Time is fleeting, and if you let it escape, it never returns. Call me soon."

"How? Wait, don't go," he said, biting back the *please* he wanted to add, but she'd already leapt through his shattered window and taken wing in the morning sky.

◆ ◆ ◆

Marc had been at the pub to drown his sorrows, as always, but the bloody things refused to die. Now, in the wake of Pendula's bizarre entry and exit from his life, he found his sorrows had clawed their way to shore and, far from drowned, were invigorated by their time at sea. It was always this way. He had to drink more every time, and every time it wore off faster. He'd always loved the drink, and the drink had always loved him, but since Fiona . . . well, his flirtation with alcohol had gone from a casual affair to a devoted marriage.

He left the key on his bed untouched, slipped into pyjama pants, and headed to the kitchen to make coffee. A black lacy bra was tossed carelessly over the breakfast bar. It had been there, undisturbed, for a year. It was *hers.* Not Pendula's (did clockwork fairies wear bras?), but Fiona's. His wife—his *dead* wife. He couldn't move it, couldn't bring himself to pick it up and put it out of sight, let alone throw it away.

On that night a year ago, Fiona had left a note stuck to the pot of soup in the fridge: *love you, see you in the morning, remember to pick up Mary from after-school care, doofus!* She'd left her dirty bra on the counter in her rush, driven off to her shift at the Hospital, and had never come back. There'd been nothing exceptional about Fiona's accident, just crappy conditions and a tree waiting for her car to slam into it as she skidded off the slick road. But losing her was exceptional, very exceptional indeed, at least to Marc and six-year-old Mary.

Mary's face flashed into his memory again, scrunched into a red ball and made ugly with her screams, as Fiona's sister Helen dragged the little girl kicking and screaming down Marc's driveway.

*Don't think about it don't think about it don't think about it!*

Marc grabbed a handful of his crotch, shifting until he felt more comfortable. It was tender down there, but in a good way. He'd been dead a year himself, too, in a way—in *that* way. He wasn't used to the activity. Hell, who *was* used to having blood sucked out of their . . .

Grimacing, Marc swigged his coffee in two gulps and headed for the shower.

◆ ◆ ◆

An agonising grind of days in the office talking to idiots about their gas accounts followed. Marc swung between contemplating the clockwork fairy, suicide, and murder as the months cycled by.

Yes, murder, there was a thought to keep him warm at night.

Helen. It was always Helen's throat he pictured his hands closing around. Helen, with her cold eyes, hard hands, and archaic views on "disciplining" children. How could anyone have thought her better able to care for Mary than he was?

"Forget you ever had a wife and daughter," Helen had hissed at him as she slammed her car door on his daughter's screams. Mary's little fists hammered on the car window and when that failed, the girl actually began to head butt the glass, her lips forming the word *daddy* over and over again. Helen ignored her, no doubt filing the "bad" behaviour in her mental catalogue of sins for harsh punishment with fist and rod later. "Mary's mine now. I knew the courts would see you for the louse you are. You're useless. You're nothing. Fiona probably drove into that tree on purpose. Killed herself, rather than have to face her pathetic excuse for a husband. I told her not to marry you, but oh no, she wouldn't listen to me, and now look what's happened. Well, you'll never see your daughter again. I'll see to that. Do you hear me? *I'll see to that!*"

At first he'd tried to fight, tried to see Mary, tried to get her back—all the more when he saw her bruised eyes and hollow cheeks in the glimpses he snatched of her before Helen slammed the door in his face and called the police—but it had been one brick wall after another. *An alcoholic with little hope of rehabilitation at this time*, the court shrinks had said. *Stuck in a time warp of losing his wife over and over again, and constantly trying to douse the memory rather than deal with it. A danger to himself and to others. Reports of threats against his sister in law, who is caring for the child. Sister in law confirms history of violence, leading to the child's current erratic behaviour, and flights of fancy about the villainy of her Aunt.* Lies, but that hadn't mattered. And the most damning two words he'd ever seen in print: *Not fit.*

Forget you ever had a wife and child.

Hating himself, Marc had eventually tried to do just that. To do otherwise—to dwell and agonise, to rage and regret—became just too much to bear. But a seed of hatred and rage planted itself in his heart, and it grew thick and deep in the fertile red soil.

And now every night, when he returned to his empty house, the golden key sat on his bedside table, a question waiting for him to answer it. He told himself there'd been no clockwork fairy, that it was a drunken hallucination, that he'd found the key on the ground somewhere as he'd staggered home after another bender, that it was all nothing, just like him. Nothing.

But.

In the end, it was the slow trudge of days that pushed him over the edge. It was all just finally . . . enough. He hated Helen, he grieved Fiona, he longed for his little daughter with an agony that was fresh each day, he raged against the injustice of it all, he struggled to live with himself, and it. Was. *Enough.*

He picked the key up, held it to his chest He needed both hands to grip it and his biceps quivered with the weight of the thing.

"Er . . . Pendula?" He said, feeling an utter idiot.

Nothing happened. Of *course* nothing happened.

He dropped the heavy key to the floor, and climbed into bed, sighing.

◆　◆　◆

The immense weight of her woke him in the small hours of the night. That, and the clanking of her parts, the whirring of her cogs, the ticking of that cursed heart-clock—slower than last time he'd seen her, but still steady, and what had she said about it slowing down before? That was important, because it meant she'd be wanting . . . oil. Again.

She straddled him, her gold-tipped teeth glinting in the moonlight that washed his room ghostly grey-white. "You certainly took your time, didn't you, Marc?" She tapped one of the many wristwatches that competed for space on her arm. "Time is fleeting. Don't you know that? I keep telling you, but you don't get it. Nobody ever does." She shrugged, her wings grating against each other with a tortured metal scream that vibrated to the very roots of Marc's teeth.

"You're . . . "

"If you say "real", I swear to whatever pathetic deity you worship, it'll be the last word you ever utter." Pendula leaned down, adjusting her position, her thighs sliding against his until the knives and spanner strapped there dug into him painfully, her metal rib cage crushingly heavy atop his own fragile chest. Holding her face within kissing distance of his, she inhaled, copper-scented steam gusting from her mouth when she released the breath again, stinging his eyes and making them water.

"You're sober," she said. "Well, wonders will never cease."

"It's the day before payday. I can't afford to drink again until tomorrow." And didn't he know it. His body ached, his mouth was parched, and his thoughts capered uncontrolled like imps through his brain.

"Ah. I see. What a charming existence you lead. But don't their faces haunt you, Marc? How do you keep them at bay without your poison of choice?"

He gaped up at her, wanting to shove her away in outrage, but unable to move beneath her bulk. She kept on grinning, those strange teeth seeming ever sharper and more dangerous.

'But a wish will help you, won't it?' Her hand caressed his cheek, and then her finger traced a line down his torso, worming into the tiny space between their bodies and reaching for his groin. Marc bucked, the movement doing little to budge Pendula, but she chuckled and withdrew her hand with a melodramatic flourish.

"You already got all you're getting from me, and you already *owe* me a wish." Marc struggled to get the words out. Pendula's weight was making it difficult to breathe.

"Aw, not volunteering any more oil?" Pendula's coin-eyes twinkled, reminding Marc of pennies placed on the eyes of the dead, and he shook his head. "But you enjoyed yourself so much last time, Marc. Oh well. You're right, of course. I owe you a wish."

"I want—"

"Be careful." Pendula's voice was amused. "Time is—"

"Fleeting, bla bla, yeah, I got that part."

Pendula inclined her head slightly. "Go on," she said.

"I want my daughter back from that hag."

"Of course you do. But frankly, I find that wish boring. What's in it for me?"

Marc's eyes widened in indignation. "I don't give a shit what's in it for you! You said you owed me a wish!"

"I did say that, but did I say *what* wish I owed you? No. I owe you a wish, and I'll honour my debt, but guess what, kiddo? I get final say on whether your wish is suitable. And that one isn't. Try again."

"You fucking liar! You can't just play with words like that!"

"Never met a fairy before, have you?" Pendula stretched atop him, her wings spreading to their full formidable span, cogs turning sleepily. The little heart-clock on her forehead seemed even slower now, and her hand fluttered to it in an absent gesture. Marc's eyes fixed on it, and an idea began to form in his mind, which was a nice change from the usual parade of angst and self-loathing that marched there any other time.

"What if there *was* something in it for you?"

Pendula raised an eyebrow.

"I see your clock is slowing down again. What if there was a way for you to grant my wish and also secure yourself as much oil as you can consume, for the next, oh, I'd say thirty years or so?"

Pendula's flinty eyes regarded him suspiciously. "You can't trick me," she said. "Just so you know. Just in case you're thinking of being clever."

"No tricks," Marc said. "If you let me up so I can catch my breath, I'll explain. It's pretty hard to have a conversation with you crushing me."

Pendula regarded him a moment longer, then swung her leg over him with a metallic screech, and rose to her feet. The relief was immediate—air, sweet air, rushing into his lungs, and the blessed lack of weight on his body!—and Marc revelled in it for a moment.

"Hurry up," Pendula snapped. "Time." She didn't bother finishing her personal catchphrase, and Marc was grateful.

"So I'm thinking of something a little like this," Marc said, sitting upright.

Pendula listened as he spoke, and after a moment, she smiled fully, her teeth flashing and her face stretching into something truly terrifying.

◆  ◆  ◆

Marc rapped on the wooden door, then, abandoning any pretence of politeness, he used both fists to hammer on it. He heard movement inside the house, hurried footsteps approaching behind the door. The outside light flickered into life, and the door was pulled open, just far enough for Helen to peer out, blinking sleepily, the chain still holding the door secure should anyone try to force their way in. She saw Marc and scowled.

"What are *you* doing here? The restraining order is still active, you know. Do you want a repeat of last time, with the police? You never learn, do you?"

A curtain twitched at an upstairs window. Mary, too frightened from a year of beatings to throw the curtain wide, but unable to resist the chance to catch a glimpse of her daddy. Marc's heart twisted with love and rage, and he smiled at Helen, who flinched as if he'd moved to strike her.

"Good evening, Helen. I just want you to remember that I tried for a year to do this peacefully. I tried to get my daughter back from you, you child-abusing cow, but you just enjoy torturing her and I too much, don't you? I've often wondered what's in this for you. Why do you *want* Mary? You clearly hate children. But I realised that's why you love this so much. You hate Mary, and you hate me, and this way, you get to take a daily hand in our misery, don't you?"

"I'm closing this door, then I'm calling the police, and then I'm going back to bed." Helen's voice was dull. "That's how little I care for anything you say. You're drunk, as usual."

"That's where you're wrong. I'm dead sober, and I'm glad of that, because it makes this moment *sharp.*"

Two things happened simultaneously. Helen moved to close the door, and Pendula stepped out of the shadows that she'd so seamlessly merged with up to that moment, and halted the door with one hand. Helen's eyes widened at the sight of Pendula, and her mouth dropped open.

"Oh," Helen said. "Oh!"

"Open the door, or I'll tear it from its hinges." A hungry urgency had crept into Pendula's voice. Her double-helix hair flamed and bristled around her face. Her half-unfolded wings trembled and clinked. Her free hand lowered to the knives strapped to her thigh—not that she'd need them to harm Helen, but they were a solid threat the woman could grasp.

"No." Helen's innate mulishness overpowered her fear and wonder. "Move your hand or I'll close the door on it. I'm calling the police."

Pendula smiled. "I was hoping you'd say that." The fairy lunged forward, throwing her weight against the door. The wood groaned and splintered, and the door shot open, knocking Helen from her feet. She skidded backwards down the hardwood floor and landed hard on her side, her head hitting the wall with a *crack*, and lay blinking in shock.

Pendula and Marc entered the house, Pendula shoving the front door closed behind them with the edge of one of her wings.

Upstairs, a door squeaked open, and light footsteps scurried above their heads. Marc looked up, biting his bottom lip, and made to move for the stairs. Pendula clamped a hand on his shoulder, stopping him.

"No. I get mine, *then* you get yours." The hands on the clock-face dangling on her forehead were barely moving at all now. Marc sucked on his teeth in frustration, but nodded.

Helen hadn't moved, still lying dazed on the floor. Pendula crouched, rattling and squeaking. Her iron bustle nudged the floor, and her tutu-like skirt bunched up around her hips, baring her long striped legs. She reached for Helen, extending her arm to show the woman the wristwatches strapped there.

"See this?" Pendula gestured. Helen's eyes moved obediently to Pendula's arm. "Time is fleeting, Helen, especially stolen time. You stole Marc's time, and his daughter's. Not just their individual time, but their time together. That's a powerful transgression. Do you understand?"

Helen gave a weak smile, and nodded, her eyes rolling a little before refocusing on Pendula. She was obviously not herself—for one thing, she wasn't berating or striking out at anyone.

"Marc wants his time back, Helen. His time with his daughter. I'm going to give that to him. And do you know why?"

Helen struggled to speak, her lips puckering and twitching. "Trans . . . transgr-gr—"

"Oh, it's not because you've transgressed, Helen. I could give a shit about that. It's because I need some fucking oil. And you? You're a big ol' sack of it. You're, what, 40, 45? Yeah, I reckon you'll be good for a few decades, if I control myself, if I only take what I need when I need it."

Helen gave another idiot smile, and then, as Pendula reached for her, she gasped and her eyes closed. Her head flopped onto the floor and she lay still.

"She *would* pass out at the good bit," Marc muttered. Pendula looked over her shoulder at him, her eyes glittering through the latticework of the wing that partially obscured her face.

"This part wasn't your wish, was it, Marc? Unless you've changed your mind. Unless this part *is* for you rather than for me."

"No," Marc said. "No." And stepping around Pendula, he hurried to the staircase, tripping up the steps, heart pounding in his chest. He heard the sounds begin below, cracking and tearing and wet slurping, but then:

"Daddy?"

That one blessed sound obscured all else, defied all ugliness, and he fell onto the upstairs landing, grasping his little daughter's shoulders and pulling her to him, burying his face in her soft hair and wrapping his arms tightly around her. She clung to him with birdlike fingers, and they both cried, and time stood still for just one perfect moment, and that was enough.

◆ ◆ ◆

There were no loose ends to clean up. Pendula made it so. First she took her key back from Marc. Then, as she slipped it back into her spine, sighing contentedly, things just . . . *shifted*.

There had never been a woman called Helen. Fiona had died, and that was terrible, almost too terrible to bear, but Mary had never gone away, had always been with Marc, and they grieved and loved *together*. At least, that was what the outside world—and Mary, it was kind of Pendula to add that touch—thought. Marc remembered all too well, but he would carry that burden. It was worth it for what he'd regained.

"Where is she?" Mark said, watching Pendula rub the spot where her key was reinserted, her fingers kneading and massaging.

"Who?" She smiled her sparky smile at Marc. He didn't return it.

"The Queen of England. Who do you fucking think? Helen, where is Helen?"

"She's with me now." Pendula ran her fingers over her ribcage corset, caressed her jutting hips, and patted her iron bustle. "My dimensions are misleading. She's in here, like a battery slotted into me. Alive. Suffering, Marc, oh yes, such suffering. And when I need oil, I'll simply take it from her. Symbiosis, of a sort, except it benefits me, and hurts her. It will hurt her more and more as I drain her in years to come. Does this please you?"

"Yes." Marc didn't hesitate. "Does it please *you*?"

"Oh, yes." Pendula beamed, all gold-tipped threat. "It was a good wish. Very practical. More symbiosis—you get something, as do I. And we get past those pesky little rules that would normally prevent me doing something like this."

Marc found Pendula's definition of symbiosis disturbing, but he didn't speak. He wanted her gone. Mary was in the kitchen, awaiting her cereal. He wanted to sit and stare at his daughter eat, just watch her for hours, soak in her proximity, memorise her every mannerism, every inflection and lilt of her voice. He thought maybe he might even move that old bra off the kitchen counter so he could use it to prepare Mary's breakfast. Maybe it was . . . time.

"Well, it's been swell, Marc, but I gotta go. Time is—"

"Fleeting. Yeah, I know. Look, uh . . . thanks." Marc extended his hand. Pendula looked at it, and shook her head.

"Don't thank me just yet. Haven't you ever read *The Monkey's Paw*? Wishes . . . they're sticky things."

"Yeah." Marc was only half-listening. He could hear Mary laughing at some cartoon on the TV, and he smiled, his heart full.

"You *really* don't know fairies." Pendula spread her wings, preparing to lift into the air. Marc waved at her, not listening at all now, his head already turned toward the kitchen and his daughter. His wish.

"I keep telling you humans, time is fleeting, but you never listen, you never hear. What you really should be thinking about is the fact that your sister in law still lives within me. She's giving me oil, and as you should know now better than most, I owe her for that."

Marc didn't hear a word. He moved inside the house, closing the door.

Pendula lifted into the sky with a deafening clatter, the heart-clock on her forehead ticking faster than it ever had before. She yelled her words to the wind, grinning. "What you should be wondering, Marc, my dear, is . . . what will your sister in law wish for?"

◆　◆　◆

Many miles below, Marc entered the suddenly silent kitchen, and screamed.

# AFTERWORD

*Pendula came to me at a convention, during a panel about steampunk for which I was in the audience. Whilst most subgenres ending in "punk" irritate me by definition, I found steampunk interesting and engaging, with lots of room therein for either deep exploration and social commentary, or superficial playfulness and blithe disregard for heavier matters. I've erred more on the playful side here (sorry!). Pendula is a cool-looking fairy who behaves precisely as you'd expect the fae to—tricksy, my precious. I was thinking about "The Monkey's Paw" when I wrote this. Be careful what you wish for. I guess I also toyed with the potentially negative consequences of revenge, and how it can go astray, or play out in unanticipated ways.*

# PHANTASY MOSTE GROTESK

The Black-Eyed Kid was present at the beginning and the end. He saw everything—always had, probably always would—but it didn't do him or anyone else much good.

Josh Tarnell assumed the knock at his front door at 8:30pm was the pizza guy delivering his pepperoni deep pan: extra cheese, easy on the sauce. He threw a robe on over his boxer briefs and pulled the door open with one hand, rummaging with the other in the bowl he kept full of change on the hall table.

"Just a sec. I know I've got enough here, won't be—"

It was not the pizza guy.

A small boy stood on the stoop, head cocked to one side, hands shoved in the pockets of his ragged denim shorts. The wan glow of the flickering streetlights revealed a network of scratches criss-crossing their way up the boy's pale legs, and a large brown stain on his lettered t-shirt (*I CHOW DOWN AT BLIMEY'S DINER!*). The boy's eyes were completely black. They gleamed with a wet, fishy coldness as Josh took an involuntary step back, heart slamming against his ribcage.

"Can I come in?" The boy's lips peeled back from his teeth in a grin, revealing a delicate train-track of braces. Josh wanted to scream and slam the door in the kid's face, but even as adrenaline spurted like battery acid in his veins, his mind insisted there was a logical explanation.

*Contacts. He's wearing contacts, and one of his buddies dared him to knock on the door and spook whoever opened it. Well, mission accomplished. But don't let on. You know how boys are; you were one not so long ago.*

"Nice one, kiddo. You really had me going for a moment there. I'm expecting company, though, so . . . "

"The pimply redhead on the bike with a pizza in his basket? He won't be coming along any time soon. He ran into some trouble."

*What the . . .*

"Hmmmn. Let me guess. You and your buddies drank his blood, right? Sucked him dry. Ooga booga!" Josh wiggled his fingers at the kid, and had the unnerving feeling that if he kept it up for a moment longer, the kid would lean forward and bite them off. *Crunch.* He recoiled, clasping his hands protectively over his heart.

"No. Can I come in?"

"No? But isn't that your deal? You're being a vampire, right? The creepy eyes, the need to be invited in. I got it, I'm down with it."

"Oh, I'm not a vampire. Can I come in?"

Josh frowned. The little brat was starting to freak him out. He was almost robotic in his persistence, and those eyes were something else.

"Look, I appreciate the effort you've gone to and all—nice job with the eyes—but I just want a quiet night in with a book and some pizza. How about you go try your trick on someone else now, huh?"

"Why don't you just shut the fuck up and let me in, Josh?" The boy's shoulders were drawn up around his ears, and he'd started moving his hands around in his pockets. They were rippling, as if he had tentacles hidden inside them.

Josh tightened his grip on the door handle.

"You kiss your mother with that mouth?" He wanted to clobber the little shit. How dare he turn up on his doorstep uninvited and scare the bejesus out of him?

*And just how did he know my name?*

"I never had a mother. Seriously, you've got to let me in. If you don't—"

Josh shut the door. As soon as the latch clicked into place, a volley of violent blows rained down on the other side of the wood. Josh stumbled away from the door, hand flying to his mouth, robe falling open.

"Go away," he whispered, and then, as the onslaught reached a crescendo, "Fuck off! Leave me alone! I won't let you in!"

Silence fell like a guillotine blade.

*Call someone. Anyone. That kid could still be out there, and even if he's gone, he could come back. You don't want to be alone if that happens. No, not at all.*

Josh was punching Erin's number into his phone before he even realised what he was doing. He thought about hanging up before she answered, but as he dangled in indecision, her concise voice spoke into his ear.

"What do you want." It wasn't a question, but a statement of inevitability. She'd known he'd call, eventually. And, as always, she'd been right—though the night's events should surely be noted as extenuating circumstances.

"Something just happened. I . . . can you come over?" The handset was suddenly slippery, sliding in his sweaty palm. He kept one eye fixed on the door, and wondered if the kid's flat black orbs were looking back at him on the other side. Fear snaked up his spine, cold and fast.

"What happened?" Erin was worried despite her better judgment; Josh heard the concern in her voice. He felt like shit for bothering her, but he was glad his welfare still mattered to her.

"Nothing. I mean . . . something . . . but it's hard to explain. Can you come over? Please."

"If this is some sort of game, I'll kick your ass, Josh. I'll be there in half an hour."

"Be careful," he blurted, but she'd already hung up.

◆  ◆  ◆

"A kid," Erin said flatly, staring down into the steaming cup of tea she held in her hands. He'd always enjoyed her hands. Small, white, and delicate, like fine bone china.

"Not just any kid," Josh said, hearing the whine creep into his voice and hating himself for it.

"A kid with black eyes, then. But they must have been—"

"Contacts. Yeah, I know. The thing is, I'm not so sure they were. He was weird. He made me feel . . . horrified." *God. I'm wasting her time. She'll storm out in disgust any minute. And who would blame her? I'm talking crap.* "He wanted to come in. He almost smashed through the door," he added, desperate to justify his panic. It was already receding, fading into nothingness, and it left only embarrassment in its wake.

"Yeah. There's blood on it, actually," she said, still looking at her tea.

He blinked.

"On the door? Are you serious?"

"'Fraid so. I saw it on the way in. Thought it must be yours. I assumed . . . " Erin let the words hang in the air. Across from her, Josh shifted on the couch, hugging an overstuffed cushion to his chest like a shield.

"I don't do that anymore."

"That's good, Josh. That's really good. I'm glad."

She looked at him then, and he felt like crying. So much history trembled in her gray eyes. So much love, but hate, too. Had it always been that way? Worst of all, he could see she didn't believe him. Not a single word.

"I'm better now," he murmured.

She smiled in response, but her eyes retained their glassiness. He knew the wall she'd built against him could never again be breached. Their time had been and gone. He'd fucked it up for good.

"You're seeing someone else."

"Oh, Christ, Josh. Just when I think we might be able to have a civil conversation."

"You are, aren't you? I can tell. I can smell him on you."

"Maybe all you smell is your own *bullshit*," she said, slamming her cup down on the coffee table, milky brown tea slopping over her rigid fingers. She stood up, rifling in her bag for her keys, and shoved one arm into the sleeve of her jacket.

Josh lurched to his feet, trying to ignore the buzzing that had begun in his ears. The Big Feelings were welling up, and it would feel so much better if he could just let a little trickle of them out, ease the pressure . . . but no. He'd been serious when he said he was better. He hadn't felt that hideous, wonderful release in months. He dealt with the Big Feelings in other ways now. Saner ways. Journals. Therapy. Pizza. Ways that didn't involve Seth and bubbling red blood welling up from clean, straight cuts . . .

*Stop thinking about it. La la la don't think about it la la la block it out la la la.*

(let me in . . . oh not by the hair on my chinny chin chin!)

Shuddering and rubbing his forehead with shaking hands, he gave Erin a sickly smile.

"Ez, I'm sorry. Please don't go. I don't . . . I've had a shock tonight. I was stupid a minute ago, and I apologize. Can we pretend I never said anything?"

She stopped her angry preparation for departure and stood staring at him, mouth ajar, coat hanging half on, half off.

"You've never apologized to me before," she said, just as he thought the silence might stretch forever. "Not once."

"I must have. Maybe not much, but I must have at least a few times in the three years you were stuck with me." He tried for a rueful chuckle, but it ended up sounding like a death rattle, and he shut up fast.

"No. Never. Not once."

"Well. I'm sorry now. Will you stay?"

"Yes," she said, letting her coat slide to the floor. A moment later, her bag followed it, landing with a soft *whump*.

"Let's go to the Long Chat Place," she said suddenly, and the Big Feelings were gone without a trace.

The memory of the kid's dark eyes sank back into his subconscious, and he felt a new sensation rush up from his feet, a sensation that swirled in his belly before shooting through his heart and reaching his brain in a starburst of brilliant intensity. What was that? Was it . . . joy?

"Ok. I'll get my keys," he smiled.

"It doesn't mean . . . "

"Don't say it, Ez. I know. You don't need to say it."

She lowered her eyes, and he hurried to get his shit together before she changed her mind.

◆　◆　◆

The Long Chat Place was one of their spots; one of the random sites they'd courted, embraced, kissed, talked, and exchanged little pieces of each other's souls. It was a sporting ground, a grassy oval dotted with goalposts and white markings, sprawled at the end of Josh's street behind a barrier of willow trees. At this time on a Sunday night, it was deserted and still. The moon was a pale, bloated corpse, drifting above them in the fetid waters of the starless sky. A heavy breeze soughed through the twisted branches of the guardian trees and gusted about the open field, bringing with it the stench of something spoiled and oozing.

Josh ignored it.

Nothing could be ugly tonight. Not with Erin by his side, here in this sacred and mundane place. The Big Feelings nibbled on the insides of his mind, whispering to be let out, but he repressed them, too.

"Let's sit here. We used to sit on this exact spot, do you remember? Once, we even—"

"Josh, what's that?" Erin interrupted him, pointed into the gloom, squinting.

He found himself noting the straight length of her arm, the tilt of her hips, the way her brown curls intertwined and spun in the wind like double helixes. He wondered idly if he could overpower her, tackle her from behind and push her down on the moist grass, pin her under his weight and have her one last time. If she screamed, he could tangle his fingers in those curls and grind her face into the soil, muffling her voice as he slid in and out of her, the ghoulish moon watching.

He felt heat begin to throb in his groin, and shifted, trying to ease the pressure as he strained against his jeans.

*She might even like it. She always was into the weird stuff. She pretends to be so straight, but she's got a kink in her a mile wide. What's she playing at anyway, leading you out here in the middle of the night, to this place of all places? Fucking tease.*

The Big Feelings weren't nibbling anymore; they were biting and clawing, tearing their way free. He had to do something. It was her or him. Him or her. God, just a bit of relief, that's all he needed. One way or another . . .

"Josh." She was at his elbow, squeezing his arm, her lips close to his ear.

He jumped. What had he been thinking? What had he almost done?

*(let me in)*

"I . . . what did you say?"

She pulled back, studying him, her fingers tight on his forearm. She was anchoring him. He'd slipped away for a moment, gone surfing on the Big Feelings, and they both knew it.

"I said: 'what's that?'"

'That' was a large circus tent, rising up out of the ground like a tumour. It was swathed in darkness, and its canvas flaps waved in the breeze like beckoning hands, inviting Erin and Josh into its gaping maw.

Squinting as Erin had a moment ago, Josh made out the figure of a man standing near the tent's opening. He was motionless.

Waiting.

"It's a tent," Josh said.

Erin sighed.

"Y'think? Wow, lucky I have you with me to explain such mysteries. I can see it's a tent, Josh, but what is a Big Top doing in the middle of the footy oval at the bottom of your street?"

"I have no idea," he said, moving forward.

Her fingers slipped away from his skin, and he felt a moment of acute loss. Nevertheless, he strode through the grass, and she had to trot to keep up with him. A jolt of perverse pleasure made his nerves sing as he heard her breathing roughen and saw her white sneakers flash in the dark, almost a blur.

*Yeah, that's it. Jog. You left me, remember? So now you can hustle, bitch. Mush! Mush!*

"Josh, wait! Do you think we should go near it? There's someone there. Maybe we should—"

"I bet that's where the kid came from. It's a circus. That's got to be his dad, or his boss, or something. I'm going to have a word with him about what the little jerk's been up to."

"But—"

"You don't have to come," he snapped. He cast an angry glare at her, and saw the shocked O of her mouth, the hurt tilt of her head.

"Josh?" The word bore the weight of a thousand questions and accusations. That caused the fight to go out of him, and he wondered just what the hell he thought he was doing.

*Go home. See her to her car and let her drive away. Go inside, eat your cold pizza, scribble in your journal until the Big Feelings die. Go to bed. Everything will be ok.*

"Good eve," the man outside the tent said as they approached. "Won't you step inside?"

"Yes," Josh said, his tongue heavy in his mouth.

God, the buzzing in his ears was deafening. He needed to sit down and have some water. Erin's hand was on his arm again, and her small nails dug into his flesh as she coughed, trying to get his attention. He liked the feeling of her hot skin against his. Even the sting of her nails was sweet.

"Hello," Erin said, nodding at the man.

Now that they were closer, Josh saw the guy was a short, round barrel, clad in a giant baby's onesie. Bright light spilled out from the tent, and as Josh's eyes adjusted, he noticed that the fabric of the man's suit was not only pink, but had little yellow rocking horses dotted all over it. An enormous dummy, easily the size of Josh's foot, hung around the man's neck on a thin chain. His head was bald, emblazoned with strange tattoos.

*Freak. He's some sort of circus freak, for sure. Man, I love this shit.*

"We're just out for a walk," Erin informed the man, who smiled in response. "So thank you for the invitation, but we'd better be on our way. Are you open tomorrow? Will there be a show? Maybe we can come back then."

"There's always a show," the man said, his eyes swinging back and forth between Erin and Josh. "But the best ones are on at night. Right now is a great time. The perfect time, in fact. Would you like to see?"

"Yes," Josh said again.

Erin hissed next to him, her nails gouging so deep that they must surely have drawn blood.

The man stepped aside and waved his hand in a sweeping gesture of welcome. Josh was already moving forward, Erin's nails snagging on his skin before they slid away.

"My name is Seth," the man said.

Erin let out a choked gasp, and Josh smiled.

"Of course it is." In that moment, everything inside Josh's mind was red and silver. The flash of light on surgical steel, the wet glee of gushing blood, the sharp, blessed release.

Seth.

How he'd missed Seth. This man was not *that* Seth, of course. Or perhaps, in a way, he was.

"Are you coming in, Ms. Duhammond? Mr. Tarnell seems to be quite interested."

Josh didn't turn around to see Erin's reply. He could already picture the pained look on her face, and he wasn't sure he wanted to see Seth's. He stood under the tent flaps, listening to them snap in the breeze, waiting. He kept his eyes on the yellow canvas floor beneath his feet. It wasn't time to look around yet. Whatever the signal was, it hadn't been given.

The moment stretched. Josh's breathing slowed. The sound of his heartbeat in his ears joined the rhythmic motion of the tent flaps.

Erin sighed.

"All right," she said, her voice thick and wet. "All right. I'll come in. I'll do it for Josh's sake. But you already knew that. Didn't you, *Seth*? Somehow, you know rather a lot."

"Ladies first, Ms. Duhammond."

"Oh, call me Erin, you bastard. We're getting personal, after all, aren't we?"

"Yes, Erin. You're right. Quite personal."

Erin's hand slipped into the crook of Josh's elbow once more, and his heartbeat sped up to a jackhammer cacophony.

"Let's begin our tour," Seth said softly, raising the tent flaps and gesturing them inside.

◆ ◆ ◆

"The first question that must be answered is both delicate and mundane." Seth had hopped into a giant brass cradle positioned just inside the entrance, where he perched like an imp, his fingers fluttering to the giant dummy as if for reassurance. "That is, the question of payment."

"Payment?" Josh only had a balled up tissue and a paperclip in the pocket of his track pants, and he doubted that would suffice. "I don't have anything on me . . . "

"I beg to differ, Mr. Tarnell—Josh, if I may. You have a great deal of value on you at all times. You too, Erin. The real question is: what are you willing to give?"

"Nothing," Erin snapped. "We're not willing to give anything. Look, you've got a quirky thing going on here. You've got the look, you've pulled some tricks, and I can appreciate that. But we've had a rough night, and I can't help but feel you're taking advantage—"

"She still has your scalpel, you know, Josh. She didn't get rid of it. She lied to you. It nestles in a bed of black velvet at the bottom of her wardrobe. She took it out and showed it to her boyfriend once—showed him the rusty stains on the blade. She told him all about how they got there. All about *you*, Josh." Seth circled the teat of the grotesque dummy with one calloused finger, caressing it like a lover's nipple. "She cried on his shoulder, and he *comforted* her all night. Over and over. Isn't that the darnedest thing?"

Josh turned his head far enough to see Erin's face. Her chin was shaking and her eyes were wide. She looked at him, hopeless, imploring. Her skin looked unnaturally pale against the vivid yellow interior of the Big Top, and the Big Feelings buzzed and chirruped in his head.

He craved steel in his hand.

"Josh, I'm leaving. I can't believe you're going along with this. I came over tonight because I was worried. Remember? I was worried about you. But this is . . . crazy. You can come with me. Now. We can still—"

"You can have her," Josh said suddenly, surprised to hear his own voice. He felt soporific, floaty. "Would that do? You can take her. But only for a little while. Only long enough for me to have a look around. Then you have to give her back. She's mine, you see."

"I quite understand. Thank you, Josh. That's an appropriate fee."

"What the fuck—are you completely insane?" Erin screamed.

Josh winced in irritation. The loud, jagged sound was all wrong in this place. He wanted it to stop.

"*Have* me? I'm *yours*? Do you even know what the hell you're talking about?"

"Not really."

"I'm *leaving*. Get that through your thick skull. I'm gone. Take care, Josh. Take a lot of care. In fact, get professional care. You need it."

Erin turned to go. Josh watched with dispassionate eyes as she paused, her back to him. Her hands—pretty, tender things—fluttered forward like timid birds and began to feel their way across the seamless canvas in front of her. They found no opening. The tent flaps had disappeared, leaving no trace of an exit. Her shoulders rose in a sharp inhalation, fell again as the breath blasted out of her. She seemed to deflate, folding in defeat. Finally, she turned, facing Josh and Seth, her eyes narrowed, her lips thin. Her quivering chin betrayed her unease.

"Ok. I don't know how you did that. I don't know how you've done any of this. I'll admit that. But it doesn't make you clever. It makes you sick. I'll say this once, and if you don't do as I say I'll scream and bring the neighbourhood down here: let me out."

"Scream away, dear girl. We rather like that in here, and nobody out there will hear a thing." Seth smiled, a broad, moist expression that threatened to split his face in two. "Payment has been given and taken. You're here until Josh leaves. You can wait where you stand, or you can come with us as we journey through the show. That much is up to you."

For the first time, Josh looked around. They stood in a short, high-ceilinged corridor. Nothing but blank yellow canvas surrounded them. Aside from Seth's bizarre cradle, no furnishings broke up the dazzlingly bright space. At the far end of the hall, a red velvet curtain hung, embellished with gold writing that Josh couldn't quite make out. The air was cool and sweet. The sound of children laughing and something like the jangling of an ice cream van's music—*Greensleeves*, perhaps—danced across the room to Josh's ears.

"Josh? Can you even hear me?" Erin appeared at his elbow again, niggling like a horsefly. "Just come back, ok? Come back to me. We'll leave together."

"I'm going in, Ez. This is something special. You don't have to come. But you can't leave, either. I don't want you to, so you can't." He knew she was furious, knew that if they'd been outside this otherworldly tent, she would have given him one of her disappointed, sad looks and walked out on him. She'd always called the shots. If Josh was good, she stayed. If Josh was bad. she left. Reward and punishment. Erin giveth and Erin taketh away.

Well, not in here. And if that pissed her off? Good.

"We'll just take a *little* bit of you," Seth said, smiling impishly. "Nothing you'll miss. The curl of your hair. The shine of your eyes. The softness of your skin. Not such a bad deal, is it? Fair trade, I think."

*Is he serious about those things? Will he really take them from her? How? Why? No. He's kidding.*

"What does the curtain say?" Josh asked, pacing down the hall. Ever since Erin had pointed the tent out to him, his legs had moved with a mind of their own. In fact, his forward movement had almost always been out of his control. That was precisely the problem.

Nearing the thick fabric, he read the large swirls of golden stitching that looped through the velvet:

Salioso's House of Monsters, Moste Grotesk and Phantastique

"This is the sort of thing I always wished would come to town as a kid. I read about travelling freak shows, amazing monsters, all that stuff. But they're not real. They're horror movie fodder." Josh reached out and touched the curtain. It felt like molten chocolate, the burgundy folds pouring between his fingers in a rush. It was liquid, suspended in semi-solid form. It sent a honeyed golden whisper through his fingertips and into his bloodstream.

"I'll be surprised and deeply offended if you retain that sentiment once you've seen my performers, Josh," Seth said. "But enough shilly-shallying. Shall we begin?"

Seth brushed past Josh and slid the curtain aside. Its brass circlets whickered along the wooden rail it dangled from, and it seemed to sigh as it opened. Now Josh could smell fairy floss, buttered popcorn, and sawdust. The children's laughter and ice cream van music was gone, replaced by a steady drumbeat and an unfamiliar shuffling noise.

The Big Feelings were blessedly silent.

Erin punched him on the bicep. Hard. For a moment the room shimmered, fractured, and he felt enormous regret as the foul odour that had coated the Long Chat Place filled his nostrils. Then everything was solid again.

Erin pushed past him, scowling.

"If I'm here, then I'm coming with you—but I'll be damned if I'll follow you around like some captive damsel," she bit.

Again, he had the overpowering urge to grab her curls, hurt her, defile her.

"You can follow *me*."

"Our first stop will be the Hide behind," Seth said, before Josh could act on his urges.

"What's a Hidebehind?" Josh asked.

There was no answer, and Josh walked a little faster, keeping Seth's curious onesie-clad form in his sights, along with Erin's bouncing curls.

◆  ◆  ◆

"In answer to your previous question, Josh, *this* is a Hidebehind."

Seth motioned to the empty air in front of him with a theatrical flourish. Josh's shoulders slumped.

*It's all crap, after all.*

They stood in a small lounge. A red velvet couch took up most of the room, bursting with stuffing and mangled silver springs. A grandfather clock leant against the far wall. Candles sputtered in gouged-out holes around the clay chamber. A rumpled gray blanket was bunched at one end of the couch, as if someone had leapt hastily out from under it.

"There's nothing in here," Erin said.

Josh nodded, sighing.

"Yeah. This was fun for about five minutes, but now I see—"

"Ah, but you don't *see* anything, Josh. That's rather the point. Instead, what can you hear?" Seth nibbled on his foul dummy like an aperitif, grinning at Josh around the bulbous thing.

And . . . there was a sound. Followed by another. And still another.

Raspy breathing; the subtle swish of a body shifting its weight; a low snarl that rolled around the room, lingering.

"There *is* something in here," Josh murmured. Erin backed up against him in silent confirmation, her spine pressing against his belly. He felt her trembling. He didn't know whether to comfort her or crush her. He settled for wrapping his arm around her shoulders, holding her to him.

"The Hidebehind. American folklore. Never seen directly, but notorious for appearing in the corner of the eye. That couch is our Hidebehind's universe. He sleeps on it, sits on it, and most of all, hides behind it when his lair is invaded. He's really very territorial and can be quite aggressive." Seth's tone was part rote tour guide, part proud parent.

"So . . . this is a room with a monster in it, but we can't see it." Erin had regained enough composure to sound scathing.

Seth seemed delighted by her remark. "Not at all. You can see him, but only in your peripheral vision. Few people use their peripheral vision actively, but it's really very easy. If you allow your eyes to become unfocused and relaxed, fixed on nothing in particular, and, paradoxically, pay close attention to everything *not* in your line of sight . . . "

Josh tried it. The little room blurred and he felt his consciousness retreat inwards, as if pulled by invisible claws.

Then something immense and misshapen lurched out from behind the couch. It was shimmering and indistinct, swaying and changing with unseen eddies of light and air. Where its head should've been, two muscular arms sprouted. Where its arms should've been, a legion of small heads bobbled, malevolent eyes glittering. It moved forward on writhing tentacles, its gyrating torso a mass of decaying teeth. It was at least seven feet tall.

Josh jumped and blinked, his eyes swimming back into focus. The creature was gone, but a roar sounded from behind the tattered couch. Erin gasped and turned, burying her face in his chest.

"It's not real," she said. "It can't be real. It's an optical illusion. A trick of the light."

"Yes." He said. "It must be."

Try as he might, he couldn't make his eyes unfocused again. Seth sat on the couch, smiling. Finally Josh hissed in annoyance, and Seth stood as if a signal had been given.

"The shock of seeing the Hidebehind often makes your body refuse to let you see it again. Deliberately, at least. But don't worry. You'll no doubt get a final look as we leave this room."

Seth scurried to the curtain at the far end of the room, and waited for Josh and Erin to follow. Erin raised her head from Josh's chest and looked up at him with wide grey eyes.

"Are you going further in?" She didn't load the question, didn't throw in any sarcasm.

Josh traced a finger down the nape of her neck, wondering at the effect she had on him. Good Josh and Bad Josh loved her with equal passion.

"Yes," he replied, wishing he could have given her the answer she wanted.

She stiffened.

"Let's do it, then."

As they followed Seth through the curtain, the Hidebehind leapt into Josh's peripheral vision. It was fast, and it charged towards them, its countless faces contorted. It hated them, meant to destroy them. Josh looked directly at the thing, and, with a scream of frustration, it disappeared.

"Easy," he breathed. "Done."

The curtain closed behind them, and they stood in a dim hall, with yet another curtain awaiting them at the far end. Seth hitched up his onesie, which had begun to wilt down toward his fluffy feet, and regarded them sternly.

"Now, there is the matter of payment. We operate on an instalment basis. The first instalment—Erin staying with us—was paid as your entrance fee. Now that you've seen the first exhibit, another instalment is due. Shall we say . . . "

Before Josh or Erin could react, Seth stretched out one of his flabby hands and stroked Erin's hair. Erin gasped. Seth stepped back, dipping his head in a satisfied nod.

"That is most acceptable," he said, spinning neatly on his heels and heading for the next curtain.

"What did he do to me? I feel . . . funny." Sweat stippled Erin's brow. She swayed like a tree about to topple. Her skin had developed a green tinge. Josh reached out to steady her, but recoiled with a startled exhalation.

Erin's bulging eyes implored him. "What? What's wrong with me?"

"N-nothing. I just . . . let's keep going." He wasn't lying, not really. The change she'd gone through wasn't big in the scheme of things, wasn't overtly horrific. Aside from looking ill, the only thing wrong with Erin was that her hair wasn't curly anymore. It fell in straight sheets, heavy and dull, a shroud draped over Erin's head. She struggled to hold her head up as they staggered forward, as if the weight of her tresses—somehow so horribly *reduced*—pulled her down.

"I'll look after you," Josh told her, knowing it was an empty promise.

"I know you'll try. I feel like me being here with you might be the only thing that can help you now. I'm sorry I wasn't always there in the past. I'm sorry I couldn't stay when you were—"

"That's all over now. I told you, I'm better." He didn't want to hear her talk about the time the Big Feelings ran his life, the era of steel and blood and tears. Something was wrong with him, yes.

Something was very wrong with this place, sure. But it wasn't *that* wrongness. It wasn't the

*(LET me IN)*

ills of old, and that had to count for something.

He hurried after Seth, ignoring his sickened heart.

◆ ◆ ◆

"And now to the Ferris Wheel." Seth threw the curtain aside. The sound of screeching metal drifted toward them on the rancid breeze that flowed through the Big Top. Erin grimaced and held her nose.

Josh frowned. "A Ferris Wheel is not a monster."

Seth giggled. "It is in Salioso's House of Monsters. Everything here is *moste* grotesk and phantastique, my dear friends." He ushered them in.

The room beyond the curtain was enormous. The roof was so high it couldn't be seen. The walls were hundreds of meters apart. Josh cupped his hands to his mouth and shouted wordlessly. His voice bounced again and again off the un-boundaries of the room. The vast expanse of yellow—always that cheerful yellow!—finally swallowed his yell after what felt like an eternity.

"This place has got to be ten times the size of the whole tent," Erin said.

"Yes," Seth responded. "Easily. Now, shall we ride our good friend Ferris?"

Josh looked sidelong at Seth. "You say it like the Wheel is a pers—"

*Oh God.*

Josh stopped marvelling at the gigantic room and looked at the Wheel in the centre of it.

Its red metal struts jutted up into the heavens, dotted at their ends with carriages like grossly oversized cherries. Fairy lights twinkled all over the structure, and somewhere, calliope music played as the Wheel groaned through endless rotations.

Josh moaned.

A man was crucified on the Wheel.

His torso, positioned at the centre of the contraption, was pushed forward by the convex hub behind it so that he seemed to be jutting his pelvis suggestively at them. His head was slumped forward onto his chest, dark clumps of hair obscuring his face. His arms and legs were impossibly stretched, tethered to the Wheel, tapering from the centre to the outer limits. The red of the struts was not paint but the man's blood, flowing in ceaseless rivulets. The metal carried the blood like mechanized veins, feeding it to the membranous carriages. The Wheel bore the blood-filled sacs around and around, and the tortured man spun with them, stretched and helpless.

"Meet Ferris," Seth said, his feet marking a jig of excitement on the canvas floor. "He's a relatively new addition to our show, but I think you'll agree he's a good 'un."

"That's the sickest thing I have ever seen. I know it's not real . . . but it's sick. You should be ashamed. Do children come through here?" Erin prodded Seth in his fuzzy chest.

Seth's mouth opened wide in a cackle, and he stroked her finger when it jabbed his sternum. Erin shuddered, swaying on her feet again. Josh moved to catch her. She felt like a bony bird in his hands, brittle and barely there at all. He turned her around gently. Her eyes rolled toward him, and he suppressed a scream.

They were pure black, gleaming flatly in her head, and the image of the boy on his doorstep earlier that night (was it the *same* night? It seemed so distant now) flashed through his mind.

"What have you done to her?" Josh reeled her in like a tiny fish, securing her in his arms, glaring over her head at Seth. The little man smiled serenely back at him.

And then Ferris began to shriek.

Josh looked back at the lengthened man on the Wheel, and saw Ferris' head rise. The man's eyes whirled in their sockets, his mouth twisting in an impossibly wide grimace. Blood spilled from his eyes, nose, mouth and ears. He struggled against his impossible bonds, causing the Wheel to shudder on its rotation, but not halt.

"Make him stop, make him stop, please, make him stop . . . " Erin whimpered into Josh's ribs. Josh's mind tilted a little more. The Big Feelings rushed forward, seizing him in his moment of weakness.

He clenched and unclenched his fists against Erin's back. The craving for a blade to be in each of them was a physical pain. He wondered how much force it would take to crush her into lifelessness; not much, given her current fragility.

If he only had a blade . . . if he had a blade, he could turn the Big Feelings on himself, release enough of his own blood to appease them and ensure he spilt none of hers . . . if she hadn't taken his Seth, his scalpel, his release . . . if . . .

"You won't hurt her, Josh. Our business is not yet done here. There are more instalments to be made on the agreed payment. You'll control yourself." Seth's voice was polite, but beneath it a layer of iron lurked.

The Big Feelings receded a little, and Josh looked at the smaller man, fuming.

"You're mad. This is disgusting. We want to leave."

"Oh, I'm afraid that's quite impossible. There's only one way out of here, and that's straight ahead. We can't exit until we've been through all the exhibits. Now, we can leave this room and move on to the next if you wish, but it seems a shame to leave Ferris without enjoying the full extent of his talents . . . "

Seth darted forward and placed his hand on one of the sac carriages, his fingers splayed on the membrane. The carriage wobbled and belched under his touch, then bowed inward, giving way. Seth's arm disappeared into the thing up to the elbow.

"It's very warm inside the carriages. They have their own special heating, you might say. Quite womblike, and the filling tastes simply delicious. Ferris works so hard to keep the carriages supplied; won't you at least have one ride to show your appreciation?"

The man on the Wheel gave a final ululating cry before his head fell forward again. Then all was silent except for the perpetual dripping of his blood and the gambolling of the calliope tune in the background.

"I'm not going near that thing," Josh whispered.

Seth sighed and withdrew his hand—clean and smooth—from the blood sac with a juicy *squelch*. "As you desire. What a waste. Well, onward!" With a loud suck of his dummy, Seth was off, scampering toward the far curtain.

Erin went limp in Josh's arms. He swept her up and, carrying her like a baby, followed Seth. He kept his eyes fixed on the floor and didn't look at the profane Wheel again. Erin's eyelids fluttered. Josh glimpsed the blackness of her eyes and shivered. Yet . . . he was still excited. He wanted to see what lay on the other side of the curtain. He wanted to keep going. He was glad Erin was unconscious so that his niggling conscience could be quieted for a moment.

The Big Feelings snarled like prowling panthers and he smiled, stroking them in his mind.

*I'll let you off your chain soon. I know I'll have to. But . . . not yet.*

The curtain rose and fell, and they materialized in a dark corridor, in between

*(worlds)*

exhibits.

◆　◆　◆

"I suppose you want another payment now," Josh said, his voice a dull glimmer in the gloom.

Seth raised an eyebrow at him, surprised.

"Why, no. I'm not greedy. As you saw, I took the liberty of securing the next instalment while we were visiting young Ferris back there."

Contemplating Erin's half-closed gimlet eyes, Josh nodded.

"Yeah. So you did. Then why have we stopped here?"

Seth leaned forward conspiratorially.

"As I said, I'm not greedy. I don't take payment where it's not due, and what's more, I like to give back where I can. So I'm going to give you a gift. A piece of her to keep for your very own. You'd like that, wouldn't you, Josh?"

The Big Feelings drew back, and Josh clutched Erin to him, hissing.

Seth chuckled.

"Oh, not like that. I would never harm her, Josh. You're doing that all by yourself. This was your idea, remember?"

"Why, you—you—"

"Now, now. Back to my boon to you. Did you know she's thought about you every day since she left you that final time? She's driven to your house on numerous occasions, parked at the end of your street, and watched your comings and goings. Just to make sure you were alright. Isn't that the sweetest thing?"

Josh felt Erin's pulse thrumming weakly beneath his fingertips and pictured her lurking, watching him. Caring for him. Her unmoving form was an accusation in his arms.

"She watched to see if you had started cutting yourself again. She had Seth—*your* Seth, the blade, the relief, not *me*, of course—but there are other cutting edges in the world, and she wondered if you were using them. When she was certain you were not, she stopped following you. But she still dreamt of you every night, cried into her pillow over you every morning, dug her nails into her boyfriend's back and pretended it was you every time they—"

"Stop." Wetness trickled down Josh's cheek. Tears. That was new. He'd sooner let blood than cry. It was a rare occurrence, but better to do it while Erin couldn't see, couldn't hear, couldn't look at him with worry in her eyes—although, now that they were unadulterated black, he wondered if her eyes could contain any emotion at all. The thought brought forth a choked sob, and Seth patted him on the shoulder.

"There now. Let it out. We like the release of bodily fluids here. Anyway, she still loves you. She would have taken you back in a heartbeat. Oh, she would have pretended to put up a fight, and you would have played along like the little pup you are, but she always intended to be with you in the end, Josh. You might have been completely healthy. You surely would have had a long and fruitful life together. But . . . ."

Josh's tears became a flood, pattering down on Erin's unresponsive skin.

"That'll never happen now, as I'm sure you've deduced. So there is my gift to you: the knowledge of what you had and lost. Some people never realise such mysteries for themselves. It's a great boon. Cradle it to you as you cradle her, and let's move on. You know, I think we'll only see one more exhibit. Maybe two. It's different for everyone, but you and your lover took the least time yet. Interesting."

With that, Seth skipped forward, vanishing through the next curtain.

Still shaking with sobs, clinging to Erin's stirring body like a life-raft, Josh followed.

◆　◆　◆

"Don't wake up, Ez," Josh crooned into her flat hair. "Just keep sleeping, love."

But she did wake, twitching in his arms until he gently placed her on her feet. She looked at him with fathomless black eyes and his mind gave a final tilt, swinging him in earnest toward madness.

"Are we free?" she said. "Did we get out? Has it all gone away?"

"I'm afraid not, my dear. But you're lucky enough to have

awoken in time to see the next exhibit." Seth sounded bored. He plopped his dummy into his mouth and gnawed at it as if it were a juicy bone, sucking and slurping with abandon.

Erin's face drooped.

Seth spoke around his dummy, the words mangled and wet. "Without further ado, may I introduce . . . Salioso's room of Doppelgangers! Of course, since you're a smaller group than we're used to, there are only two here today, but I'm sure they'll prove extremely entertaining nonetheless."

Barely bothering to complete the flourish of his hand, Seth crossed the mirrored room and sat on one of the wooden chairs on the opposite side, the only furnishings in the chamber. One of the mirrors shimmered and wavered, and two figures stepped out.

Josh gasped. Erin stared, flat-eyed.

Their precise doubles stood facing them. Erin's had her newly straight brown hair and black eyes, but, unlike Erin, throbbed with life and energy—and was completely naked. She taunted Erin, gyrating inches from her, cupping her nude breasts and leering, her pink tongue lashing over her ruby lips.

"Cold, dead fish," the thing sneered. "I'm more than you ever were. He never wanted you. He always wanted me. He saw *me* when he looked at you. I'm here now. You're as good as dead. Ugly, stupid bitch!"

The creature leant forward on the final word and spat in Erin's face. The saliva slithered down Erin's cheek as she stood motionless. Furious, Josh slapped the woman-thing open handed across the face. Far from deterred, the creature dropped into a crouch and clasped Josh's calf, rubbing herself against him, panting.

"Oh, you know I like it rough," it moaned. The thing's hands were hot and its body was slick; Josh felt his own body respond despite himself. "You were thinking about giving it to me rough, remember, in the Long Chat Place? You wanted me then. You want me now. Stay here, lover, and have me! Have me as long and as hard and as often as you want. Anything you like. I want you. She's nothing compared to me. It's me you've wanted. Take me!"

The thing reached for his belt and unbuckled it in one smooth pull. He wavered, Big Feelings flooding his brain while blood rushed to his groin. She felt amazing. Her hand made his closed zipper a distant memory and he felt the cool air on his bare legs as she tore his jeans off. He rocked back on his heels as her fingers grasped him, as her sex massaged his leg, as her lips wrapped around him . . .

Then he heard the distinctive sound of a punch next to him, followed by a muffled moan and tearing fabric.

"No! Stop! Please, Josh, don't hurt me!"

Did Erin really see that man-thing—and whatever it was trying to do to her—as being *him*?

Did *he* really see the thing kneeling before him now as *her*?

With a snarl, he shoved the female Doppelganger's head away from him and turned to Erin. The male Doppelganger—the Josh-thing—had her on the floor, one hand gripping her throat, the other yanking the remains of her skirt from her. The creature was naked like its female counterpart.

"Get away from her," Josh roared, aiming a massive kick at the creature's head. His boot connected with a jarring thud and the thing rolled over several times, coming to rest against the wall.

Sinuous, tempting arms clutched his shoulders from behind, and a velvet voice murmured in his ear. "That was gallant. I've always loved your chivalrous side. You'll slip into me like a hot knife into butter. I'll never leave you, never deny you, not like *her*. I'm soft and delicious, but I'm hard and strong, too. You can do what you like to me and I'll bounce right back—and I'll *love* it."

The thing's tongue snaked from its plump lips and lapped at Josh's earlobe. He shuddered, a jolt of white heat rocketing through his body and numbing his mind. He wanted to turn and grab the creature, throw it to the ground, and climb aboard. He wanted to say the dirtiest, vilest, evilest things to it and watch its face as he did. He wanted to hurt it and love it and own it. He wanted . . . he wanted . . . want . . .

"Josh," Erin whispered from the floor.

He wanted to *kill*.

He spun around and tore the creature's spindly arms from his shoulders. He saw surprise on the Doppelganger's face as it turned to run. Before it could get away, he reached out and caught a fistful of brown, lank hair. The creature screeched and flailed, twisting away from him.

Josh stepped forward, hooking one foot under the Doppelganger's pedalling feet and pulling them out from under the thing. The pseudo-Erin fell face-first to the floor, howling. Not hesitating, Josh dropped one knee into the creature's back and landed with the full force of his body right between its jutting shoulder blades.

As the woman-thing gave a final scream, Josh released the creature's hair and reached forward, grasping its chin in one hand and forehead in the other, and

yanked

back.

The creature's neck broke. After the loud *snap*, all was still and silent at last.

"Interesting," Seth commented from his perch. "A waste, to be sure. She was a delight. But . . . very interesting indeed."

Josh fell back from the dead creature in disgust and crawled toward Erin. She sat in the tatters of her skirt, her arms wrapped around herself, black eyes bottomless and her face slack. When he neared her, her mouth twitched, but she said nothing.

"I'm so sorry, Ez," he croaked. "I love you, and I wish I'd never brought you in here. I wish I'd been strong enough to stand up to the Big Feelings and to Seth, but you know he was always my weakness and my release, and I couldn't deny him." He was babbling gibberish now, and yet, it made sense and it was important that she hear him, where ever she'd gone.

"Heads up," Seth remarked casually.

Josh only had a moment to look up before the male Doppelganger's fist knocked him onto his back. His jaw rang with pain, and the world blurred into a hazy web of yellow.

"She's mine," snarled the Doppelganger. "Always was. Always will be. I own the bitch. What's left of her, anyway. What's left will do just fine for my purposes."

The thing's laughter was oily and low, oozing like pus.

Rage propelled Josh up and at the creature. It was waiting for him, dropped low in a fighting crouch, its appendage dangling like an added insult between its muscular thighs. It was him, of course, but . . . better, harder, stronger, and with far more hatred than he'd ever felt for anything pumping through its supernatural veins.

He hit it head-on, and it fell, crushed under his body. Without pausing to think, he made his thumb and forefinger into prongs and rammed them into the thing's eyes. He felt the membrane burst, and pushed on, through the jelly and oozing liquid, into the squiggly mush of the creature's brain. He ground everything his fingers touched to a fine paste. The creature screamed, gurgled, and finally fell silent. Its body jerked under him. The sensation was revoltingly intimate. He rolled off and staggered to his feet, gasping for breath.

The Big Feelings were quiet, and for a moment he cruised, drifting on the blissful waves of nothingness.

"Well," Seth said, standing. "I think we're just about done. Let's adjourn for our final business, shall we? If you could help Ms. Duhammond to her feet, we'll be on our way."

Josh reached down and pulled Erin into his arms for the last time. She felt like a bag of feathers. She was almost gone. He squeezed her and it was like hugging a cloud of vapour. She was diminishing as the seconds ticked by. Whatever had been Erin Duhammond was almost extinct.

And he'd done it.

His tears formed a shimmering curtain, shrouding his eyes as Seth led him and the bundle of skin and bones he carried through the last red velvet curtain in Salioso's House of Monsters, Moste Grotesk and Phantastique.

◆  ◆  ◆

"Don't touch her," Josh said. "No more of your payments. You've taken enough."

"Yes, I have. Payment has been made in full. I took the final one while you enjoyed your time with Ms Duhammond's Doppelganger. You didn't even notice."

*(the softness of your skin)*

The life was gone from Erin. It winked out in her black eyes as Josh looked down on her, and then, without a sound, she disappeared.

"What have you done with her?" Josh fell to his knees, tears burning his cheeks like acid rain.

"I haven't done a thing. You did it all, Josh. You made choices every step of the way. You followed your desires and your impulses. You designed and delivered the payment. I merely obliged you. Erin is now part of Salioso's show. And so are you."

The room around them was bare: yellow walls, yellow floor, yellow ceiling. No furniture. Average size. But it was gravid with life; it ebbed and flowed and bent and stretched before Josh's eyes. It was almost as if it itched to take shape, but waited for direction.

"Where is she?" Josh's voice was a whisper. His tears had dried up.

"Nowhere, as far as you're concerned. Although I rather think she might form part of your exhibit. I have a sense for these things, after the time I've spent here."

Twirling his dummy on its chain, the little man broke into a whistle. He strolled to the far end of the room and pressed his hand to the wall. It melted at his touch, exposing a gaping hole. He stepped into it and threw Josh a cheery wave.

"Farewell, young Josh. I'll see you again. So many souls come to Salioso's House, and they're all eager for a show. You'll entertain a great number of them, forever and forever and forever. You and your Big Feelings, boogeying on down in the ultimate Big Top. It's a beautiful thing. Oh, look. Your exhibit is taking shape. And yes, there she is. Splendid."

"Who is Salioso?" Josh's lips were stiffening, and his brain seemed to be grinding to a halt. He forced the words out, knowing they were probably his last.

"You asked that a little late, m'boy! And it really doesn't matter. He's no one and nothing you'd understand. But he owns you. And, unlike you, Josh, he never gives up that which is his."

The wall closed with a *thud*, and Seth was gone.

Josh had been wrong. As his body snapped and cracked, driving him across the room and into a position outside his control—as his brain petrified and changed, motivating him in ways he could not override—his *real* last words slipped from between his bloodying lips.

"Ez," he sighed. "Erin."

◆  ◆  ◆

"Step right this way, please! Keep together now, this one gets a bit messy and I wouldn't want you to get lost in the spatter. Yes, that's right, sit down there, nice and comfy. All settled? Good, we'll begin. Allow me to introduce—the Cutting Man!"

The dwarfish entertainer, now wearing a garish purple tutu and leotard, his tattooed bald head shining in the light reflected from the yellow canvas, motioned grandly to the stage at the front of the long room. A group of twenty people sat spellbound, gazing up at it, waiting for their entertainment to commence. The tutu-clad man's eyes roamed the crowd, and, unseen, he made a gun out of his thumb and forefinger and mimed shooting each person in the head. The nametag on his left breast read HI! MY NAME IS STEVE-O! Josh would have told the crowd that he'd known the man as Seth once upon a nightmare, but he was unable. It didn't matter, anyway.

Josh stood on the stage, still, quiet, waiting. In his hand, a giant scalpel—so big it was more of a sword—sparkled. Etched in large black letters on the blade was the word *Seth*. He raised the blade at a right angle to his body and paused. She wasn't here yet.

The crowd was hushed. A little boy whispered to his mother and she shushed him, not wanting to miss a moment of the coming show.

Ah. There.

Erin crossed the stage on gliding feet, her diaphanous white gown billowing behind her. Her hair was a glossy brown, plentiful with curls. Her eyes were grey and bright. Her skin was flushed with beauty and life. Her smile was wide and generous, and her hand was on her heart.

It always began this way.

"I love you," he told her. As he uttered the words, his hand swung above his head, and brought the vicious blade down on Erin. It struck with an audible *crack*, cleaving her skull in two. Her head stayed stubbornly on her body, branching off in two directions like a forked tongue. Her hand—small, pale, delicate— jerked away from her heart and fluttered to her wounded head. The gash was clean, and she smiled at him around it.

"I love you, too," she said. She felt no pain.

Josh took it all.

He felt the fountain of blood spurt from his own head, felt the searing, crippling agony. He swayed on his feet, but didn't— couldn't—fall. He would not be permitted to collapse to the ground until this was over. Until she was a twitching, unrecognizable pile of pieces on the floor, and he was a red geyser of suffering.

His love was his blade, and he scored them both with it, but he felt the pain. For that, at least, he was thankful.

"Mummy, is it real?" The little boy was crying.

His mother's voice was shocked, but calm. "Of course not, darling. It's just a show. The nice man *might* have warned us it wasn't going to be suitable for children—" she threw a shrewish look over her shoulder at 'STEVE-O', who smiled disarmingly in response, "—but it's not real. You just hide your face in Mummy's shoulder here, and—"

"No," the boy said, sniffing. "I want to see."

Yes. Of course he did. They all did. And Josh would give them what they wanted. He had no choice. "I want to protect you," he told Erin, this time lopping off her right arm. She looked at the dry stump in mild bemusement, then turned her radiant smile on him.

"I'm safe as long as I'm with you," she said.

His right shoulder was an orchestra of pain. Blood gushed to the floor in torrents of bubbling claret, and he gritted his teeth. It was all he could do. The ability to scream had been taken from him. Everything had been taken from him, other than the abilities he had used most in life: the release of his own blood, and the damaging of the one he held most dear whilst hurting himself.

This was his great and secret show.

In the back row, behind the spectators and the little man in the tutu who clapped his hands in delight at each new blow, a familiar boy stood. His face was contorted with grief, and he wrung his hands in distress. Blood red tears dripped from his black eyes. His t-shirt declared to the world his preference for BLIMEY'S DINER.

"Should have let me in, Josh," he whispered. "I tried to warn you, to save you. I try to save them all. They never let me in."

The man in the tutu's tattooed head spun 180 degrees on his shoulders, his neck bunching in pink ridges. His eyes locked on the Black Eyed Kid, and his mouth widened in an immense snarl. The boy slipped away through the red velvet curtain.

"I really must do something about that 'un," the man said, adjusting his STEVE-O badge and turning back to the bloody onstage action. "He's a pest, to be sure. Still, he never does any real harm. There's no stopping them when they're determined to see the show."

In the background, the tune of an ancient calliope ground on and on, and the scent of popcorn and sawdust drifted on the thick, rancid air.

# AFTERWORD

*It's no doubt self evident that I have a soft spot for Ray Bradbury. Carnival horror is an old, gaudy trope, and this was my take on it, because I devoured it whilst growing up. My protagonist is not a healthy, functional, likeable man. His ex-girlfriend, however, merits similar judgement. They are both masochistic and unlucky—but aren't we all? There's no real rhyme or reason here, just grotesquerie, spectacle, and suffering. In a collection entitled* Bread and Circuses, *it's a perfect fit, don't you think? Guilty fun is sometimes the best sort . . .*

# THE BLIND MAN

I can't tell you where it all started, because it didn't start with me. Rage, hatred, revenge, sorrow . . . these are great and ancient things, bigger than just one man. I can tell you a little bit, though. That much I can do.

◆ ◆ ◆

I was always in trouble as a kid. Once, when I was fourteen, I went too far. It was nothing out of the ordinary at first, just me and Nathan Geeves pushing and shoving behind the school gym, one on one, with the usual audience. It got out of hand when my mates Luke and James grabbed Nathan, held him so he couldn't fight back, and egged me on. I should have just thrown a cursory punch to appease my buddies and the jeering crowd, and left it at that. But I didn't. Something took hold of me, something cruel and wild that was excited by Nathan's helplessness, by the naked terror in his eyes.

My head throbbed and spun, and I saw my father's face, superimposed over Nathan's.

"Please, Greg," he begged. "Don't. Stop."

"All right, I won't stop," I told him. I got a good laugh for that one.

I beat the hell out of Nathan that day. I can still hear the sound of his skull cracking like an egg under my fists, hear his piercing screams, until that last punch when he went limp and silent and Luke and James let him go, watched him slither to the ground and lie there. I broke a couple of my knuckles. That hurt. Nathan wound up in hospital, hooked up to beeping machines and metal pulleys. His face was livid and swollen into a jellied lump. He didn't look a thing like my father any more. His parents thought I was the antichrist. Maybe they were right.

Broken jaw and nose, the doctors said. Broken ribs. Punctured lung. Fractured cheek bone and skull. Detached retina. Fragments of orbital bone floating behind Nathan's right eye. Cerebrospinal fluid leaking from his ears. Severe brain bleeds with the possibility of irreversible damage. The list went on, and on, and on.

The police came and dragged me from my house, and my mother cried into her tea towel, a low droning *uh uh uh*. I had to go to children's court. My mother didn't come with me. She said she loved me, but she couldn't support me in the terrible thing I'd done. Luke and James ran off to their dad's houses in another state. Suddenly, the crowd that had applauded me working on Nathan was against me, each of them trudging up to the witness stand and regaling the court with their recollections of my savagery. I got one hundred hours community service and a suspended twelve month juvenile detention term. The local media said it was too lenient by far, a travesty. If this was what I could do at just fourteen, imagine what I'd do in my manhood!

My mother made me lasagne after my sentencing, with extra béchamel. She was still crying into her tea towel, but her *uh uh uh* was happier now. She'd thought she was going to lose me forever, like she lost my dad. He was in jail serving two consecutive life sentences for killing my little brother and sister. They had been two-years-old. Twins. He strangled them. He loved his crystal meth, did my dad, but it didn't love him much—or my kid brother and sister.

Don't look at me like that. I don't want your pity. Don't assume it's why I am the way I am. It's no excuse. There *is* no excuse.

I knocked on Nathan's door to apologise, a few days after my sentencing. His mother opened the door, boggled at me, slapped me on both cheeks, spat in my face, and slammed the door shut. I could hear her crying from the other side of the thick mahogany. She didn't *uh uh uh* like my mother. She wailed. Her cries sounded like they really hurt, like ropes of barbed wire were being pulled through her tear ducts.

I *was* sorry. I couldn't tell Nathan, or his mother, so I'm telling you. I was very, very sorry.

◆   ◆   ◆

I had to do a minimum of ten of my community service hours every week. I did two hours, Monday to Friday, at The Willows aged care facility. That's where I met Mr Salioso.

He was a withered old thing, bent into his wheelchair like a weed yanked from its soil and forced into a too-small bucket. He always wore the same tattered brown dressing gown, with little bits of mashed pumpkin on it. No matter what they served for meals at The Willows, Mr Salioso always had pumpkin on his dressing gown. That was weird, but as I found out, it was one of the *least* weird things about him.

"Hello, Greg," he croaked. He sounded like Clive Barker, post throat polyps. He was wearing hokey sunglasses, despite sitting in the darkest corner of the old folk's lounge. "Thank you for coming to talk to me."

"I don't have a choice," I told him, slouching into the seat next to him. He didn't smell funny, like the rest of the patients here. He smelt . . . sharp, like a mint candy cane that had been sucked until it formed a lethal point. "I'm doing community service hours."

"Yes, I know," he replied, and we sat in silence for a while. He was smiling, a little curl at the corner of his pale lips. I sighed, drummed my fingers on my thigh, watched the old folks staring into space while cranky staff shovelled pureed mush into their mouths. I checked my watch. Only two minutes had passed.

"So," I said, finally unable to bear it any longer, "What're you in for?"

"This isn't a prison, Greg," Salioso said, amused.

"Isn't it?"

That odd, twitchy smile at the corner of his mouth again. "I've been here such a long time, I don't recall how I came to be here. Someone must have put me here, once, someone who perhaps thought it was the best thing for me."

"Or someone who hated your guts and didn't want to look at you anymore," I said.

"Yes. Maybe that was it."

BREAD AND CIRCUSES ◆ FELICITY DOWKER

More silence. This guy was good. I shifted in my chair, sighed again.

"What's with the sunnies?" I reached out to tap on Salioso's glasses, but damn if his arm didn't shoot up, quick as a snake, his bony white fingers like fangs, circling my wrist, biting deep. I gasped.

"I'm blind," he said mildly, giving my wrist one last little love squeeze before shoving my hand back towards me, releasing it. "Can't you tell?"

"No." In my mind, he grabbed my arm again. Crazy fast. Faster than anything I'd ever seen before. "Not at all. You don't move like a blind guy."

"How should a blind guy move?"

"Slow. Careful. Doddery. Unseeing."

"I'm only blind, Greg. It doesn't mean I can't see."

Yeah, right, and what the fuck did *that* mean?

I chewed the inside of my cheek and waited for the two hours to tick by with excruciating slowness. When my watch grudgingly relented and told me it was two o'clock, I stood up and walked away without a word to Mr Salioso.

At the door, I stopped, turned, looked back at him.

He lifted a hand and waved at me. Smiling, smiling.

◆ ◆ ◆

"How was it today?" My mother, bustling around the kitchen, was probably telling herself I was at the old folk's home out of the kindness of my heart. She lived on those little delusions.

"It sucked. They assigned me to this creepy old blind dude. He's really pale, like, you can see through his skin, and he smells funny, not bad, but funny, and—"

"He's old, Greg. He can't help it." She wasn't listening, not really. She never did.

"He could see me."

"I thought you said he was blind?" Well, maybe she listened a bit. She just didn't hear.

"That's what he told me, and he wears blind-guy glasses, but he knew where I was, what I was doing. He told me he could see."

"Blind people's other senses are extra sharp, honey. He could probably smell you, or hear you, or something." She handed me a steaming plate, lamb chops with mashed potato and peas and carrots. Smiled. Ruffled my hair.

Yeah, I thought, that had to be it. He used his other senses.

My dinner tasted funny that night. Like pumpkin.

◆ ◆ ◆

It was my fifth day spending time at The Willows. I crunched an apple in between words. "You can smell me, right? That's how you 'see'. You smell, and you listen, too."

Mr Salioso pursed his lips, nodded.

"Yes, I can smell you, and hear you. Better than anyone, better, even, than other blind people. I can track your blood, you see. It speaks to me. It paints pictures behind my eyes. In that way, I see you perfectly." I noticed that the orange smears on his dressing gown were so smooth, so clean. Like they'd been put there with deliberate care, fresh that morning, as part of his toilette.

"Track my blood, right. They didn't tell me you'd gone soft in the head, but I guess that's the norm in here." I dipped my head to take another loud bite of my apple. Salioso moved in my peripheral vision, a white-brown-orange blur, and my apple fell into my lap, seeded entrails ripped out, flesh quartered in coarse chunks. Sweet juice dripped from the old man's long fingers. Reaching slowly this time, he leaned into my lap, wiped his hand on my jeans. His smile was close to my face, and I could see the shiny points of his canines.

"Oh," I breathed.

"Yes," he said, drawing back into his wheelchair once more. He was slow now, the movements as careful as the neat smears of pumpkin on his clothes.

Those hours flew, my brain racing with fear, with questions, with excitement. I said nothing, though. I wanted to say the right things or nothing at all. Suddenly, I cared very much what Mr Salioso thought of me.

◆ ◆ ◆

"Why do you sit in a wheelchair?" I was proud of that question. I'd worked it out in my head just right as I lay in bed the night before. Not, *why are you in a wheelchair*, because he wasn't *in* a wheelchair. He could get out of it if he wanted to, walk, dance, leap tall buildings in a single bound. I knew it the same way I knew he wasn't human—because it was true. Because all the signs pointed to the truth.

"For the same reason that I wear this disgusting old rag, and for the same reason I smear muck on myself," Mr Salioso said. He was minty-fresh as ever, like he'd squeezed a whole tube of toothpaste onto his gleaming fangs.

"It's all part of your disguise."

"Yes, Greg. Very good." He sounded bored, but I knew he wasn't. He'd led me to this point. We were where he wanted us to be, he and I.

"And the glasses?"

"I'm blind. I really am, you know. That happened . . . before."

"Yes, but they're not essential, are they? And they don't seem very 'you'." I was afraid, of course; always afraid by then. Mr Salioso wanted something from me in exchange for the glimpse he was permitting me into his truth. That was the way of the world. I knew that at fourteen as I know it now.

Salioso laughed, a little chuff of hoarse breath. "You really are a rather smart boy, aren't you? Not your garden variety thug at all. Why do you conceal your intellect, Greg? Do you *want* everyone to think you're like your father? Is that it? Do you fear their expectations if they look beyond that?"

A sharp chill shot through me. My blood seemed to congeal in my veins, and everything slowed and quietened, until all I could hear was the harsh *whumph whumph whumph* of my heart, thudding in my ears. How had he known about my father?

After a long, tense moment, I sucked in a breath and blew it back out, my lips vibrating. Salioso knew because . . . well, because he was Salioso. He knew because he knew, and I decided that he had mentioned it to rattle me. The glasses," I insisted.

A pause, and Salioso curled his flaccid lips at me. Approving. "All right. Come closer."

I wanted to run. Instead, I leant into his minty personal space until my nose almost touched his. His teeth were white blurs in my straining peripheral vision. His tongue darted around behind them, pink and moist, tasting my breath.

Salioso lifted a hand and, with one finger, pushed his glasses up onto his forehead.

His eyes were totally black. They bulged, wet and fishy, glistening in his lashless sockets. Cataracts hugged the gangrenous orbs, thick with canker. I swallowed the cry that tried to bubble free from my throat. It slid back down my gullet, heavy and painful.

"The staff think it's an eye disease, contracted in my childhood. That's the story I've fed them, and they've gobbled it up, because, like you, they fear fully using the knowledge they already possess." He let his dark glasses fall once more onto his bony nose, and I flopped back into my seat, aware of my rapid heartbeat and the rancid sweat coating my body like frosting. I could taste metal in my mouth. I wondered fleetingly if this panic, this primal horror, was something like what Nathan had felt when he knew I was going to hurt him very badly. And what my little brother and sister . . .

"I wear the glasses for them, and for the other patients," Salioso continued. "It's a courtesy, you see."

"What . . . " I found I couldn't speak, and I swallowed several times, rapid fire, *gulp gulp gulp*. "What do you want from me?"

"You came to me, Greg. What do *you* want?"

"I had to come here, and I had to talk to you. They assigned me."

"You didn't have to talk to me like this, though, did you? We could have chatted about the weather, your schoolwork, my festering childhood. We could have discussed nothing at all, if you'd chosen to simply serve your sentence in sullen silence. But you wanted to talk, really talk, and at some point you've got to ask yourself . . . why?"

Two hours, up. We were over halfway there. I had forty more hours to serve at The Willows, sitting rigid in the seat next to Mr Salioso's wheelchair. Forty hours to voice the words that had been forming in the swampiest part of my animal brain. I knew Salioso already heard those words and knew what I wanted. He would wait for me to speak the request, though.

It was a courtesy, you see.

◆ ◆ ◆

I dreamed that night.

My mother lay down on the floor and wrapped herself up in the rug like a big ol' sausage roll, and I saw that it wasn't really a rug, but an enormous tea towel. *Uh uh uh.* She wriggled her arms free from the not-rug and waved them around, conducting her own honking sobs. *Uh uh uh.*

"Gweg?"

Oh, no. It hurt, it hurt bad. I didn't want to see them, didn't want to miss them, didn't want to know their pain. But I turned around anyway, couldn't not, and there were my little siblings, Amy and Todd, their hair matching spirals of sunshine, their cheeks pink and round, and I felt my own silent tears start to drip, drip, drip.

*Uh uh uh.* My mother receded and disappeared, as she always had when we needed her.

"Gweg? Wowee Daddy?" They wanted to know where our father was, and I suddenly thought maybe this wasn't a dream, maybe this was a chance to save them. I lunged for them, gathering them into my arms like the dolls they would forever be. They clung to me with wet kisses and high pitched giggles, and I ran to hide them in my bedroom, except the floor beneath me turned into hungry sludge, and I sank down, down, down.

"Give them to me, boy." The big bad wolf had arrived and oh, what big teeth you have, Mr Salioso, except it wasn't him, not him, but Daddy, and Daddy had gone mad.

The sludge sucked me into it, devouring me to the neck, and I couldn't turn my face away, couldn't close my eyes, couldn't scream because the sludge filled my mouth with cold malice when I tried. Amy and Todd ran to Daddy, all open adoring arms and puckered up kissy lips, *luboo Daddy, wowee, Daddy!*

Daddy was a drugged-out demon with popping tendons and bright eyes, and he took off his belt and wrapped it around Amy's slender neck. Then, when she was a broken doll all shattered on the floor, Todd's neck received Daddy's fatal love.

"They're not really kids," he told me as he squeeeeeeezed death into my beautiful brother and sister, who had loved *Play School* and cuddles and chocolate crackles. "They're aliens. You can't see, but I see, I know, and I'll save us."

I let the sludge pull me right under then, and it was orange. Pumpkin. It tasted like mint.

◆ ◆ ◆

I had twenty hours left. Time to get down to business. "Can you bring back dead people?"

"No. Not the dead." Salioso laid a hand on my arm. It felt like frozen clay. "I'm sorry. I can't help them."

I choked back a hard ball of grief. I'd known he'd say that, but I wouldn't have been able to live with myself if I hadn't made absolutely sure.

*Tick, tick, tick.* The clock on the wall was so loud. How loud must it have seemed to him, day in, day out? Who had put him in this place? Had it been before or after he'd become what he now was? How did it feel to be given eternal life, but be old and blind when it came? Why did he stay there at The Willows?

"My father . . . " That ball again, jagged and hot, surged up my throat. My hands fluttered to my neck, grabbed it, tried to massage the pain away.

"Mmmn."

"He . . . "

"I know. You don't have to discuss that. I won't put you through it." How kind he could seem. How hungry he was. It rolled off him in silver-bright waves. His fingers were hooked into claws, trembling, eager. "I can see it in your blood."

"I want you to kill him. I want him to be terrified and miserable when he dies. I don't want it to be quick."

"Of course." *Tick tick tick.* "Tell me where he's incarcerated."

"Okay." I told him, and it was done.

◆　◆　◆

"Greg." My mother, shook me out of my slumber, her voice strange. "Wake up."

"Mmmnh?" She had turned my bedside light on, and as my eyes adjusted, I saw her face. Her cheeks were wet with tears, but she looked . . . radiant.

"Your father—"

"Is he dead?"

She recoiled a little at that, but only for a moment. "Yes, honey. They found him in his cell an hour ago. They think one of the other prisoners got to him, with a . . . a knife, or some such. His blood . . . "

I smiled at her. After a long, long moment, she smiled back.

I guess I'd never really understood how much she'd suffered, too.

◆　◆　◆

After they planted my dad in the ground, I was woken in the middle of the night again, this time by Mr Salioso sitting on my bed. He'd turned my bedside light on, too. He didn't need it to see in the darkness, but he knew I did. A courtesy, you see.

"You're not in your wheelchair." It was a stupid thing to say, but I needed to break the silence. I sat up, clutching my blankets to my chest. The air seemed cold and sharp in my room. Minty.

Salioso gripped my shoulder. I think he was trying to comfort me. He failed.

"Hatred makes us blind, Greg," he rasped. He wasn't wearing his glasses. His black eyes were obsidian mirrors, reflecting my pale, terrified face. "It starts with pain. Our pain, the pain of others, world-hurt, whatever. That's when it begins to grow. The hate, the rage."

"He was a monster," I whispered. Hot tears scalded my cheeks. "He made our lives hell, and then he murdered the two innocent little creatures that loved him the most."

"Yes, he deserved his death, and I was happy to deliver it. But what got him to that point? What pain did *he* suffer, to shape him? He wasn't born a drug-addicted child killer. Maybe he saw something that set his rage to burn . . . do you see?" He squeezed my shoulder. My bones ground together audibly. I gasped, nodded.

"Like you," Salioso said, and my nod turned into vehement side-to-side shaking. *No!*

"I'm nothing like him," I hissed. I tried to move away, but the blind man held me fast.

"Ah, Mrs Geeves would beg to differ," he said. For a second, I wanted to ask *who?*, but it came to me. Nathan—who had looked a little like my father. Nathan's mother—her spittle on my face, her loud cries of agony.

"I didn't mean to hurt Nathan. I'm sorry." I was sobbing aloud by now. *Uh uh uh.*

"Oh, you did mean to hurt him, but you're certainly sorry. Neither fact matters much to Mrs Geeves. Nathan didn't recover in every way that matters, you see. His body healed. His soul didn't. He killed himself this morning." The words fell from Salioso's lips like thunder, cracking and booming about my head.

I understood, then. Understood everything. I opened my mouth to scream, to bring my mother running, but Salioso's hands were there, sealing my lips. Then his hands were everywhere, impossibly fast, irresistibly strong. He pushed me back down onto my mattress, and his fingers traced loving circles around my bulging eyes. His fangs were bared, his mouth gaping open, too wide, too deep.

"She wants you to live," he said. "She thinks death is too easy for you. She wants you to live, and to suffer."

Salioso's fingers moved like white lightning, and he plucked my eyes out, one after the other in quick succession. I felt the harsh suction and the terrible give as each one went, but the pain took a while to filter through. Shock and the sheer speed of Salioso's movements kept me in blissful ignorance for a short while. Then my body realised that, yes, those long sharp fingers had slid in between my eyeballs and their snug sockets; and no, it hadn't been nice when my reluctant orbs were yanked until their nervy tethers gave way. And, emphatically, the juicy hollows where my eyes had been protested their discomfort as they wept bloody tears and pulsed and swelled with their loss.

The sudden and terrifying blackness of eternity was in me, around me, consuming and surrounding me. Excruciating agony crashed over me in a hard, red wave. I was drowning, my cries for help emerging only as short, wheezy exhalations.

"You saw nothing while you had these." Salioso's voice came to me as if from a great distance, whooshing through a wind tunnel. There was a mushy popping sound, and I knew Salioso had crushed my eyeballs in his fist. Somehow, that was the worst of it. "It is fitting that, now you have had them taken from you, you shall see all. Blindness is a disease, and it cannot be contained now, but it can also be its own cure, as you will learn."

My mattress creaked as Salioso bent over me. Something firm and wet probed the pulpy beds where my eyes had been. He was licking my wounds. He pressed his lips to my eye sockets then, and sucked hard. The pain was cosmic. I shot into oblivion gratefully.

◆ ◆ ◆

So there you have it. Nothing more than an old blind man's fractured memories, the broken shards scattered before you in hopes that you may make of them a worthwhile picture. There is a moral to my story, I suppose, except that darkness leads to more darkness, pain to more pain. There must be other paths, but not having walked them myself, I'm afraid I can't show you the way.

Salioso did not make of me what he himself was, except for the blindness. And so I will die, perhaps soon, since seventy-four years have passed since I lost my sight and saw everything in the same moment. My mother died decades ago. There is no one else. So I sit and rot here, in The Willows, my days a blur of pureed vegetables, desperate sounds, and hospital odours.

Today, however, someone came to visit me. He sat beside me and held my hand. His skin was cold. He smelt of mint.

"You've got pumpkin on your clothes, old friend," he croaked.

"Yes," I said.

We sat in silence then, my visitor and I, as the slow minutes ticked by. His hand in mine was an invitation etched in cold blood. I didn't accept. I wish I had. I hope he visits me again tomorrow.

Perhaps the only way to truly get anywhere in this ruined world is for the blind to lead the blind.

# AFTERWORD

*I was invited to write this story to suit the very particular theme of the* Scenes from the Second Storey *anthology—namely, each writer had to craft a story around a specific song from the God Machine album after which the collection was named. The music we were using as inspiration was quite a long way from any I would normally choose to listen to, which actually helped in formulating a story based on the unique mood of the song. Unsurprisingly, my contribution revolved around revenge, but without any joy in its execution. I'd been reading a lot in the newspapers about increasing brutal violence amongst youths, and it was weighing heavy on my mind, so that is in this story, too. I also have a recurring name, "Salioso", which pops up inexplicably in my stories from time to time (it's in this one, and it's in "Phantasy Moste Grotesk", though the bearer of the name bends and changes in each story). I thought it might be nifty to consider a different sort of vampire—one who was already old and infirm before being changed, a long way from those vamps popular in books and TV shows at present. And I guess, in general, I wrote about what I often write about—dysfunctional families, painful childhoods, and Very Bad Things.*

# RED DELICIOUS

The boy's arms were inside the dragon, and shadows stalked him with intent to kill.

His brown hair was pulled back in a messy ponytail, his eyes closed, his lanky jean-clad legs splayed on the muddy spur road. The metal flank he leaned against was not really that of a dragon, though that was what he'd called it as his friends had chained him to it. He seemed a fiery spirit himself, his hot exhalations pluming white in the freezing night air.

Ivy saw what the boy couldn't see yet: two big men moving toward him, one gripping an iron bar, the other a cricket bat. She crouched in the trees, waiting, watching. Eucalypts towered around her, spindly ghosts in the moonlight. She inhaled their menthol scent, and smelt pines, too; Leatherwood, Blackwood, Celery Top, Myrtle, Sassafras, Huon. Melodic names that reminded her of Saturday mornings spent at Salamanca Market on Hobart's waterfront with her parents, browsing the stalls' wood, sheepskin and opal wares, listening to Arauco Libre's lively Chilean music, eating steaming donuts laced with cinnamon and sugar—and, oh, Dagwood dogs skewered on wooden sticks, oozing thick tomato blood.

All that sensation, all that light. One and a half decades ago, when she'd been 18. She was still 18, but back then, she'd also been alive.

She remembered the sharp brine of the Derwent River in the air, fairy lights in the trees, and a dreadlocked woman at one of the stalls handing out SAVE THE WELD fliers. "Huon Pine are a remnant of the supercontinent Gondwana," the woman had said. "Undisturbed, they can live for more than 3,000 years." How impossible that had seemed to Ivy at the time. Now she wondered how many more thousands of years than that she herself would linger.

Forever, perhaps, whatever that meant.

She stopped breathing. It was unnecessary, and it brought yearning for all that was lost to her. Better to focus on this night, full of the forest's noises and the promise of blood.

Earlier, she'd watched Ponytail and his friends' machinations, completed by jerky torchlight; digging the hole, pouring quick-set cement, inserting shackle rings, driving a doorless old car over the top of their handiwork, securing Ponytail to it, and leaving him.

And now, the two brutes had appeared.

"You tree-huggers and your bloody "dragons"," Iron Bar said, and Ponytail gasped. His feet twitched, sending a huntsman spider the size of Ivy's hand scuttling for cover. Gorgeous creatures. Didn't spin webs, just hunted.

"Who's there?" Ponytail's head snapped back and forth.

"*We* don't call 'em dragons, though," Cricket bat said. "*We* call 'em "how far off the ground do we have to lift that car before the hippy's arms pop out of his sockets"."

Ivy stepped out of the trees. The forest leaned in on both sides of the logging road, blocking the moonlight. Ivy could see just fine, but Ponytail, Iron Bar, and Cricket Bat could see only murky outlines—not that any of them saw her at all.

Ponytail was rigid against the car body. "What are you doing out here in the middle of the night?" He tried to sound brave, bless him, but he only sounded desperate.

"Hunting," Iron Bar said, slapping the bar against his palm. Cricket Bat chuckled. They stood directly in front of the boy now.

"I'm not hurting anyone," Ponytail said. "This is a peaceful protest. There's no need for violence."

"You hurt our families every time you *protest* against our livelihood," Cricket Bat said. "It's only fair we hurt you back."

"And what about what you're doing to this land? What about—"

Ivy didn't get to hear the boy's arguments, because Iron Bar adopted a baseball batter's stance and swung the bar in a huge arc at Ponytail's head. Blood exploded outward from the right side of his face, his head snapped to the left and ricocheted off the car body, and he slumped in his chains, unconscious. Iron Bar spat on him.

"Bulls eye!" Cricket Bat yelled, and raised the bat above his head like an axe.

Ivy closed the gap between them in a blur of rapid movement, leaves whirling in her wake, mud spurting into the air. Iron Bar and Cricket Bat spun around, gaping at her. They saw the shape of her long tangled hair flying on the wind, the impression of dark checks on her flapping flannel shirt, but most of all, they saw her pale yellow eyes, glowing in the darkness like miniature moons.

"So you're here to hunt?" She said. "Great. So am I." She shouldn't talk to them, shouldn't prolong this, but the harder their hearts were beating when she bit into them, the bigger their arterial spray would be, exploding against the back of her throat and gushing into her, life itself. And oh, but she wanted life.

"Get the hell out of here," Iron Bar said, but is sounded like a question.

Ivy shouldered past them, craning her head over Ponytail's shoulder, looking down into the car, her eyes lighting their own way. In their confusion, Iron Bar and Cricket Bat didn't touch her. Two holes were torn in the wreck's underbelly, through which Ponytail's arms were placed, chained to the shackle rings in the cement.

"Ah." Ivy straightened, turned to face the men, standing between them and their victim. "Must dent your working day in a big way, moving them every time they do this."

"Didn't you hear him?" Cricket Bat pointed at her with his bat. "He said get the hell out of here. This is nothing to do with you."

"Oh, but it is." Ivy smiled. They didn't see her fangs; to them, her teeth were just white smudges in the night.

"What, he your boyfriend or something?" Iron Bar took a step closer. "Well, he shouldn't have played in the forest with the big boys. And neither should you." Another step. Another.

"Yeah," Cricket Bat said, raising his bat as Iron Bar reached for her with blood-spattered fingers. Behind her, Ponytail gurgled as he woke.

"I don't see any big boys here," Ivy said. "Just sacks of shit who feel tough when they beat on chained-up kids."

"We'll show you what big boys we are, sweetheart," Iron Bar said, dropping his bar to the ground and reaching for Ivy's throat. She reached for him in turn, and for a moment they looked like lovers locked in a heated embrace. She broke his neck before he could scream, the crack like a gunshot, carried away by the wild night wind. He fell bonelessly to the ground. Cricket Bat roared. She held her arms wide, welcoming him. He swung at her with his bat, but she slapped it aside like a mosquito, sending it flying into the forest. His arms dropped to his sides and he stared at her, stunned.

"Oh, come on," Ivy crooned. "You've got more than that, *big boy*. Show me."

Cricket Bat crouched, dropped his head below his shoulders, and rushed at her. When he reached her, she snatched a fistful of his hair and yanked. His body continued its charge, bouncing off the car next to Ponytail, who shrieked as it fell to the ground, blood jetting from its neck stump. Cricket Bat's head dripped and swayed in Ivy's hand like a grisly piñata. She held it above her, letting blood patter on her face, tilting her head back and opening her mouth, sighing as the red droplets coated her tongue.

"Oh my God," Ponytail moaned behind her. "Oh my God."

She lowered Cricket Bat's head and turned to look down at Ponytail. He sobbed and muttered, the ruined right side of his face still bleeding heavily, his mouth moving with obvious difficulty.

"It's ok," Ivy said, kneeling before him.

"Oh my God," he said again, then: "Thank you."

"Don't mention it," she said, and, reaching out with her free hand, broke his neck. Her teeth slid into him at almost the same moment his vertebrae snapped, half his lifeblood gone down her throat before he even knew he was dead.

◆ ◆ ◆

"Red Delicious." Tesla flicked through the dog-eared appointment book on the front desk, hunching her right shoulder to wedge the phone's handset against her cheek. "I dunno, dude, we're booked out months in advance. We might be able to squeeze you in if it's small . . . "

Ivy took her foot off the pedal, the tattoo gun in her hand falling silent, and watched Tesla over the bare hump of her client's rounded hip. Tesla was tiny, looking only 12 of her 19 years. Her fire-engine-red hair stuck out in fuzzy spikes where the phone was pressed into it. Ivy smiled at her. Tesla didn't smile back. She was still pissed about being left to run the shop alone last night while Ivy hunted and fed—though of course, Tesla didn't know that was what Ivy had been doing.

"I love this song," Ivy's client said. Jane, Jill? Ivy didn't much care. "*Pure Massacre*." The girl hummed along. Her blood spotted her skin like an orchard of tiny rotten apples, reeking of codeine abuse. Ivy sprayed water on the half-finished tattoo, wiped the blood away with a paper towel, and flung the soiled towel in the bin at her feet.

"Silverchair were great, once," Ivy said, bending her head, the tattoo gun buzzing in her hand as she recommenced her work on the girl's thigh. She stopped breathing so she didn't have to smell the girl. "*Frogstomp* was their only good album."

"You would say that—you've really got that '90s grunge vibe going on."

"Thanks," Ivy said, resisting the urge to press harder with the tatt gun.

"You know what I mean," Jane/Jill said. "Hey, I like your shop logo. It's hardcore."

"Thanks." *Shut up, shut up, shut up, you little bag of rotten blood, shut up.*

"What is it, exactly? It's a bit twisted, I can't tell. No, wait, I can guess—it's partly an apple? Cos your shop's called Red Delicious. And the Huon Valley is the Apple Valley, and Tasmania is the Apple Isle, right?"

"Good guess." Maybe pressing harder with the tatt gun wasn't such a bad idea.

"So what is it?"

"What?"

"The logo? Apart from an apple, I mean."

Ivy sighed. "It's a bleeding heart, shaped like Tasmania, with a tattoo needle stem at the top."

"In other words," Tesla said, finished with her phone call, "It's a fucking apple, ok? Now unless you want a shaky tattoo that goes all the way to the bone, I suggest you shut it and let Ivy work in peace, yeah?"

Jane/Jill gaped, her eyes darting from Tesla to Ivy, then buried her face in her arm and was silent. Ivy raised an eyebrow at Tesla. Tesla smirked. All was forgiven, then.

*Israel's Son* blared through the shop. Tesla sang along as she worked on a stencil for her next client. Ivy smiled. Being dead had its downfalls, but running your own night-time tattoo shop wasn't one of them. She'd built a solid rep in the five years she'd owned Red Delicious, and people never baulked at the opening hours. They figured geniuses were always eccentric, and coming into the shop under cover of darkness added to the mystique, as did Ivy's "cool yellow contacts and fake fangs". The customers all left satisfied and they all paid top dollar. Dead or not, a vampire still needed to make a living.

Jane/Jill's swirly floral obscenity was almost done. The girl winced and twitched melodramatically as Ivy worked, the white butcher's paper stretched under her crackling on the red vinyl it protected. The phone rang, and Tesla answered. She always did. Aside from it being part of Tesla's job to handle the phones, Ivy had the same issue with phones that she had with mirrors. They didn't work for her. No reflection—visual, verbal, or otherwise.

"Red Delicious. Hi, mum. No . . . calm down . . . *what?*" Tesla dropped the phone.

"Tes?" Ivy stopped tattooing.

Tesla looked at Ivy, her eyes wide and moist. "Mum says Pete never came home last night."

"I thought your brother often went MIA."

"The police called Mum. They think they found Pete in the Weld. She has to go identify the . . . the body."

If Ivy's heart was beating, it would've stopped. "What would your brother have been doing in the Weld?"

Tesla was too distressed to notice Ivy's odd reaction. She retrieved the phone, her mother still on the other end, and said she'd be home in fifteen minutes. She hung up.

"Tes?" Ivy laboured the point. "Why would Pete have been in the Weld?"

"I don't fucking know," Tesla snapped. "I . . . " She clapped a hand over her mouth, grabbed her bag, and left.

This was bad. Ivy liked Tesla, a lot. She also liked keeping her work and her feeding separate. That was why she hunted in the Weld in the first place. It was close enough for a vampire to run to within minutes, but far enough away to make running into the few humans Ivy still knew—at night, no less—so unlikely as to be impossible. Her two halves were never to touch. What's more, hurting Tesla was unthinkable. The girl was like a punky puppy, and if Ivy was honest with herself, she probably didn't just like her, she probably loved her.

It might be the love of an owner to her dog, vampire to human, but it was still love.

But Ivy had never met Tesla's brother. She didn't know what he looked like. It was possible, during last night's hunting trip, or a previous one, that . . .

"Get out," Ivy muttered. Jane/Jill looked up at her in confusion. "Your tattoo's done. No charge."

"But . . . can I have a mirror to look at it? And I couldn't possibly not pay."

"I said, *get out.*"

Jane/Jill looked into Ivy's "cool yellow contacts", and obeyed. Fast.

◆  ◆  ◆

Ivy needed to go out in the light.

Like most young vampires, she'd been obsessed with losing the sun when she was first turned. Even in Tasmania, Australia's sun was harsh. It hadn't been easy, but she'd found a way. She couldn't change her body since dying. Hair and nails grew back, wounds healed, but for some reason, tattoos stuck. Something to do with the interplay of vampire blood, metal-heavy ink, and the deep layer of dermis she injected it under. Ivy had decorated her skin with tattoos everywhere she could reach—largely red, because it had the most metal—and had Tesla tattoo the areas she couldn't. She'd done her face and neck in white ink, from shoulders to hairline. It meant that with a thick hat, a lot of sunscreen, and several layers of clothing, she could walk in the day for limited periods of time before the burn started to get too deep to bear and sweet-smelling smoke started to seep from her pores.

She ran to Tesla's house and hid behind a wattle bursting with yellow flowers. A female voice, an older version of Tesla's, drifted from an open window in the one-sided conversation of all telephone users.

"I know." A sob. "It's horrible. Those mutilated bodies. Someone's child, each and every one of them, and I know it's awful, but all I could think while I was looking at them was *thank God they're not mine*. Tesla's gotten it in her head that Pete's up there, though, in the Weld, because the bodies keep turning up, and he's still not home, and she's driven off up there in such a state . . . "

Ivy ran for the Weld, invisible with speed, the trip brief as ever, but still giving her a moment to think. She never left bodies lying around. She wasn't *stupid*. She buried them deep, and covered her tracks with inhuman expertise. It had troubled her when bodies had started being found in the Weld weeks ago, but the authorities had been curiously eager to write them off as animal attacks, accidents, exposure, drunken fights among campers gone wrong. It sounded flimsy to Ivy, but people bought it.

And now Tesla's brother was missing, and Tesla was in the Weld looking for him. It would be bad if Ivy had inadvertently killed Pete, but niggling at the back of her mind was the question: if she hadn't, what had?

◆　◆　◆

It felt like hours had passed before Ivy found the first body. Her skin had begun to feel hot, even in the damp, dim forest, and she thought she detected a hint of the roast pork smell that meant she'd begun to fry in the blood of her victims.

The body was a girl in her late teens, face untouched except by dirt and leaves. The rest of her hadn't fared so well. Her clothes hung in ragged streamers, and her flesh had been torn from her bones in chunks, especially around her neck and inner thighs. She looked like she'd been mauled by a powerful animal. Of course, there was nothing bigger than a fox in the Weld. Maybe a wild dog or two, escaped from a nearby farm, but that was a stretch. Certainly nothing equipped to do this.

Ivy hadn't killed this girl. She never forgot a victim's face.

She darted through the forest she knew so well. She found more bodies, and recognized none of them.

The heat in her skin deepened, became a definite burn. Sickly-sweet odour filled her nostrils as she inhaled. Her head swam and her limbs felt floaty. She'd have to turn back and seek the shelter of her dark bedroom above Red Delicious, with its blackout curtains, double brick walls, heavy door, and a bed that sang to her across the kilometres.

"Hello, Ivy," a male voice said.

Ivy stiffened. "Ethan," she whispered.

"You're adorable, you know that?" Ethan wandered out from behind a tree as if this were all part of his morning stroll. "Fifteen years as a vampire, and you're still here in this redneck hole, clinging to your human memories, keeping human pets."

"Why are you here?" Ivy stepped sideways, circling, keeping the male vampire in front of her at all times. He was tall and broad, clad in blue jeans and a battered brown leather jacket, his hair short and spiky, his mouth set in a pleasant smile that was betrayed by his long canines and creamy-bright yellow eyes. He wasn't wearing a hat, and his skin looked untouched by sunscreen. He was ancient, though he looked no more than 30. His skin withstood the sun far better than Ivy's. His voice had a strange accent, somewhere between Irish and American.

"I got bored. It happens, every decade or so. Thought I'd see how my newest daughter was doing. But you're not doing anything, are you? You make me wonder why I bothered giving you this gift at all."

"You didn't give me anything. You took everything from me."

Ethan rolled his eyes. "Always the same old song from the newbies. "Wah! I didn't want to be a vampire!" Get over yourself."

"You killed my parents!" Ivy's hands curled into fists as she stepped closer to Ethan. "You murdered them, and you turned me, and you had me *feed on their corpses*! Then you left. What did you expect me to do?"

"Be a *vampire*," Ethan hissed, closing the gap between them. "Not the snivelling, creeping, human-loving thing you are. This always happens. Humans always disappoint, even once they're vampires. A tattoo shop? A few loggers and hippies taken in the woods now and then? *That's* your eternity?"

A weak cry sounded nearby. Ivy's head snapped around in the direction of the sound. Tesla!

"Oh, yes. I haven't finished with that one. Came looking for her brother who, unfortunately, is rotting somewhere in these woods already. He died begging. But I liked her. She had guts. So I didn't spill them." Ethan laughed at his own pun. Ivy snarled. "I was almost done with her when you showed up. She's drained, but I haven't refilled her yet."

Ivy's mouth hung open as the meaning of Ethan's words dawned on her. "You've . . . *turned* Tesla?" She'd smelt blood on the air, but it had been masked by all the other strong scents in the area—decaying flesh, old and new blood, Ethan himself, her own slow-burning skin. Now she focused, and yes, there was Tesla in that blood, and pain, and horror, and grief. Her lips peeled back and she bared her fangs at Ethan in open aggression.

"Well, no, she's not turned yet, she's just dying. Without vampire blood, she'll be worm food, probably within minutes." He wiped his mouth with the back of his hand, a smear of red stark on his white flesh. "She was a *tasty* one, too."

Ivy leapt, but Ethan was ready for her. He caught her like a father might catch his child as she ran into his arms, and threw her in the air. She flew for a moment, small whorls of sweet smoke spiralling dizzily in her wake, and then crashed into a tree. Bark exploded around her upon impact, the tree splintering and toppling to the ground. Ivy shook her head, panting, and got to her feet. Blood trickled from a cut on her forehead, obscuring her vision. She ran a finger along the cut as it healed, catching the blood before it stopped flowing, and licked her finger.

"You're burning, my daughter," Ethan taunted. "Better run back to your burrow and hide. I'll look after your little pet while you're gone."

"Ivy?" Tesla's voice was thin, but closer now. The undergrowth rustled as the girl dragged herself closer to Ethan and Ivy. "Help me. I'm cold."

"Help her, she's cold!" Ethan mocked.

Ivy rushed at him again, feigning right. In his arrogance, he didn't doubt her move. He lunged right to counter her, and she curled around and came at him from the left, wrapping her arms and legs around him, sinking her teeth into his throat. He screamed, and grabbed her head in his strong hands. He pulled, and Ivy's skin began to sizzle in earnest as her neck stretched. But Ethan's blood was powerful, and it gushed down Ivy's throat, strengthening her and weakening him with equal speed.

He might still have beaten her, if the group of ten loggers hadn't chosen that moment to burst into the clearing where the battle was taking place, chainsaws, axes, and picks in hand. One of them carried Tesla, the girl pale and bloodied, her hands clinging to his neck like little bird claws.

"It's him," Tesla cried, "That's the one who attacked me, the murderer who's been leaving bodies up here!"

Ivy detached from Ethan's throat with a slurp and regarded the loggers with glowing yellow eyes and long fangs coated in gore. They stared at her as Ethan kept his vice-grip on her head. The smell of pork filled the air, and Ivy's skin radiated red, like sunburn gone radioactive.

"That's my friend," Tesla whispered. "She was trying to save me."

Looking at each other, then Ethan, then Tesla, then Ivy, then at each other again, the loggers finally decided to act first and question later. They waded in, weapons raised high. Ethan released Ivy and tried to turn to defend himself, but Ivy clung to him like a spider monkey, and he staggered, giving the first logger time to bring his axe down on Ethan's head as several other loggers started up their chainsaws.

Ivy let Ethan go, the weakened older vampire falling to the ground as the humans closed in around him, ignoring his screams. She ran to Tesla and gathered her in her smoking arms. The girl was unconscious now, but Ivy whispered to her as she ran, nonetheless.

"It's ok," she said, as the Weld fell behind them and they neared the safety of Red Delicious. "It's ok."

◆ ◆ ◆

Ethan blinked, tried to knuckle the blood-encrusted sleep out of his eyes, but found he couldn't move his hands. He turned his head from side to side and saw silver manacles encircling his wrists, the chains tethering him to the surgical table he lay on. Something rattled when he tried to move his legs—more manacles around his ankles. If he pushed his skin against the silver too hard, it sizzled and smoked. There would be no muscling out of his bonds.

He opened his eyes wider, taking in his surroundings. Red vinyl. Pin-ups. Silverchair blasting from the wall-mounted speakers. Photos of tattoos on the walls. A weird image that might've been a heart or might've been an apple emblazoned everywhere he looked. Blackout curtains drawn across the windows.

Ivy and Tesla, smiling down at him with matching fangs.

"Wha," he said, and found that his throat burnt so much he couldn't go on.

"That'll be the wild rose and hawthorn branches we've shoved down your neck," Tesla said. "Great thing about the Huon and the Weld and, well, pretty much everywhere in the Tassie wilderness: plenty of natural vampire deterrents to be harvested. Easy to avoid if you're running past them and know they're there, not so easy to avoid if they're inserted inside you."

"You'll find talking painful, and screaming impossible," Ivy added. "But please, feel free to try. It never stops being funny."

Ethan did try, and a fire raged in his throat that required him to squeeze his eyes shut and be still for a few agonised moments before he could move again.

"Bitches," he rasped.

"No," Ivy said. "Vampires. Wasn't that what you wanted us to be?"

"How?" Ethan ground out the word.

"Simple. Ivy brought me back here, gave me her blood. You'd already drained me, so that was that. I was one of you. And to be honest, I'm quite pleased about that, which will probably piss you off more than anything." Tesla handed a bottle of clear liquid to Ivy, reaching over Ethan to do it. He bared his fangs at her, and she chuckled and patted his arm.

"And then," Ivy continued, doing something with a metal object that Ethan couldn't move his head far enough to see properly, "We went back to the Weld. If the loggers had still been there, well, sadly, they would've had to go, despite their fortuitous assistance. But they'd gone, and they'd left you there in an undignified pile of bloody flesh. They'd messed you up pretty bad, but they hadn't removed your head, and they hadn't put wood through your heart, and they hadn't set you alight, so you were still alive, though they didn't think so."

"They'd obviously just left you there to rot. Guess they figured we wouldn't mind," Tesla said. "And they were right."

Ethan hissed, coughing as the fire scourged his throat.

"So we brought you back here, and we made sure you couldn't yell or escape, while we dealt with the rest of the mess you created," Ivy said, unscrewing the bottle and carefully pouring a little of the liquid into a plastic cup, where it mixed with the red ink already there. The sharp odour reached Ethan, and he sucked in a startled breath. "We found all the bodies you'd left up there, and we buried them."

"I took my brother home to my mother," Tesla added, her voice soft. "And she told me I looked paler than usual, and asked if I was alright. Can you imagine? I deliver her son's mauled body, bloated and already decomposing, and she asks me if *I'm* ok. I've lost a mother as well as a brother, because I can't see her anymore. The grief might destroy her."

"But you've gained a sister," Ivy said, dipping a long metal needle into the cupful of ink.

"A different sort of mother," Tesla agreed.

"And when your mother's time comes, if you decide to, you can turn her, too."

"Please," Ethan said. "Not . . . " He coughed as his throat refused to let him continue.

"Garlic?" Ivy inserted the needle into the tattoo gun and pumped the foot pedal experimentally, smiling as it buzzed into life. "'Fraid so, *dad*. I think we'll start with a nice, big chest piece. The ribs are the worst, you know. Some people throw up, others pass out, some just cry like babies. You're a big strong vampire, so you'd normally be fine, but with the garlic I just put in the ink, well . . . "

Tesla nodded and pointed to a large sticker on the wall above Ivy's head: YOU BET IT HURTS!

"We'll start with a nice traditional heart with "mum" on a banner in the middle, for my mother, and for Tesla's, you son of a bitch," Ivy said, brushing her hair out of her face and leaning close to Ethan's chest, tattoo gun in hand. "From there, we'll do a stylized memorial tatt for Pete. I haven't decided what we'll do for my dad yet, but we've agreed that all the names of our victims go on you, too, as they happen. You're going to be our in-house pincushion. That's a lot of garlic ink."

"But you're vampires too," Ethan whispered. "You kill too."

"Two wrongs don't make a right," Tesla said. "You made us. The sins of the father aren't going to be visited on the daughters, they're staying right with the father."

"Sucks to be you," Ivy said, and she and Tesla shared a giggle at the pun before Ivy put the needle to Ethan's pale skin.

It turned out that he could scream, after all.

# AFTERWORD

*Oh, this one was just good clean fun to write and, I hope, to read. Given the story was specifically written to a theme (vampires in Australian setting), I of course decided upon my home state of Tasmania as the setting. Tasmania is much neglected in Australian speculative fiction, which perplexes me, because it's a place rich in fodder: its dark and bloody history, its unique mythology, the endless beautiful but harsh wilderness, its isolation, the weird and wonderful creatures that call it home, and . . . well, I could go on all day. I also wanted to toy with tattooing, another personal love of mine, and I thought it could tie in pretty interestingly to the vampire theme (they both involve blood, pain, and permanent change, after all). And I saw my protagonist before I sat down to write: a sort of '90's grunge vampire, far from the glittering Edward Cullens of the world, and of course, a female. I did originally hope to squeeze some exploration of serious issues in (conservation and logging in Tassie, for instance) but this story just didn't want to be that* story, and that's ok.

# AFTER the JUMP

*Commercial Diver.*

That's what I scribble on my tax return every year, in the box titled OCCUPATION. And, strictly speaking, it's the truth.

But it's not the whole truth; not even close.

If I told you I was a HAZMAT Diver, it would be more technically accurate, but would still only steer us further away from the reality of what I do. You see, the diving isn't important. It's the most basic essential facet of my work, but it's ultimately meaningless.

It's the people that matter. Their empty, broken bodies. Their stories. Their tragic faces. And the swampy mud of the riverbed; deep, rich and wet.

That mud is like decadent chocolate; the bodies mired in it, the fillings. Sometimes hard. Sometimes soft. Sometimes oozing. Always delicious—at least, the riverbed seems to think so. It holds fast to its prizes, refusing to release them without a struggle. Oh, the power of that dense mud, the incredible suction it exerts, the *sound* as its treasures are finally pulled loose . . .

Yeah. The name of what I do is one thing. The experience is quite another.

◆　◆　◆

It's called the West Gate Bridge. It spans the Yarra River, a harsh slash of grey against the smoggy sky, connecting Melbourne's inner city to the Western suburbs. It's a cable-stayed box girder contraption, 2,583 metres long and 58 metres high. It carries four lanes of motor vehicle traffic in each direction.

But who gives a fuck, right?

I'm telling you the dry, boring shit only for the sake of context; so that when I tell you there is an average of one suicide on the bridge every three weeks, you can picture the distance those desperate souls need to walk to find the highest point to jump from. You can probably hear the endless roar of the traffic; maybe you can even smell the exhaust fumes, feel the *whoosh* as the cars go by and the *hummmm* as the bridge vibrates under their onslaught. And when the soon-to-be-corpse looks down from the great height of the West Gate to the filthy, churning Yarra below, I think perhaps you can feel your own head spin with vertigo and your heart clench with a sort of primal fear that screams without words or sound.

I know I can.

I've thought about it a lot. I wonder if the actuality is worse than my imaginings. I know, of course, that it must be; far, far worse.

I've heard it said that the only truly important question in life is whether or not to kill yourself. If so, then every ruined body I've retrieved from the bottom of the Yarra is the shell of a great philosopher, who solved the only real riddle in existence with final aplomb. I can't claim as much.

Here's how it works.

When someone jumps off the West Gate, they fall one hell of a long way. I've already told you how high the bridge is in metres, but all that matters when you're a human body plummeting from the bridge is that it's *one hell of a long way*. So, after falling for eternity within a brief moment, the body hits the water. It can get pretty messed up on impact, sure; but that doesn't concern us right now, because if they just end up in the water (or, if they miscalculate entirely, the riverbank), they don't need me to go get them. They float. Eventually. But I can tell you now, most of them don't *just* hit the water. Because—remember?—they fall such a long way. They're like fleshy torpedoes; they keep right on going. They part the water like a willing woman's legs, and they penetrate the fecund muddy cradle that lies beneath. And there they stay; implanted like sperm in an egg, only the merge is not one of life but of death.

And we can't just leave all those bodies planted in the mud down there, in the river our city plays in, gazes upon, drinks from (never mind the fact that it's already a polluted cesspit). No, somebody has to go and remove them. And that somebody is me.

I'm not the only one, of course. Victoria Police contract 10 divers from Any Dive, the HAZMAT diving company I am part of. But most of the other guys only do a West Gate suicide dive now and then; they also do the other stuff Vic Police need chumps like us to do for them—the raw sewage dives, the chemical infested pipelines, the simple body removals (usually murders, not suicides) from more placid lakes and waterways. Me? I'm a fulltime West Gate diver. I manage the Any Dive team. I'm on call. I'm *devoted*.

Not that it really matters, but my name is Ryan Deer. I'm 38, I'm single, and I live in a two bedroom apartment in West Brunswick. One bedroom for me. Another for the West Gate suicides who live with me always, their twisted limbs cavorting in my dreams, their agonised faces floating behind my eyes, breaking my heart over and over.

They are all my darlings; I have a memory slot in the computer of my brain allocated to saving each and every one of them. We tousle in the hungry soil of the riverbed together and we share an intimacy (them dead, me alive—in theory) that I never find above the roiling waterline of the Yarra. I have loved them all well.

But none as well as she.

◆ ◆ ◆

It was a 4am dive, one summer Sunday.

We usually do them in the very late or early hours, when traffic on the West Gate is a sluggish crawl and we're not likely to be noticed. Berko—self-dubbed "King of the Yarra"—squatted on the boat as I dove, cigarette dangling from the corner of his wizened mouth, directing the big industrial spotlight on me and the sprawling riverbed. I've got my own kit, torches included, but that spotlight is vicious, and it slices deeply into the water without mercy. It's enough to see all I need to see. You'd be surprised just how much I *do* see under that glare.

The first thing I see is her hair. Well, some of it. It's lying on the riverbed about a metre from the rest of her. It's a lonely thing, swaying to and fro with the water's movement like flaxen seaweed. It's anchored down by the hunk of scalp it's still implanted in; the bloody underside of the skin flap glued to the dark mud of the riverbed. I guess the impact of her body meeting the water—akin to smashing into a mass of concrete at great speed when you jump from such a height—caused half her scalp to shear right off her skull.

It's far from the worst thing I've seen down here on the scummy underside of the Yarra, but it might be the saddest. The portion of scalp and the endless riverbed, clinging to each other like star-crossed lovers while the owner of the scalp resides—alone, separate, discarded—elsewhere.

I hook the piece of scalp with my pick-up-stick, bagging it and sending it up the line to Berko. I'm not interested in that lost piece of her. It forsook her, and it must fend for itself now.

I move over towards her, approaching slowly; respectfully. Only her legs are visible, pointing up at the water's surface like accusations. They are naked, and streaked with deep furrows where her body has caved under the assault of the long jump. Blood and mud and pain are visible in her wounds. One of her feet is aimed backwards, bent double; her left leg is moving in a fluid way that boned limbs should not be able to achieve. At the point where her thighs should meld with her buttocks and pubic mound, there is only the riverbed; a muddy chastity belt, devouring her sex and the rest of her body; hiding her in the netherworld beneath the sod.

She's a head-first jumper. I don't see many of them. Most suicides literally step off their platform, or leap—but almost always feet-first. They hit the water in a messy heap, sideways or footways or any which ways—but rarely headways.

I have a sudden image of this woman, tall, blonde, and nude; arching her back as she reaches above herself with pale arms, looking at the sky before soaring away from the bridge in a perfect swan-dive.

Do-it-yourself fatality, head-first.

She must have been something. No doubts. No half-arsing. Just diving right into death, naked and determined. And how did she manage to climb to the middle of the West Gate with no clothes on? Did anyone try to stop her? Was she naked before she even got onto the bridge? Why?

Without thinking, without even pausing, I peel off one of my gloves and cup the curve of her right calf in my hand. She feels smooth and cool, and somehow *hard*. We stay like that for a while, she and I, clad in water and skin to skin. I have to fight the urge to wrench out my mouthpiece and press my lips to her legs; lick healing into them, taste her, know her. The compulsion to surrender my oxygen for her is overwhelming.

Then Berko jiggles the spotlight, impatient, and I know it's time to get to work.

*I'm going to get you out*, I mouth, chewing on my life-giving bit, the urge to spit it out still strong. *I'm going to free you from this river. I promise. Trust me.*

The alabaster tendrils of her legs move in my direction, and I know she is relying on me. I won't let her down. I've never let any of them down—I always get them out—but it's never mattered to me as much as it does right now.

Reluctantly, I flip the switch on the pack on my belt, activating voice communication with Berko as he bobs high above me. His voice barges down the umbilical line connecting me to the boat, ornery and indignant, violating my suit and flooding my head.

"Bin 'avin' fun down there, 'ave ya? What the fuck're ya doin', anyway? Courtin' the stiff?"

"Sorry, Berk. I've cleared the surrounding area now. Ready to excavate." My lips move with difficulty around my mouthpiece, and my voice is a clumsy wet murmur in my ears. I hate talking this way. The tinny electronic wail of it all is a profanity down here in the under-Yarra world.

"Cleared the area, yuh. If ya mean ya copped a feel of some dead legs, then you've cleared up *real* good. Think I can't see what yer up to from up here? I can see *everything*. Got it? Don't leave yer voice box off again. I'm not just gonna sit up here with me thumb up me arse while ya jerk off. Hear me?"

God, it's so wrong that he's even here; cranky old fart. I could steer the frigging boat myself, avoid his interference. They won't let me do a dive alone, though—safety reasons. I want to throw myself over her, wrap my body around her legs and shield her from his probing eyes and compassionless brain. *Fuck you!* I want to shout up to him. *Fuck off! Leave us alone! You don't belong here—you have no* right!

Instead, I wait without comment for him to feed the equipment down to me. After a moment, when he feels his point has been made, I see it break the surface above and begin to weave down. There are technical ways to explain how we get the bodies of the West Gate suicides out of the mud, but I'll keep it simple, because I don't care, and neither do you. Not about that stuff. We're here for them,

(*her* )

you and I.

Basically, we blast them out with a high-pressure hose. Berko's boat sucks in the river water—a hydraulic vampire, drinking the Yarra's blood—and spews it back out with enormous strength from the mouth of the hose that I've secured near the body. The riverbed is strong, but it's no match for the false strength of man-made power. My job is twofold. I have to try not to vaporise the corpse by putting the hose too close; it has to be near enough to get rid of the mud holding the body, but not so near that it hits the body itself. And, when the hose clears enough mud, I have to pull the body free. Then I take it up and after that, it's Berko's responsibility. He ferries his cargo to Vic Police, and who knows what they do with the bodies after that. Return them to their families for burial, I guess. If the suicide *has* any family.

The mouth of the hose nuzzles at my neck, a grotesque proboscis. I wrap both my hands around it and position it on the river floor. I used to need to spend time calculating precise measurements for positioning—in fact, I'm still meant to do that—but experience has given me a sixth sense for it now. I spend time with the jumpers, I dwell in their watery grave, and I just *know* where I have to put the hose in order to liberate them.

I follow this intuition now, and anchor the hose down. This does take a while, because if the hose comes free once the water is surging through it, I'll become the second corpse down here today. One blast of that water full in the chest and I'm the HAZMAT rather than the HAZMAT Diver.

"Hurry th'fuck up, Deer. I want that body onshore by sunrise."

"It takes the time it takes, Berk," I reply, the closest I get to snapping at him. It's unwise to bitch at the man who controls your air, your communications, your very body temperature with the warm water he sends into your suit. But more than that; if Berk complains about me enough, I could get taken off the West Gate team. And that would mean no more time spent under the water with the jumpers.

I need them. They need me. I'd be a fool to let anyone mess that up.

I test the last bolt on the hose's tether, and yank on the umbilical line six times, signalling Berk. The old bastard must have been waiting with his hand on the lever, because I feel the hose come alive in front of me immediately. Swearing, I propel myself backwards with all my strength (which is considerable, after years of this job).

As the first gout of water hits the mud around *her*—a near invisible stream of pure power, water in water—I stand on the riverbed and watch, my heart tight with anticipation.

In a matter of moments, she won't just be a pair of legs. I'll see the rest of her. I'll *hold* her. I'll save her.

God, I can't *breathe*.

When her legs thrash violently and begin to tilt like a felled tree, I jerk on the umbilical cord six times again. The torrent of force pouring from the hose ceases, and the hose wilts, its ardour spent.

I move forward, pushing against the stubborn water, wanting to get to her.

I catch her just as her legs crumple and fold in on her torso. I gently spin her, turning her right side up, pulling her head out of the hole she'd tunnelled with her death-dive. She's bundled in my arms, a long baby, the hair left on her head trailing across my bare hand where I've forgotten to replace my glove.

"Send the stiff up, then git that hose dismantled and git your arse up here, Deer," Berko's voice grates in my ears, shattering the perfect moment. "Sun-up soon. Time t'go."

Her eyes are open. They're fixed on me; black rings in the white of her face. One of them is filled with blood, bulging against the thin skin of her eyeball, but still beautiful. Her lips are pale, torn a little in the corners where the water barrelled in and stretched them, but they're curved in a smile, and that's beautiful, too. Her mottled cheekbones are high and wide, and her nose is straight and proud—even when it's pushed over to the right, broken. The white of her skull where half her scalp was torn off gleams at me like a bony hat, jauntily tilted to the side. Her remaining hair is long and golden, curling around me like tentacles. Her body is firm against my arms; I wish I could shrug off my suit and feel the coldness of her dead skin—that iciness that is so cold it's hot.

When she moves her hand to my face and speaks, I'm not even surprised. I've been waiting for this; for one of them to feel me, to respond to me. To reach them, and have them reach back.

*We don't want to get out,* she murmurs, her voice a liquid melody in my veins. *We want to get all the way in.*

"All the way in? You mean, under the riverbed?"

"Wha'the fuck're ya jawin' about, Deer?" Berko's voice is an obscenity, and I drop one hand to my belt, silencing my voice box before putting my hand back on her body.

Her hand reaches for my mouthpiece, and in a flick of her shattered wrist, it's gone. I'm breathless, and my first instinct is to panic; to gasp in lungful after lungful of dirty water. To choke. To drown. I see my mouthpiece, floating within arm's reach, and then her fingers brush my cheek. She draws my head down toward her, her lips waiting for me, her eyes closing.

*Kiss me. Say goodbye to me. Take my secrets. Sing me home.*

And I do. I take her in, mouthful after mouthful. We twirl in our sacred place beneath the water, beneath the city, beneath the world. She gifts me with her secrets, and I offer her mine, feeble though they are in comparison. The hum of the nothing that is everything fills my ears, and as we dance alone together, I sing her home.

◆　◆　◆

I'm fired, of course. Berko really did see everything from his craven perch up there on the rolling boat. When he tells them he saw me remove my oxygen bit and smooch a corpse, I'm handed a tidy severance package and some complimentary counselling sessions. Trauma, they said. Understandable after spending as many years on the job as I had. Nobody held it against me. There would be no . . . repercussions.

When I laughed in their faces, they thought it was evidence I truly had lost it. But I couldn't help it. They were just so damned *funny*, sitting there quacking at me, utterly clueless. Poor bastards. But how could they know? They'd never been down there, beneath the world. There was always someone else to do their dirty work for them. And nobody else had spent as much time down there as I did; nobody even came close.

Nobody else had known the jumpers the way I had. Nobody had touched *her* the way I did. They didn't know anything, and it wasn't their fault. I pitied them. I told them so.

Berko was in the room. He didn't speak while they fired me. He just sat and stared at me, the corner of his left eye twitching now and then. From the little you know about Berko, you can probably already guess that was mighty strange behaviour for him. They left us alone in the room for a few minutes at one point. Berko leaned forward and put his hand on my leg. He was trembling.

"What was it like?" His voice was awed and he took great care to enunciate clearly. "Did she show you . . . y'know, what's there? I saw things twisting and shining . . . in the mud . . . God, they were *reaching* for you! Such beautiful things, they was."

That old bastard. He'd seen more than he deserved.

"I don't know what you're talking about," I said, smiling serenely into Berko's watery eyes. He snarled at me, all reverence gone.

"Why you fuckin' . . . who d'you think y'are? D'you know how long I've been workin' that river? Long before your daddy forgot to wear a condom, I was there. I've seen and heard things you wouldn't believe on and under that water. It ain't fair. Hear me? It ain't *fair*. Why should *you* be the one—"

They came back into the room then, and Berko jerked back into his seat, his mouth snapping shut and his eyes sinking back into his head. I offered to tell them what we'd been talking about, but they just exchanged odd looks and shook their heads.

I didn't offer to tell them the secrets she'd sang to me, though. I didn't go that far. They hadn't earnt it the way I had. They weren't ready.

But *I* was. Oh, God. I'd been ready for the longest time.

◆ ◆ ◆

There are no walkways on the West Gate; it's not a walking bridge. As if it matters. As if the lack of designated areas for sad feet will somehow prevent people from scaling the bridge and leaping to their deaths.

There has been a call for "suicide fences" on the bridge for a long time, but they (the powers that be, the builders of fences, the rulers of bridges) have refused to erect any such thing. Think about that for a moment. Some simple fencing might save some desperate lives, but they won't oblige. Why? Don't they *want* the suicides to stop? Don't they care? Is it too much expense to save the sort of washed-up souls who shuffle off the West Gate every other week?

Or is it just that they know that it all goes much further
*(deeper)*
than it seems? Do they somehow understand that a fence wouldn't change a thing?

The mud is hungry, and deep, and we know that something better lies on the other side of it. If we could just . . . get . . . in.

She told me that, my darling in the river, whispering her secrets to my soul as I kissed the pulpy meat of her dead lips. I cradled her in my arms, she who didn't quite make it through the mud, and I sang her home. A song drawn in bubbles and silt and cold aquamarine. Not the song she dove in search of, but a song that put her searching essence at rest, all the same. My song was my love. She knew I cared, and in death she found the connection she
*(we)*
lacked in life. She was the culmination of my years under the Yarra; the end of my journey through the stories of the West Gate suicides. I always knew they had wonders to share with me. I knew I was there for a reason. I knew I was special, because they were special.

All of them.

I knew, and I was right. About that, and about other things, too.

Like what it would feel like to climb the West Gate and stand balancing on a ledge, the air expansive and shimmering around me, the water surging up greedily at me from far below.

◆　◆　◆

It feels awful, and exhilarating, and terrifying, and wonderful, and primal, and all-encompassing. Just like I thought, and not at all like I thought. Perfect.

I'm naked; but not only that, I'm hairless. I've waxed everywhere—head, body, even my eyebrows. Pulling out my eyelashes (one by one with tweezers, slowing down to wait for the tears to clear each time) was the hardest part, but I wanted to be as aerodynamic as possible. No clothes. No hair. I'd remove my skin, if I could. I realised why she—my darling under the Yarra—was naked, you see. It was to make her travel further, faster. To get deeper under the mud.

But I've got an edge that she, poor angel, didn't have: my diving weights. I've lugged them all up here, to the top of the West Gate, in 20kg lots. I've got rather a lot of them, you see, over the years. Easily my own body weight. And I've gotten *strong*, diving under the Yarra and digging up its human treasures. I've put all the weights on the ledge I plan to leap from, and I'm confident that I can strap them all onto me and still be able to propel myself off the bridge with enough force to make my jump count. Even just falling with style will be enough, with all that weight on board.

The interesting thing is that it's taken me the better part of several hours to climb up and down the West Gate, naked, hairless, carrying weights and arranging them on a jutting platform. And do you think anyone has stopped their car, hung their head out their window, asked me if I'm ok? No. Of course they haven't. They haven't so much as slowed down, honked their horn, or flashed their lights; I'm not sure if they've even seen me. And it's midday; I'm noticeable. Don't get me wrong, I don't *want* anyone to stop me; I don't *need* their help.

But it just says a lot to me that they haven't offered.

Sooner or later, someone *will* call the Police, and I don't want that interference, so I know I need to act now. Enough musing about man's inhumanity to man—it's not as if it's news to me. I've seen the riverbed. I know how this gig—life—works. It stinks.

I've worked out the spot she would have jumped from, and that's where I am now. She came the closest out of all of them—all the jumpers I've seen—to getting right under that mud; getting all the way in, getting *through*. I'm heavier than she was. I'm streamlined. I've got my weights.

And the riverbed and I . . . we understand each other. I think it has wanted me for a long time. I know I've wanted it.

It feels like time is stretching, slowing, stopping; as I stand and look down at the river so far below me. My body feels pain from the burden of the weights and the chill wind on my naked skin, but it's a distant sensation to me; like a dream someone else is having in the next room. I can't hear the cars anymore; I can't feel the bridge platform under my bare feet. There's only me and the riverbed. The frothing water looks like a thin sheen of smoke over the mud that I know lies beneath, and I take a moment to calculate the exact angle I should fall at; the best way to shoot myself into the boggy target and hit it dead on. To penetrate and transcend.

Well, what do you know? Some people have stopped their cars after all, clogging up the flow of traffic on the bridge. I can see them in my peripherals, intruding only slightly on my holy communion with the Yarra. A woman is waving her arms above her head and screaming at me. Nice of her. She thinks she's trying to save me. You and I know better, don't we? I'm bound for shiny, beautiful things in that mud. Preventing me from reaching it would be a travesty.

Ah. See that man, to our far right? He's gotten out of his car, too, but he's not looking at you and I. He's peering over the edge of the bridge, down at the water, at the mud. He's wearing reflective sunglasses, and in the lenses . . . can you see that? Silvery tendrils of pure light, undulating and pulsing in a constant thready rhythm from their riverbed home. *He* sees it. He hears it, singing and cooing and whispering. He's already taking off his jacket and reaching down to untie his shoes. He shoots me a dark look. Knowing. Jealous. Sly.

I can't let him beat me. I was here first. And I've got weights.

I'm the happiest I've ever been as I shuffle forward and prepare to take my final steps this side of the mud. I can hear a murmur in my ear; my Yarra darling, singing *me* home this time.

And where is that home—where will I actually go, when I break through the mud, get all the way in at last?

Maybe it's the same marshy flesh that we all sprang from, as embryos implanted in our mother's wombs. Maybe the river is that same life-giving amniotic fluid we all swam in, once upon an unremembered time. Maybe it's an eventual rebirth I'm headed for, but not into this broken world; somewhere new, better, somewhere *good*.

Look, I'll be honest. I don't know. But I *will* know.

After the jump.

In the seconds when my feet leave the bridge and the air starts to tear at my skin like the razor-sharp tines of a thousand pitchforks, it occurs to me to wonder why that radiant something that I want so badly would also want *me*. Hell, it even wanted Berko, a man who freely admits to slipping his three year old granddaughter laxative-laced lollies for the joy of watching her face crumple and her legs pump as she runs for the toilet.

As I near the water—so quickly!—and those beckoning silver swirls solidify into something immense and hungry and suddenly not at all shiny, I ponder the fact that even now, the Yarra's next lover is parting the air only metres above my head, matching my own sacrifice with every pound of his falling flesh. How quickly he was hooked. How easily my own offering was bettered, before it was even complete.

In the very final second, my blonde riverbed angel reaches up from the water. She's going to grab me and pull me under, wrap me in her arms and share eternity on the other side of the mud with me. She'll answer all my questions, quell all my foolish doubts. But . . . no, she's trying to push me away! Her ethereal hands grasp my ankles, but they slide through my skin like smoke through mesh.

Her savaged mouth is open in a perfect O. It closes and opens, closes and opens again, and I can see what she's saying:

*nonononononononononononono*

Then a gargantuan column of writhing mud shoves her aside, and she's gone, leaving a seared after-image on the back of my eyes.

I'm hitting it it's hitting me we're together

I know now

I've made it

the mud is dirty silver

Oh, God! It's so col—

# AFTERWORD

*This story was written as therapy; out of anger; and also, out of love and fascination for Melbourne, the place I've called home for the last twelve years.*

*Therapy: because a monstrous excuse for a man threw his four-year-old daughter off the West Gate Bridge in January 2009 as his two helpless young sons watched, and I think I can safely say it traumatised the whole city of Melbourne, definitely including myself. At the time, my own daughter was not quite two, and my son was almost four. I related so much to the grieving mother and the poor little girl, and I couldn't comprehend the unfathomable evil that is a father betraying his trusting infant. I couldn't even bear to think about it (and still can't), but something like that is all through the news and all through our hearts and minds whether we want it to be or not. So I channelled it through a not directly related story, to distract and to process. There was no way I would glorify or trivialise that horrific act by writing a directly related story, so I focused on the bridge and the Yarra itself, as entities in their own right.*

*Anger: because so many people have gone to the West Gate Bridge seeking death, and it could've been so easily stopped, long before now. Indeed, the mother of the little girl who lost her life on the West Gate is now suing VicRoads for that very reason: she believes, had VicRoads not repeatedly ignored advice to install safety barriers on the bridge, her little girl could still be alive today. Those barriers are now in place, fast tracked after the little girl's death, and the bridge suicides have dropped by 85%.*

*And love and fascination: because Melbourne has always reminded me of Gotham City, a city with a darkness that holds unmeasured strangeness. I don't know what was under the water in this story, but whatever it is, when I look at the Yarra, I can believe it's there. That's the thing about Melbourne.*

# ROTA FORTUNAE

Harold stepped through the door, nudging his round spectacles higher on the bridge of his nose as a clanging cowbell announced his presence. Inside the concrete building, the air was thick with congealed age that squirmed up Harold's nostrils and coated his throat like mucous. Industrial washing machines lined one lime-green wall, rumbling and bouncing their way through cycles. The chipped linoleum floor was scattered with shelves bearing random goods: faded cereal boxes, shrivelled potatoes, and tins of shoe polish lay together, strange bedfellows huddled under threadbare blankets of dust.

A woman stood behind a counter at the far end of the store. Her steel grey hair was pulled into a bun that wrenched her flesh up into a vague semblance of features. She looked hard beneath her loose skin, like a bank vault encased in jelly. Several wristwatches were lashed to each of her forearms. A badge was pinned to the left breast of her shapeless nurse's uniform: Welcome to Zarathustra's!

"Excuse me." Harold crossed the store and stood across the counter from the woman, knuckling his glasses into place again. "This is a little embarrassing. I can't quite recall how I got here, but I'm trying to get to a doctor's appointment. I wonder if you might—"

"You need to go out the back and take the elevator." The woman's voice was stagnant with boredom. She moved a cloth around on the countertop. It stayed within a well-worn circle surrounded by unrelenting filth.

"Oh. Unusual location for a doctor, isn't it? Above a—what is this place, exactly? A laundromat and general store combined?"

"We have lots of things here," the woman intoned. A fat black fly crawled across her slack cheek and burrowed into her hair, buzzing intimately.

"Yes . . . well, as I said, I'm not sure how I—"

The woman jerked a thumb over her shoulder, indicating a doorway lined with dangling beads. The gesture was clear: *Go. There. Now.* The weathered skin on the back of her hand cracked under the sudden movement, leaking a runnel of watery brown blood. The watches on her arm slipped, seeming to strain towards her open wound.

"Right," Harold said, less politely. The woman's eyes fixed on her cloth as she engaged in a frenzy of ineffectual scrubbing. Harold stepped around the counter. *One foot in front of the other*, he told himself, heading toward the beaded doorway as the laundromat-store canted askew around him. *You're sick. The doctor will help.* A gaudy Hawaiian mural was splattered in visceral colour on the beads, all bleeding red sky and tortured bent palm trees. Harold reached out and parted the tacky curtain with trembling hands.

"What the . . . " Harold stared. A tantalising knowledge danced within the darkest recesses of his mind; a memory, capering and taunting him with its secrets.

*(been here before)*

No elevator. No stairs. Nothing. Just the small, stark rectangular chamber, and the sound of Harold's rapid breathing.

◆ ◆ ◆

Well, not *nothing*, exactly; just nothing useful.

The room resembled a junk store. Broken appliances and furniture cluttered the narrow space. A boxy TV with dials removed crouched like a wood-panelled gargoyle. Beneath it, a three-legged card table leant in stubborn defiance of gravity. An army of old-fashioned transistor radios marched atop a splintered sideboard, interspersed with misshapen clusters of semi-melted wax fruit. Posters advertising cigarettes—You'll wish you had an extra lung when you suck on Nico's Slims!—flaked from the walls like dying flowers.

About to quit the room and demand that the laconic woman at the front counter give him proper directions, Harold spotted the chair opposite him. The black leather gleamed like the oiled skin of a sunbather, dimpled with metal studs. On a shelf behind the wing-backed chair, a silver microwave sparkled, clean and modern.

Harold stepped closer and read the buttons on the machine.

UP, half of them announced.

DOWN, the other half declared.

"What is this?" Harold's voice had acquired a strange timbre in the fusty air. It frightened him.

*The doctor . . .*

Harold looked down at the floor. A fracture ran through the concrete in a ring around the chair he leant over. Harold let his heavy head flop backwards, staring up at the cobwebbed ceiling. The same faint circle marred the roof, directly above the chair.

*Alright.*

Harold sat in the chair. The leather felt sensuous and mobile against him, and he shuddered. Twisting around in the seat, spine crackling and popping, he pressed a finger to one of the buttons marked UP. The button was warm and soft. Harold recoiled and faced forward, sitting stiffly.

The chair rose, borne aloft on the ascending circle of floor beneath it. It carried Harold up, and he craned his neck, realising for the first time that he might be crushed against the ceiling. The ever-increasing height Harold perched at sent zaps of electric panic darting through his brain. As if sensing his alarm, the chair seemed to press closer to him. He squirmed, loathing its clingy touch. The ceiling slid open above him, the round segment dropping and shifting aside. A puff of dust coated Harold's upturned face, tickling and making him sneeze.

Then he was up and out, blinking in the sudden bright light.

◆  ◆  ◆

*Finally*, was his first thought, but something felt very wrong.

*(even if you remember it won't help you)*

Harold sat in a doctor's office. Rosy floorboards shone from beneath the edges of several overlapping rugs. A mahogany desk littered with medical detritus—stethoscope, prescription pad, thermometer—consumed a quarter of the room. Warm sunshine beamed in through several wide windows. A line from an old Jim Carrey movie leapt unbidden into Harold's mind. *This is a lovely room of death, take care now, bye-bye then.*

The doctor's room had two doors, both closed, one on either side of Harold. To the right, Harold could hear *The Time Warp* from The Rocky Horror Show blaring, the beat pounding against the wood like an intruder demanding entry. To the left was silence. Harold looked from one door to the other, his head swinging like a pendulum. Left, peace. Right, *Time Warp*. Left, peace. Right, *Time Warp* . . . and something else.

Rising from the chair and moving over to the vibrating door, Harold steeled himself against the raucous music, and pressed an ear to the wood. Two voices rumbled beneath the merry beat.

" . . . so I told her, you can just get something over-the-counter for that, it's nothing but a common fungus."

"Good work, Elsie. You've saved her time and mine. She's a worrier, that Mrs Jinks, but she means well, dear old love."

"Yes, doctor. Now, I need you to look at this pathology report that's come back for Mr Krupp . . . "

*The doctor and receptionist.* Harold stumbled away from the door, the merciless music repelling him. *I've got an appointment. I should pop my head out and tell them I'm here.*

Instead, Harold scurried across the room, crouching low, his heart a frightened bird fluttering against the bars of his ribcage. Grasping the door handle of the other door—the *quiet* one— Harold moved to pull it open.

Music shrieked into life. Harold's hand dropped from the doorhandle, his mouth stretching into a startled O. On the other side of the once-quiet door, Cher wailed throatily at him about everything she'd do, if only she could turn back time.

Jagged red letters were slashed across the door, right in front of Harold's eyes. *TEMPIS FUGIT,* they informed him, their paint still wet, trickling down the polished wood like too-bright movie blood. Harold's knees quivered, and he knew he wouldn't be opening that door.

*(not this time but you have other times, oh yes, oh ho)*
*The doctor. I have to . . .*

"Oh, fuck it," he said, standing and striding back to the chair he'd rode in on.

Squatting down until his nose almost touched the sparkling floorboards, Harold saw the faint ring around the base of the leather chair. About to straighten up and settle into the chair— never mind the fact that there was no queer microwave with elevator buttons here, he'd *find a way*, dammit—Harold saw the floor-circle shimmer and disappear.

*No!*

*(you* could *have gone if you'd tried sooner, but you're too late. You always are. And where would you go, late boy?)*

The doctor's office was silent. Harold tore open the door on the right hand side.

There was no throbbing *Time Warp* now. A shocked silence permeated the hall. A few metres away, a portly man with a gleaming pink skull and gin-blossomed cheeks leant on a counter, pen poised in hand. Across the counter stood a small elderly woman, tightly bound in prim skirt and jacket, one hand fluttering to smooth her blue-rinsed curls. Their mouths hung open as they stared at Harold standing bedraggled and panting in the open door.

"I have an *appointment*!" Harold shrieked. "D'you hear me? An appointment! I demand to be seen, *now*!"

◆ ◆ ◆

"Well," the doctor said, "I think perhaps we'd best check the book, Elsie."

The little receptionist's deft hands flicked through a leather-bound tome on her desk. Her veiny finger traced a page from top to bottom, and she shook her head ruefully. "No, doctor, there's no other appointments today. You've seen everyone."

"Harold Jensen!" Harold spoke with more self control, but he couldn't quite stop the trembling in his hands. "My name is Harold Jensen. Look for that."

"What time, Mr Jensen?" Elsie's courteous enquiry was mocking. Harold frowned at her as the hall spun once, twice, three times. He staggered, and steadied himself against the doorframe.

"I'm not sure. I can't remember. I'm sick."

"Yes, Mr Jensen, everyone who comes here is. But I really do need to know . . . oh, there you are!" Elsie's twisted finger stabbed the page with sudden glee. "You were scheduled for 2pm! But, oh dear, it's 4pm now, Mr Jensen."

"You're rather late, aren't you?" The doctor spoke with evident grief. *There's not a lot that can be done now,* his tone implied.

"I don't know. Am I?" Harold's nerves gave a sudden agonising shriek. "I don't wear a watch." He sidled out of the doorframe and along the wall, feeling with his hands, his eyes glued to the doctor and receptionist. They stared back at him, their too-wide smiles hungry, their skin hanging loose on their bones like costumes that didn't fit. Harold saw the wristwatches on their arms, at least ten aside, and noticed the five clocks on the wall behind Elsie.

*(tempis fugit, Harold Jensen, and you're tempis fucked!)*

"You're late," the doctor insisted, and his smile was gone, leaving gaping emptiness in its place.

"Late, late, for a very important date," Elsie trilled.

"What are you?" Harold whispered, creeping ever backwards. "Where am I?"

"Chained to the wheel," Elsie sang. A fly hopped from her mouth and crawled onto her wrinkled cheek, its wings a buzz-saw scream. Another pushed forth from her left nostril, droning to her forehead and grooming itself below the balcony of her blue coif.

"How do I leave?" Harold felt yet another closed door in the wall behind him, and his convulsing fingers searched for a handle.

"You don't," Elsie said, and her mouth yawned open, a dark chasm ringed with gangrenous teeth. Countless blowflies streamed forth in a mindless wave, their plump bodies grotesque and round, their wings carrying them toward Harold with mnemonic relentlessness.

"But I will," Harold promised her as his fingers finally found the doorhandle. He spun, wrenched the door open, and threw himself through it, pulling it closed so hard that his arm reverberated with the impact. Flies peppered against the other side like bullets. He slumped to the ground, tears streaming from his eyes and fogging up his glasses.

"It's no use," a woman's voice announced. "There's no escape."

Harold screamed.

◆ ◆ ◆

"Sorry!" The woman was no older than twenty-five. She stood with her hands held out towards Harold, her blue eyes lined with red. "Don't be scared of me. I'm like you. I've been here for a long time and there's just no way out."

The room fell silent as the flies stopped hammering against the door. Nothing moved beyond it. Harold used the closed door to stand, sliding up with the wood supporting his aching back.

"Where are we?" His voice was quiet, but they both jumped.

*(twitchy, aintcha)*

"I don't know. I can only remember bits and pieces of my time here. Like *those* things out there." She pointed at the door behind Harold. "They're not even people." Her shoulders jerked as she spoke. Harold saw that a section of her blonde hair had been torn out at the roots near her temple. Globules of clotted blood stippled her pale skin. Her face was mottled with purple-black bruises and long, deep gashes lined her bare arms.

"We've been kidnapped," Harold said, but he knew it was a long shot. "Someone brought us here. We're drugged."

"No. That's not it. I'm not sure we're even . . . " she trailed off, shuddering. "Anyway. I'm Amber." She stretched one hand closer to him. He took it and squeezed, and didn't let go.

"Harold."

"Well, it sure is nice to meet you, Harold. Now what the hell do we do?"

"I'll get us out. I have these hunches—"

*(BEEN HERE BEFORE LATE BOY KEEP TELLIN' YA)*

"—and I know there's a way out. We just have to find it."

"Yeah," Amber said dully. "Ok. Sure. Whatever."

"Trust me," Harold said, and pulled Amber with him across the room. He paused to see if the door behind them would burst open and the awful not-doctor and his sidekick would rush in, all death-flies and waxy un-skin, but nothing happened. Sighing, he dragged Amber on into the ill defined half light.

◆ ◆ ◆

They'd stumbled through endless corridors and chambers when Harold finally saw it. "Get in," he urged Amber, pointing to the refrigerator standing in the corner of the empty room.

"You're kidding," she said, yanking her hand free of his. "It's a *fridge*."

"You think that means anything in here? *Really* look at it. This room is a pigsty—everything is filthy and old, except that fridge.

It's sparkling new. You don't think that's significant? I got in here using a microwave—"

"You *what*?"

"—and we're getting out using that fridge. There'll be buttons somewhere inside. Some will say 'down'. You're getting in, and you're pressing one of those buttons. You're doing it first, because I don't trust you to do it if I'm not here to make you, and I don't want to leave you here."

Amber stared at him, her face hard. She opened her mouth to speak, and the door handle across the room rattled. "There you both are," the doctor said as he stepped in, the skin of his face now hanging in juicy red-white flaps around his collar. His eyes swivelled in his exposed skull, and a long purple tongue emerged and lapped at his skeleton-teeth. "We've been looking for you. You're both late, you know."

"*Tempis fugit*," Harold said. Elsie appeared behind the doctor, buzzing with flies. Only her eyes and hair were visible, blue and ugly.

"Oh, that's *good*," Elsie enthused, flies cramming themselves into her mouth as she spoke. "You're learning. Now, come here. We can help you."

"Get *in*," Harold hissed at Amber. She backed across the room. The fridge door hung ajar, and she kicked it fully open. Harsh fluorescent light spilled out, revealing a gleaming white interior devoid of shelves. Harold could see the panel of buttons on the rear interior of the fridge. Amber clambered into the fridge. The rear of her shirt was torn open, her exposed back a mess of oozing weals and pulpy wounds. Blood ran down her legs and pooled atop her white cotton socks. Harold tasted bile in his mouth.

"Help us," he sneered at Elsie. "I can see you've *helped* Amber real good. But you won't be helping us anymore." There was a quiet *pop* in the corner of the room, and the fridge light flickered. When Harold turned to look, the fridge was empty.

*Good. She's out. Now run over there and get the hell out of here yourself.*

(SEE YOU AGAIN REAL SOON)

"Get him *now*, Elsie," the un-doctor hissed, and Harold made a run for it. He threw himself across the room with the last remaining strength and speed in his weary body. He leapt into the fridge with such force that it rocked and threatened to tumble, and he braced his feet against the smooth interior, holding his curled-up body in place. He reached for the panel of buttons now facing him . . . and stopped.

*Oh, shit.*

There had to be a hundred of them. Most of them showed clock-faces with various times. A few said TEMPIS FUGIT. As he watched, one of them wavered and changed to read OH SHIT. Many said TOO LATE.

"You can't get out," Elsie said behind him, her crypt-breath scouring the nape of his neck. "You're ours. *Mine.*"

Then Harold saw it. "Sorry, you're not my type. A little old," he said over his shoulder as he thumbed the small button at the bottom of the panel. "And the flies are a real turn off."

DOWN, the button said in glorious redemptive letters.

"No!" Elsie's furious howl of loss was already receding.

The ride this time was fast and furious, and Harold was smashed against the fridge's interior so hard his spectacles cracked. He didn't care.

◆　◆　◆

Harold fell out of the fridge and sucked in ancient dust as he landed face-down on the floor. It tasted like freedom, and he laughed, giddy. Lifting his head and squinting through the unbroken section of his glasses, Harold took in the room he'd caught the microwave-elevator from. The chair was gone—upstairs where he'd left it, presumably—but the microwave remained on its perch, twinkling at him.

"*Now* where the hell are we?" Amber leant on the unbalanced card table, arms crossed over her chest. She was smiling. Old tears had engraved pale stripes in her grime-darkened face. She looked like a pleased Zebra.

"Can you feel it too?" Harold clambered to his feet and grinned. His bunched cheeks shifted his glasses on his nose, and suddenly he was looking through shattered fragments at a warped world. His grin wilted, and he adjusted his glasses.

"Well, I feel better than I did up *there*," she answered, jerking her thumb at the ceiling. "I feel like we're close to freedom, if we can just get this right."

"That's exactly it." Harold pointed at the garish Hawaiian bead curtain. "There's a woman in the shop beyond. We'll talk to her."

"Is she . . . " Amber bit her bottom lip. "One of us?"

"I think so." Harold headed for the curtain. "Though I'm not sure she knows it."

"You *think* so? Harold, wait!" Amber sounded frightened, but he ignored her, pushing through the beads and entering the shop. The woman was still at the counter, wiping in slow circles, eyes downcast. After a moment, Amber appeared at Harold's elbow.

"That's her," Harold said redundantly. Amber raised an eyebrow.

"She doesn't look right," she whispered.

"No. But that doesn't make her one of them." Harold crossed the shop, the rumbling of the washers on the wall vibrating up through the floor into his body. He stood once more across the counter from the woman. He waved a hand in front of her vacant face. She didn't look at him.

"HEY!" Amber cupped her hands between her lips and the woman's ear. The woman jumped, nostrils flaring, and dropped her cloth. Her eyelashes fluttered, and knowledge swam into her eyes as she stared in horror at Harold and Amber.

"You can't be here," she muttered, fingers crawling on the counter like pale blind worms.

"Well, we are." Harold told her. "And we're leaving, and you're coming, too."

"Yes," the woman said, one of her grey hairs snapping loose from her tight bun and drifting to the floor. "Leaving."

Amber clasped the woman's elbow, her fingers sinking deep into the flaccid flesh. She threw Harold a disgusted look, and steered the woman around the counter. Harold strode ahead and opened the door.

CLANG. The cowbell above the door was loud and discordant in the dusty silence. Harold's heart stammered in his chest.

◆　◆　◆

"Who are you?" As soon as they crossed the threshold of the store and stood on the red dust outside, hot air buffeting their skin, the store woman shrugged free of Amber's grip.

Harold exhaled in relief. "I'm Harold, and this is Amber. We don't remember how we got here."

"Hi," Amber said, waving. In the outdoor air, her cheeks took on a healthy hue, and her blonde hair fluttered on the breeze like fragile butterfly wings.

"Hello, Harold, Amber. I'm Bea. Now . . . there's a chairlift of some sort round the back, and I think . . . yes, I'm quite sure. It's the only way out of here." Bea swept a hand in front of her, indicating the horizon. The red dirt they stood on tapered away to nothing, and beyond it, sparse grassland stretched as far as Harold's searching eyes could see in all directions. The land was flat and empty. Harold thought you could wander it forever and never find any end, any divergence.

"Harold?" Amber stared at him. "Do you think we should . . . ?"

"We have to," he told her. "What else can we do?"

"It's just . . . " Amber leant and whispered in his ear. "This feels familiar, too. I feel like . . . this isn't right."

"You're just nervous, after all you've been through. All *we've* been through." He patted her arm.

Bea walked ahead of them, leading them around the building. Her ample hips swayed beneath her strange uniform. A fly droned around her head, trying to land. She waved it away.

"Hurry," she threw over her shoulder. "We don't want to be late."

◆ ◆ ◆

The basket stood at the base of a steep hill that reared up behind the building. It was purple, and Harold though of the doctor-thing's tongue.

"That's it," Bea said, inclining her head toward the basket. It was connected to a thick steel cable that ran up to another, higher, cable suspended from poles driven into the earth. The rickety 'chairlift' ran up and over the hill, out of sight. "We have to get in and go."

"I don't like it." Amber hung back.

Bea glared at the blonde woman. "It's the only way."

"There *isn't* a way," Amber insisted, tears spilling down her cheeks, carving new tracks in the old dirt there. "We're here forever."

"Amber, if I have to pick you up and carry you, you're getting in. I'm not leaving you." Harold pointed at the purple basket. Amber laughed.

"Oh, I'll get in. What difference does it make, really?" She crossed the red dirt and stepped into the basket. It wobbled beneath her, the steel cable tightening, the basket already beginning to lift.

"Quickly!" Bea waddled over to the basket and vaulted in, surprisingly nimble. Harold ran after her, having to reach up to grasp the rim of the basket as it took off above his head. Bea grasped his wrist and hauled, and he swung his legs up, climbing-tumbling into the basket. It rocked like a cradle, at once soothing and unsettling. The wind grew sharper as they rose with startling speed.

"There, look," Bea said, pointing down at the shrinking store. "It's a one-storey building. How could you have gone upstairs?"

"We . . . didn't mention the fact that we did," Harold said. "Besides which, you're the one who sent me upstairs in the first place."

*(catching on now, late boy)*

Bea chuckled. "Don't waste time thinking about it. Time is fleeting, you know."

"Oh God," Amber moaned, hunkered on the base of the basket's interior, arms wrapped around herself. Harold crouched next to her, pressed his body against hers. She was cold.

"I'm sorry," he told her. "I should have listened to you."

"It's ok," Amber said. "I don't think you ever do. And I don't think it matters. Everything leads to the same point here, eventually."

"Hush, now," Bea said, smiling down at them. "You're right where you're meant to be. Just enjoy the ride." A fly wriggled out of her ear. She slapped, smearing it on her cheek in a gory black stripe. Harold saw the fly's tiny white guts and closed his eyes.

"Hold me, Harold," Amber moaned. Harold wrapped his arms around her. She clung to him, and, heads bowed on each other's shoulders, they rode in silent despair as the basket rose ever upward.

◆ ◆ ◆

"Why, hello, late boy." The voice was harsh, and Harold had heard it before, on a loop in his head. He looked up to see a large red-gloved hand descend and ensnare his shoulder. He was yanked from the basket and sent sprawling in the dust. "And my little late girl, back as always. You're both most welcome." Amber hit the dirt beside him, gasping and clawing at her waist where Red Gloves had grabbed her. Harold shuffled across the dusty ground to her side. She gazed at him with wide, unblinking eyes.

"Welcome to the top of the hill. This is my place, and yours for the next few moments, too. I . . . " Harold looked up to see Red Gloves—a tall, plain man with a jaunty bowler hat perched atop his head like an accountant dressed as a circus ringmaster—sigh. "Oh, I *do* get sick of this spiel. Every day the same damn thing."

"You deserve it," Bea said, clicking her tongue. *Tsk, tsk.* "It's your due for never knuckling down to the mundane rhythm of your living years. And it's better than some. God, all I did was fail to clean my shop regularly. You're not doing so bad."

"Shut up, bitch, I know that." Red Gloves snarled sidelong at Bea, who rolled her eyes. "Doesn't mean I like it. Look, here's the deal, ok?" He turned back to Harold and Amber. "You're to be thrown to the dogs. It's your punishment—*this* time around—for always being late when you were alive. You," Red Gloves pointed at Harold, "Always turned up late for doctor's appointments, or not at all. And you," the tall man jabbed a finger at Amber, who flinched, "Were a good five minutes late for work every day. *And* you left early!"

Harold looked around for the first time. A ring of oversized kennels surrounded them, bedecked in loud colours. Red Gloves skipped across the dirt and paced the line of kennels, rapping on the roof of each. He muttered under his breath.

"What is this place?" Amber struggled to her feet and stood swaying, looking at Bea. "At least tell us that much."

"The fifteen thousand, nine hundred and seventy sixth circle of Hell, dear." Bea yawned. A millipede tumbled from her lips and squirmed sightlessly in the dust at her feet. "Reserved for shirkers, latecomers, and the untidy. Not such a bad place, once you get used to it. Although you probably never will," she added, eyeing their bare wrists. "Without time, you've got no perspective to cling to, have you?" She patted her own wrist, caressing the multitude of watches strapped there.

"Hell." Harold's voice was flat as the first low growl carried to them from the kennels. "We've gone to Hell for being a bit late sometimes."

"Well, of course you have." Bea looked at them as if their brains had suddenly started to drip from their noses—which wasn't such a ridiculous prospect in this place. "It's not about *whether* you come here—every single last one of us does—it's only about which circle you go to."

Something emerged from the kennel nearest Harold and Amber. It was a hulking, misshapen thing, padding on all fours with cruel stealth. Its claws drew crooked lines in the dust, stretching a metre from its . . . paws?

"Oh God," Amber cried. "It's human."

Harold realised she was right. The 'dog' was a bent and twisted woman, horribly disfigured. It reached his feet and sniffed, staring up at him with baleful eyes. Its face was painted—a dog's cartoon face, of course. Its teeth were hoary tusks, jutting from under its top lip. A string of saliva swung like spider silk from its chin. It snarled, a wet sound deep in its throat.

"Now, just wait a second," Harold said.

"You haven't got a second," Red Gloves jeered. "You're far, far, far too late."

The dog-thing leapt. Amber screamed. Harold was borne to the ground by heavy, stinking weight. Savage pain burst into being in his neck as the dog tore into him with its many teeth. Harold felt hot wetness flood onto his chest and spatter his face. He couldn't fight, couldn't move, pinned by the thing's body. A desperate sob bubbled out of him, unheard and unheeded.

The light started to ebb from Harold's world. His fingers tingled and went numb as his arms sagged at his sides. The world around him slid sideways again, and he had the sensation that he was suspended on an immense wheel, spinning endlessly through time and space.

"Remember, Harold!" Amber's voice was distant. "That's our only chance to stop all this . . . remember next time, before it's too late!"

(next time, *that's funny because next time will be this time will be last time if we have no time at all*)

A thud, a scream, and wet snuffling ended Amber's pleas, and Harold slipped into oblivion with gratitude.

◆ ◆ ◆

Harold stepped through the door, nudging his round spectacles higher on the bridge of his nose as a clanging cowbell announced his presence.

# AFTERWORD

*This story was a dream I had, apropos of nothing. I added some details and changed others, but it still represents, more or less, an accurate retelling of the original dream from start to finish. It's the only time in my life I've had a dream, woken up, thought it remarkable, and written it all down with the intention of making it a short story. I almost feel like I "cheated"—like the story was placed into my head fully formed and all I had to do was take an ethereal sort of dictation from the* real *author. Which isn't true at all, of course—I still had to put in the usual hard slog and edit and rewrite and polish, etc. I'm quite taken with reflecting on time from an emotional and mental perspective (as opposed to scientific), and playing with that, with a touch of uneasy subconscious dread thrown in. It's a theme that's creeping into a lot of my newer work, this piece included. I hope to continue to grow that idea and develop it in future stories. Oh—and "Rota Fortunae" means "wheel of fortune". It's an ancient concept/allegory still reflected on today . . . and not just on game shows.*

# NEPENTHE

Dahlia buried the key to her heart beneath the weeping willow in her backyard at 3am on a Tuesday. The loneliness of the hour suited Dahlia's sense of melodrama, and she enjoyed the sly night wind's sharp black teeth against her bare skin. She hiccupped out a satisfying sob or two as moist dirt caked under her fingernails. Her muscles sang of their exertion to the rhythmic beat of *throb-burn-ache*.

"Bury it deep," said the Secret Squirrel, appearing at her elbow, his electric red tail bristling. His teeth were bright pegs in the gloom, and his gimlet eyes sparkled with anti-light. "If you don't, it will rise and find you."

Dahlia cast an irritated glance at the creature. "I don't need your help," she hissed. Her words snaked through the chill air, tangible with venom. "I know what I'm doing."

The Squirrel looked up, the tilt of his downy head mischievous. "Waxing gibbous," he said to the anaemic moon above. "A good choice, I'll admit. And yet, I'm not sure that you *do* know what you're doing. It is not as easy as you might think to lock up your heart and throw away the key."

"Well, nonetheless, it is done." Dahlia leant back on her haunches, damp soil squirting into the intimate spaces between her toes and making her shiver. The night wind's bite grew hungrier and more perverse, and she regretted her ceremonial nakedness.

"Now you cannot love, and neither can you hate. You are absolved of the weight of your secrets, but you are cursed with the burden of emptiness. You are a shell, and you may think that a boon, but in truth—"

"Shut up, stupid beast. I've fed you. I've completed the ritual. Now go away." Dahlia lashed out, her clawed hand lusting for the Squirrel's soft cheeks. The creature was suddenly perched on the fence far away from Dahlia, untouched and unruffled. Dahlia snarled, but even as she clambered to her feet, she felt the ire draining out of her. She swayed, her limbs drooping like the willow's as nullity thickened her blood.

"So be it," the Squirrel sighed. "When you want your heart back, you know where to find me."

"I'll never want it back," Dahlia said, her eyes clouding over.

The Squirrel grinned at her. "Oh, you will. Everyone does, sooner or later."

In a flash of phosphorescent chestnut fur, the Squirrel was gone, and Dahlia was alone. This didn't bother her. Nothing could bother Dahlia now.

She staggered inside and fell into bed, dirt pattering from her skin to her white sheets like black rain on tundra. Sleep took her in its gritty arms and cradled her reluctantly, for the heartless are loathsome to touch.

◆ ◆ ◆

One year, one month, one week, and one day later, Dahlia met Angus at the corner store. He mistook the gaping void behind her eyes for intriguing aloofness, and although Angus didn't much care for news, he developed a sudden commitment to buying the Daily Express at the same time Dahlia did every morning.

Angus conveyed his adoration to her through handwritten poetry, his perfect iambic pentameter reaching with black-and-white fingers for the cavity in her chest and finding . . . nothing. Spurred to new heights of ardour, he left trails of pink-red-white rose petals on Dahlia's front porch leading to thoughtful personal gifts: autumn leaves the colour of her hair pressed between the pages of *Wuthering Heights*, chocolates he'd made himself with gemstones winking at her from each gleaming cacao peak, exotic herbal teas to compliment her every mood. Dahlia picked up each gift and regarded it blankly before slipping into her house and closing the door.

Once inside, she stood staring into space as Angus' bounty tumbled from her stultified fingers to the dusty floor. She thought of the key buried in her backyard, and of the Secret Squirrel's words.

Angus asked Dahlia if she would like to go to dinner with him. Dahlia informed him that she didn't care, and he took that as a promising sign. After several dates, Angus pushed his luck and asked if he might move into Dahlia's house with her, since his own lease was up and they were getting on so well. Dahlia announced that it really didn't matter to her one way or the other, and Angus was ecstatic.

Watching Angus' broad shoulders bunching and shifting beneath his shirt as he scrubbed the grime of neglect off her floors, Dahlia thought she might feel grateful, if she could feel anything at all. Angus turned and bestowed a radiant smile on her, his hand lifting to push a stray lock of russet hair from his sweaty brow. Dahlia thought she might find that irresistible, if she could love.

The day dropped into night, and the sly wind wheezed against the windows.

"I'm going outside," Dahlia told Angus. "Don't follow me."

The ground beneath the Willow was caked with frost and hard as a diamond at first, but Dahlia couldn't feel pain, so she punched and scraped and gouged until her broken fingers broke through. The soil grew warm and soft with Dahlia's blood the deeper she dug, and her hands soon found treasure.

Pulling the filthy brass key out, Dahlia stood and held it aloft.

"Unlock my heart," she said in a bored voice, and waited.

The Squirrel failed to appear, and after a while, Dahlia trudged back inside, the heavy key bouncing in her dressing gown pocket. She would have been disappointed, if she could mourn.

◆　◆　◆

Dahlia couldn't breathe.

Her eyelids flew apart like broken shutters. The Secret Squirrel sat on her chest, crushing her lungs with its considerable weight. It held her key angled downward in its fuzzy paws, a dagger aimed at her heart.

"Are you sure you want this?" it whispered.

Unfortunately, Dahlia was unable to feel fear, or suspicion. She looked at Angus lying fast asleep next to her, his eyelashes dark smudges of soot on his pale skin. She looked back at the Squirrel, whose nose was twitching with excitement. It gave her a ravenous smile, its teeth creamy-sick-yellow in the early morning half-light. Its eyes were sunken craters and its cheeks were no more than jutting bones.

"Yes," she gasped, the words struggling free from her compressed diaphragm. "I want to feel Angus' love. I want to love him back."

It occurred to Dahlia that *wanting* was a sort of feeling in and of itself, and something important stirred in her brain, demanding her attention. She would have frowned and concentrated on figuring that something out, if she cared—but, of course, she didn't. Couldn't.

"So be it," the Squirrel intoned, and plunged the key into her chest. It sank through her flesh and parted her bone and met with the pulsing red muscle beneath. The Squirrel gave it a savage twist, and suddenly Dahlia felt quite a lot of things all at once. She whooped and wailed, her hands and feet drumming an idiot rhythm on the mattress.

Angus jerked awake and sat up, knuckling his eyes and staring in horror as the object of his affection danced toward her death beside him. He reached for Dahlia and opened his mouth to speak, but froze as the Squirrel leapt nimbly from Dahlia's thrashing body.

"Wait," it said. "I've given her back her secrets. You should know what it is that you think you love."

Blackness oozed from Dahlia's chest, welling and congealing around the shaft of the key. Her skin bubbled and rippled, bruising purple-green-brown and sinking in on itself like rotting fruit. Angus was apoplectic with shock by the time Dahlia's body collapsed into gangrenous slush, an indecipherable Rorschach pattern on the bed linen.

"Now," the Squirrel said, "see her heart."

It lay in the decomposing muck, vivid scarlet, pulsing and thrumming as the key fell out of it with a soft *plink*. As Angus choked back bile, Dahlia's heart shimmered and changed. Suddenly, a mongrel dog was crouching low in its place, yelping in pain as its small body received blow upon blow from an invisible assailant.

"Dahlia liked to play with stray dogs," the Squirrel said, shaking its iridescent head.

The dog warped and elongated, becoming an old woman, lying fragile and prone on the sheets as a hypodermic syringe gripped by an unseen hand slid into her arm. The woman's filmy eyes rolled back in her head as her miasmic body was wracked with spasms.

"Dahlia nursed people to their doom," the Squirrel announced. "Healthy people. The elderly were her favourites."

Tears streamed from Angus' eyes.

The old woman wavered and shrunk, becoming a boy of no more than five years old, his eyes wide with terror and his plump lower lip trembling.

"No," Angus murmured, finding his voice at last. The Squirrel's ebony eyes twinkled.

"Dahlia's favourite place for kidnapping children was the shopping mall. She snatched dozens of them, and grew ever more crafty and vicious."

"Make it stop," Angus pleaded, looking away.

The Secret Squirrel lifted a paw to its tufted chin, considering. "Would you like to forget it all?"

"Oh, yes," Angus breathed.

"Would you like to remove the part of yourself connected to this?"

"Yes."

"Lock it away? Never see or feel or know it again?"

"Yes, yes, yes."

The Squirrel leant forward, its wet nose almost touching Angus' own. The whimpering phantasm of a small long-dead boy evaporated with a *whoosh*, leaving the juicy mass of Dahlia's wicked heart in its place once more. The Squirrel's breath carried the fetid odour of the grave. Angus pursed his lips and concentrated on not being sick.

"I pity you, man-fooled-in-love, and so I'll take it all," the Squirrel said, its long pink tongue unfurling and lapping delicately at Angus' lips. "I've an appetite for such things, and it's been a while between meals."

Once begun, Angus discovered that divesting oneself of one's secrets was a very painful process indeed.

◆ ◆ ◆

Angus buried his key alongside Dahlia's dead heart beneath a rosebush at 4pm on a Saturday. The sun was whimsical on his bare skin, and he revelled in its amber kiss, his mind filled with melancholy thoughts of unread newspapers and Dahlia's limpid green eyes. Already his agony was receding to a dull focus, his chest hollowing out. Blood flowed from a thorn-prick in his finger, dripping onto the key and staining its silver hilt crimson as he hid it beneath the willing earth.

"Bury it deep," said the Secret Squirrel, its chubby face solemn. Something slimy and loathsome marred its gravestone teeth.

"I have," Angus answered, rising to his feet, his joints crackle-popping as the feeling ebbed from his body and joined the silver key in the ground. He would have wept if he could, if he was able to identify the relief coursing through him.

"It's never deep enough," the Squirrel said. "I'll come back when you're ready."

Angus raised a lethargic hand in farewell as the Squirrel bounded away over the fence. He sank to the ground as the sun melted into the horizon. Curling into the foetal position, Angus opened his clenched fist, revealing a tiny copper key hung on a strand of curious chestnut hair. He'd seen it—the greatest secret of all—glinting and winking amid the dense forestation of the Secret Squirrel's chest fur. He'd pilfered the necklace from around the creature's throat, after it began to feed on him, but before his senses had abandoned him to his pain.

"You'll come back, alright," he told the deepening dusk. "But not for my sake. And I will definitely be ready."

# AFTERWORD

*"Nepenthe" is, to put it simply, a drug for forgetting. It's been mentioned throughout a lot of literature over the ages, but I personally first came across it in Edgar Allen Poe's "The Raven" (my favourite poem). I find it a beautiful word, and an intriguing concept, and that's what this story is built upon: beautiful words (I hope!) and an intriguing concept. The title's application here is probably fairly obvious, in the void of non-emotion, non-memory, and thus non-pain between the literal and metaphorical hiding away of hearts and unlocking of them. This is a strange little piece, hard to love, and not my usual style. I like it for that reason. It's jagged, it doesn't sit right, and it makes me uncomfortable. I hope it has the same effect on readers.*

# THE FEMALE OF THE SPECIES IS MORE DEADLY THAN THE MALE

Waking up dying is the worst feeling in the world.

I don't know where I am. There's light and noise and too many people, but all that matters is the air that I can't get into my lungs. The pain and the panic. I'm choking, clawing at my throat. Tears stream down my cheeks. A woman—she's all in white and has a little clock clipped to her chest pocket, a nurse?—leans into my narrowing field of vision. She takes my hands away from my neck, holds them firmly but kindly, squeezes them. We're moving, me being wheeled flat on my back, she running alongside me.

"Don't cry," she says, as tears slip from her own eyes. I see death in those eyes, and pity, and they both terrify me. My limbs are tingling and my head is buzzing and I don't want this unknown woman to be the last thing I ever see, and there's no air, *no air!*

"Shhh. Please . . . don't cry."

◆　◆　◆

The car found me. I think that's the way these things always work. You can't just go out and buy something like that. It's not for sale. It smells you, it hunts you down, and then it owns *you.*

I'd been home from the hospital for only a few hours. Dominic had just left for work. He was subdued, but given that he'd almost killed me, that was to be expected. Guilt seeped from his pores, sour and stale, and it sickened me. Still, I comforted him. *It's alright, I love you. It wasn't your fault. It was my choice too, and I made it.* And the biggest lie of all: *I'm ok.* I couldn't help myself. I was the one with a bleeding hole in my womb and my heart, but I needed to make him feel better about it. Otherwise he might leave me. All else beyond that unthinkable thought was panicky technicolour oblivion, yawning open like a mouth waiting to consume me. A mouth lined with countless teeth.

Anyway, the car.

I sat at my computer to check my emails, looked out the window, and there it was in the driveway where Dominic's car had been less than an hour ago. My stomach twisted, but then again, it'd been doing that pretty much non-stop since The Procedure a week ago. My hands trembled on the keyboard, stopped moving altogether. Everything slowed around me, receding into obscurity, the car the only clear point upon which to look. And I did look. I stared at the car in a moment that stretched like chewing gum. It seemed I could hear faint music, or maybe it was whispering voices, or just the sly wind.

I'm not a car person. I don't use words like "beautiful" to describe them. But this one was. Glossy black, with a fat red stripe running the length of the roof. It was boxy and old in structure— vintage. Large silver lettering just above the front bumper spelt: DODGE.

"Dodge what?" I asked my empty living room. Didn't those fancy American cars usually have cute names, like Viper, or Ram, or Daddy Pays My Bills?

Sunlight hit the car's windscreen and it flashed briefly. Winked.

I went to get dressed and investigate.

◆ ◆ ◆

It was cold outside, the wind sharp on my skin. I pulled my inadequate cardigan tight around me and forged ahead. The wind grew stronger the closer I got to the car. Or maybe that was my imagination. I was still a little feverish and weak from my brush with mortality, after all. Either way, I liked the cold. Always had. It reminded me I was alive, and the wind? Well, the wind was the song of life, akin to the first sound we heard when we came into consciousness *in utero*—the relentless booming rush of our mother's blood flow.

"How'd you get here, girl?" I reached out and ran my fingers along the car's side. It was like rubbing a racehorse's flank, the duco stretched taut over the power that lay beneath. Or maybe it was more like the accidental touch of a large spider's hairy shell, that unexpected, dark intimacy.

Even over the howling wind, I heard the *click* as the driver's side door opened.

I circled the car and slipped inside. Red leather bucket seats. Two red fluffy dice bedecked with white spots dangling from the rear-view mirror. The steering wheel stark white.

I was inside the beast. Everything was flesh and bone, and it felt like home.

I reached for the ignition. The key was in it, of course, waiting for the touch of my hand. I inclined my head to look. Just a nondescript silver key, slotted snugly. Two charms dangled from the keyring. A tiny spider, black, with a red gash down its rounded back. A die, red, with white spots.

Well, alright then. This was *my* car. Redback spiders were a totem of mine. They were Black Widows—feminine power. *The female of the species is more deadly than the male.* Dice, too, were symbolic to me. Chaos, neatly contained, awaiting the flick of a wrist to decide how it manifested. Endless possibilities. Endless power, and endless responsibility.

I hadn't thought much about these things in a long time. Six months ago, when my mother died, such self indulgence seemed almost evil. And then there had been the dramas with Dominic, the slow suffocation that was my fear of losing him, and everything that had followed . . . no, I hadn't thought about myself in a long time. Not *me*. Only the dreadful things that were happening to me and all that I had lost and might yet lose.

I caressed the steering wheel. The car sighed around me. This whole thing should've been weird, but it wasn't. It was mine, and I deserved it, dammit. I noticed silver lettering in the centre of the steering wheel—had it been there before? I hadn't noticed it—and leaned in to read it. WARP. That felt right too. This car was a Dodge Warp.

"I'm driving you," I told the car, "and nobody can stop me. They might take you away, later, but I'll survive that when it happens, like I've survived everything. Right now, it's you and me, darling."

I grasped the key in the ignition, but the car's engine was already purring. When had that happened? I thrust my foot toward the accelerator, but the engine roared a moment before I made contact, the pedal dropping away of its own accord beneath my shoe.

"Fine!" I found myself yelling the word—sobbing it—and my belly gave a dull *thump* of pain. I crossed my hands over it, hunching forward. I felt the bleeding start again, seeping into the mattress-sized pad the hospital had given me, and what did it matter, now? Except that it hurt, it hurt, oh, it hurt so much. I wanted to wail for my mother, but she was . . . nowhere. Gone. The double-punch of absence hit me like a freight train, as it always did. "That's fine. You drive. Take me where I need to go. You obviously know where that is. So do it. Go."

And we did. My new friend Dodge and I slid backwards out of my driveway and spilled into the street like silk on wheels. A tight turn, and we were on the main road. The radio crackled into life. A woman spoke, her voice low and soothing.

"Lin," the woman said. "Lin. Are you listening?"

"Yes," I answered, because that was me. Lin Johnson, at your service.

"I'm Dodge, Lin. Please don't cry."

The combination of the repetition of my name and the woman's familiar voice was hypnotic. My head grew heavy, and I let it fall back against the headrest as we cruised the streets.

"We can go back, you and I. Go back and make a change. Everybody wants that. Everybody looks back and wishes they'd done something differently. Even those who insist they wouldn't change a thing only say so because they think they have to. Isn't that right, Lin? Do *you* want to make a change?"

"Yes," I said. My voice had a little slur in it now.

"You'll need to offer something in return, Lin. Something . . . personal. Something that means as much to you as the change you want to make."

"Dominic." That word was hard to say, the letters sluggish on my tongue.

"Yes! A good trade. A *fair* trade." Dodge's voice shifted, became my mother's. "I love you, baby girl. I miss you. I see what he's done to you, and I hate it! I hate I hate I hate I hate . . . " My mother's voice retreated, and Dodge's radio let out a scream, an alien siren that felt like it would shatter my skull.

Dodge sped up. The g-force pressed me back into my seat with hard fingers. My heart tripped and thudded. A jogger ran backwards past the car. The wind gusting outside was somehow inside the car too, and it hit me from behind, fanning my hair around my face until I couldn't see. The blood pooling in the pad in my underpants ran back into me, hot and sensuous, pulsing.

We were hurtling along, and just ahead (or just behind . . . everything was displaced in space and time), a red brick building loomed over us.

♦ ♦ ♦

Careening through a dizzy blur of moments:

A long Sunday morning in bed. Dominic's hand cupping my breast. Ouch! Me flinching away. Dominic propped on one elbow, raising his eyebrow, concern in his voice. Oh, how I loved his voice! "You know what *that* means, Linny, don't you?" "No. What?" "Pregnancy." "Don't be ridiculous, that's impossible . . . "

Weeing on the stick, alone in the toilet. The two pink lines right away. My hands shaking. "Oh, my God. Oh, my God. Oh, my God!"

The constant nausea and fatigue, like nothing I'd ever known before.

Lying on my back on the paving stones in the backyard, warmed by the sun, hands on my belly, smiling.

Assuming Dominic and everyone else would share my joy.

"You said you couldn't get pregnant without medical help. You tricked me. This is your fault. What will my parents say? No. If you keep the baby, I'll leave. Or, I'll stay, but I'll be an arsehole. I'll hate you." Dominic's beloved face cold and hard as he said the impossible words to me, each one disembowelling me anew. The cold shock of his betrayal. The utter desolation. The fury at the cliché he turned out to be—the cliché he made me into as I cowered and puled.

Dominic screaming at me not to make out to my friends that he was the villain in all this, my tearful pleas for him to stop, to reconsider, to be kind to me like he used to be and to want this baby as much as I did, to understand. It was only six months since my mother died, and my doctor *had* told me I'd never get pregnant without help, the baby was a miracle, a sign, *please don't do this I love you!*

The unbearable realisation that he couldn't be swayed and I was losing him, losing him, and he was all I had left, he'd been so good to me while I grieved, he was so special, way too good for me, so wonderful. Usually. All the time, except now. When it mattered most.

My girlfriend asking me at work what I'd decided. My voice dull and monotonal as I replied. "I just want it gone. Now. I want the pain and sickness to end, since there's no point to it." Screaming inside, *save me, save me!*

Sitting outside the red brick building in the car with Dominic. Him back to his gentle, caring self, but it was fake and frightened now, a grotesque pantomime. "Are you sure about this?" Me turning on him, unable to believe he'd actually had the nerve to say that. "Of course I'm not sure! You know I don't want to do this! But what choice have you given me?" The guilt marring his face not strong enough to stop him as he opened my door and led me into the clinic with his head bowed.

Dominic paying half the fee. Me paying the other half, because Dominic told me to.

And then—*oh no, don't put me back there*—everything slowed as I fell down completely, into the darkness of a past so recent that I was still bleeding with its wounds.

◆　◆　◆

After a brief and tearful session with a counsellor who seemed to find my grief embarrassing, Dominic and I spent an eternity on a sagging couch staring at terrible Monet prints, studiously ignoring each other, and then: "Lin Johnson?"

I paused just a few moments. Long enough for Dominic to make everything alright, to stop this, to put the knife away rather than cut out my heart with it. But he gave me a thin smile and looked away. We died then, he and I. I had tried so hard not to lose him, and in the end, he lost me. The tragedy was that neither of us even noticed.

"Ms Johnson? Are you ready?" The nurse was looking at me, her face slack. She must see this every day. She had a button pinned to her chest, one of those irritating cryptic advertisements: SAVE TIME—ASK ME HOW!

*No, I'm not ready! I don't want to do this! Dominic? Please!*

"Yes," I said. My body got to its feet and carried me towards the nurse. Away from Dominic. Away from myself.

The nurse took me to a small white room, all tiles and metal, and told me to change into the white hospital gown she handed me. It was starchy and cold, and left my back and butt exposed. It had barely touched my skin when the nurse burst back into the room and led me, barefoot, down the hall to a large room. More tiles and metal, but this room also had a smiling doctor and a chair that looked like a torture device in the centre of the room.

"Ms Johnson." The doctor gestured to the chair. I sat in it and reclined awkwardly. An enormous bright light hung above me like an artificial sun. Long arms extended from both sides of the chair, and my wrists were strapped to them. I was a criminal about to be executed by lethal injection—no—I was Jesus on the cross! I giggled, and then hiccupped. The nurse raised an eyebrow.

"Legs," she said, her tone cold now. She thought I didn't care. That was pretty damn funny, when you thought about it, and I bit my lip to stifle further giggles. The crazy urge to ask the nurse exactly *how* she suggested I save time was overpowering. I slid my legs onto the stirrup-like holsters at the base of the chair, and she strapped my ankles down. Roughly. Then she shoved my legs apart and the doctor glided in between them on a rolling stool.

Spreadeagled. Exposed. Alone.

Something big stood in my peripheral vision, a machine, *the* machine. I refused to see it, but still, the long hose jutting from the thing like a proboscis sneaked into my awareness before I squeezed my eyes shut.

A needle slid into my skin like a serpent's fang, and I flinched.

"Count down from ten," the nurse said, but she was already fading.

"I've changed my mind! I don't want to do this. *I want my baby!*" But my screams were silent. My lips wouldn't move, my whole body was paralysed. My eyes rolled back in my head and my eyelids fluttered closed. Everything was tingling floatiness.

I felt the doctor's rubber-gloved hand on me, then . . .

♦ ♦ ♦

. . . I opened my eyes and sucked at the air, but it wouldn't enter me, it wasn't there. I gasped, again and again. Nothing. It was so bright, so loud. My eyes and ears hurt. I couldn't breathe. My mouth tasted like rotten rubber and my throat was full of something that burnt. Where was I? I had no idea. It didn't matter, I just needed to breathe!

"Lin." A man standing over me. He was vaguely familiar . . . a doctor? Where had I seen him before? "There was a complication. You vomited under anaesthesia and you breathed that vomit into your lungs. That's called aspiration, and it's why you can't breathe. It's triggered an asthma attack, and it's also clogging your lungs. We're putting you in an ambulance to go to hospital. Do you understand?" I couldn't answer him. He leaned in close. "Don't worry. The procedure was completed before you aspirated. There're no problems there. This is nobody's fault. Just one of those things." He gave me a paternal smile.

Oh. Yes. That's right. I was in the abortion clinic.

The doctor was gone. So was my baby. *No problems there. Nobody's fault. One of those things . . .*

Where was Dominic? Not here, never here.

I wanted my mother, wanted to scream *mummy* like a toddler who'd gotten a fright. But my mother was just a void now, infinite, formless, and empty.

I was nothing more or less than pain, forever and ever, amen.

Nurses buzzed about me like bees, stinging me with needles loaded with steroids to try to help me breathe. Ventolin was sprayed into my mouth, over and over, so many blasts that my heart felt like it would hammer its way right out of my chest. Absurdly, a line from Stephen King's IT flitted through my mind, something abstract to do with spiders and asthma: *This is battery acid, you slime!* My body convulsed so hard that my teeth clamped shut on my tongue, preventing further Ventolin onslaught. The nurses looked scared. Surely they weren't meant to look like that. They were like flight attendants, meant to smile and reassure while the 'plane went down in flames.

The ambulance arrived and I was bundled in. My stomach cramped painfully, and I felt warm wetness spurt between my legs. Air was finally getting into my lungs, just a little, but enough for the black pinpricks that had been dancing before my eyes to recede. As the panic lessened, my thoughts came rushing in like a tsunami.

I clutched at my chest as a sob burst forth, a poisonous bubble exploding, filling me with canker.

"Don't worry," the ambo said, his face gentle. "I know your heart is beating like a drum, but you can't really overdose on Ventolin. You'll be alright."

I lost myself to crying, then, and he let me be.

◆ ◆ ◆

Dominic arrived in the ER as they hooked me up to an antibiotic drip. His face was grey and unreadable. He held my hand and stroked my hair. I wanted to lean over and tear his throat out with my teeth. Instead, I turned my head to the wall, and lay silent. Letting him off easy. Like always. *You slime.*

"You'll be here for about a week." Yet another doctor, standing behind an orderly who had brought in a wheelchair to take me to the ward. "You've got aspiration pneumonitis, and you'll need high dose IV antibiotics every few hours." No mention of *the procedure*. It didn't matter to anyone but me.

Dominic went with me to the ward, sat by my bedside, read to me for hours from *The Hobbit*. It was a favourite book of his.

"Go home," I told him. "Get some sleep. I'm ok." Liar, liar.

He slipped out of the room with relief evident in every movement.

That night, and every other night, I awoke every few hours to find a tall male nurse who looked like a serial killer standing over me with a needle in my IV. In my dream-haze, I was sure he was poisoning me, and always, always, disappointed when I woke up in the morning, still alive.

◆ ◆ ◆

*. . . in the void and the void is my mother so I'm in my mother, again, and she is in me, and so is something else, and it's safe here, but temporary, and she's speaking to me, the void is speaking to me . . .*

*. . . we're here together, in the timeless mess, and it's not a mess at all, not really, there are patterns, deceptively fragile in appearance, glimmering in the unlight, like a web, and something with countless eyes and dripping mandibles rules this place, something so black it's red, the female of the species is more deadly than the male, this is battery acid, you slime . . .*

*. . . is this the change you desire . . . the trade you make . . .*

*I nod, except I don't because I have no form, but it's done, anyway.*

◆ ◆ ◆

Sitting at my computer again, gazing out the window, confused. Cold.

Had there been a car in the driveway? Was that what I had been looking at? I thought so, but there was nothing there now but red-black smears of oil glistening on the cement. Someone must've taken a wrong turn into the driveway, and then gone again—leaving my driveway cement stained, and I'd have to scrub it later—and in the meantime I'd vagued out. Taken a trip to la-la land, as Dominic used to say.

Dominic.

God, I hadn't thought about him in months.

It was strange, really. If I concentrated hard, I fuzzily recalled having cared very much about Dominic, once. But that memory was a deeply buried thing, already decomposing, and I couldn't touch it with any real strength, because it crumbled to nothing when I tried.

I never would've thought I could survive him leaving. But he had left—when, exactly? Where had he gone? I didn't seem to know, and it didn't seem to matter—and here I was. Here *we* were. Alive. Intact. I rested my hands on my swollen belly, feeling the blood swirling and rushing in there, my hands moving as my baby rolled beneath them. A girl, I knew it was a girl. I hadn't asked the sonographer who did my ultrasounds—had specifically told her *not* to tell me the baby's sex—but I knew, all the same. Had known from the start, holding that stick in my hand with two pink lines, nine months ago. One line for me, one for my daughter.

A tear tumbled down my cheek and splashed onto my belly. Not for Dominic. I couldn't remember crying for him at all. No, my tears were always for my mother, who wasn't here to meet her granddaughter, who died before I even fell pregnant. I felt her, though. I heard her voice on the wind that soughed around the eaves of this old house at night, as I drifted into sleep and my daughter moved inside me. She waited for me in my dreams. My mother, frozen in time, always in her dressing gown and always smiling, holding her arms open wide—impossibly wide—wide enough for me and my engorged belly to snuggle inside. I was maiden, mother and crone in those dreams, defenceless but safe in my mother's arms, heavy with child and body-wisdom, and ancient with grief and mortality. I needed nothing more. Even my loss was a jewel that I wore with pride. It was a pretty thing—an essential thing. My blood-red heart, my ruby.

But Dominic . . .

He'd given me an ultimatum: him or the baby. I'd chosen the baby. The details were murky in my mind. I suppose it must have been difficult, at the time, but I felt none of that now. Only mild amusement, like there was a joke in all this that I didn't remember, but I still felt the mirth that accompanied it . . . mirth from a distance, almost like it was someone else's.

The radio crackled into life in the kitchen, yanking me from my reverie. It did that often now. I really should call someone in to see to the house's obviously faulty wiring, but in a strange way, I found it comforting. Sometimes it felt like there was something here with me, and I didn't want it to go away.

The radio was *loud*, though. I rose from the chair with difficulty, levering my bulk with straining arms and grunts of exertion. My back and hips ached, and heaviness bore down inside my pelvis, a welcome pain. Soon, soon my little one would be born. I had my midwife on standby, ready to drive the short distance to my house when the time came. A birth pool sat fully inflated in the spare room. Everything and everyone was waiting, it seemed, but there was infinite time. I felt no sense of urgency. I cherished the time with my baby connected to me in the most intimate of ways. I didn't yearn for the severance that must come.

I waddled into the kitchen. As usual, the radio reception was dreadful, the broadcast indecipherable, reduced to wordless whispering and animal shrieks. I was used to it, but it could still be quite . . . spooky.

I unplugged the radio. Simply switching it off didn't always work, and I was too big to be lumbering in and out of here over and over again to see to the thing's noise.

I went to my bedroom, drew the curtains, lowered myself onto the bed and arranged the harem of cushions into the intricate system that was the only way I could lay comfortably now. Cushions bore the weight of my belly, and slipped between my legs they balanced my hips and back. I closed my eyes, draped a hand over my belly. My baby's back curved against my palm. My skin was flush with heat and life.

I relaxed as the wind murmured against my window, morphing into my mother's soothing voice as I flirted with sleep. Something tickled my cheek. I slapped at it drowsily, wiped my hand on my pants, felt something smear there. I didn't open my eyes to check what it was. This old house was full of little spiders, as if somewhere, a great mother spider had birthed.

A half-asleep thought, that, and not one I liked.

Just as dreams claimed me, I thought I heard the radio in the kitchen blast into life again, but that was impossible.

My mother reached for me in the dream-web that awaited me. Her arms were longer than I remembered them having been when she was alive, and her dressing gown had a fat red stripe up the back that looked like a wound on the brink of bursting open . . . but she was *here*, just like my daughter.

All was well, even the things that weren't, because I had chosen them.

◆　◆　◆

Dominic squeezed his eyes shut, pinched the bridge of his nose between his fingers, opened his eyes again.

Nope, didn't work. He was still here. Where-ever *here* was.

But he remembered this place, didn't he? It was red brick, and there were overstuffed couches and overbright prints on the wall, and the sound of someone sobbing. They wouldn't stop crying, the sound seeping through the walls and crawling along Dominic's spine, infuriating and unnerving him.

"Can't you make her shut up?" The words slipped from him before he could control himself. A nurse materialised before him, clipboard in hand. He wasn't sure how he knew she was a nurse, since she wore red and black rather than white, but he knew it, nonetheless. She looked familiar, a smiling older woman with features he seemed to know very well, but he had no idea who she was.

"No," she said. "Nobody can make her do anything now. Especially not you."

He frowned. "I don't know what you . . . " But he did. He'd lost someone. That was bad, but he'd done something . . . broken something fragile, trespassed somewhere terrible, and that was worse. Who was he? Where was he? He didn't want to know, but he *did* know, and that was the worst thing of all. This . . . guilt, this . . . regret.

"Dominic." The nurse brought his focus back to her. Tears seeped from her large hazel eyes. He knew those eyes. "Please don't cry, Dominic."

"I'm not," he said, but he was. His face dripped with tears and his lips trembled, and he felt a terrible wrench of grief, deep in his gut. Wetness stained his jeans, and, looking down, he saw red slowly staining his crotch. He gasped, clutching himself, but there was no pain, as if the blood was a phantasm. *Out, out, damn spot!*

"This is how it was for her, Dominic." Still crying, the nurse ticked something off on her clipboard. A radio thundered into life somewhere, no music, just alien screams, the cacophony not quite drowning out the sounds of nearby sobbing.

"Can you turn that racket down?" Dominic put his hands over his ears, but they did nothing to muffle the sound. Something sharp pricked his palms, and as he snatched his hands away from his ears, two small objects tumbled into his lap, shining in the blood there. He hunched forward, staring at them. Little charms. A Redback spider and a red and white die. Recoiling in a horror he didn't understand, he knocked the charms to the floor.

The room didn't feel straight, didn't feel even. He felt seasick, unstable.

"Save time! Ask me how," the nurse said.

"Please," Dominic whispered.

"It's just one of those things. Nobody's fault," the nurse said, and she picked him up as if he were a thing made of feather and air. He flailed, yelling, but it was useless. She carried him down a long corridor, which twisted and tilted around them.

"Please," he whispered, "I don't want this. Please. No."

The nurse carried him into a room and dropped him into a chair. It was a hellish thing, a recumbent crucifix with sharp metal edges, and he immediately tried to leap out. Strong, sinuous restraints wrapped around his wrists and ankles. Raising his head, he saw with very little surprise that they were snakes, black things with bright red bellies.

Something giant glided in between his spread legs, belching rancid smoke.

"Count to ten," the nurse said, standing at his side now. "Then count to ten again, and again, and again." The snakes that held him in place hissed and darted their angry heads at him, their fangs piercing his skin. Hot venom laced through his veins, burning and pulsing. He screamed.

The nurse leaned down, her face pressed right into his, and he saw the hatred and fury in her smiling eyes.

Lin's eyes.

Lin!

He remembered, oh, he remembered the squat spider-like car that had brought him here, a glassy-eyed unspeaking Lin standing constantly outside the vehicle as everything around her somehow ran backwards, and he was sorry, so sorry . . . but mostly he was angry. And surprised.

Somehow she'd done this to him, and how *dare* she?

"It's the forcing that did it," the nurse said. "On top of all the pain she already felt, you pushed her. You broke her. A thing like that . . . that sort of warp *echoes*, Dominic. We heard it. We answered." The plunging, scraping thing between his legs clattered closer. Something sharp and hungry nudged his thigh. His limbs grew heavy and his head fell back against the hard chair. The nurse's face filled his vision, and he knew her, oh yes, he knew her.

Lin had looked just like her mother. The spitting image.

◆　◆　◆

Somewhere else—some *time* else—a newborn's cries filled the early morning air.

It was a good trade.

# AFTERWORD

*I wish to state firmly and unequivocally: this is not a pro-life story. It's pro-choice. I'm pro-choice. I believe in women's bodily integrity, and that means I believe every woman should have the right to decide what she does with her body, including as it pertains to conception, pregnancy, and birth. I would be horrified if anyone took any other view away from this piece and deemed it mine. This story is intended as a speculative exploration of just one of the many ways women's hard-won choices are warped and used against them or simply obliterated altogether; usually in ways we're not supposed to discuss in polite company. (To which I respectfully say: get fucked.) There are kernels of truth in this story. For instance, I once travelled back in time in a magical car. No, not really. But other parts, I may or may not have personal experience with, as so many women do. And yet I'm still here. We're still here. The female of the species is more deadly than the male . . . and I'd caution you to never forget that fact.*

# THE EMANCIPATED DANCE

"Stupid car. Stupid, stupid, *stupid* car!"

Penny aimed a savage kick at the Datsun's worn tyre. The little rust bucket remained unmoved by her emotion and by its burnt-out engine. Thin tendrils of smoke had begun seeping from under the battered hood hundreds of kilometres before, but she hadn't had the time nor money to stop and investigate. *Just a hundred k's more,* she'd silently bargained with the shuddering vehicle. *An hour or so, and we'll be home. Please, get me home. Don't die yet.*

But the traitorous machine had gone ahead and broken down, stranding her here on a stretch of long, flat country road. She wouldn't make it to dinner at George's parents' place, and he would be furious. That was bad, but maybe she had worse things to worry about right now. Like leaving her mobile phone at the presentation she'd just given in Malachi Springs. Like having no water or food, other than the few lint-covered lifesavers dwelling in the depths of her handbag. Like nothing and no one in sight for as far as her frowning eyes could see.

Like the sun edging towards the horizon, threatening to disappear and immerse her in darkness.

Her chest began to ache as her lungs inflated with panic. Her brain froze, unable to move beyond the hopelessness of her situation.

*I'm stuck here, and I have no way of calling for help, and I haven't seen anyone else on this road for hours, and it's almost night, and there's nothing here, and George will kill me, and oh God—really kill me this time, not just yell, not even just hit, but really kill—what do I do?*

Behind her, a crowed cawed: a rifle crack in the silence. Penny shrieked and spun around looking for the bird. It stood on the roadside, a metre or so away from her and the useless car, regarding her with gimlet eyes. As she stared, it cocked its gleaming head and croaked at her again.

"*Walk,*" it rasped. "*Walk, walk!*"

"You didn't just say that," she told it. "You didn't talk. I'm tired from working and driving too much. I'm imagining—"

"*Walk! Walk, walk, walk! Walk-walk!*" The crow was insistent, amused—mocking?

Angry at her own cowardice, she waved her arms above her head and stomped her feet, trying to frighten the bird away.

"Shoo! Go on, get out of here! Shoo, ghoul! Carrion eater! Rat with wings!"

"*Walk,*" the crow reminded her before lazily unfolding its wings and taking to the air; leaving her alone once more.

She placed her shaking hands on the roof of her car, resting her forehead on the cool metal. The sun was no more than an amber half-disc, ever-dwindling below the edge of the darkening sky. The breeze that toyed with her hair and snaked under her sensible dress was brisk; within an hour, it would cross the line into unpleasant coldness. The paddocks and forest around her rustled and twitched, promising to release their crawling secrets with the fullness of night.

She didn't want to be there when that happened, and she didn't care how irrational the aversion was. Out here, it felt perfectly rational. Things change when you're alone in a strange landscape. The rules of normality slip away, to be replaced by more primal, ancient truths.

*I have two choices. Get in the car, lock the doors, and bunk down for the night—a sitting duck in a tin can in the freezing cold, with one eye open on the lookout for a passing car or an uninvited visitor—or I can . . .*

*walk-walk!*

*. . . hit the road on foot and hope to find a house or an emergency road phone or another human being before it gets too dark and cold. At least that would be doing* something.

She was walking before her thoughts had fully formed. She'd known she would; she just hadn't wanted that damned crow to see her doing it. She wasn't willing to surrender the illusion of control just yet. She was walking because she *chose* to, not because a bird told her to.

It was bullshit, but it was all she had for now, and she clung to it as she trudged away from her car and down the lonely road.

◆ ◆ ◆

She'd been walking for about an hour, maybe two. It was dark, and the road beneath her weary feet had changed from asphalt to gravel a while ago. She hoped that she was staying on course by veering back to the gravel whenever her shoes found soft grass, but she had no way of being sure. There were no lights, only the moist gloom that pressed in on her on all sides. Her senses were heightened by the night around her, and each noise was like a circular saw applied to her raw, screaming nerves.

*Why the hell didn't I just stay in the car? It's the first thing they tell you when you're a kid: if you get lost, stay in one place! Don't move around. Especially not alone, at night, in the deserted countryside . . .*

Unbidden idiot tears welled, and she knuckled her eyes, disgusted.

*I'm a wreck. George is right; I'm a fool. I can't do anything right. I deserve whatever I get—*

And then there it was: a large three-storey brick manor, jutting out of the black night, a few hundred metres down the road. Lights blazed from every window, and spirals of smoke curled invitingly above the roof.

*They've got a fire, a crackling fire for me to curl up in front of while I wait for George to come and get me, and he'll be so angry, but anything is better than being here. Where ever "here" is.*

She broke into a run, dashing through the darkness towards the haven of civilization ahead. Her galloping imagination, giddy with relief, pictured a wealthy family—perhaps three generations dwelling in one enormous house—gathered in their plush drawing room (whatever *that* was) for drinks and conversation around a cosy hearth before bed. She would clatter up the steps onto their broad porch and hammer on their front door, and the father would urge the grandparents, his wife, and the children to stay in the house while he went to investigate their unexpected night-time visitor. He would open the door with a cocked rifle in his hand and a cautious look on his noble face; but upon seeing the damsel in distress shivering on his veranda, he would sweep her into the house's warm safety with one dressing-gown clad arm. The children would clamber all over her as the grandmother wrapped a rug around her shoulders and pressed a cup of steaming hot chocolate into her hands. There would be a phone, and she would be saved.

As she reached the garden and stepped onto the path winding toward the front door, she could almost see the half melted marshmallows bobbing in the hot sweet drink and smell the acrid tang of the grandfather's pipe smoke.

But her cosy visualisations soon evaporated as she climbed the steps and mounted the porch.

It was the smell. The *real* smell, not the ones she'd imagined.

The veranda was heavy with a thousand scents: the crackling odour of ozone after a storm; the tingle of exotic spices; the warm musk of unsanitised humanity. Above it all rose a fecund metallic smell that throbbed in the air and filled her with recognition.

It was blood, yes—but more than that—it was menstrual blood.

She'd smelt that uterine tang on herself once a month for countless years now, caught whiffs of other women when it was their time. The place was ripe with it. Penny found it exciting, repellent, and disturbing; a strange, heady bouquet.

She remained lost in sensation for several minutes before noticing the card.

It was made of thick silver paper, folded in two and propped on a straw mat that lay before the front door. Purple script, spidery and large, sprawled across the card:

Welcome to The Sisterhood

"What Sisterhood?" she mused aloud, turning the card over in her hands and inspecting it. She didn't hear the door open, didn't notice the woman standing framed in the doorway until she spoke.

"*The* Sisterhood," the woman said, smiling.

Penny dropped the card in surprise. "Oh—I'm sorry, I didn't mean to intrude; only, my car broke down a few hours from here, and I'm lost, and I wondered if I could use your phone. I—I've got change, to pay for the call. Would you mind?"

The woman dipped her head a little, still smiling. Penny looked at her properly for the first time and saw that she was dressed in ceremonial garb. Her black hair was groomed in long straight sheets, and her face was heavily made up—all dark smudged eyes and glimmering red lips. She wore a robe, deep purple in colour and made of heavy, flowing fabric. A large hood rested on her shoulders. Her wrists, neck, fingers, and ears dripped with jewellery.

*What the hell did she mean, 'The Sisterhood'? She sure isn't a nun. Is this some new-age kinda thing?*

"You're not intruding at all, Penny. We were waiting for you to arrive before we began. Please, come in. You'll need to walk through the house to reach the fire; the others are already there."

The woman spoke with both a comfortable familiarity and a sympathetic compassion for Penny's obvious confusion. The combination frightened Penny more thoroughly than overt menace ever could have. She felt *known*: exposed, found out, naked to the core. The night at her back called greedily for her to return to its hidden dangers, and the beautiful woman—*mother*—in front of her gestured kindly for her to enter the solitary house . . . and Penny didn't know which option was the wiser.

"I just . . . need a phone," she said, almost whispering.

"Oh, I'm so pleased you didn't resort to all the obvious questions, Penny." The woman reached out and grabbed her hand. Her skin was warm and smooth, and her pull was insistent. Penny was tugged through the door and into the house before she could so much as squeak. The door closed and they stood together, hand in hand, in a long, polished hallway. There seemed to be only one other door, at the far end of the hall; through it, Penny could hear the hub of women's voices and see the flickering light of a large fire. And that *smell* . . . it was so dense that she could almost see it floating on the air in ruby droplets. It coated her throat, and she gagged, coughing.

*This house is immense. How can there be no rooms? Surely there's more than just a front and back door and a hall . . .*

"Obvious questions?" Penny forced herself to speak.

"Yes, you know—how did you know my name, where am I, how did you know I'd be coming, what fire, what were you waiting for—the usual. I know those questions are on your mind, but you didn't *ask* them, you're not so blatant. I knew you were special. That's why you're here. And my name is Ceri. *That's* a question you don't need to ask; it's only polite that I tell you." The woman—Ceri—chuckled, a deep sound that rolled from the depths of her belly.

"The phone?" Penny's lungs were rock-hard with panic, her chest a taut barrel of tension. Her heart pounded a staccato beat through her alarm, assaulting her eardrums with its jungle rhythm.

Ceri leaned down—*she's so tall*—and pulled Penny against her, embracing her firmly. Penny's face was buried in the coarse purple folds of Ceri's robe, and she felt the woman's strong arms around her shoulders, pinning her. Sharp nails rested on the bare skin at the nape of her neck, and she shivered.

And yet . . . it was a calming embrace. Ceri was abloom with a thousand fragrances, each one more familiar and comforting than the last. Her body felt soft and malleable, and Penny wanted nothing more than to sink into it, to give herself over to this strange woman and this bizarre night.

To let go.

"Yes," she murmured into Ceri's robes.

Ceri sighed and released Penny from her arms. "Come." She took Penny's hand once more and led her down the looming hall. "This way. They're—*we're*—waiting."

The corridor seemed to lengthen as they walked along it. The perspectives were all wrong; the roof shifted from high to low, from convex to concave. The walls merged from paint to wallpaper to a nameless, spongy substance; Penny thought she could see them moving in and out—*breathing*—and looked away quickly. The floor, once a rich red velvet runner over bare floorboards, was now a boggy flesh-coloured surface coated in red-brown mucous, sucking hungrily at the soles of her shoes. The sound of the women's voices and the heat of the fire were getting closer, but the hall . . . the hall was an eternal walk.

She was unafraid, and that was curious, because she was *always* afraid. Of George. Of the night. Of being alone. Of the world around her. Of humankind. Of herself. Of worming, burrowing, nameless things that dwelt within her own heart.

"But I don't have a robe." She felt absurd, yet Ceri squeezed her hand as though the remark had been perfectly normal.

"You won't need one. Tonight, you're a guest. If you like what you see, then you can stay, and join in next time. The choice is yours. Ours is to dance; yours is to *see*."

Penny had a moment to think one last time of what lay outside the surreal house—*car, my car is broken down, didn't I need to call someone? Aren't I lost?*—and then Ceri led her through the door at the end of the hall and into what lay beyond.

◆ ◆ ◆

Penny sat on the warm earth, removed from the hooded figures encircling the fire; her fingers toyed with the crumbling soil. The fire was surprisingly small—almost a mere formality—yet, it burned bright and hot. The flames had a lavender tinge to them, yet she was not surprised. She felt safe; at peace. Above all, she felt interested. Something essential was going to happen here, something that would illuminate her life with meaning and fill her hollow bones with purpose. Something *real*—at last.

Ceri was one of the figures around the fire; but Penny could not tell which. Their robes were identical; the hoods cupped their heads and curled down all the way to their chins, concealing every inch of countenance. They didn't move. They didn't speak. The fire hissed and crackled, a passionate symphony of hungry flame and willing wood in the otherwise silent night. The only smell was the thick bloody femininity that hung in the air like a curtain, surrounding the scene. Neither music, nor chanting, nor pomp and ceremony were needed to punctuate the gathering.

The dance was all that mattered right now, and this stillness was part of it.

"We are woman. We are The Sisterhood. We will be free."

It was Ceri's voice, deep and mellifluous. It was all of their voices, unique and united. It was a shout, and it was an unspoken thought.

The purple-red flames flickered in acknowledgement, and Penny's blood thrilled in her veins. *Oh yes, oh yes, oh please, oh yes.*

"Womankind, unmask!"

Gem-clad fingers with painted nails emerged from voluminous sleeves to lift the concealing hoods. In the shimmering, changing air, Penny watched as one woman removed her oversized sunglasses, plucked out her blonde hair extensions, and rubbed her lips free of their thick coating of gloss; another woman removed her hijab and wiped the black kohl from her eyes; yet another woman removed the disc that nestled in her distended lip and smoothed the ritual scarification from her cheeks with magical fingers. A dozen . . . no, a hundred . . . no, a *thousand* women's heads were revealed, bathed in dusky fire-glow. The women knelt for a moment, digging their hands in the soil at their feet, and scooping up handfuls of dark dirt before standing again. As they began to rub the soil into their faces, Penny saw the jewellery and nail polish melting from their bodies. It snaked in runnels of extravagant colour down their robes and was absorbed by the implacable earth.

They stood, heads bare, skin scoured clean, bereft of ornamentation, mutilation, and artifice. Women of ebony skin, of brown skin, of white skin, of pink skin. Women of long hair, short hair; tresses curly and straight, bristling in a riot of colour. They were unenhanced, they were imperfect, and they were formidable.

*It's beautiful. I want to be a part of it. It's not a difficult choice.* She moved, preparing to get to her feet, to find Ceri in the expansive circle of women to tell her she wanted to join in *now.*

"Sit," the crow at her side said. "*Sit-sit, be still. Watch, watch-watch. More comes.*"

She wasn't startled by the bird this time. She stared at it, and it looked back at her. She nodded, settling back into her seated position. The crow nodded in return. They sat, side by side, and their gazes returned to The Sisterhood and the fire. The women had begun to move. Their bodies swayed within their robes as a low hum emanated from their unhindered throats.

"*Watch-watch,*" the crow said again, but Penny needed no more urging.

The gentle to-and-fro of the women's rocking bodies escalated until they were moving on hidden feet, walking with slow solemnity around the fire. Their purple robes rustled as they passed by Penny, and a light breeze created by their circular motion stroked at her face.

"Unmask!" Ceri's voice rang out again, strong and delicious in the charged night.

Without ceasing their movement around the fire, the women began to remove their robes. One by one, they raised them over their heads and threw them into the fire. The moment the flames touched the fabric, the robes disappeared without a trace. The small and modest fire consumed robe after robe after robe and never struggled—never guttered nor smoked. The women gave without hesitation, and the fire took in kind. This was a mutual dance.

Naked and gleaming in the fiery moonlight, the women danced faster, bare of everything that was not a natural part of them. They were flesh and heat and teeth; writhing, pulsating, thrumming with life. They were power. They were energy. They were *free*.

"Yes!" Penny yelled, only half aware she was doing so. "Yes! *Yes!* I want this. I want to join the dance! I want—"

"*Watch. More.*" The crow didn't look at her as it spoke; the black droplets of its eyes remained fixed on the thrashing bodies around the fire. But its words were commanding, and Penny lapsed into silence once more, her own body shaking with the desire to throw herself amongst the ritual.

"*Unmask! Unmask! Unmask!*" Ceri's voice was no longer hers; it was a universal cry, the shriek of a host of Furies, the croon of every mother to every child, the war-wail of an Amazon queen. The women moved so fast around the fire that Penny's eyes watered from the wind they generated and her hair whipped wildly in the frenzied air. She opened her mouth—to say what, she didn't know—but the wind scorched her throat, stole her words, and pinned down her tongue.

She barely had time to close her mouth and blink her weeping eyes before . . .

*Fuck you George! I'm going to join the dance and be free, really free.* You don't even exist here, *you never did, only The Sisterhood does, it always has . . . where am I?*

. . . the real unmasking began.

The women grasped handfuls of their own hair, dragging at it, wrenching it out in ragged chunks. The moist skin still attached sizzled as the women flung the meaty mess into the fire. The air was thick with the spatters of their blood and the cacophony of their shrieking. White patches of skull gleamed through the oozing remnants of their scalps as freshets of blood flowed down their backs. Each and every woman was smiling, their mouths stretched to capacity in beaming rictuses of joy.

Bile rose in Penny's throat, boiling and urgent. She held it down with difficulty and kept her eyes on the bleeding, bald, semi-scalped dancers.

*It's terrible, but it's beautiful, and I want to see. I need to see.*

The women's hooked fingers moved from their hair to their faces. They sank their nails into the plump flesh of their cheeks and burrowed, wriggling their fingers inside their own faces. Once they had a secure hold, they ripped. Great sheets of skin sheathed off in wet slaps, taking with them noses, lips, and ears. The women squeezed their hands into fists around the sundered meat, squashing their faces into balls of wet pulp before hurling them into the fire. Grinning skeleton skulls now perched atop naked, blood-drenched bodies; voluptuous and perversely fecund. The women capered around the fire, jerking their gore-clad skulls from side to side. Still singing. Still dancing.

Still beautiful.

Penny felt heat on her own face and didn't know if it was blood sprayed from the whirling skeleton-women or her own terrified tears. The crow next to her was cawing a continuous excited *awr, awr, awr,* and she wanted to clap her hands over her ears and scream to blot it out. However, the woman-wind was phenomenal, and she couldn't move at all. She could only sit, held in thrall, watching the great and gruesome dance.

The women inserted their fingers into their toothy grimaces and raked the flesh from the bones in appreciative chomps. They spat the red mess into the fire where it was devoured whole.

There was a pause, a moment of waiting in the relentless dance; and then the women fell upon themselves in a final feverish attack. Their bony fingers stabbed into their soft, fleshy bodies and tore out entrails, hearts, muscles, and arteries. Extravagant jets of blood arced up a hundredfold toward the calm moon; a scarlet fountain pattering down upon the deathless fire that waited hungrily to receive. They tore themselves apart in a blur of flailing white bones and screeching that came from throats that no longer existed. They capered and gambolled around the fire, a festival of meat-streaked bones.

And then, one by one, the skeleton-women leapt directly into the fire.

The flames consumed them as if they had never been. Each skeleton hung framed in the air for a moment, an ecstasy of dangling sinew, jutting hip bones and gangly limbs, and then was erased without leaving so much as an after-image on Penny's retina.

Within moments, the last skeleton had leapt into the fire and been taken whole. Penny sat, her convulsions slowing to spasmodic tremors as the wind abated and the air quieted. She rubbed her stinging, tear-sodden eyes and sniffed. The crow sat beside her, head bowed, beak parted in a perpetual sigh.

*What was the point?* She was angry, disappointed, bitter. *If I want to see women being torn apart, I can just step outside my own house on any given day and look around me. Or better yet, just stay inside my home and witness my own assault under George's willing hands. What was the-*

"*Wait,*" the crow croaked, as close to a whisper as it could manage. "*Wait-wait. More. Now.*"

And then the first creature crawled up and out of the fire.

A woman, tall, ebony-skinned, and rippling with sinuous muscle. Her hair was long and matted, woven with bones and feathers and shells. Her eyes blazed red-purple from the hard angles of her face. She held a staff topped with a human skull in one large hand; in her other, she cradled a slumbering baby. She was death, and birth, and everything in between. She was woman, free and primal. She was terrible, yet beautiful, beautiful, beautiful. She was everything.

She was Ceri.

Penny stared at her, mouth agape, drool slipping down her chin and rolling to her chest unnoticed. Her heart was a fragile bird, fluttering against the bony ribs of its cage. She wanted to touch the incredible creature; to fall at its--*Her . . . Her, Her,* HER*!*--feet and keen with grief and joy and awe.

Ceri smiled at her, and Penny felt something deep inside her unfurl, delighted. She had been seen. Everything was alright.

Another creature pushed itself forth from the fire, birthed from flame and ember. Penny watched without surprise or confusion as a dolphin wormed on its belly across the dry earth to rest beside the Ceri-Goddess. It smiled up at Ceri with teeth long and jagged, and then it fixed its yellow, slanted eyes back on the fire.

A girl-child with two heads and four arms and legs scampered from the fire, giggling and grooming itself with a tongue as long as its body.

A willow tree, miniature and perfect, grew from the flames and trundled on spidery roots to take its place in the regrowing circle. Eight red eyes glimmered in the gnarled bark of its trunk.

A cat the size of a horse.

A burning ball of gas with a dark sphere at its core.

An ape with a score of piglets feeding from its multitude of teats.

Penny watched them all burst from the fire and resume their places in the circle--until they were all there. Until the circle was full and bustling and living with their presence.

"Sisters," the Ceri-Goddess intoned, her vivid eyes taking in all of them. "We are unmasked. We have danced the dance most sacred and profane. We are free."

The crow cackled, and Penny turned to look at it.

*"See? See-see?"* the crow gloated and flew at her eyes.

As she plunged into darkness, she felt strangely unafraid.

◆ ◆ ◆

She awoke in a large bed, swathed in thick feather duvets and crisp sheets. A steaming mug of hot chocolate, irresistible with the fragrance of cinnamon and cardamom, sat beside her on the oak bedside table. She wiggled her feet, nudging the hot water bottle that warmed them.

She knew there would be marshmallows in the hot chocolate. If she inhaled sharply enough, she could even detect the faint bite of pipe smoke in the air; a lingering memory of a cosy evening that never happened, spent by the fire sharing tales with elders who never were.

*It's all from my daydream, the one I told myself when I was lost, when I found this place. When I needed comfort. When I wanted to be saved. And now, I am. And if I want it to take this form, for now, well . . . that's ok. Why the hell not?*

Ceri sat on the bed, once again a beautiful, normal woman with straight black hair and carefully applied makeup. She smiled at Penny, patting her hand with a *click-click* of the rings that adorned her pale fingers.

"Did you sleep well, darling one? Were your dreams sweet? Are you . . . well?"

Penny stared at Ceri for a moment, then found herself smiling.

"I'm so glad you didn't ask all the obvious questions, Ceri," she said, and they laughed together. They were women-kin, sharing time in a cosy room of one of their dreams; and if the blood-red walls were more porous than they should be, and if they seemed to breathe . . . well, what of it?

"Did you enjoy our dance, Penny?" Ceri was serious now, the smile sliding from her face like rain from a window pane.

"I . . . I did. I loved it."

"I knew you would. Oh, it's so beautiful, isn't it?" Ceri was still unsmiling, but her eyes were large and glistening, fixed on faraway places and beings. She stank, but in a ripe and delicious way: of blood, and of fertility, and of the decay that compliments full-blown life.

"Ceri? Could I . . . can I stay? Can I dance? I'd like to. I want . . . nothing else."

"Of course you can. We've been waiting for you. We always wait—except for when we dance. Then, we . . . but you've seen, and you'll know for yourself, next full moon. I wonder what you'll become, when you're birthed from the fire? When you unmask?"

*See-see*

"Something free," Penny said. "No matter how much it hurts."

# AFTERWORD

*I'm wearing my feminism on my sleeve here in a fairly self-explanatory way. This piece plays with some old and overt symbolism and issues—the crow, ritual, fire, the womb, the sisterhood, the Goddess Ceridwen ("Ceri"), women's cycles, women's various forms of oppression, the raw power of woman that is both terrifying and beautiful—to the point that we women sometimes live in fear and mistrust of ourselves and each other. Often, actually. Womankind, arise! Shoulder to shoulder . . .*

# ACKNOWLEDGEMENTS

"Bread and Circuses" Copyright © 2010 Felicity Dowker.
First published in *Scary Kisses*, Ticonderoga Publications,
edited by Liz Grzyb, 2010. Podcast by *Tales to Terrify*, 2012
(forthcoming).

"Jesse's Gift" Copyright © 2009 Felicity Dowker. First published
in *Andromeda Spaceways Inflight Magazine* #40 in August
2009. Finalist, Aurealis Awards, Best Horror Short Story.

"From Little Things . . . " Copyright © 2010 Felicity Dowker.
Published in *Andromeda Spaceways Inflight Magazine* #43,
January 2010, edited by David Kernot.

"Us, After the House Came Back" Copyright © 2012 Felicity
Dowker. Previously unpublished.

"The Bearded Ones" Copyright © 2009 Felicity Dowker.
Published in *Festive Fear*, Tasmaniac Publications, December
2009, edited by Steve Clark. Honourable Mention, Ellen
Datlow's *Best Horror of the Year* Vol. 2.

"Berries and Incense" Copyright © 2011 Felicity Dowker.
First published in *More Scary Kisses*, edited by Liz Grzyb,
Ticonderoga Publications, 2011.

"To Wish on a Clockwork Heart" Copyright © 2012 Felicity
Dowker. Previously unpublished.

"Phantasy Moste Grotesk" Copyright © 2009 Felicity Dowker.
First published as a numbered limited edition chapbook by
Corpulent Insanity Press, April 2009. Reprinted at Red Penny
Papers as a serialised online novella, April 2011.

"The Blind Man" Copyright © 2010 Felicity Dowker. First
published in *Scenes From the Second Storey*—Australian
Edition, edited by Pete Kempshall and Amanda Pillar,
Morrigan Books, September 2010. Honourable Mention, Ellen
Datlow's *Best Horror of the Year* Vol. 3.

"Red Delicious" Copyright © 2011 Felicity Dowker. First
published in "Dead Red Heart", edited by Russell B Farr,
Ticonderoga Publications, 2011.

## AVAILABLE FROM TICONDEROGA PUBLICATIONS

978-0-9586856-6-5   TROY BY SIMON BROWN (TPB)
978-0-9586856-7-2   THE WORKERS' PARADISE EDS FARR & EVANS (TPB)
978-0-9586856-8-9   FANTASTIC WONDER STORIES ED RUSSELL B FARR (TPB)
978-0-9586856-9-6   LOVE IN VAIN BY LEWIS SHINER (LIMITED HC)
978-0-9803531-0-5   LOVE IN VAIN BY LEWIS SHINER (TPB)
978-0-9803531-1-2   BELONG ED RUSSELL B FARR (LIMITED HC)
978-0-9803531-2-9   BELONG ED RUSSELL B FARR (TPB)
978-0-9803531-3-6   GHOST SEAS BY STEVEN UTLEY (HC)
978-0-9803531-4-3   GHOST SEAS BY STEVEN UTLEY (TPB)
978-0-9803531-5-0   GHOST SEAS BY STEVEN UTLEY (EBOOK)
978-0-9803531-6-7   MAGIC DIRT: THE BEST OF SEAN WILLIAMS (TPB)
978-0-9803531-7-4   THE LADY OF SITUATIONS BY STEPHEN DEDMAN (HC)
978-0-9803531-8-1   THE LADY OF SITUATIONS BY STEPHEN DEDMAN (TPB)
978-0-9803531-9-8   BASIC BLACK BY TERRY DOWLING (LIMITED HC)
978-0-9806288-2-1   BASIC BLACK BY TERRY DOWLING (TPB)
978-0-9806288-0-7   MAKE BELIEVE BY TERRY DOWLING (LIMITED HC)
978-0-9806288-3-8   MAKE BELIEVE BY TERRY DOWLING (TPB)
978-0-9806288-1-4   THE INFERNAL BY KIM WILKINS (LIMITED HC)
978-0-9806288-4-5   SCARY KISSES ED LIZ GRZYB (TPB)
978-0-9806288-5-2   DEAD SEA FRUIT BY KAARON WARREN (LIMITED HC)
978-0-9806288-6-9   DEAD SEA FRUIT BY KAARON WARREN (TPB)
978-0-9806288-7-6   THE GIRL WITH NO HANDS BY ANGELA SLATTER (L/HC)
978-0-9806288-8-3   THE GIRL WITH NO HANDS BY ANGELA SLATTER (TPB)
978-1-921857-93-5   THE GIRL WITH NO HANDS BY ANGELA SLATTER (EBOOK)
978-0-9807813-0-4   DEAD RED HEART ED RUSSELL B FARR (LIMITED HC)
978-0-9807813-1-1   DEAD RED HEART ED RUSSELL B FARR (TPB)
978-1-921857-99-7   DEAD RED HEART ED RUSSELL B FARR (EBOOK)
978-0-9807813-2-8   MORE SCARY KISSES ED LIZ GRZYB (TPB)
978-1-921857-94-2   MORE SCARY KISSES ED LIZ GRZYB (EBOOK)
978-0-9807813-3-5   HELIOTROPE BY JUSTINA ROBSON (LIMITED HC)
978-0-9807813-4-2   HELIOTROPE BY JUSTINA ROBSON (TPB)
978-0-9807813-5-9   HELIOTROPE BY JUSTINA ROBSON (EBOOK)
978-0-9807813-6-6   MATILDA TOLD SUCH DREADFUL LIES BY LUCY SUSSEX (L/HC)
978-0-9807813-7-3   MATILDA TOLD SUCH DREADFUL LIES BY LUCY SUSSEX (TPB)
978-0-9807813-8-0   YEAR'S BEST AUSTRALIAN F&H EDS GRZYB & HELENE (HC)
978-0-9807813-9-7   YEAR'S BEST AUSTRALIAN F&H EDS GRZYB & HELENE (TPB)
978-1-921857-98-0   YEAR'S BEST AUSTRALIAN F&H EDS GRZYB & HELENE (EBK)
978-1-921857-00-3   BLUEGRASS SYMPHONY BY LISA L HANNETT (LIMITED HC)
978-1-921857-01-0   BLUEGRASS SYMPHONY BY LISA L HANNETT (TPB)
978-1-921857-97-3   BLUEGRASS SYMPHONY BY LISA L HANNETT (EBOOK)
978-1-921857-05-8   THE HALL OF LOST FOOTSTEPS BY SARA DOUGLASS (HC)
978-1-921857-06-5   THE HALL OF LOST FOOTSTEPS BY SARA DOUGLASS (TPB)
978-1-921857-03-4   DAMNATION AND DAMES ED LIZ GRZYB & AMANDA PILLAR (TPB)

WWW.TICONDEROGAPUBLICATIONS.COM

# THANK YOU

The publisher would sincerely like to thank:

Elizabeth Grzyb, Felicity Dowker, Trent Jamieson, Jonathan Strahan, Peter McNamara, Ellen Datlow, Grant Stone, Sean Williams, Simon Brown, Garth Nix, Angela Slatter, Lisa Bennett, Karen Brooks, Jeremy G. Byrne, Kim Wilkins, Marianne de Pierres, David Cake, Simon Oxwell, Grant Watson, Sue Manning, Steven Utley, Lewis Shiner, Bill Congreve, Jack Dann, Janeen Webb, Lucy Sussex, Stephen Dedman, the Mt Lawley Mafia, the Nedlands Yakuza, Brian Clarke, Shane Jiraiya Cummings, Angela Challis, Kate and Andrew Williams, Kathryn Linge, Al Chan, Alisa and Tehani, Mel & Phil, Kelly Parker, Hayley Lane, Georgina Walpole, everyone we've missed . . .

. . . and you.

IN MEMORY OF
EVE JOHNSON (1945–2011)